Praise f

"A beautifully told and imagined story of secrets, faith, love, and devotion. With a compelling plot and cast of characters, *Before the King* is a tale not to be missed."

—Tosca Lee, *New York Times* bestselling author of *Iscariot*

"In *Before the King*, Heather Kaufman presents a moving tale of two sisters, one of whom has a front-row view of Jesus' ministry and crucifixion. Joanna's story is a reminder that God does use ordinary people in extraordinary ways . . . if they are willing."

—Angela Hunt, *New York Times* bestselling author

Praise for *Up from Dust*

"Kaufman's biblical tale is based on the scriptural account of Martha, the sister of Lazarus and Mary . . . . a novel that will be greatly appreciated by readers who enjoy Christian fiction. . . . Kaufman's writing is skillful and compelling, conveying Martha's deep emotions and inner conflicts."

—*Booklist*

"Heather Kaufman gives us a biblical story with a heart for today's world, pulling out an array of joy and hope, sorrow and loss. Ultimately, this book consumed me with absolute delight. . . . *Up from Dust* is a ray of hope for every Martha who seeks and follows Jesus."

—Mesu Andrews, Christy Award–winning author

"*Up from Dust* is a story of struggle, of old family hurts that haunt life for aching years. Ultimately, this novel pits our unhealed wounds against the hope that only Jesus can offer. Heather Kaufman is a truly fresh voice in biblical fiction with great promise."

—Tessa Afshar, *Publishers Weekly* bestselling author of *The Hidden Prince* and *The Peasant King*

"*Up from Dust* invites us into Jesus' inner circle with fresh insight on the life of Martha of Bethany. Taking us on an intriguing journey through heartbreak and healing, this strong debut from Heather Kaufman leads readers directly to the joy of the empty tomb."

—Connilyn Cossette, Christy Award winner and ECPA bestselling author

"A heartfelt story of faith . . . Through Heather Kaufman's gorgeous and masterful writing, the world of first-century Judea comes to life. . . . To say that I fell in love with Martha is an understatement. This was Kaufman's debut novel, and I look forward to what she writes in the future!"

—*Historical Novels Review*

BEFORE
the
KING

Books by Heather Kaufman

BEFORE *the* KING

JOANNA'S STORY

HEATHER KAUFMAN

BETHANYHOUSE
a division of Baker Publishing Group
Minneapolis, Minnesota

Published by Bethany House Publishers
Minneapolis, Minnesota
BethanyHouse.com

Bethany House Publishers is a division of
Baker Publishing Group, Grand Rapids, Michigan

Printed in the United States of America

Library of Congress Cataloging-in-Publication Data
Names: Kaufman, Heather (Heather M.), author.
Title: Before the King: Joanna's Story / Heather Kaufman.
Description: Minneapolis: Bethany House Publishers, a division of Baker Publishing Group, 2025. | Series: Women of the Way
Identifiers: LCCN 2024026653 | ISBN 9781540903570 (paperback) | ISBN 9780764244551 (casebound) | ISBN 9781493448937 (ebook)
Subjects: LCGFT: Bible fiction. | Novels.
Classification: LCC PS3611.A8277 B44 2025 | DDC 813/.6—dc23/eng/20240624
LC record available at https://lccn.loc.gov/2024026653

Unless otherwise indicated, Scripture quotations are from The Holy Bible, English Standard Version® (ESV®), copyright © 2001 by Crossway, a publishing ministry of Good News Publishers. Used by permission. All rights reserved. ESV Text Edition: 2016.

Scripture quotations labeled NIV are from THE HOLY BIBLE, NEW INTERNATIONAL VERSION®, NIV® Copyright © 1973, 1978, 1984, 2011 by Biblica, Inc.® Used by permission. All rights reserved worldwide.

Scripture quotations labeled NLT are taken from the Holy Bible, New Living Translation, copyright © 1996, 2004, 2015 by Tyndale House Foundation. Used by permission of Tyndale House Publishers, Carol Stream, Illinois 60188. All rights reserved.

This is a work of historical reconstruction; the appearances of certain historical figures are therefore inevitable. All other characters, however, are products of the author's imagination, and any resemblance to actual persons, living or dead, is coincidental.

Cover design by Jennifer Parker

Cover image of Herod's Palace Interior © Israel Museum, Jerusalem / Holyland Tourism 1992, Ltd. / Bridgeman Images

Cover image of fortress (Monzón Castle) by PRISMA ARCHIVO / Alamy

Published in association with Books & Such Literary Management, BooksAndSuch.com.

Baker Publishing Group publications use paper produced from sustainable forestry practices and postconsumer waste whenever possible.

25 26 27 28 29 30 31   7 6 5 4 3 2 1

This one is for my sisters,
Laura and Anna,
with love.

Do not hide your face from me in the day of my distress! Incline your ear to me; answer me speedily in the day when I call!

Psalm 102:2

prologue

60 AD
ROME

He's sitting in the center of the room when I enter, his parchments and pots of ink scattered across a scarred table. He wants my stories. He wants to write them down. But first he asks after our friend, the one who brought us together, and I smile. Our friend is well, I tell him. More than well, for she recently became a *savta*. Like Naomi dandling Obed on her knee, the woman whose life seemed barren has been given a legacy.

I settle across from him, this beloved physician, and watch his stained fingers carefully dip the tip of his stylus, tapping once, twice, then bringing nib to parchment, face expectant as it lifts to mine. What was it like, he wonders, and uses the word to describe me that so many do.

Brave.

My eyes mist, for I am not brave, and I tell him so. I am an ordinary woman whom God chose to put in extraordinary places. Any strength to be found in my story is His alone. I only did what I could with what I had, and this, I now know, is how His Kingdom advances.

Each of us doing what we can with what we have by His power.

So no, I am not brave. I am needy—desperate for Adonai to meet me with His strength. My story is how He did just that.

Through years of sorrow and fear, when the face of God seemed a distant star, whose brilliance was meant for others but never me . . . He was there. And now I will never tire of sharing the story of His faithfulness, for it is a living flame, meant to spread.

My story, however, begins in a place of fear, hiding, and uncertainty, for my heart had yet to learn its greatest lesson—that God is as near as our own breath.

PART
ONE

ONE

SPRING 13 AD
BEIT NETOFA VALLEY, ISRAEL

The sun kissed the fragrant earth with fervor, promising a full day of excitement and importance. I blinked into that bright light, smiling until my cheeks ached. Abba normally didn't bring Dalia and me along when he traveled, but today was different. Today we would all go to see our family's new country villa.

"Things are about to change for us, my little swifts," Ima declared, clapping her hands as she used her affectionate name for us. Dalia and I were restless—roosting in high places like the small bird that made its home in the clefts of rocks, never settling down, eager to move. We jumped now, giddy with this new adventure.

"How, Ima? How will they change?" Dalia hopped from foot to foot, her honey-colored hair gleaming beneath the sun. I pranced by her side, my black curls bouncing off my back.

"We are moving to a city even bigger and grander than Cana. Buildings taller than you can imagine! So many things to see and do."

We were young enough that the thought of change brought

only curiosity, so we absorbed this news without understanding all that it entailed.

"Will we live in the city? What about the villa?" I squealed, unable to contain my delight.

"We'll live in Sepphoris, but the villa is not far away in the country. Some farmers will tend it for us, and we will visit it whenever we like. Today you will see it with your own eyes."

"And you, Ima? You will come too?" Dalia questioned, spinning on her toes.

Ima laid a tender hand on both our heads. "Of course," she chuckled. "We'll have Vidette pack us food. How does a picnic sound?"

We cheered at the thought of supping outdoors with Ima.

A litter bore our family from Cana to the city, and as the strong walls of finely chiseled ashlars rose tall and grand before us, my breath caught. Herod Antipas' palace towered above the walls, its gold-plated roof slyly winking beneath the sun, bearing secrets we would soon discover.

"That's Sepphoris?" I squeaked, cowed beneath such brilliance.

Ima bent so our faces were cheek to cheek as we beheld the city together. "Yes, and our new home will be close to the acropolis. That's the very center of the city."

"When? When will we go live there, Ima?" Dalia wondered, sticking her head out of the litter.

"Soon," Abba answered as he pulled her back inside, his thin lips quirking upward. "Uncle Leshem is gifting the estates to us soon, and then we will move."

I'd never met Abba's uncle, who was a chief priest and member of the Grand Sanhedrin in Jerusalem. It was Uncle Leshem who was appointing Abba as a member of the Sepphoris Sanhedrin. Abba had been talking nonstop about our family's "change of fortune."

Our litter descended into the sprawling and lush Beit Netofa Valley just north of Sepphoris. I gaped as we approached the grand estate. As soon as the litter stopped, Dalia and I tumbled out into the clear air and ran into the gardens. The trees seemed to beckon us with wide-open arms, and the air was sharp with the scent of ripening fruit.

For once, Ima did not chide or call us back. Instead, she sat on a cushioned seat as a servant held a fan to shield her from the sun. With crinkling eyes, she watched us tussle in the long grass.

"Let's play hide-and-seek," Dalia suggested, her brown eyes sparking with fun.

I nodded my agreement, and we both ran to Ima's side, tugging her hands, imploring her to join us in the game.

With a groan and a grumble, she rose to her feet, but her eyes were soft as she began counting out loud. We shrieked and ran like spilled oil from a jug, spreading out and away, looking for the best hiding place.

My gaze snagged on a pear tree. I threw myself at it, small hands grabbing at the lowest branch as my sandaled feet clawed at the rough trunk. Finally, I managed to heave myself up onto the branch and lay there for a moment, panting and exultant, before I continued my climb.

I was only seven, and small for my age. The climb proved to be a difficult one as I strained my tiny stature as far as it would go, reaching toward one branch and then another. The tree was in full bloom, and easily hid me. I sat contentedly, swinging my legs.

"Let me up, Jojo!" Dalia's breathless voice drifted through the leaves. I peeked down to find her at the base of the tree, hands clasping the first branch, face red with exertion as she tried to follow me.

"Go find your own spot."

"But yours is so good," she whined.

I rolled my eyes as I watched her struggle to pull herself up. "We don't want to be in the *same* spot, Dalia. Go find your own."

"If you . . . would just . . . *help* me!" she spluttered, straining at the branch. With a yelp, her grip broke, and she fell back, lying for a moment, still on the ground.

"Dalia?" I slid lower on my branch.

She sat up, regaining her breath and sobbing as she examined her hands. "Ouch! My hands are cut." She glared up at me, and I ducked.

"Fine!" she spat, voice full of tears. "Since you're being so *mean*, I'll go find my own spot." She scampered away.

It was too bad that she'd scraped her hands, but I was too irritated to entertain guilt for long. Dalia was always following me around, even though she was older by a whole year. We were often mistaken for twins, for we were equal in height and, apart from our hair color, looked similar. We had the same round face and large brown eyes, the same full lips and pert nose.

"Oh, girls, where are you?" Ima's voice rose like a song, her tone light as she approached. "My little swifts, I'm going to find you!"

I held my breath as Ima drew near, searching this way and that. I'd been right to send Dalia off. I'd still be hauling her into this tree if I'd let her stay.

One heartbeat and then two. Ima sighed and left, heading in the direction of the villa.

I released my breath in a long sigh and giggled with delight. Long moments passed, and I spent them kicking my legs and staring through the branches into the bright blue sky. The fruit grove spread like a bountiful blanket at the foot of a hill, and on the top of that hill stood the impressive villa with its stucco walls and tiled roof. Terraced gardens and paved pathways led up to it.

This day, with all four of us together, was special.

Our parents had borne children later in life, when hope of a family was all but gone. Because they had stopped expecting children, Dalia was the biggest of surprises, and when I had arrived soon after, they'd been consumed with shock and joy. We were prized and important.

Even so, Abba was often too busy for us. As a priest and a member of the Sadducees, his time was valuable and rarely spent with his daughters. Now he would have a more prominent role in this new city, so I was certain we would see even less of him. Both my time and Dalia's would also change. I'd overheard our parents talking about all the new things that would become available to us in Sepphoris.

"We will be able to employ a tutor for the girls," Abba had said. "With two daughters and no sons, I'm determined that they become educated and marry well. And with this appointment, we will have the means and opportunity to see that happen."

Soon Dalia and I would become knowledgeable in Greek and Latin, for we would marry important men one day.

"Why shouldn't we aspire to Herod Antipas' court?" Abba had gloated, eyes alight with ambition.

But today we were together. I kicked my feet harder, setting myself slightly off-balance, grabbing the trunk for support with a laugh. Today we were a family, the four of us, even if Abba would spend most of his time inside with the tenants.

Wobbling to my feet, I clung to the trunk and strained to catch a glimpse of the villa. Had Ima found Dalia yet? Too much time had passed. Impatiently, I slid back down the tree, scraping my hands in my haste. What a fuss Dalia had made earlier! A little scrape wasn't so bad. With a sharp huff, I ran in the direction I'd last seen Ima go.

I'd made it halfway up the hillside when the shrill sound of Ima's scream pierced the air, causing me to jerk to a stop. Never had I heard her scream like this. The sound came to rest in the bottom of my stomach, where it simmered and leapt like one of Vidette's boiling concoctions.

Trembling entered my limbs as Ima continued to scream. I managed to pull my legs free from the earth and ran and ran. Up the hillside and along the front of the villa to an enclosed courtyard on the side. The gate was open and swinging on its hinge. I stopped at the gate, but my heart continued to race, pounding ahead of me, leaping to the middle of the courtyard where Ima stood screaming for Abba.

Dalia lay stiffly on the ground, her head cocked at an awkward angle, eyes wide and unseeing.

She's dead.

I placed both my hands over my gaping mouth to stifle the scream that tore at my throat. But no, she wasn't dead, for as I stared at her face, she jerked once and then twice as if someone grasped her with two strong hands, trying to shake her awake.

"Itamar, come!" Ima screamed as she sank to her knees by Dalia's side. "No, no, no," she moaned, rocking rhythmically on her knees. "Not like Sarah. No, God, please."

Ima continued to moan her own sister's name while voices rose from inside. Soon Abba had joined Ima in the courtyard, his face crumpling in disbelief as he beheld Dalia, who was still jerking. "What happened?"

"I found her this way! I found her this way, Itamar! What can we do? I can't go through this again!" Ima was babbling and crying all at once, her words barely recognizable.

"How long has this been going on?" Abba cried.

"I don't know," Ima sobbed. "I found her like this."

"We were playing," I whispered, but no one heard me, no one saw me. "We were playing, and I wouldn't let her up and she fell." I sank to my knees. Had Dalia become injured because I wouldn't help her into the tree?

Abruptly, Dalia's jerking stopped, and she lay motionless at our parents' feet. Hot tears burned my face as Ima gathered Dalia into her arms, crooning to her in a raw voice.

She's dead.

I sat miserably at the gate, watching Ima grieve. Dalia's small round face was pressed into the crook of Ima's neck.

I killed her.

I stared at my sister's face. I wanted to scream and claw at the earth. I wanted to run down the hill and throw myself back into the tree and wait for this horrifying day to be over. I wanted to fly far, far away, like a true little swift, and never return.

But then Dalia opened her eyes.

Two

Our parents were filled with hope that Dalia's episode would never happen again. "There is no cause for alarm yet," the physician assured us.

For her part, Dalia seemed completely recovered. She was my bright-eyed sister, my friend and shadow. Our family spent a worrisome week, gazing at Dalia like she might crumble at any moment. As the days stretched on with no reoccurrence, however, we turned our attention to the move. Abba sent some of our belongings ahead, and Ima regaled us with stories of the grand city we would soon inhabit.

Just as Dalia's episode became a painful memory, she had another—this time in the kitchen while trying to nab a sweet. It was the same as before. Dalia lay stiff and jerking, eyes unseeing, remaining this way briefly before reviving.

"I've seen this before," Ima moaned in Abba's arms late into the night. I perched unseen outside the door, knees anchored against my chest, eyes wide and dry. "Sarah had similar fits."

"Hush, Zahava." Abba's voice was deep and comforting, but I heard the quaver he tried to hide. "It must be a passing illness. Sarah outgrew the seizures."

"Yes, but it took years, and I've heard of those afflicted throughout their whole lives. Their whole lives, Itamar!"

Ima's despair burrowed into my bones, leaving me shaken and morbidly observant. I began monitoring myself, wondering if I would be next. When would I lie senseless and shaking on the ground? I awaited an attack that never came. Instead, the illness continued to bypass me and afflict my sister.

One day, at the marketplace, Dalia collapsed in the middle of the street. Shocked screams sounded, and many stepped back, fearful that whatever tormented Dalia might spread to them too. Ima and I crouched by Dalia's side, forming a protective barrier, tears streaming down our cheeks as we waited for it to pass. And then I heard it for the first time, whispered like a bad omen. *Demon.*

"I know we don't believe in the spirit world, but, Itamar—they looked at her like she was indeed possessed," Ima wailed to Abba.

As Sadducees, we did not believe in the spiritual realm, nor in God's direct intervention in human affairs, but doubt flickered in Abba's eyes that night.

The next week, as we were alone preparing for bed, Dalia dropped to the ground again. I placed both hands, warm and heavy, on her face, staring into her unseeing eyes as I waited for the spasms to pass, holding her body close when they did.

My limbs were firm, my mind and body intact. *Please, God, let it be me next time instead of her. Please!* I prayed, hopeful that He would listen and take pity.

With a pinched expression, Abba sent notice to Uncle Leshem that our family's move must be postponed since his daughter was ill. Abba called for the best physicians, but no matter what we did, nothing worked. Dalia continued to experience intermittent episodes at different times of the day and night.

As we continued to go without answers, Abba was sapped of vitality. He began keeping Dalia close to home. No more trips to the market or playing in the fields. By slow and painful degrees, Dalia's sphere of movement dwindled to the confines of our walls. The only place he allowed her to go was to synagogue.

On a bright summer day, we were standing in the back of the synagogue while Abba read from the Torah. His sonorous voice filled the room as he read the account of the fall of humankind. Dalia was restless and uneasy by my side, one hand to her stomach, the other reaching to me, her eyes holding a flicker of fear. I was beginning to understand the signs and was reaching back to her when she fell.

She landed hard against a woman who yelped with surprise, jumping back and knocking over a lampstand. It crashed to the ground, dangerously near Dalia's head. Ima screamed as Dalia jerked closer to the flame.

And then Abba was there, righting the stand, dousing the flames, the words of Moses scattered across the stone floor behind him.

Demon.

In the marketplace, the word had been spoken by strangers. Now, neighbors we had known for years tossed the word one mouth to another.

Demon.

The word tore through my heart with terrifying speed. There was a dreadful certainty in everyone's face as they watched my sister convulse. I wanted to scream my resistance, but the core of me rattled with fear and uncertainty.

Later that evening, after a lengthy meeting with the elders and priests, Abba returned home with defeat etched on his face.

"I have prayed ceaselessly over Dalia, but to no avail," he groaned. "I cannot have others thinking I have a demon-possessed daughter!" Abba's voice cracked. "I could not live down the shame of it."

"Ah, the shame," Ima said in a harsh hiss. "Is that all you can think about? When our daughter is being robbed of life in front of our eyes?"

"You are turning this against me," Abba grunted. "I am confounded by this, but the elders were clear. They insist on an exorcism, even knowing my stance on the subject. They are adamant. If she has any more public episodes, we won't be able to contain the gossip that spreads."

That very week, several priests came with incense and prayer. A mixture of defeat and hope filled Abba's face, his lips moving in silent petition as he observed their efforts.

"We cannot continue like this, Zahava," Abba spoke afterward in a deeply troubled tone. "By now Uncle Leshem knows this is no temporary illness. Word has reached him that Dalia suffers from some inexplicable ailment. What I've feared has come to pass. He now threatens to withdraw my appointment to the Sanhedrin."

"She's only a small girl," Ima sobbed. "She's not a threat to anyone."

"You know as well as I that there can be no hint of scandal associated with our family—nothing that would indicate my unsuitability for such an esteemed position. In granting me this post, Uncle Leshem is tying his own reputation to ours. He will not hesitate to withhold my inheritance to preserve his name. Everything we hoped for would be gone."

Ima emitted a wet, gurgling wail as her tears choked her breath. "What do we do?"

Abba grew quiet. I stood outside their door, small and silent.

"Itamar?" Ima's voice trembled.

Abba released a deep moan, and I realized he was weeping. Deep fear and curiosity compelled my hand to open the door. They were sitting on a low bench, Abba bent double, forehead against his knees, while Ima collapsed over his back with a hand covering her face.

I stood breathless before their grief. Closing the door, I fled to my room, where I wet my blanket with tears.

◆

The morning sounds of the village trickled through my window as I sat curled on a seat, chin propped on the sill. With languid eyes, I traced the movement of people on the streets and tried to ignore the worried voices in the room next door.

My parents' early morning argument had woken me. In truth, I'd barely slept, tossing and turning all night long, dreaming of Abba's tears. Now I gazed out the window as dullness settled in my chest.

"I don't want my daughter sequestered away like we are ashamed of her! We cannot isolate her. I saw what happened with Sarah." Ima's voice was unwavering, but Abba's was stronger and filled with authority.

"Which is why we must take different measures than your family did. We must learn from their mistakes. What I propose may seem severe, but it avoids your own father's error and ensures not only her protection, but ours as well. You saw what happened at synagogue. Next time she could be burned, trampled, or worse. The seizures are too uncontrollable and unpredictable."

"Should we shove something aside simply because we do not understand it? Or is God trying to get our attention, Itamar? The way He did with the burning bush? What if Moses had turned away because he could not understand fire that did not consume?"

"You would liken Dalia's condition to the holy fire sent by God?" Abba's voice broke with disbelief.

"No, I—"

"I understand enough to know that Sepphoris is no place for Dalia."

Ima sucked in a sharp breath. "Are you concerned about our daughter or your own reputation?"

"I have every right to be concerned with both. With this new role, I will be one step away from Herod's court. Our position isn't something to be careless about. We must be wise, Zahava."

Below in the street, an obstinate mule pulled at his bit. I watched quietly as his owner beat him, curses carrying in the wind.

"Joanna?"

I raised my head slowly to gaze at Abba in the doorway. Out in the hall, Ima softly wept.

"Yes, Abba?"

He closed the door behind him with a sigh and stood quietly for a moment, staring past me and out the window. We were seldom alone together. I took the opportunity to study his face. It was lined and tired. His black beard was filling out with gray.

"I have something important to tell you." His eyes rested briefly on me, pain entering his face before he quickly looked away. The screams of the mule from the road distracted me, but Abba's next words reclaimed my attention.

"We'll be moving to Sepphoris soon. It's a large city and very busy. Much busier than Cana or anything else you're used to. It's not . . . safe for your sister to be there."

"What do you mean, Abba?"

"We cannot take Dalia with us."

Even though the words entered my ears, I could not understand them. "But she is a part of our family."

"And she will remain a part of the family . . . but not in Sepphoris." Abba ran a shaking hand through his hair. "I was hoping your mother would help me explain this to you, but she refuses to come in. You remember Aunt Sarah?"

I nodded, mind whirling. Ima's younger sister lived in the fishing village of Gennesaret, off the northwestern coast of the Sea of Galilee. She was married to my uncle Ebner, a fisherman. We hardly saw her, and Ima rarely mentioned her, except these last weeks.

"Dalia will remain a part of the family, but she will go live with Aunt Sarah, where she will be much safer than in Sepphoris."

Tears leapt to my eyes. "I don't understand."

"It's not for you to understand, child." Abba swallowed hard and cleared his throat. "It's for you to accept. This is what's best—not only for Dalia, but for the whole family." He crossed the room to place a large hand on my head.

"You are young, and there are many things you do not understand. But you will. You will in time. For now, it's enough that you accept what has to be."

I gazed up at him and tried to see the tenderness in his face. It was there if I looked hard enough. "Will we visit her?" I managed past the lump in my throat.

Abba's hand slipped from my head, fingers catching in my glossy curls. "Perhaps. . . . Once things have settled. This is hard to accept, but you will adapt—we all will. Dalia will be happy with Aunt Sarah, and you will receive the best care and attention in our new home."

He hooked a finger beneath my chin, tilting my face upward. "You will do well and will grow into a lovely woman, just like your mother."

"Yes, Abba." My voice squeaked.

Abba withdrew his hand quickly, turning to hide his face from me. He hovered by the door as if he had more to say, clearing his throat once before leaving me alone.

I peered out the window and realized the mule was gone. Willingly or not, it had left. I clenched my teeth until my jaw ached. Abba said Dalia would still be a part of our family, but how was that possible if she was so far away? Why must we send her away?

Quietly, I unfolded my legs and padded to the door, glancing

26

down the hall to ensure I wouldn't be seen before quickly ducking into Dalia's room.

The window was shuttered against the early morning light. I paused to let my eyes adjust. Dalia's bed rested against the far wall, her small form unmoving beneath the blanket. On trembling legs, I crossed the room and stood silently, staring at her face.

"What does it feel like?" I'd asked her once, curling against her side in the dark, our heads tilted together.

"It feels . . . strange in my stomach and my head. But it happens so fast. Most of the time I don't know it's coming."

"Does anyone . . . talk to you? Do you hear any voices?" The question I truly wanted to ask lodged in my throat, unspoken. *Do you hear demons?*

"No, of course not." She'd crinkled her nose.

I looked at her now, so serene in her sleep. Was Dalia something to be scared of? Was she something to hide? No, she couldn't be. She was my silly, happy, beautiful sister. I wanted Dalia to stay with me. But I wanted her to get better too. Was living away from me truly better for her?

I squeezed my eyes closed. God seemed so big in the stories from Torah. He was big, powerful, and could do anything He pleased. He had saved our people from slavery and given us this land. He had created Adam with a word from His powerful mouth. So couldn't He, with a single word, heal my sister? Abba claimed God was no longer involved in people's everyday lives, but . . . maybe He was. And maybe He would do this one thing for me.

Crawling into bed, I snuggled against Dalia until our noses touched, voicing another prayer from the deepest part of me, asking for something I wanted more than anything else. The beginnings of this raw prayer came soft and stumbling, spilling from my unpracticed lips. "God, please, please, please."

He'd kept me safe and whole, while Dalia remained stricken.

If He wouldn't afflict me in her stead, then maybe He would do something better. "Make Dalia well again. Please, God. Make her better. I love her. Please keep her with me."

Tears leaked from my eyes and fell on Dalia's nose where it rested against mine. Her expression scrunched up briefly, and she sighed, softly smacking her lips in sleep. A fierce, new determination sprang up within me.

Did God see me? Did He hear the prayers of little girls? Or only of men like David and Abraham? Perhaps if I prayed hard enough and long enough, then maybe God would hear me. Then maybe He would come and help.

THREE

Summer 22 AD
Sepphoris, Israel
Nine Years Later

The midmorning sun flared off the bronze mirror, blinding me with its brilliance. I squinted and adjusted myself on the cushioned seat, blinking away the rosy spots in my vision, focusing once again on the fine features reflected back to me.

"You will make quite the impression," Ima murmured by my side.

Behind me, Eden, my young handmaid, twisted my curls into tight braids. My scalp itched as her slim fingers pulled tight, but I resisted the urge to scratch.

"I was going to save this for later, but I simply can't wait." Ima slid an ornate box onto the table, opening it to reveal a collection of jars. "You're so beautiful already, but why not highlight that beauty?" Ima beamed. "A little kohl for your eyes and color for your cheeks. Judith says these colors grace the features of Queen Phasaelis herself. What do you think?"

"Thank you, Ima." I gave her the dimpled smile she loved. Judith, the wife of Herod's leading economist, was an endless fount of information when it came to cosmetics and perfumes.

I'd seen these exact shades on her daughter, Mireya, a few weeks ago. Certainly, Ima had noticed as well, which had prompted this gift.

As Ima left me to Eden's deft ministrations, I turned my attention back to the mirror, watching as my hair took shape into a lovely array of braids. When she'd finished, Eden took a step back with lowered gaze. "Would you like me to apply your cosmetics, mistress?"

Eden had recently entered our home, and I was still getting accustomed to her quiet manner. She looked young, with eyes so large and cheekbones so pronounced that she appeared to be in a constant state of surprise.

"I'll do it myself." I dismissed her with a wave.

Once alone, I slowly explored the contents of the box, noting the delicate spoon and dish for mixing powder and oil. Scooping kohl into the dish, I drizzled oil over the powder, slowly mixing it with the spoon and then dabbing the inky black mixture gently with a small wand. I'd seen the process done on Ima many times. Solemnly, I drew a line around one eye and then paused, pursing full lips in inspection.

I was beautiful. It was a fact of life, and I understood the deep joy it brought my parents. The fields grew golden with barley at Passover, the Sea of Galilee teemed with fish, and Joanna, daughter of Itamar the Sadducee, chief priest in Sepphoris, was stunningly beautiful.

The decadence of the cosmetics was one of many ways our family had embraced the opulence of our new home, separating ourselves from the Pharisees and those from the lower class who adhered to their teachings. Abba often spoke disparagingly of what he termed the "lives of deprivation" lived by the men in the solemn black and white robes, faces full of unattainable holiness as they proclaimed the merits of a life to come.

"Why deny oneself now in anticipation of a future life? Man is not

God that he might live forever!" Abba's view was shared by most of the Sanhedrin, for most were fellow Sadducees, who believed there was no eternal life, only the one given now.

Because life was lived but once, it should be lived to the full. Therefore, Abba, and others in his sphere, patterned family life after Herod's own court, embracing the Hellenization that most common Jewish people despised. This meant I was afforded much more freedom than was typical for Jewish girls, such as outings to the glamorous four-thousand-seat theater or attending elaborate dinner parties, as was the case tonight.

Right eye finished, I moved to my left, hand trembling slightly in concentration. The party tonight was in honor of Livia, the beloved daughter of Ravid bar Simeon, Herod's lieutenant and my future father-in-law.

Unlike his demure daughter, Ravid's son, Othniel, was a wolf—hungry and impatient. He was often seen in the acropolis, prowling next to his father, who was an overseer of goods in the thriving Sepphoris marketplace. Possessing the form of someone who spent ample time at the gymnasium, Othniel and his impressive build set many girls' tongues ablaze. I'd listened to such talk with partial interest, for despite Othniel's angular and arresting features, his character was unproven and his hunger for more power elicited unease within me.

What irony, then, that he had chosen me for a wife. And how fitting that Abba had immediately and joyously agreed.

Finished with the kohl, I leaned back and applied small dabs of color to my round cheeks and full lips. Othniel would appreciate the efforts I was taking, and the thought put a confusing twist into my stomach.

This union was everything that Abba had hoped for, and I would not disappoint him. After the marriage contract was finalized, we would hold a betrothal ceremony, solidifying our legal union until the marriage followed a year later.

With a sigh, I shoved thoughts of Othniel aside and gently pressed my lips together, pushing the color deeper into my flesh before leaning back to gaze at my handiwork.

"You're so beautiful, sister!"

I stiffened. For a moment, my painted eyes slid closed.

Imagination—it was a stubborn beast that insisted on conjuring up Dalia even though I hadn't seen her in two years. I turned and stared, half expecting to catch her in the doorway but knowing she was many miles away.

On and off for seven years, Ima and I had traveled north, bearing gifts and money to Aunt Sarah and Uncle Ebner. Initially those visits had throbbed with hurt and tension. There were deep and aching wounds between everyone, and Uncle Ebner barely seemed able to tolerate our presence.

We persisted until the wounds became scars—ever present but bearable.

Slowly, Aunt Sarah had loved Dalia into acceptance, until she'd felt less abandoned by her first family and more like she'd been gifted with a new one.

The first time Dalia called Aunt Sarah *Ima*, discomfort had stretched wide in my chest. Happiness that my sister had a place she belonged warred with a loss that felt endless. Slowly, Ima had come to terms with that loss. I, however, continued to live with a hole in my chest. I craved our meetings, desiring the straightforward simplicity of Gennesaret and the companionship of my sister.

When Uncle Ebner had died three years ago, Abba had sold our country villa and given the funds to Sarah so she and Dalia would never want for sustenance. Instead of seeing them more after the large gift, we saw them less.

Last year, Ima had made excuses as to why we couldn't go. This year, it had been the same. A weaning had begun, and with my imminent betrothal, I understood why. Life was changing in directions where the past could not follow.

The past . . . it was littered with years of unanswered prayers. My first halting pleas had multiplied into a torrent of earnest cries. Many nights I'd prayed myself to sleep, staring hard at the ceiling or squeezing my eyes shut as tightly as I could. I'd prayed standing, sitting, lying prostrate. I'd prayed staring out the window toward Gennesaret. I'd prayed kneeling in the direction of the Temple in Jerusalem. I'd called upon God as Yahweh, Elohim, and Adonai. I'd prayed until the faith within me dried up and cracked open like a stretch of thirsty ground.

How many years had it taken before I'd realized that God was too big to bother with me?

Too many.

Hope deferred had made my heart sick. Prayers no longer spilled past my lips, for I'd come to my own place of acceptance. Hope would try to make sense out of life's randomness, but this was a fool's endeavor. Better to accept what was than wish for something that would never be. Perhaps Abba was right and our lives were ours to direct without God to assist.

I'd asked her once. After noticing fresh burn marks on her arms where she'd fallen into a flame, I'd asked Dalia how she could continue to believe in a present God when such awful things happened.

"I have to believe," came her simple reply. *"In order to live, I have to believe that He is present and that He cares."*

Misguided, I thought. I'd kept my observation silent, unwilling to cause her one more moment of pain, but she'd seemed to catch my disbelief, had looked at me with that narrowed expression that saw too much.

"He gives as well as takes," she'd told me. *"I have experienced comfort that I cannot explain. In being denied a full life here, God has given me a glimpse of the fullness to come."*

There it was again—a life to come, a life beyond the immediate, an eternity in the presence of God. Abba rejected such teachings, as most in our sphere did, but then there was Dalia—utterly, undeniably convinced, and my heart had pounded hard with the thought. *What if?*

Closing the ornate cosmetics box, I slowly wiped my fingers clean of the kohl's black residue. My prayers may have ceased, but thoughts of Dalia lingered. I often welcomed them when they came. I let them climb into my mind and then sat with them, waiting until they eventually left.

And they always did. The thoughts left while I remained here in the life that should have been my sister's.

◆

Sepphoris teemed with activity, pulsing like a throbbing heart in the palm of Herod's hand. Spread out in a grid, the city was bustling with commerce, for it was on a major trade route. As Herod Antipas' capital, it was the seat of political power.

"We are privileged indeed to call the jewel of Galilee our home," Ima often said.

Our family's fine house was only a few streets away from the acropolis, the fortified heart of the city. From my latticed window, I could see the gleaming white limestone walls of the basilica, and not far beyond that was the synagogue where Abba spent most of his days. Ravid's extravagant home, however, was inside the acropolis, not far from Herod's gold-roofed palace.

As we approached the elaborately carved doors of Ravid's home, light glinted from outdoor torches, throwing shadows across Abba's face. For months, his features had been pinched, as if he was struggling to hold onto something that was determined to fly free. Tonight, however, he looked loose and relaxed.

Under the combined glow of moonlight and torches, Ravid's steward led us into a small vestibule with a brightly patterned mosaic floor. Music and laughter drifted from deeper inside the home. As we entered the grand reception room, I cast an observant eye over my surroundings.

The stucco walls were a stunning white with broad deco-rated panels mimicking stonework. The ceiling was carved into a breathtaking honeycomb pattern. Low tables surrounded the room, and in the center sat a group of musicians playing a lively melody.

"Itamar, you bless us with your presence!" Ravid approached Abba and extended the kiss of welcome. "And Joanna, my beauti-ful future daughter-in-law! Come and make yourself comfortable. Livia will be delighted to know you're here. She's been eagerly awaiting your arrival."

I allowed myself to be guided to a table full of Livia's com-panions. Beneath the flickering candlelight, the young women sparkled with their jewels, their high-pitched laughter dancing off the walls.

"You look stunning tonight." Mireya lifted a goblet in a toast to me as I settled onto a cushioned seat by her side.

With a touch of humor, I noted that we wore the exact same shade on our cheeks. "As do you."

"I hear you are to be congratulated," Mireya continued, cap-turing my arm and drawing me close. "Othniel bar Ravid is a fine match indeed. There isn't an unmarried woman present who isn't jealous of you." She cut her eyes down the length of the table to punctuate her point.

My gaze followed hers reluctantly. She was right. More than a few young women were casting jealous glances my way. I shifted uncomfortably in my seat.

"Is it true that your friendship with Livia facilitated the match?" Mireya took a long swallow of wine, settling into my side like a cat beneath a sunbeam.

Mouth dry, I nodded to a servant who swiftly filled my goblet. "I suppose it's true that my acquaintance with his sister put me within Othniel's presence." I lifted the cup to my lips, hiding behind its silver rim.

"You are a smart one. I'll give you that." Mireya laughed lightly. "Befriending the young girl was a good move."

"I didn't . . . you speak as though I used Livia."

"Didn't you?" Mireya raised a languid brow.

"No, I most certainly didn't."

"Well then . . . a happy accident." Mireya giggled, the wine already going to her head.

I twisted away, attempting to hide my irritation. Part of the reason I enjoyed Livia's company was because of her youth and sweet temperament. She had yet to learn the sharp ways of the court, one that saw women as pawns for maneuvering. Upon meeting her, my heart had pounded with protectiveness.

A loud laugh drew my attention to the head of the table, and I tensed as I saw who sat by Livia's side. Susanna, daughter of one of Herod's councilmen, was leaning familiarly into the guest of honor, commanding her full attention.

"Susanna is too late, isn't she?" Mireya quipped, lifting her empty goblet to a servant. "Why the fuss to impress the girl when her handsome brother is all but betrothed?"

Weariness poured smoothly into my limbs, weighing them down. I'd had no ulterior motive with Livia. Surely, she knew that. I caught my lip between my teeth and waited for her to look my way, but it was Susanna who turned. The breath stuck in my throat.

Susanna often made a point of singling me out in public settings. Her tongue cut sharper than a two-edged blade, and her penetrating gaze could level the strongest man. Her look became haughty as her eyes held mine, one brow lifting as her lip curled.

Weariness turned to heat beneath Susanna's assessing gaze. I widened my kohl-lined eyes and returned her stare with a set jaw. She laughed slightly, my bravado amusing her, and focused her attention back onto Livia.

"Why the dark expression tonight?" Othniel's voice crawled

unexpectedly into my ear, and I startled. "Your features are far too lovely to be twisted into such a frown."

Quickly, I smoothed my expression as his eyes eagerly roamed my face, his extended hand inviting me up and out from behind the table.

Our interactions had been few, but even so I knew this—Othniel was well aware of the effect he had on most women; indeed he was enjoying it now with Mireya, who stared at him with flushed cheeks and parted lips as I left her side to join his.

He watched my every move, more like a cub than a wolf, eager for me to engage with him. "You have nothing to say?" he prodded, his jaw flexing.

"You gave me a compliment on the underside of a slight, my lord. A lady, no matter how lovely, is allowed her dark looks without needing to explain herself."

At my smart reply, the wolf reappeared, eyes lingering on the jewels at my throat. He eased forward with a release of air from his perfectly formed lips. "Tell your father to hurry with the negotiations over the marriage contract." His tone dipped as his hand captured my elbow. "He is being overly fastidious."

I pulled back, a flash of discomfort filling my breast, both at his physical proximity and harsh words. "He has a right to take his time, and you would do well to learn patience." The swiftness of my retort surprised me, and I bit my tongue, hoping my tone had been sufficiently playful rather than reproachful.

Othniel studied me, eyes wavering briefly before settling into a gleam of anticipation. "A man is allowed some impatience, don't you think?" His gaze slid down the length of me, a slow smile spreading across his bronze face as his eyes returned to mine, approval in their depths.

I glanced to Abba, who was across the room with one of Ravid's colleagues, a dark, tall man who towered above him like an oak. His clothing marked him as a courtier, and Abba was obviously flattered by his attention—too flattered to notice his future son-in-law's brashness.

"Livia will want to know you're here." Othniel shifted the conversation, glancing at his sister. "If Susanna will ever stop dominating her ear." The slight condemnation in his tone sparked my curiosity, but before I could explore his meaning, he'd already turned to his favorite subject—himself.

"I'll be following in my father's footsteps soon. With construction almost finished at Tiberias, Herod has already promised my family a large estate and prominent positions within his new administration."

Tiberias was around eighteen miles east of Sepphoris, a full day's journey away. Sitting proudly on the coast of the Sea of Galilee, it was a strategic location and had been under construction for years.

"It is true, then, that Herod will move to Tiberias, even with the recent discovery?" I probed, knowing the answer but curious about Othniel's thoughts.

He scowled. "That is a lot of fuss over nothing."

"Ceremonial uncleanness is hardly nothing." I arched a brow, seeing how he would respond. "They uncovered a cemetery, and Herod chooses to build anyway. You know the instruction of the Pharisees is widely accepted on this count. According to their teaching, the Levitical purity laws are to apply to all Jewish people."

Othniel observed me quietly for a moment with an assessing look. "Are you sympathetic to their teachings?"

"I've been taught to view their instruction as unnecessarily burdensome." I gave a safe answer that smoothed over whatever deeper feelings I harbored. "However, the fact remains that most people are upset by this discovery."

"Herod is well aware of our nation's customs. An observant Jew should have no fear of coming into contact with the dead when Herod has ensured that towers of industry and culture are firmly established above them."

In Othniel's impassioned words, I recognized my father's own ardor for Herod's administration. In Abba's eyes, Herod represented our nation's continued future. *"Better to have one of our own in power than Rome,"* he often said. What others saw as moral compromise by a power-hungry ruler, Abba saw as strategic interplay between the Jewish people and our Roman overlords. *"Our duty is to God, yes, but appeasing Rome allows us to fulfill that duty."*

With the discovery of the cemetery at Tiberias' construction site, however, Abba had shown flickers of doubt. As a Sadducee, he did not extend the purity laws to all people. He was, however, meticulously concerned with ritual purity when it came to the priesthood.

"How will the priests be able to maintain purity atop such a site?" he'd mused to Ima. *"Do the benefits of the location outweigh such concerns? Herod must think so if he's willing to upset the people so deeply."* As Herod staunchly pressed forward, however, so had Abba's approval and any discussions of doubt ended.

Marriage to Othniel meant I was destined for Tiberias, despite how I might feel about the matter. I did not relish the thought of living atop a cemetery or of being used as a means for advancement by this young man who was still watching me possessively.

You are being harsh, Joanna, I chided myself. *You are attributing the worst to his motives when you hardly know him.*

I released the tenseness in my shoulders and gave Othniel a smile I hoped was generous. "No matter the location, I'm certain you will do well in Herod's new administration."

At that moment, Othniel's companions came, goblets in hand, to lead him away, and with some hesitancy, he let them, eyes trailing back to me.

"What were you two talking about?" Susanna approached with a gleam in her narrowed eyes.

"I could ask you the same," I returned coolly, with a nod toward Livia.

"You are welcome to him," Susanna said in a tight, clipped tone. "Did you know that we were nearly betrothed once?"

Despite my best attempt, surprise showed in my face, causing Susanna to smirk.

"However, my father quickly dismissed Othniel when he found a much more desirable match with Manaen."

"'A personal friend of Herod himself,'" I sighed, repeating her father's words back to her. "Yes, your family made sure everyone knew of the betrothal."

Susanna had delivered her news about Othniel with airy aloofness, but as her eyes strayed to him, a hint of pain smoldered in their depths. She turned quickly back to me, a mask of control firmly in place. "You are more than welcome to my leftovers."

Her pointed words were flint to stone inside me. "Certainly, I will take what you cannot have. Othniel is robust and handsome, is he not?" In this quiet statement, I thrust the dagger deep, for Manaen was much older.

"Your betrothed has several children from a previous marriage, correct? Even though they aren't much younger than you, I'm sure you'll make a fine mother." I drove the dagger home.

Susanna clenched her teeth until the muscles along her jawline ticked. "You are not as modest as others think you are. Joanna, the beautiful and docile daughter." Instead of laughing dismissively, she held my gaze with an unsettling steadiness. "I find you to be . . . interesting." She departed quickly, and I was left with mouth hanging open. Her disdain I could handle, but her curiosity was new, and I was disoriented beneath the spark of her interest.

My hands were trembling. Splaying my fingers, I noted the

slight waver and balled them up into brief fists before stretching them out once more. *Control yourself, Joanna. Get a firm grasp on your tongue. These parties and these people . . . they are your reality, but you don't have to become like them. You know this.*

I would find Livia, who was still sweetness and innocence. I would congratulate her on her birthday and stay by her side for the remainder of the evening.

She was standing in a small cluster of women as I approached. "Joanna!" Her face brightened upon sight of me as she broke away to grasp both my hands in her own.

Pulling her close, I pressed a kiss to her cheek. "Happy birthday, Livia. Are you enjoying yourself?"

"Oh, I am! Abba gave me the best gift. Look!" She thrust out her arm. Encasing her slender wrist was a shiny gold band with twining vines and delicate leaves engraved upon its surface.

At the sight of the glinting piece of jewelry, the breath caught in my chest. I blinked rapidly.

"Isn't it lovely?" Livia's fingers traced the design.

"It's . . . yes, it's . . . beautiful." *Not now.* Memories of the past were clamoring for entrance, pounding upon the door of my mind. *Not now. Not here.*

"Are you all right?" Livia's smooth face scrunched with concern. "You look pale."

"I'm fine." I took a steadying breath. "I became lightheaded for a moment. Too much wine, that's all."

"Sit, and take some food!" Livia stretched a hand to the lavish table where fresh fish, poached eggs, roasted figs sticky with honey, and many other delicacies tempted the tongue.

I allowed her to lead me to the table as if food was indeed all I needed. But the winking of her bracelet beneath the flickering light of the lamps kept calling my mind to the ring of crown daisies at home, a gift from Dalia that was dearer than all the jewels surrounding me.

Livia served me herself, urging me to partake, and I did. Licking honey from my lips, I pulled on a smile and directed my thoughts away from young men full of ambition, ladies full of flirtation, tongues full of fire, and daisies blooming with broken promises.

FOUR

Eden's slender fingers raked through my dark tresses as she undid the tight braids in preparation for bed. Slowly, I rolled a hairpin back and forth across the table, replaying my quick words from the banquet, grimacing at the memory. I'd used my words to wound the way Susanna often did. Mireya would be proud.

Nine years of feeling caught between two worlds, perpetually restless like a little swift.

I moved my hand from the hairpin, fingers hovering over the drawer, aching to open it, to trace the faded flowers within.

"Oh, Jojo, everything will be all right." Dalia's voice, tender and brave the last time I'd heard it. I was fourteen and she fifteen, and yet the old, familiar name still dropped from her tongue. *Jojo.*

It would be the last time we were together, but we didn't know it. I was of marriageable age and fearful. Dalia could never envision my life in Sepphoris, no matter how many stories I collected and shared with her.

Even then, Abba had begun his tireless hunt for a worthy suitor, and I was terrified. My fear found release in the slender arms of my sister. I'd sat tucked against her side, shivering and miserable as I recalled the barrel-chested man who had approached Abba for my hand and whom he had turned away as inferior. But there would be more, and eventually there would be one whom Abba did not turn away.

"Breathe, Jojo. You're going to make yourself sick."

I'd tried to comply, but my breath was snatched from my chest. I'd heaved with the effort to draw air.

"Here, look at me." Dalia's voice had been so calm as she'd plucked a small bouquet of crown daisies from a patch at our feet. Methodically, she'd begun braiding them into a chain, the way we used to do as children.

"Remember?" she'd asked.

Mutely, I'd nodded, watching her thin fingers pluck at the blooms without damaging them. Slowly my breath had evened.

"I'll make you a crown, Jojo. A crown of crown daisies." Her practiced fingers had flown quickly over the flowers, transforming them before my eyes. When finished, she'd nestled the circle of bright yellow blossoms atop my dark curls, breath catching. "You're so beautiful, sister!"

I'd managed a grin through my tears, gently fingering the flowers where they lay among my curls.

"One day you will marry a good man. He will love you deeply; I know it. It will be God's good gift to you, and I will be there to see it." Dalia's bright expression had slipped, easing from delight to sadness. "These flowers are a promise between us. Promise me that when God sends you that good man that you will send for me. And I promise I'll come to you." I could tell that she was trying to be strong, trying to ease us over the edge of yet another good-bye.

I gave in and opened the drawer. After two years, the dried daisies were all but crumbled, falling apart like the promise they represented. Behind the few faded blooms was a beauty and simplicity that was far removed from my life.

Quickly, I shut the drawer and swallowed the lump in my throat.

Othniel—strong, handsome, and with a promising future—

was the culmination of many years of effort. At the age of sixteen, I was older than most girls who entered marriage simply because Abba had been overly selective. Many suitors had arisen over the years, but none were high enough to please Abba . . . until now.

Threading her fingers deeply into my hair, Eden massaged the tender spots on my scalp. "Are you well, mistress? You seem distracted. Would you like a cup of tea before bed?"

"No, thank you. I'm simply wondering—" I broke off. Eden was new to me and young, but she was the only listening ear I had at the moment. "I'm wondering why happiness is so elusive. I should be happy with a match that everyone deems desirable."

"But you're not," Eden stated softly, fingers stilling.

"Not yet," I whispered.

Eden was silent for a long moment, fingers absently playing with a lock of my hair. When she did speak, her voice seemed older, the words she delivered hard learned. "I think sometimes happiness has to grow over time."

I twisted to peer up at her. "What do you mean?"

Her face blanched.

"Don't be nervous." Awkwardly, I patted her hand. "I welcome your thoughts."

Eden swallowed convulsively, a confusing array of emotions crossing her face. "I . . . I suppose I meant that sometimes we have to *choose* happiness, and even then . . . we often have to wait for it." Now her cheeks flamed, dark eyes meeting mine then shifting away. "We aren't always able to harvest happiness immediately, but we can nurture it while it grows."

"You are wise beyond your years." My brow lifted in admiration.

Ducking her head, Eden nudged my face forward. "Hardly, mistress, but it's kind of you to say so."

With a lump in my throat, I watched my head weave and bob

in the bronze mirror as Eden undid every last braid, until my curls were free and flowing, my thoughts not far behind.

———— ✦ ————

I dreamed of daisies and woke up coated in sweat. Ever since the match with Othniel, I'd shoved this particular memory of Dalia away. Abba and Ima would never agree to send for her, so why stir up desire within my own heart when it would lead to disappointment?

But the memory was here to stay. For days it lingered, refusing to remain locked away in a drawer, rattling about in my mind, encouraging me to follow it back to a field of flowers and forward into a future that maybe—just maybe—could include my sister once again for a moment.

Still, the request was risky, for Dalia had never come to us. Indeed, my parents had expressly forbidden me to disclose that I had a sister.

"Your father is in such a high position that if others knew of Dalia's affliction, it would endanger both his position and your chances at a good marriage." In Ima's wide and weary eyes, I saw years of suppressed emotion. *"A man will not want a bride whose sister is so afflicted, whose children might one day also exhibit the signs. . . ."*

"Was it like that with Abba and you?"

"No." But Ima's face had grown tight.

I was well instructed of the danger Dalia's condition presented to our family and yet perhaps now, with the betrothal at hand, my parents would be amenable to the request. Perhaps I could convince them that the greatest risk was behind us, and I could honor the promise I'd made to my sister after all.

Nearly a week after the banquet, I awoke resolved, hurriedly dressing for the day and dismissing Eden before she could tend to my hair or cosmetics. While my resolve remained high, I went in search of Abba, knowing I'd most likely find him supping alone in his study off the main reception hall. Approaching silently, I was surprised to see the door ajar and had raised my hand to knock when a voice I didn't recognize stopped me short.

"Thank you for agreeing to meet with me today."

The voice was low, smooth, and deeply accented. I scrunched my nose, trying to ascertain the nationality of its speaker.

"I'm honored that you would seek my advice," came Abba's gratified response.

A swift peek through the cracked door showed the back of the tall man Abba had spoken to at the banquet. Guiltily, I moved away, preparing to leave, but the man's next words stayed my steps.

"The discovery of the cemetery weighs heavily upon the king. I, among others, urged him to withdraw from the site completely, but the location is too strategic and the progress too advanced."

Abba grunted deep in his throat. "So now he runs into the problem of population. You are newly appointed as his financial minister. How do you feel about his recent decision?"

Financial minister? I placed a hand over my mouth. Abba was receiving an important guest indeed.

"What I personally feel is of no account," the man replied smoothly, with practiced diplomacy. "My job is to keep a firm grasp on his finances."

"I've heard he is liberating slaves on the condition that they settle there. He is extending free housing and land—even suspension of taxes—for the poor who have few alternative options."

There was a long pause, during which the man shifted in his seat. "You speak with some hesitancy," he finally replied.

"I'm commiserating, not reprimanding," Abba quickly asserted.

"This is why I'm coming to you. The administration needs to know who they should approach among the priestly and aristocratic families about relocating to Tiberias. The king's purse alone cannot populate the city. It must be offset with families that won't see the recent discovery as a concern."

A swirl of conflicting emotions pooled within me. My new home would be populated with mostly paupers and slaves?

"You will encounter some difficulty when it comes to the priesthood." Abba's voice was controlled. "However, some names in the aristocracy are coming to mind. I will give it more thought and get back to you."

I was too distracted by the conversation to notice the scraping of the chair, the minister's voice as he offered his thanks. When his large frame appeared in the cracked doorway, I scurried like a startled rabbit, leaping to the side and out of the way, seeking shelter behind a decorative plant as the door opened. I pressed myself against the wall as the men took their leave of each other.

Abba returned to his study, and the minister hesitated for a moment in the hall. I peered at him through the fronds, surprised to see that he was younger than his voice sounded—perhaps ten years my senior. He emitted a deep, weary sigh and scrubbed a large hand slowly over his face. Something about his sad demeanor tugged at my chest.

He muttered something to himself, and recognition flared—he was Nabatean. Our neighbors to the southeast were a common sight, for Herod's own wife was Nabatean, the daughter of King Aretas IV. Was this minister new to court? He seemed to wear his station reluctantly, if the expression on his face was any indicator. Why was he lingering so? His hand raked through his hair, which was black and thick and stood on end in the wake of his long fingers.

What was he waiting for? The longer he tarried, the more irritable I became, legs locking into place, feet beginning to tingle. I jumped when he moved, bumping awkwardly into the potted plant.

"Who's there?" His deep-set eyes found and fastened onto me where I shrank in the shadows.

"Oh, I'm sorry, sir . . . Minister." I shuffled out of hiding and ducked my head, now achingly aware that I wore no cosmetics and that my hair flowed free.

"No need to apologize." His features softened at the sight of me, composure returning even as his hair continued to stick up in all directions. "You're Itamar's daughter?"

I nodded mutely and kept my gaze trained away from his face. It landed instead on his broad shoulders, which flustered me, causing me to shift my eyes to the ground.

He had the build and bearing of a warrior but with the manners of a courtier. Impressively tall, with skin the color of rich acacia wood, he exuded calm strength under tight control, and I was cowed—utterly intimidated without quite understanding why.

I glanced up just as his tousled hair flopped back over his forehead. The small movement made him seem younger, and the tight knot in my chest eased.

"You overheard our conversation?" he pressed. "You appear distraught."

Did I? Flustered hands found my cheeks, which were warm to the touch. "How did you . . . ?"

"The furrow in your brow." He tapped his own lightly. "And the look in your eye. I'm trained to notice such details."

Hurriedly, I attempted to smooth my expression. "I admit that I did overhear your conversation. I apologize—I didn't intend to eavesdrop. As to being upset . . . I suppose . . . I didn't know that the king intends to . . . ." Now I was talking *too* much. Quickly, I shut my mouth.

"You didn't know of the king's plans to populate the new city." He finished my thought. "And it upsets you."

Careful, Joanna. I glanced up at the minister's face. Was he trying to trap me into expressing disapproval over the throne's decision?

But his gaze was kind and understanding. It was a face that invited confidence.

"I've alarmed you. I'm sorry." He spoke again, brow knotting with his apology.

"I'm not upset, merely curious," I quickly answered, eager to be done with the conversation before this man elicited something incriminating from my lips. "I will, after all, be moving to Tiberias upon my marriage."

Something in his face shifted.

"You've come to the right man," I continued, nodding toward Abba's study. "My father will be able to assist you well."

The minister's eyes cut to the closed door briefly before returning to me. "Your father is a good man, I think. Desirous for the welfare of his family."

"He is certainly desirous for the *advancement* of his family," I clarified and watched as surprise lifted the minister's brow.

"Most see advancement as corresponding to welfare." He broadened his stance, settling into the conversation. "But you do not see it in such a light?"

"I often don't know *what* I think." The admission left my lips before I had a chance to reconsider it. "Women do not have the luxury of following their convictions or true desires." Where had this brashness come from? I swallowed my dismay and dipped my head, preparing to leave, but he was leaning forward, eager and interested.

"That—I believe—is a true pity. Some of the most vibrant minds I've known have belonged to women."

"This is not Nabatea." I smiled ruefully. Women from his culture enjoyed economic and legal privileges unheard of throughout most of the surrounding region.

"No," he chuckled. "No, it most certainly is not."

A noise from Abba's study jolted our attention to the closed door, and a deep flush spread across my cheeks. I shouldn't be standing here talking to such a prominent man. *He* shouldn't be talking to an unmarried woman with her father right behind the door.

I ducked into a quick bow, not daring to look him in the face again. "Minister."

From the corner of my eye, I could see him watching me as I swiftly sidestepped the plant and hurried from the hall.

The conversation about Dalia would have to wait.

———— ✦ ————

Abba tore a hunk of bread into pieces, dipping the largest into the bowl of lamb stew, bringing it to his mouth, only to set it back down half-eaten with a wince. By his side, Ima chattered about a recently widowed friend and all the woes she was experiencing with her estranged son but stopped abruptly as she saw Abba's face.

"Are you well? Do you need to lie down?"

"I'm fine, simply tired. I'll retire in a bit but not before we share our news." Swiftly, Abba motioned for a servant to bring him a bowl of water. He wet his fingers, dried them, pointed at me. "We've come to an agreement on the terms of the marriage contract. We can set a date for your betrothal ceremony at last— the sooner the better."

"It will be a beautiful and grand affair," Ima added, eyes shining.

"The family has requested a shortened betrothal period," Abba continued. "Nine months rather than the typical year."

"Nine months?" I squeaked. "Why the hurry? Won't there be talk if we rush the wedding?"

"Nine months is hardly rushed," Ima assured. "It's enough time to prove your chastity. There shouldn't be any gossip."

"You are older than most who enter marriage," Abba reminded me. "It doesn't surprise me that Othniel is impatient to start a family with you."

I gazed at the table with flaming cheeks. Susanna, when she found out, would be furious. Nine months placed my marriage soon after her own.

"Do you have nothing to say?" Abba asked expectantly.

My shoulders eased downward as acceptance landed heavily upon me. "I'm glad things have proceeded as you've hoped, Abba." I raised my eyes, looked firmly into his own, searched for courage. "But I have one request to make. Once the betrothal is complete . . . might we send for Dalia? Invite her to the wedding ceremony?"

Ima sucked in a sharp breath, held it, released it on a trembling question. "Itamar?"

But Abba was shaking his head. "I understand you think the risk will be lessened once the betrothal is complete, but I assure you, such an invitation would be imprudent. We cannot compromise this union before the marriage ceremony."

"Just this one time, Abba, please." I swallowed with difficulty, feeling like a young girl again pleading with God to do this one thing for her—just this one thing.

Abba winced sharply, but whether it was from physical discomfort or from his denial remained unclear. "I'm sorry, my girl, but the answer must be no." Ima sat silently by his side, refusing to look me in the eye.

I'd been foolish to follow memory into hope. I'd opened the drawer, opened my heart, and I'd known better than to do so.

"You have been generous with Aunt Sarah and Dalia after the death of Uncle Ebner," I stated softly. "Can you not be generous with me in this?"

"Whether you believe it or not, I *am*, Joanna. It is love for you and your future that compels me."

"What about a love for Dalia?"

"She is well provided for. You know that." Abba had a hand to his side, face growing pale. "I will lie down now, Zahava." He rose slowly. "We must put the good of the family above all else, Joanna."

Swiftly, I looked away and bit my lip. Some days, I allowed myself to believe wholeheartedly in my parents' good intentions. While other days, as now, the hurt in my breast was sharper than all else. In such moments, I could no longer rationalize their choices and didn't even want to try.

An unexpected sob clutched my chest as tears flooded my eyes. Lurching to my feet, I pushed past Abba and out of the room.

Like Herod populating his grand city with former slaves, Abba would do whatever it took to build up appearances. This was the life I was living—this propped-up façade, this illusion of flourishment above a bed of death and decay.

FIVE

With the denial of my request came a crack in my soul. I'd made a promise to Dalia. How could I break my word?

With shaking hands, I started and stopped numerous letters, not fully knowing if I would send one in spite of Abba's firm answer. My room became littered with crumpled parchments full of sentiments that seemed either too hollow or too much. My heart hardly knew how to begin, or if I dared to defy my father.

Five days of strained silence reigned in our home, during which time my chest constricted every time I thought of Ima. She'd always been a link to my sister. If not for her, our visits to Dalia would never have happened. But now, when she could have used her voice to come to my aid, she'd remained silent.

I avoided Ima until one day I came across her in the courtyard. The afternoon sun slanted into the heart of our home, highlighting the fine features of her face. She reclined upon a cushioned bench, head against the stone wall, face open to the sun, hands cradling a cup of cinnamon tea. I attempted to leave, but Ima tapped the space next to her with a sad smile.

Wavering briefly, I finally perched on the bench at the farthest point from her. If she noticed my aloofness, she didn't draw attention to it. Instead, she stared thoughtfully into the sky for a long moment before speaking.

"Family relationships are often unbearably complicated. We must learn to live the best we can among the tangle of past grievances." She directed her eyes to her cup, swirled the dark liquid within.

"Even if we did send for Dalia, I doubt Sarah would let her come. She and Ebner were always protective, fiercely so, and there was deep discord between them and your father."

She broke off, and my eyes widened in surprise. It wasn't like Ima to speak so candidly. My body tensed, fearing any movement might spook her into silence.

"You know the stories—how Sarah suffered as your sister does. Ebner came to love her the year before she outgrew her ailment."

"I've prayed the same for Dalia," I murmured. "That she would outgrow this malady that grips her."

Ima's eyes closed, lids pressed tight. When she opened them again, they shone with tears. "But by that time, the damage to the family had already been done. Sarah was found to be with child. Her life had been difficult, and Ebner was the only person who seemed to reach her, the only person she truly loved. I think that desperation drove their actions. Ebner was beneath our family, not a man my father, an elder of the town, would have chosen. They married quickly. They didn't have a choice. Shortly after, they lost the babe, and some say her years of subsequent barrenness was just punishment for the nature of her sin."

I quieted at this new picture of my aunt.

"Ebner hated the gossip and what it did to Sarah. He lived with that bitterness all his days. You saw how he was when we visited. He could barely stand the sight of us. In fact, he told your father he never wanted to see him again."

"Is that why Abba never visited with us?"

Instead of answering, Ima hid behind her cup, taking a long swallow. "Ebner came from a different class," she continued, swirling the last dregs of her tea. "He didn't understand the world we belong to, nor did he wish to. And yet even with the animosity between our families, they have been good for Dalia, and I do not regret that decision." Ima chewed her lip until I thought it'd sprout blood.

"You *never* regretted it?" My tone lifted in disbelief. I'd seen the way Ima had wept after those first early visits, the way she'd held onto her grief, keeping it close and away from the light.

She sighed. "Perhaps, at first, I did regret it, but then after . . . when I saw how Dalia flourished in her new home and understood the joy she brings to Sarah. She, who had lost the one babe and had no more children of her own, now has a daughter to love. And Dalia has . . . a mother who can understand."

Her voice clogged with tears. With a swift, rough hand, she wiped her eyes and turned to me with a firm expression. "Dalia is where she is supposed to be. It is for the best, and we cannot risk her having an episode here and exposing our family to the gossip."

My heart rose in protectiveness, the way Uncle Ebner's must have. I, too, was tired of the gossip, the lies and speculation that dictated our lives.

"Do you know what some people say about you?" I'd asked Dalia once.

When I'd asked her this horrible question, her soft voice had gone hard. *"What others think of me has no bearing on who I am."* She'd grasped my startled face in her slender hands and stared at me with glinting eyes. *"Remember this, Joanna. What people* think *changes all the time. What is true never changes."*

I looked now at Ima and wished with all my soul that I could explain it to her. That I could tear open my breast for her to witness all the things I struggled to articulate.

"Perhaps it . . . it doesn't matter how others view Dalia." My voice cracked with effort. "Perhaps love and truth . . . perhaps these things matter more than appearance, more than—"

"Truth?" Ima stated as if hearing the word for the first time. "What others *perceive* to be true is a powerful thing, Joanna. It is nothing to toy with. You best learn this now. It doesn't matter what something *is*—only what it appears to be."

Setting my jaw, I stared at the paved ground, noted the grime in the mortar between the stones. "I would think the *actual* truth would be even more powerful," I murmured, but Ima didn't appear to hear. Her face, when I glanced at it, was tilted once more toward the sun, as if begging it to blind her with its relentless heat.

❖

Later that evening, I entered my room to find Eden crouched over the table. Upon my entrance, she spun with a yelp, thrusting her hand behind her back.

"What do you have there?" I questioned gently and watched as fear entered her wide eyes.

When she remained silent, I slowly approached her and gently pried one of my crumpled letters from her clenched fist. "What were you intending to do with this, Eden?"

"Oh, mistress, I'm sorry!" Eden fell to the ground, her neck and cheeks darkening in a rapid blush. "I shouldn't have been snooping. I mean, I wasn't *snooping*. The parchment . . . it was sticking from a drawer, and I went to close it. Oh!" She broke off in dismay, pressing her face to my feet.

"Eden, get up!" I yelped, distraught at the sight of her prostrate and trembling form.

She attempted to obey but was shaking so violently that she couldn't rise past a crouched position.

"You were . . . not intending to take this to my parents?" I questioned softly.

"Never!" Eden's eyes flashed to mine, and in their depths, I saw a mixture of fear and strength. "Mistress, I would never do such a thing. I overheard you with your mother, heard the request you made about your sister. Oh, mistress! It isn't *right* that they keep you from her!" The words came leaping from Eden's lips like a warhorse chomping for battle even while she remained in a humble position at my feet.

I extended my hand, waited until she grasped it, and then pulled her to standing. "Why does this upset you so?"

Eden tried to tug her hand free, but I clasped it firmly in my own. "I-I should comb your hair for bed." She blurted the inane comment and then flushed as I laughed.

"You cannot distract me from my question! Why do you care so deeply about my sister?"

"Your parents, they took a choice away from you as a child, and now they're taking another choice away." Her free hand leapt to her chest. "I shouldn't have said that."

With a long sigh, I released her hand. "You and I, we are getting to know each other. One thing you must learn is that I'm not so easily angered." My lips quirked. "Well, at least I try not to be." My expression shifted into seriousness. "But please know one thing right now—I won't mistreat you, Eden, like some might."

I went to the drawer, slid it open, and stared down at the remains of the daisy chain. "If I keep my promise to my sister, I go against my father's wishes. The repercussions . . . they could be disastrous, but . . ."

"But perhaps it is worth the risk," Eden whispered. "One shouldn't be robbed of family."

"As you were?" I questioned. "Is that why you're so passionate? I don't know the details of your history—what your life was like before now." I paused and tried to catch her eye. "But I recognize the ache in your voice."

Eden cleared her throat. "You are my mistress, and if you demand it of me, I will share my past."

"I won't *demand* anything from you, Eden."

"Then I . . . I prefer to let my history be my own."

"Very well."

A little sigh escaped Eden's lips.

"And now, yes, you may comb my hair for bed." I grinned and sank onto a seat.

Grateful, Eden settled behind me, and for a moment all that sounded in the room was the swift shush of the comb through my curls. As my limbs relaxed, I reached for the crumpled parchment and ran my thumbnail along the edge as my heart moved toward its decision. I gazed at Eden's distorted reflection in the bronze mirror. Would she help me? Something deep and hopeful in my chest told me that she would.

Six

WINTER 22 AD

Abba swiftly set a date for my betrothal, but only days before the ceremony, two priests were killed in broad daylight near the basilica. The men involved had dragged and dumped the bodies onto the steps of the Roman temple next door with shouts of "No lord but God!" The event was one of many in a long line of recent attacks in Sepphoris, but this one struck differently. Mireya's uncle was one of the deceased. I, along with others, attempted comfort, but the public nature of the attack and inhumane treatment of the bodies left Mireya's family inconsolable.

The local Sanhedrin was kept busy, conferring with Herod as to how to end such violet outbursts, which meant Abba spent long hours at the palace, returning home bleary-eyed and strained.

"This is not good for you, my love. You need rest." Ima's large eyes welled with concern.

"There can be no rest until we reach the bottom of this. Herod grows livid, Zahava. He sees this as both a moral and political failure, but what can the Sanhedrin do? These men are elusive."

"These men" were Zealots—those who claimed to be zealous for God and the purity of His people.

"They seek to purge the land of Rome, as if such a thing were possible," Abba complained over dinner, where he barely touched his food. He'd grown thin in recent months. No matter how hard Ima plied him with food, he remained gaunt, and in his worried speech, I could tell pressure from the throne was affecting him.

"All they do is make things harder for our people by their brutality." Abba pushed back from the table. "They claim God alone as their authority but refuse to submit to His representatives on earth. Such men cannot be trusted."

"Do you think *we* are in any danger, Abba?" I questioned, recalling Mireya's thundering sobs. "They target Jews whom they regard as Roman sympathizers, so could it be *our* family next time?"

"No," Abba assured, but the look in his eye spoke otherwise. "The Sanhedrin will sort this out."

And yet the hatred evident in these attacks left me feeling exposed, like my family had personally done something despicable, worthy of great violence. The notion that we were hated doggedly pursued my mind.

Were these men right in their desire to drive out Rome, punishing those who believed otherwise? Or was Abba right in wanting to cooperate with Rome to ensure the peace and prosperity of our people? What chance did an insect have in crushing the hand that held it? Then again, the sting of a wasp did hold some power.

"You are frowning and brooding tonight, mistress." Eden gently ran a damp cloth over my brow, removing the day's cosmetics. "Is it thoughts of your betrothal that quiets you so?"

Since our candid conversation, I'd assessed Eden with a new and interested eye. There was a dormant fire within her that she banked with great care.

"I'm preoccupied with thoughts of our family. I fear some look at me and only see an arrogant Roman sympathizer."

Eden moved from my brow to my lips, lifting the color off them with firm pressure. "I don't find you to be arrogant, mistress. Some may view outward status as indicative of arrogance, but I have known poor men who were full of pride."

She dipped her cloth in a bowl of water, gently wringing it out before bringing it back to my face. "Sometimes . . . men who have nothing become too focused on their lack. I don't think anyone is exempt from arrogance, no matter their station."

"Still, some would condemn us without even knowing us."

"Didn't the Lord tell the prophet Samuel that He doesn't look the way man looks? Man looks on the outward appearance, but the Lord sees the heart."

Ah, she was so young, and her words so hopeful. I had been that way once.

"He may see and hear, Eden, but make no mistake—His ways are higher than ours, and He does not always answer."

◆

The day of my betrothal arrived on a thundercloud, perfectly imitating the restlessness of my heart. Eden spent hours on my appearance and, as a finishing touch, dusted my dark curls with flecks of gold and nestled pearl pins in their folds. I emerged from my room swathed in the finest linen and with a gauzy head covering that kissed my face with every move. Ima greeted me at the bottom of the stairs with a sigh of approval before leading me into the reception hall.

I entered the room as if walking into a dream. My body registered my movements, but my mind was detached and distant, observing the proceedings from outside myself. Ravid had brought a handful of guests as witnesses. They all turned as I entered, and my eyes immediately snagged on the minister from Nabatea, the kind man who'd spoken so freely about the vibrant minds of women.

"Some of Ravid's colleagues," Ima whispered. "Herod's chief architect as well as his financial minister are here." Her eager commentary did nothing to assuage my nerves.

The minister seemed taken aback by my regal appearance. The last time he'd seen me, I'd been barefaced and hiding behind a plant. I shifted my gaze from his wide eyes to find Othniel regarding me with obvious relish. Swallowing with difficulty past the lump in my throat, I allowed Ima to guide me to his side, where he grasped my hand possessively in his own.

It was a warm hand, strong and smooth. I stared at it, unwilling to meet Othniel's hungry eyes as I pushed back the strong swirl of emotion forming in my body. I began to shake as Othniel withdrew a golden ring and slid it onto my finger. My hand was trembling so violently that he had to try twice before meeting success. A slight frown passed over his features.

What was wrong with me? I had known this day was coming, had submitted myself to this man of Abba's choosing. He was handsome, and he had chosen me. What more could I desire?

Abba drew forward the marriage contract and spoke a blessing over us, but the ceremony itself was mercifully short, serving only to bind us legally. Nine months from now, the marriage ceremony would take place, and I would enter Othniel's home . . . and his bed.

A spasm of what I now recognized as fear shook me as Othniel signed the contract. What wayward spirit held me that I could not settle into joy? He turned to me with a confident grin and extended the stylus.

I don't want this.

The realization blazed across my mind, as bright and undeniable as a sunbeam piercing a darkened room.

Year upon tired year of ignoring my own desires had schooled me to stop recognizing them. If I desired nothing, then I would not have to face disappointment. How foolish! For I could see now that I was still riddled with desire. I wanted my sister. I did not want this man. Oh, if I had been honest with myself and everyone else sooner. Would it have made any difference?

"Joanna." Abba's voice, firm and low, tore through my mind and lifted my eyes. I took in Ima's confused face, Abba's pinched features, and Othniel's disgruntled expression at my prolonged hesitation.

My eyes flew about the room, searching for landing, coming to rest on the minister where he stood in the back, silent and observant. His eyes were shaded with compassion, the same look he'd given me in the hall.

"Man does not see as God sees." The words Eden had recited found a home in my heart. I could not see inside this man who was about to become my betrothed. I could not see into our future. I could not see enough to bring me peace.

With numb fingers, I took the stylus from Othniel and bent over the contract.

Elohim. The name came trembling to the surface, dusty from disuse. *Elohim.* I used His ancient name, the name of power and strength. *Elohim.* I breathed, shaking and searching for solid ground. *I cannot see. Help me.*

I signed and stood, head light.

"God be praised!" Abba declared, clapping his hands and leading our guests toward the more intimate dining room off the courtyard.

It was done, and now we would celebrate.

Men and women typically dined at separate tables, but because of the occasion, I was given a prominent position beside my betrothed. We reclined next to each other, symbolizing our legal union. As the food was brought in and the drinks poured, I expected relief to fill me, but my chest continued to tighten as if a hand clutched it with greedy fingers, tangling and capturing my breath.

My arm was too unsteady to support myself in a reclined position, so I sat next to Othniel's relaxed form and raised a cup to my lips. The wine seemed to land on top of my stomach. I reached for a piece of bread, trying desperately to settle my nerves, but the bread became paste in my mouth. Another sip of wine only served to mix with the paste and turn it into a disgusting concoction that I barely managed to swallow. My stomach refused entrance to the bread and the wine, which seemed to hover uncomfortably inside me. Lingering breadcrumbs stuck in my throat, and I coughed once, twice, while trying not to gag.

"You will do well in court." Othniel angled his body to look up at me. "I observed you long before we met and was glad when you befriended Livia. You have the bearing and the beauty to stand among the finest in Herod's court."

I gave him a weak smile, eyes watering as my stomach roiled. Othniel must have mistaken my expression as deeply felt emotion, for satisfaction flooded his features, and he shifted so that his hand slid beneath the table. My body tensed as his fingers brushed against my knee. Because I was seated next to his reclined form, he had full access to my leg. I shot an alarmed expression in Abba's direction as Othniel ran a finger along my calf. Heat filled my cheeks, and my head began to swim as his hand grew more curious. Did no one notice his impudence?

I attempted to shift away from Othniel's eager fingers, but his hand followed and recaptured my leg. Inadvertently, I caught the minister's concerned gaze. Of course, he'd notice, this astute man with the kind eyes.

"Be patient, Othniel." I laughed nervously, twisting so the minister wouldn't see my distress as the contents of my stomach came to rest solidly in my throat.

With a groan, Othniel released my leg with a final squeeze

and returned to the food. "The marriage ceremony cannot come soon enough for my liking." He took a long swallow of wine, eyes never leaving me.

I was going to be sick. No amount of willpower could quench the upheaval inside. I stumbled to my feet, surprising our guests. Mustering up a smile to communicate all was well, I skirted the room as quickly as I could without running. Once outside the dining room, I ran to the bath across the courtyard, barely making it before I retched onto the tiled floor.

Long-elusive relief poured through me, and I collapsed onto a stone bench with a groan. In the wake of the relief, however, came embarrassment. Resting my head against the wall, I placed a hand to my brow. My skin was clammy, like clay after a brief rainfall. I needed to walk back into the dining room with my head held high. And I would. But not right now.

I allowed myself a moment of deep breathing before rising onto weak legs. My head was still spinning and light, but at least my stomach no longer rebelled. Slowly I entered the courtyard, stopping short as I saw the minister outside the dining room, head swiveling in search of someone. Looking for *me*.

His dark eyes found me and deepened with their discovery. Humiliated that I'd been caught in such a weak state, I mustered up the last dredges of my strength and crossed the courtyard. He met me in the middle, concern evident on his face.

"Are you well?"

"I'm fine," I managed to say and gave him a deeply dimpled smile.

This smile—it worked on most people, but apparently not on him. He observed me through narrowed eyes and tapped the space between his eyebrows. "You smile but your brow is still worried. Do you need anything? Would you like me to fetch someone?"

"No, I'm fine now," I assured him. "Something I ate disagreed with me."

His expression lifted with disbelief. "Something other than the food distresses you."

I opened my mouth in astonishment at his insight and forwardness.

"Forgive me." He raised a hand and ducked his head. "I'm trained to detect when people are lying—a habit that is hard to release."

This man was supremely comfortable with himself and sure of his own observations but without any of Othniel's arrogance.

"I suppose I am anxious . . . as any new bride would be."

Again, his expression lifted in disbelief, but this time, he checked his tongue. Still, a desire to explain myself flared to life. Before I could think better of it, I'd blurted out, "Well, it's true. Any bride would be anxious."

He continued to gaze at me with those deep-set eyes. I could still detect his disbelief, and it began to frustrate me. Why was he so sure of himself? He didn't know me. "Are there no anxious brides in your country?"

A flit of pain crossed his face as he took a step back, a barrier sliding into place between us. What had I said to cause this shift in his mood? Regret nipped at my mind, and my tongue loosened in an effort to outtalk my own embarrassment.

"It's the way of the world—a woman's desire must follow after her duty. I do not know Othniel, but I will come to know him as his wife. Of course, there is anxiety when a woman binds herself to an unknown man." I thrust a hand to my chest, grasping at my ornate necklace.

The minister had remained silent beneath my stream of words, eyes filling with a sorrow I couldn't begin to understand. At last, he spoke as I stopped to gulp breath, fingers tangled in jewels.

"I know what it is to choose duty over desire." He paused, the firm set to his jaw indicating that he was carefully choosing his words. "I did not mean to cast judgment upon your fear. As for

Othniel, he is young and eager. In his eyes, life is a challenge to conquer. He has not learned the lessons only sorrow can teach."

My breathing slowed as I studied his face. Even though he kept his tone neutral, I sensed his disapproval of Othniel. "Ima says that marriage is the garden where love and understanding grow," I stated slowly. "And perhaps that is true. Perhaps we will grow together. Even though I am fearful of the unknown and do not relish the idea of living in Tiberias . . ." I broke off, blinking up at the minister, surprised at the sudden pressure of tears behind my eyes.

"Your God promises His presence wherever you go, does He not?" The minister looked down at me with warm eyes. "He is a God who keeps His word. When He makes a promise, He stands by it. The faithfulness of your God is what makes your people distinct. Surely you can find rest in the promise of His presence, no matter where you go."

"He's promised our nation His presence, yes," I muttered. "But does that promise extend to one woman?" The question came out harsher than I'd intended. I choked back the bitterness too evident in my voice. "It's arrogance to expect personal attention from Adonai."

The minister frowned. "But according to your own writings, He is the God of Abraham, Isaac, and Jacob. He is the God of individuals as well as nations."

"He is the God of men through whom He chooses to build His nation," I retorted, suddenly weary. "I wouldn't expect you to understand."

Genuine hurt crossed his face. "Because I am Nabatean, I cannot understand the ways of your God?"

Shame filled my cheeks with heat, and I opened my mouth to correct myself, but he was still talking, his former careful restraint abandoned.

"It's *because* of my background that I see the beauty of your

God. We Nabateans carve our gods into stone and adopt deities from Egypt as if borrowing a neighbor's cloak."

He drew close, hands spread wide, and my heart thudded, neck cricking upward to stare into his face. I swallowed hard under the weight of his conviction as he continued to speak words full of fire and faith.

"I grew up under a plethora of gods as unfeeling and unresponsive as the stones that bore their image. Your God is the only one I have encountered who moves like a spirit. He refuses to be engraved on stone but chooses to engrave His people on His own hands."

Distantly, I registered the words of the prophet Isaiah. How did this foreigner know our Scriptures so well?

"A God that infinite is worth trusting." He was standing breathless and close, towering over me. I could almost feel the heat rising from his expansive chest.

"How did you come by such strong faith?" The question left my lips before I was conscious of forming it. "I envy your confidence. My own faith is a flickering flame."

He backed away a couple of paces. "Then you are safe."

"What do you mean?"

"You are safe, for a faintly burning wick He will not quench. A bruised reed He will not break."

Again, the words of Isaiah spoken with conviction from the lips of a Gentile. He left the courtyard, and I remained behind, utterly baffled that a foreign man had more faith than I.

SEVEN

The stylus shook in my hand as I began yet another message to Dalia. I would finish this one and then I would send it. With Uncle Ebner gone and Abba so generous with his funds, surely Aunt Sarah would view the message as an olive branch. And if they came, then perhaps true repair in the family would follow.

Without question, Eden had agreed to help me. As I finished my message and rolled it up tightly, my eyes landed on the fruit of her work. Blinking at me in the predawn light, Abba's signet ring nestled in a small dish on my writing table. No one had noticed a small servant girl slipping into his room to retrieve it. No one would notice when she carefully put it back. With Abba's seal, my missive would be given the utmost care, and perhaps would persuade my aunt to let Dalia come.

Gently, I drizzled a pool of hot wax onto the seam of the parchment before firmly pressing the seal into the soft wax. I straightened and stared at my bold handiwork, heart settling with resolve as the wax hardened.

◆

Months passed, my seventeenth birthday came and went, and still no response from Gennesaret. The longer the silence stretched, the more my heart ached. "Aunt Sarah must have kept the message from Dalia," I confided to Eden. "I'd hoped Abba's seal would have persuaded her, but maybe it had the opposite effect. Maybe it angered her more."

"Give it time," Eden soothed.

Time—it was all I had. Time to replay Othniel's hand, heavy on my knee, his voice thick with anticipation. Time to imagine life in Tiberias, further alienated from Jewish religious life.

Abba remained withdrawn as he attempted to uncover the nest of insurrectionists who conducted intermittent attacks in the city. The physical toll upon him was obvious, even prompting visits from the doctor, which Ima tried unsuccessfully to hide from me.

"He's overexerting himself," she explained. "But there's little we can do if he won't agree to rest."

Pressure from the throne intensified at the news that Sejanus, prefect of Emperor Tiberius' guard, would be passing through Sepphoris upon his return to Rome. Notoriously cutthroat, Sejanus had no tolerance for uprisings of any kind—a fact not lost upon Herod, who had become agitated and impatient with the Sanhedrin's efforts.

For a while, there were no definite leads, but several eyewitnesses to the last attack finally came forward and an arrest was made. Abba, along with the other twenty-two members of the Sepphoris Sanhedrin, convened at the city gate to hold trial. Word reached us that the accused was young, not yet twenty. He'd stood rigid with clenched jaw as the charges were brought against him. Steely-eyed and expressionless, he'd given no testimony of his own and instead endured hours of debate with not a word to add in his defense.

When Abba returned later that evening, his face was grim. "He will be acquitted."

"Surely not!" Ima's eyes widened as she raised herself from

a cushioned bench. "Judith will be horrified. It was her brother who was killed. The family needs justice."

"Many are unhappy, and Herod will be furious, but the law is clear. We need at least two eyewitnesses whose testimonies align."

"But you had such witnesses."

"It became clear that their testimonies were contradictory and confused. Their speeches left the council wondering if they were paid to come forward. We cannot, with confidence, place this man at the scene of the attack. When we reconvene in the morning, we will push for an acquittal." Abba ground his teeth in frustration. "We should have released him this very day, but there was enough dissension among us that the decision was postponed. The law is clear, but some are fearful of Herod." He shook his head. "They grossly underestimate the throne. They assume Herod will be blinded by a desire to please Sejanus and ignore the clear teaching of the law. They let an emotional response cloud their reason."

I listened with a hollow ache in my stomach. I had seen Herod Antipas from afar on many occasions, but soon we would have cause to see him up close, for Susanna's wedding was approaching, and we had received an invitation.

"It's to be held at court," I'd gaped as I read the parchment. "And Herod himself will be present."

"Manaen is a close friend, so it's no wonder Herod would personally honor him in such a way." Ima had held the invitation reverently. "What I don't understand is why we received an invitation at all. We aren't close with the family."

I knew exactly why. I recalled my sharp tongue as I'd snidely remarked on Manaen's age. Now Susanna would be able to rub his wealth and standing directly in my face.

"We don't have to attend," I'd tentatively suggested.

But of course we would go. Abba's delight over the invitation had lifted his mood considerably. I'd spent weeks dreading the wedding due to Susanna's gloating, but now a fresh worry arose. What would it be like to dine in the same room as the infamous Herod Antipas?

The next day, a messenger arrived, intercepting Abba as he prepared to leave. "There will be no trial today. The matter has been taken care of by order from the throne. The man has been interrogated and condemned."

Abba's already pale face blanched even more. "Herod would bypass the judicial process? He would go against our ruling on the matter?" Abba left in a panic to ascertain for himself what had occurred, and the news was worse than he'd imagined.

Herod's police had forced a confession from the man. They'd spent long hours drawing forth three other names. All four had been executed in Herod's prison, their bodies thrown outside the city walls for the beasts and birds of the air.

"He knew there was no grounds to condemn the man," Abba said when he came home, bewildered. "What did he hope to gain from such a confession? He's solving nothing! Doesn't he recall the downfall of Archelaus? Surely he doesn't want the same reputation as his brother . . . too hotheaded and cruel to rule."

Vaguely I recalled the stories of Herod's older brother, whose rule over Judea was so incompetent Rome had to send in a prefect. It was one of the reasons Abba respected Herod. He'd managed to keep direct Roman rule at bay for more years than his brother had done.

"He craves the appearance of decisiveness, but in doing so, he circumvents Jewish law, and why? To prove to Sejanus that he has things under control? In reality he only stirs the people's unease and hatred."

Abba slammed a fist into the wall, then cursed and shook his hand in pain. Rarely had I seen him so distraught. "He's undoing his image in the eyes of the people in an effort to present a front of control to Rome."

"You could report him," Ima offered quietly, voice wobbling as she tried to sound soothing despite her own evident fear, "to the Great Sanhedrin. Wouldn't this qualify for their attention? They have the power to try him for what he's done." Her voice grew quieter, as if the very walls were listening.

Abba shook his head and groaned. "Herod knows we won't do that, not with Sejanus' imminent arrival. He's capitalizing on the council's delay and using Rome to flex his power." He sank his face into his hands. "It's Sejanus' arrival that has caused this. It must be. Rome doesn't normally become involved in such local affairs if they can help it, but Sejanus . . . he will surely approve of this move, and Herod is using his arrival to protect himself."

Abba raised his face to pull agitatedly at his beard. "There are many who will simply allow him this overstep, but I cannot side with him in this, Zahava. Not when he blatantly disregards our laws."

It was the first time I'd heard Abba openly criticize the throne. In his haunted face, I saw our family's dilemma. He had driven us to this moment, intentionally and carefully maneuvered us closer to the seat of power. Dare we complain from our lofty view?

The last time I'd seen such fear on Abba's face was when Dalia's affliction began. He received this news of Herod the way he'd looked at Dalia—with a deeply unsettled expression, as if he was watching something die.

EIGHT

SUMMER 23 AD

The moon pierced the dark with blinding brilliance on the evening of Susanna's wedding banquet. I moved through the night, streaming like a breeze off the slopes of Mount Hermon, resplendent in my wedding garments. Fine silk, supple to the touch, pooled about my feet and formed graceful currents around my legs. Torches and guards lined the pathway to the palace as a steady stream of guests entered the colonnaded courtyard. We moved forward, gently compelled by the swelling notes of the lyre and flute.

My waist was cinched tight with a silken sash threaded with jewels, and my feet boasted slippers that left a lingering trail of perfume. Rather than anticipation over the festivities, however, my thoughts were thick with unease. Still no word from Gennesaret, and my own wedding was so close at hand.

As I entered the grand triclinium with my parents, I took in the brightly painted frescos on the walls and the high ceiling.

"This is the grand room Herod regularly uses for entertaining," Abba informed me, as if I didn't know.

By his side, Ima hovered, mouth gaping like a fish on the hook.

"Foreign dignitaries and esteemed guests of honor have all been hosted within these walls . . . and now us," she breathed.

The room boasted two levels with an elevated floor in the back accessible by a flight of wide steps. Low tables lined the walls of the bottom floor, men sitting on the left and women on the right, and at the back of the room, towering above the proceedings, was the head table. As the guest of honor, Herod sat in the most prominent position, his stately form and imposing presence permeating the room.

As Abba left to be seated, Othniel approached with a frown. "What are you doing at this table?"

"These are our assigned seats," I answered, surprised by his harsh tone.

"They insult you by placing you nearest the door." Othniel's disgruntled voice sounded loudly as Ima and I sat.

"Never mind that." I fluttered my hand with an easy expression. "I will have greater access to the bath, which, given the state of my nerves, is a blessing." I breathed a laugh, attempting a joke, but instead of matching my smile, Othniel's frown deepened.

"It should bother you to be slighted in such a way."

In truth, I had no desire to sit beneath the gaze of the notorious tetrarch, so even though Susanna most certainly had intended to slight me, I received her petty gesture with gratitude.

"Susanna did this on purpose to belittle *me*." Othniel directed his dark gaze to the glittering bride who reclined at the head table next to her husband, the two wearing golden crowns that winked in the candlelight. "It wasn't enough to abandon me for a better match; now she must add to the wound by mocking my betrothed."

My heart caught at his pointed words. Was I nothing but a second choice?

"It doesn't matter." Othniel turned back, lips spreading in a smile. "She is nothing. She utterly pales in comparison to your beauty, and she knows it." He crouched behind my seated form, lowering his voice for my ears alone, the breath from his lips making the hairs on the back of my neck rise. "I'll have my eyes on you the entire evening."

I tried to laugh lightly in response, but it sounded more like a strangled cough. Had he given me a compliment or a veiled threat? As he stood, he brushed his lips across the top of my head, causing me to shiver.

"It's good of Othniel to be so concerned over you." Ima nodded with approval, running distracted fingers over the rows of bracelets lining her arm. "After your marriage, I'm sure you will never sit nearest the door again."

As the evening commenced, Herod was the first to toast the couple. When he rose to his feet, the room fell silent. "To Manaen, my childhood friend." Herod turned an affectionate eye to the groom. "May this marriage bring you much happiness, and may the womb of your wife be as fruitful as the Beit Netofa Valley."

We raised our goblets to affirm the blessing, and as I drank to the well-being of the bride, I found myself truly wishing her well. She had the cunning and ambition to prosper in her new role. I was sure she hoped to see me writhe with jealousy, but I did not desire to marry so close to the throne and would not give her the reaction she craved.

The feasting would last all week long, and even though we were a local family, we were given guest rooms to stay the night.

"Our position is rising indeed to be given such honor," Abba exclaimed as we were escorted to our lavish rooms off the central courtyard.

I checked the retort on my tongue. Most likely it wasn't our family's position that warranted the gesture. More likely it was Susanna's desire to keep me close and observant to all that was now hers.

On the third day of the feast, she sought me where I stood at the edge of the room, her eyes glassy from drink. "What do you think of my husband now, Joanna?" She cast an approving glance at Manaen, who reclined next to Herod.

Dancers performed in the middle of the room, limbs twisting in their agile performance as the mingling guests watched. I lifted my voice to be heard above the music even as I worked to keep the annoyance from my tone. "You've sufficiently made your point. You've made a fine match indeed."

My measured response seemed to frustrate the bride. "He's proven to be a kind, gentle, and . . . *knowledgeable* husband." She propped a jeweled hand on her hip and arched her brow at me. "Experience may, after all, prove more desirable than youth."

I blushed at her candid words.

"And your betrothed . . ." She cast an eye to where Othniel reclined across the room, his relaxed form partially obscured by the dancers. "I've heard that his supposedly high position in Herod's new administration is not quite as secure as the family would have everyone to believe."

At that moment, Othniel looked in our direction, eyes locking with mine, face easing into a slow, heated smile before becoming obscured once again behind the entertainment.

Susanna sniffed. "Perhaps *that* is why he wishes to marry you in a rush. Before your family discovers otherwise?"

The fastest way to make Susanna leave was to give no response, but the heat in my chest loosened my tongue. "Just because you couldn't have him doesn't mean he isn't a good match."

Pain flitted across Susanna's face before she buried it with a laugh. "It's of no consequence anymore." Languidly, she tipped her goblet in my direction. "Or perhaps the other rumors are true and there's a different reason for the rushed marriage."

She was goading me, but I couldn't resist asking, "What rumors?"

Her face lit with excitement, which she quickly masked with false concern. "Oh, I don't want to worry you, but you *should* know what is being said."

I shouldn't have asked. Fear corded through my belly, and I turned away, already sickened.

"They say you simply couldn't wait."

I glanced up sharply.

"For your wedding night," she clarified with wide eyes. "Joanna, the stunning jewel of Sepphoris. Poor Othniel didn't stand a chance beneath your charms."

"Enough." I took a large step back with raised hands, startling those around us as my voice cracked. "You are lying."

Nearby, I could see my mother, who was sitting with Judith and Mireya. All three had stopped talking and were staring at me with fixed interest.

Lowering my hands, I whispered urgently, "I will not have you tarnishing my character."

Susanna slid her eyes to my belly and then back to my face. "You do look . . . altered lately. But by the time you truly begin to show, you'll have enjoyed the marriage bed and no one will bat an eye." She clucked her tongue.

"Why?" My voice was hollow and low. "Why do you taunt me so?" Tears of fear and frustration caught in my throat. She had to be lying. Surely, no one thought—

My legs began to shake, sweat forming on my brow. I swiped it with an unsteady hand and took a deep breath and then another. The room was blurring.

Stand firmly before her. Do not let her see your fear.

I raised my chin, stared directly into her face.

Susanna's expression flickered with surprise.

"What have I ever done to earn your hatred?" My chin trembled, although my words remained steady.

For a moment she stood dumbstruck, apparently so accustomed to deceitful tongues that she was unsure how to answer a blunt question. Finally, she cleared her throat and shook her head. "You've *done* nothing, Joanna. It's who you are." She pursed her lips, offering no further clarification.

"You are wasting your energy trying to tear me down. Turn your thoughts upon your new husband." I raised my goblet in a toast to her. "Enjoy him and the new position he affords you, and think no more upon me."

Something close to regret entered Susanna's eyes. Swiftly she blinked it away. "You are welcome to your new wine. My old wine has proven its quality."

As she returned to her seat, all bravery drained from my body, leaving me standing on weak legs.

"What was that about?" Ima approached and extended a hesitant hand, but I brushed her away.

Air, I needed the sweetness of the night air rather than the cloying scent of wine and roasted meat.

"Come and sit with Mireya," Ima urged.

Swiftly, I shook my head and for the first time in a long time voiced what I needed. "I-I need solitude. Just a moment. A moment."

Skirting the table, I fled the room.

◆

Tears never came easily anymore. Having spent so many of them in my childhood, they were all used up. I sat alone on a bench in the garden and did not weep. Instead, I gazed at the dark form of a cloud where it settled against the belly of the moon. My eyes were wide and dry, breaths even and slow.

The palace compound was littered with small gardens. From where I sat, I could see the stretch of the main courtyard, the clusters of guests beneath the glow of the moon. I cast my mind back over the months of my betrothal, searching for any hint of impropriety and finding none on my part. Had someone else noted the familiar press of Othniel's hand on my arm whenever we were together? Did tongues wag behind jeweled hands the way Susanna had implied, or was she so spiteful she would make the story up?

How Dalia must suffer beneath the weight of others' judgment. I closed my eyes and opened my hand loose on the bench, imagining her sliding there next to me, slipping her thin hand into mine. *"What people think changes all the time. What is true never changes."*

A deep burst of masculine voices filtered through the bushes. My eyes opened to find a group of men approaching a nearby fountain, their voices rising and mixing with the sound of flowing water.

"It could be you this time next year." One of the men clapped another on the shoulder. "Reclining next to Herod himself with a bride half your age and bursting with beauty. Mention it to your cousin. She will make it happen."

"The queen has more important things on her mind. Besides, I did not come here for a bride," the man replied softly.

With surprise I recognized the minister's voice. Queen Phasaelis, Herod Antipas' wife, was this man's cousin?

They were directly in my line of sight now, four dark figures resting near the fountain while I sat in the shadows.

"Be that as it may, you will need a wife sooner or later," another man retorted. "Especially now that you've been promoted from economist to financial minister."

"That, I admit, was unexpected." The minister's voice was low, almost pained.

"The queen must think highly of you to recommend you for the position. Surely she would be happy to secure you a wife. Take it from another Gentile in this court . . . it will go easier for you with a Jewish wife."

A round man chided, "You work harder than ten men and yet take no pleasures for yourself. You've held your position for barely a year, and already you stoop like a man twice your age."

The minister straightened, released a chuckle. "I may stoop from time to time, but at least I have all of my hair."

The man barked a laugh, the moon gleaming off his smooth head. "You are five and twenty, in the prime of your life. Enjoy it while you can." He rested a hand on the minister's broad shoulder and shook him gently. "You are tightly bound. Get a wife and let her loosen that somberness in you."

The minister twisted away from the man's kind words and a shaft of moonlight illuminated his conflicted features. He appeared handsome and sad in the moonlight, and my heart stuttered in my chest for I recognized the ache in his face.

"I appreciate your concern, but I did not come here for a wife," he repeated.

The other two men stood. "Perhaps, then, you will join us. There are several women waiting back in our apartments."

I couldn't see the minister's face as his gaze turned toward the other men, but the distaste in his voice was evident. "No. That is not for me."

"I best get back to my own wife," the round man with the gleaming head spoke quickly.

As the other two shrugged and left, the round man stood with a lingering hand on the minister's shoulder. "You have a wise head, and you also have the favor of two kings, which is no small feat."

"King Aretas may have recommended me for his daughter's

entourage, but his favor changes like the wind," the minister stated, large hands on his knees, shoulders hunched.

"That's the nature of kings." The round man sighed. "Queens, on the other hand, can be loyal to a fault. Herod was wise to listen to his wife and appoint you for this new position. I've been in the court long enough to recognize Herod's trust, and you, my son, have it."

The man left but the minister tarried, head hanging low between his shoulders as he studied his hands.

I sat alert and still on the bench with a new desire tangling in my breast. I wanted to slide my hands into the minister's shock of black hair and comfort him. Shame flamed in my cheeks as the sharp coolness of the bench bit through my silk tunic. I gazed at my hands with surprise, as if I'd caught them in the very act of tousling his hair.

He lingered a moment longer and then stood with a groan and left. I watched his retreating form with my heart heavy and pounding over this mysterious man caught between two courts.

◆

The final evening of the celebration found me eager for home. If Livia had been present, I would have taken refuge by her side. Instead, I'd spent most of the time with Mireya, who seemed determined to mute the sorrow over her uncle with an endless cup.

My mind was so weary and inattentive that I nearly missed the palace servant's approach. "Mistress, the king requests to meet you."

By my side, Mireya choked. Mutely, I gaped at the messenger until Mireya prodded me to respond.

"M-me?" I finally squeaked, and at the servant's affirming nod, spluttered, "You must be mistaken."

"Yes, you, mistress. He requests to meet you . . . now."

Agitatedly, I shook my head to clear it. Why would Herod

request to meet *me*? I lumbered to my feet, which were sluggish with dread. Had I conducted myself improperly? Had Susanna complained about me?

Ima returned to the table as I left it, eyes widening as I walked past her toward the head table on trembling legs.

Covertly, I searched the room, gaze landing upon my father, who was watching me with wondering eyes that surely mirrored my own confusion. He gave me a slight affirming nod as if to infuse me with courage from afar. But his face was ashen, the hollows under his eyes standing out starkly, and my own nerves heightened as I recognized fear in him.

I approached the wide steps leading to the elevated platform and stopped, casting my eyes to the top where the man himself sat, fingers twirling the stem of his goblet as he eyed me. With a flick of his fingers, he indicated for me to approach, and so I did—one trembling step at a time until I reached the top and sank into a low bow before the tetrarch.

It was common knowledge that in King Herod the Great's first will, he'd named his youngest son, Herod Antipas, his sole heir and king . . . a will that was later revoked, a title that Herod Antipas would never receive, a disappointment from which he would never recover. His subjects, however, referred to him as king, and some still felt that he had been robbed of the title. I released that title now past numb lips. "My king."

"You've been a quiet flower over there in the corner." Herod's tone rippled, alternative meanings lurking beneath. "I've noticed you these last few days—quiet and subdued. Tell me, what's your name? This must be your first time in court, for I would have remembered such a beauty as you."

Words dried up within me as my mind snagged on all the hidden compliments from Herod's tongue. How was a modest woman to respond? My lips parted, but only a strangled noise exited.

"This is Joanna, only child of the chief priest, Itamar. I had the honor of attending her betrothal ceremony."

This voice—I knew this voice. Out of the corner of my eye, I saw the minister returning to his seat. Gratitude poured from my eyes as they met his.

"Betrothed, eh?" Herod mused. "And who is the fortunate man?"

"Othniel bar Ravid, my king," I managed to answer, ducking my head once more.

"Ah yes, Ravid is a good man, competent and shrewd in all his dealings. He has high hopes for his son."

Something in Herod's tone indicated mistrust. I glanced up sharply to find him observing Othniel with narrowed eyes.

"Ravid insists that his son has inherited his business mind. We will see if such claims prove true." Herod turned back toward me, and before I could lower my head again, our eyes locked.

I could not look away, for I had never stared someone in the face who held such power. His eyes were a deep brown, appearing nearly black in the flickering candlelight. At forty-three, he was robust, with only hints of aging. His beard was oiled and black, and the sparse gray in his hair only added to his severe countenance.

Recently, this man had met with Sejanus and now here he sat, appraising me with a lift to his lips that left me queasy. His words and demeanor were warm and inviting, but scarcely a month ago he'd had his police torture a man, a youth not much older than I. Instead of the acquittal he deserved, the youth had endured a shameful death by the hands of the man now staring shrewdly at me.

All moisture left my mouth. I swallowed with difficulty and tried to look away, but Herod was smiling now, his expression so inscrutable it held me captive.

"If Othniel has made such a match as this, he must indeed

possess good sense, don't you think, Chuza?" Herod asked the man by his side, still holding my gaze.

Trembling, I tore my eyes away and sought instead this mysterious man who now had a name.

Chuza was looking at me, but instead of Herod's scrutiny, his eyes held compassion. The fear in my chest loosened.

"What say you?" Herod clapped a hand on Chuza's shoulder, rocking his financial minister's large frame slightly off-balance. "She will make a fine addition to the court, will she not?"

Beneath his dark complexion, Chuza flushed deeply as he raised his goblet. "A fine addition, indeed."

——— ✦ ———

"A personal introduction to King Herod!" Ima squawked, squeezing my arm painfully. We were borne upon a litter, wending our weary way home after a full week of celebration. Dusk was beginning to settle, the stars small pricks of light as we turned onto our street.

"You conducted yourself well, daughter." Abba looked upon me with relief and approval. "I watched your every move, and although I could not hear the interchange, it was clear Herod was pleased with you."

"Of course she pleased him," Ima breathed. "She will do well in Tiberias."

My parents' enthusiasm grated upon me, for my heart was sore tonight. "I'm glad you think I performed well," I stated dully, peeking from the curtain, eyes hunting for the moon as my mind tried to forget the last few days. Susanna with her cutting gossip, the king with his sharp and assessing gaze. Gooseflesh spread down my back.

"Herod's minister of finance was gracious enough to facilitate the introduction," I murmured softly, heart quieting as I recalled his kindness. He seemed upright—a man of integrity. Perhaps there would be others like him in Tiberias.

As the litter stopped at our home and we exited, two dark figures rose from a nearby alleyway. I tensed as they approached us, recalling Mireya's broken expression over her uncle. A family coming home from an extravagant banquet made an excellent target, and fear lurched in my breast as the figures neared.

"Inside, quickly," Abba hurried us up the steps, just as Akim, our porter, opened the front door.

"Welcome home, master." His gaze caught on the dark figures below us, eyes narrowing with suspicion and distaste. "They are still here." He turned back to us with an apologetic expression. "They've been out here for days. They insist they are family but offer no proof. Of course I would not grant them entrance, but they refuse to leave."

A burly man, nearly as wide as he was tall and with the strength and tenacity of a mule, Akim pushed his bulk past us, shoving the torch out into the night. "I told you to leave! You go too far accosting the master at his own front door."

The two figures were standing at the base of the steps, Akim's torch throwing light onto their faces. I blinked rapidly, befuddled and disoriented as my earlier fear morphed into something else entirely. A swath of honey hair, eyes as dark and big as mine. I sank down upon the steps in bewildered joy.

"Dalia?"

NINE

I stood with a hand over my heart, pressing hard against its uneven thump, pushing it back into my aching chest. With the other hand, I held onto my sister, our fingers threaded tightly together. The pulse in her delicate wrist hammered hard against my own.

"Why would you think I sent for you, Sarah? I did no such thing!" Abba paced quickly from one end of the reception room to the other, face white, eyes restless. Nearby, Ima swayed, a hand to her throat.

"Not you, Itamar. It was Joanna." Aunt Sarah's voice was tight and confused as she watched Abba pace before her. "But the message bore your seal and so, I believed, your blessing."

"My seal?" Abba grew still. "Impossible. Can you produce it?"

"I . . . I destroyed it," Aunt Sarah admitted reluctantly. "I didn't want Dalia seeing the message, but she overheard the scribe reading the contents to me and wouldn't relent until we came." Aunt Sarah looked toward Dalia with a pained expression. "By the time I agreed to come, it was too late to send advance notice."

"I never sealed a message to you." Abba's voice grew quiet. "Joanna would never do such a thing. She would never write to you, let alone use my seal."

Aunt Sarah lifted her arms. "Then why am I here, Itamar? After all these years and with the history between us . . . why would I show up on your doorstep with the knowledge I have? For I know that your Joanna is soon to be married to Othniel bar Ravid, son of Herod's lieutenant." She dropped her arms. "How very proud you both must be." There was a biting edge to her words.

A dumbfounded expression flooded Abba's features as he slowly turned to me. "Joanna? Can you explain this? Did you take my seal without my permission? Did you send a message without my knowledge?"

"I did, Abba." The words came out stronger than I expected. I stepped forward, drew Dalia with me as if presenting her to him. *Here, Abba. The truth.*

"I made a promise to Dalia," I continued, words growing stronger. "Wouldn't you have me be a woman of my word?"

"I would have you be a woman who doesn't make rash vows she cannot keep."

By my side, Dalia sucked in a sharp breath.

"It was a mistake to come." Aunt Sarah hurried toward Dalia, snagging her hand from mine. "I thought the missive had your blessing. Now I see this was not a gesture of goodwill after all. This was simply a mistake."

"No!" Ima lurched toward her sister. "No, it was *not* a mistake."

"Zahava." Abba's voice was hushed, full of warning.

Ima flashed him a look so full of fire, we all took a step back. "Our relatives have come beneath our roof, Itamar, and we will not throw them out."

Never had I seen Ima so assertive. She faced Aunt Sarah with hands spread wide. "Joanna may have been the one to write to you, but I am the one requesting you stay."

The distrust in Aunt Sarah's eyes was evident. I sensed this trip had cost her deeply, and now she wavered, eyes flitting from Ima to Abba and back again.

"A word, Zahava," Abba spoke urgently, face crumpling as if in pain, hand reaching for the wall, body sagging.

For once, Ima did not respond to his discomfort with sympathy. "Our relatives have come from out of town for Joanna's wedding ceremony." The fire in Ima's eyes was dimming as exhaustion took its place. "No one will think anything of it."

Abba pinched the bridge of his nose, sighing deeply. "The evening grows late, and emotions run high. We will revisit the conversation in the morning." He waved a hand to our steward. "We'll have rooms prepared for you."

✦

Dalia and I lay in bed with our noses touching, like we used to as girls. Her fresh scent enveloped me—henna, almond, and aloe. "Joanna." She said my name just the way I remembered it, with a slight emphasis on the *Jo*. No one else said my name that way.

I sniffed loudly as tears leaked from my eyes, fingers lifting to trace a new, jagged scar on her temple.

"Rocks," she murmured, covering my hand with her own. "I fell onto rocks." The veins in her wrist stood out painfully, like bright blue rivers.

"Are there other injuries?" I whispered, eyes roaming her face.

She closed her eyes, nodded. "But Adonai has preserved my life."

"Your speech . . . it's different. Slower?" My hand was still beneath her own, captured against her cheek.

"Sometimes . . . certain words are hard. Hard for me to find. I think, perhaps, the seizures are affecting my memory," she admitted, eyes opening, latching onto mine. "Oh, do not weep so!" She released my hand to tuck a strand of hair behind my ear.

"I can't help it!" I sniffed again as tears dripped from my nose. "Things have grown worse for you instead of better. How can I not weep?"

Dalia grew quiet. "Some things have worsened," she whispered. "But other things have grown better. I have made a friend."

I sat up at her unexpected announcement and wiped at my face. "Who?"

"Her name is Tirza. She's around your age. She is not . . . afraid of me, as some are."

Jealousy flashed through my breast but then, just as quickly, a ray of happiness drove it away. "I'm thankful you have a friend," I murmured as I lay back down.

"She and her brother, Judah, have been incredibly kind to me. He is training to be a scribe, and he's so . . . intelligent and kind." She tripped over her words, repeating herself, a flush forming in her cheeks. "I listen to him often at the synagogue where he teaches and shares his knowledge . . . with me and anyone who is interested. Those outings, listening to him, have become such bright spots in my life."

My brow lifted at her tone. "You like him?"

Dalia closed her eyes, shook her head swiftly with a short, hollow laugh. "Oh no . . . I could never . . . *like* someone in that way. Even if I did, I wouldn't be able to marry. Not in my condition. And certainly no man would have me."

"Ebner loved Sarah while she—"

"Ima's seizures were not as frequent as mine. She was not beginning to be impaired." Dalia looked away quickly. "And Abba didn't marry her until . . . afterward."

She faced me again, eyes shining with strength. "I have passed the age when Ima's own affliction lifted. I thought it would wreck me, but in truth, it helped." She reached for me, and I grasped her slender hand between both my own.

"I realized I'd been waiting for that age when Ima's own ailment passed—like it was some mystical moment. But when it came and went and I only grew worse . . . Adonai showed me that I'd been hoping in that moment instead of Him. I'd been keeping a part of myself away from Him."

"What?" I blinked hard in surprise. "You are the most hopeful and faith-filled person I know."

She smiled slowly, eyes softening as they lingered on my features. "But faith in what? Faith that Adonai would heal me at a certain age? That's not really faith, Joanna. Faith is founded on Adonai Himself and not on the condition that He act in a certain way at a certain time."

I shook my head, throat tightening. "I'm amazed by you," I managed to croak. "You're so brave."

"Do not be amazed by me," Dalia frowned. "Be amazed by Adonai. He's the one who holds me. Do you think I could possibly face this life without Him? I'm not brave, Joanna." She swallowed hard. "Most days, I'm close to terrified. I'm weak, and I know it. I need the strength only Adonai can give." She squeezed my hand hard.

For the first time, I wanted it—deeply and ardently wanted the faith of my sister.

"I wish I was like you!" I dropped her hand to cover my face, eyes wide behind my fingers as I wrestled with this new desire. "Here I am, with all of this," I swept my hand wildly about the room before returning it to my face. "And yet . . . and yet . . ."

The life Dalia would never lead stretched before my reluctant feet.

"And yet?" she gently probed.

"Sometimes I do not want what you cannot have." My words cracked open like a ripe pomegranate, spilling its bright seeds everywhere, staining all it touched. "It's unfair. I do not understand it, and it keeps my heart from Adonai."

There—I had said it. I lay on the bed, breathless with hurt and bracing for Dalia's reproof. But she lay still and gazed at me with so much love I nearly gave in to tears once more.

"My life is not your fault, Jojo," she murmured. "You know that, right?"

I ducked my head, refused to answer.

"Adonai has used my illness to draw me to Himself and perhaps . . . He is doing the same with you—if you will let Him. I know some view my life as barren, and I confess that at times I'm tempted to do the same. But I'm learning that God bears fruit in unexpected places. Sometimes His riches are hidden."

"Still, I would trade places with you if I could. Give you all of this, and take away your pain." The words came crawling from the deepest part of me.

She smiled, eyes wide. "And I would not let you. Oh, sister, I've learned to love my life, but I can see that you have yet to love yours."

"You would have me embrace my life—this privileged position I didn't ask for and that is so separated from you." I drew in a trembling breath. "I don't know how."

Urgency flashed across Dalia's features as she grabbed my hand. "But you *must* learn to live your life, Jojo. It's the one God gave you. You have to find a way to live in it." She quieted then, threading her fingers back through mine. "I have to believe you are here for a purpose just as I am, each of us planted where God intends us to be."

I raised our clasped hands, pressed my lips to her knuckles, and wished for tears that now refused to come. Instead, they lodged in my chest, burning and trapped. Could I learn to love the life I'd been given?

Adonai, give me Your strength.

TEN

Abba agreed to let Aunt Sarah and Dalia stay. His acquiescence was a gift I hadn't dared to hope for and realized had come, in large part, due to Ima's insistence. There was a condition, however. In an effort to keep the family history of the ailment hidden, we would not disclose that Dalia was my sister.

Was a life lived free of pretense even possible? My heart ached with love for Dalia and a desire to claim her—now and always—as my sister.

"You may not like it," Ima stated swiftly, expression emptied like a dry cistern. "But it cannot be helped. Some worlds are too far apart to reconcile."

I knew the dire words to be true. We lived in a world that drew firm lines between people and did not treat those who crossed them with kindness.

Aunt Sarah agreed to stay but did so reluctantly. In her tight expression and pursed lips, I could see how she longed to leave. Late into that night, she and Ima argued, their voices rising in heated debate. Dalia was fast asleep, but I stood in the shadows and listened.

"You say we can stay, but it's only because we've foisted ourselves upon you. I was foolish to believe the message had Itamar's blessing—not when he'd made himself so clear."

"Clear? In what way? What are you talking about?"

"You gave us your money when you wouldn't give us your presence," Aunt Sarah hissed. "A generous gift to keep us away."

"No! That's not what the gift was. Sarah, it was to help after Ebner—"

"Are you certain about that?"

There was a painful silence in which I could almost hear my heart hammering in my chest.

"Itamar has always been uncomfortable around me," Sarah continued. "And now he'd deck us out in finery, hiding our humble station."

"You know as well as I that it's common for hosts to provide wedding garments." Ima's voice had dulled. "I am weary of you poking and prodding at us and our motives. Always questioning and distrusting!"

Long into the night they argued, fueled by years of untended hurt.

✦

Dalia and I embraced our temporary reunion—this fragile happiness that must and would fade away. Instead of Aunt Sarah's reticence, Dalia displayed an open and sincere curiosity. With joy she fingered my fine garments, exclaimed over the view from my window, and sampled luscious dishes from the kitchen. But it was my betrothed who elicited the most questions. I shared only the details that would delight her, holding back my worry and doubt.

"He sounds handsome and intelligent," Dalia sighed. "I always knew God would gift you a good man."

She was looking forward to the wedding with such zeal that I could almost begin to anticipate it myself. Soon after they arrived, Ima insisted we go to the market to purchase cloth for new wedding clothes so Aunt Sarah and Dalia could be fitted, and the seamstress begin work immediately.

Ima did not intend to take Dalia with us on the outing. "Your father will not want to risk it," she told me privately.

To Aunt Sarah, however, she made a different excuse. "Sepphoris has seen her share of attacks lately. Hatred toward those connected to the court has turned into violence, and we are targeted by our own people! Zealots killing their Jewish brethren in broad daylight."

Aunt Sarah listened with hooded eyes. "I'm surprised you dare to show your own face, then. It's just as well. We wouldn't want anyone seeing Dalia, would we?"

Her sharp words were flint to stone, sparking Ima into action. "If an outing for Dalia is what Sarah wants, then an outing for Dalia is what she will receive. Itamar doesn't have to know," she muttered through gritted teeth, the desire to appease and silence her sister's condemnation evident on her face.

Lately, we never went anywhere without Akim, who stayed close with a concealed dagger at the ready, but for this outing Ima added two more menservants to our bodyguard. Sufficiently protected, we entered the flow of travelers on the main colonnaded road.

Dalia took in her surroundings with wide eyes. "We didn't pass this way when we arrived," she breathed. "Everything is so . . . tall and big compared to the buildings back home—and busy."

"Things are quieter in Gennesaret," Aunt Sarah concurred. "We are not caught up in appearances." She glanced sharply at Ima.

When we reached the marketplace, Ima led us toward a stall with spools of colored thread. "We will stop here first to make selections for Joanna's wedding garments."

I was nearly finished embroidering the wide hem of my tunic, threading delicate pearls into the intricate design. As Ima and I made our selections, Dalia and Aunt Sarah stood silent and staring, their plain brown clothes contrasting sharply with the colors around them. My chest tightened, and I rushed us through the purchase, unwilling to cause Aunt Sarah any more discomfort.

A voice stopped us, however, as we prepared to leave. "Joanna, what a pleasant surprise!" Susanna greeted us. Behind her, a servant staggered beneath a massive load of packages.

"Lady Susanna." Ima bowed her head. "You honored us with your wedding invitation. It was a fine celebration. I pray you are enjoying your new husband?"

"Indeed, I am." Susanna replied to Ima but looked at me, lips pursing in appraisal. Before she could say more, however, her gaze slid behind me. "Who do we have here?"

Heart tumbling to my toes, I watched as Susanna's attention came to rest upon Dalia, eyes traveling over her humble garments and unadorned face. The gold ring in Susanna's nose glinted as her nostrils flared.

"Cousins from out of town," Ima quickly stated.

"Lovely," Susanna purred. "And is that colored thread for . . . them?" She laughed airily. "Their wardrobe certainly could use the renovation."

Susanna's remark cut deep. Aunt Sarah's face became solid as stone, while Dalia flushed and averted her gaze.

I opened my mouth to protest the rude comment, but Ima was already responding, "It's for Joanna's wedding garments. It won't be as fine an affair as your wedding, but I do hope you will grace us with your presence." Ima ignored the slight and extended an invitation to Susanna all in one breath.

"You honor me, thank you," Susanna replied, her mask of cordiality sliding firmer into place as she glided past me, raising her slender shoulders ever so slightly. Before she'd passed us entirely, she paused. "You were gracious to extend an invitation, now let me do the same. Some of Manaen's friends are planning a trip to the theater to see the new play."

"The one Emperor Tiberius praised." Ima nodded.

"This will be the first time the production appears in Galilee. Why don't you join us?" Susanna spread her hands as if the idea was a grand one. "You could even bring your cousins. Show them how fine our city is to be hosting such an event."

Far from gracious, the invitation was a mockery. Clearly Aunt Sarah and Dalia would not be able to hold their own among the court favorites.

"A fine invitation indeed," Ima replied. "But we must decline. We'll be far too busy with wedding preparations."

"Very well." Susanna signaled to her servant, who followed her with slow steps.

Ima turned to the rest of the group, seemingly unaware of the turmoil her exchange with Susanna had garnered.

"May we return to your home now?" Aunt Sarah requested past tight lips.

"But we haven't seen the cloth merchant. Does Dalia grow tired?"

"I-I do feel funny," Dalia spoke, turning toward Aunt Sarah. "I can't tell if it's from the new smells, but my stomach doesn't feel right."

Aunt Sarah grasped her arm with a frightened expression. "Let's get you to bed, dear one."

"Perhaps it's something she ate?" Ima questioned as we began walking toward home at a quick pace.

"She used to say her stomach felt funny before an episode," I murmured.

"Did she?"

With a sharp rush of air, I gave release to my anger. As Aunt Sarah hurried Dalia before us, I fell back with Ima, Akim and the others not far behind, and whispered, "Didn't you ever ask her how it felt? Because I did."

"I-I didn't realize there were signs. It all seemed so random," Ima stuttered.

Ahead of us, Dalia came to a sudden stop. We were just outside the acropolis now and nearly in sight of home. Dalia turned to Aunt Sarah and moaned. "My stomach is worse now, and my fingers are tingling."

"Is she cold?" Ima asked.

Aunt Sarah shot her a withering glare as Dalia's arms jerked violently, sending her crashing against a wall.

Ima startled as Aunt Sarah caught Dalia before she fell completely. "Oh, what do we do? What do we do? Itamar will be furious. What have I done?" Ima babbled, close to hysteria, hands fluttering.

"Even now, you are more concerned with appearances!" Aunt Sarah spat, gazing up at Ima, eyes pooling with the bitterness she'd been trying so hard to mask. "Of course you don't know what to do. You never did. Not when we were young, and not even when your own daughter needed you. There's nothing we can do but wait this out and make sure she doesn't hurt herself. You wouldn't remember, would you? Because your path has always been one of avoidance. *This* is what you and Itamar couldn't handle. Or, should I say, *wouldn't* handle?"

"You know it was more complicated than that!" Ima yelped, her face mottled with tears.

"Stop it!" I stomped my foot and threw down the package in my hand, finally locating and using my voice. "Would you both stop it?"

Blinded by tears, I knelt by Dalia's side. The past rose up, reminding me of the small girl who'd once held her sister and wept over her, praying childish prayers full of faith and fear to a far-off God to come and help her.

I gathered Dalia into my arms, sitting as still and solid as possible while she shuddered against my body. Her head bashed into my jaw, causing me to bite my lip. As blood flooded my mouth, I wept anew for my sister and for the faith that had once been mine.

ELEVEN

The episode shifted Dalia's mood. She was quieter, subdued. "They're happening more frequently," she confided that evening as I lay next to her, face pressed to her shoulder. "I used to go long months with no seizures and now hardly a week doesn't go by that I—" Her words broke, along with her resolve. "Some days I'm so tired." She closed her eyes. "And I want Him to hold me like the psalmist says: 'The Lord will hold me close.'"

I swallowed hard, remembering another part of the psalm: *Even if my father and mother abandon me.*

"Doesn't the psalmist also say that the Lord's right hand will hold you securely as you cling to Him?" I whispered, searching for hope I had yet to feel, offering Dalia words that I prayed were true. "You are clinging, Dalia. You are clinging close, so surely, He will hold you."

Her eyes flew open as she twisted to look at me. "Those are the first hopeful words I've heard from your lips in a long time!"

I snorted. "You must be having an influence upon me."

She giggled, and the sound burrowed straight to my heart.

"Will you be safe?" I asked when she quieted. "On the journey home. Will you be safe to travel?"

"Travel *is* becoming harder," Dalia admitted. "But Ima will be with me, and she is vigilant in her care."

"I can understand her worry." I shivered. Seeing Dalia so vulnerable on the streets of Sepphoris—both to Susanna's cutting assessment and her own convulsions—had left me rattled.

"I'm sorry for what you had to endure this morning," I murmured. "With Susanna. She was unbearably rude with her comments and invitation to the theater. And Ima—" I caught my lip between my teeth as I chose my next words carefully. "Sometimes she only sees a person's position and not her character. Or at least she chooses to ignore the one because of the other."

"Is it her position or her character that made Susanna's offer so offensive?" Dalia softly questioned.

"I think it's both," I grimaced. "Her poor character means she wields her position in distasteful ways . . . such as extending an invitation as a way to poke fun at someone's lower station."

"I see." Dalia's expression tightened. "It would have been magnificent to see the theater, but I can understand not wanting to respond to such an invitation."

"You would like to see the theater?"

"It seems thrilling." Dalia's face settled into a wan smile.

"I suppose it's thrilling in its own way."

Dalia's desire to see the theater surprised me, but even more so was the compassion that shone from her gaze. "She must be deeply unhappy."

"Who?"

"Susanna. You don't see it?" Dalia's eyes narrowed. "What reason would she have for slighting me other than to hurt you? And what reason would she have for hurting you other than to make herself feel better?"

"I don't know how hurting me would make her feel better."

Dalia shrugged a thin shoulder. "Susanna immediately looked pained when she saw you. And when people are in pain, they often hurt others. It doesn't make sense. Why would causing more pain ease your own?" Her voice lifted at the mystery.

I mulled over her words, trying to view Susanna from Dalia's perspective. "I suppose I've noted pain in her eyes before, but I don't know why she targets me above others."

"Perhaps she's threatened by you."

"Hardly!" I barked a laugh. "She's made a finer match than I have. She's beautiful and wealthy."

Dalia clucked her tongue. "You don't see it, do you?" At my confused expression, she explained. "Susanna may be pleasing to the eye in her own way, but, Joanna . . . next to you she appears as common as a sparrow fluffing herself up with borrowed peacock feathers." Dalia laughed at her own word picture.

Hearing my looks praised from Dalia's lips snapped something fragile within me. "Ah, my beauty!" I scoffed. "I've heard enough about that for a lifetime. Sometimes I fear it's the only thing people see." I averted my face.

The room grew quiet. "I'm sorry, sister." Dalia rested a hand on my shoulder. "I didn't mean to make light of something that pains you."

"I shouldn't complain." I shook my head, angry with myself.

"Do you view your beauty and position like an affliction—something to endure?" Dalia peered into my face, trying to ferret out the truth, before finally leaning back with a sigh. "Perhaps they are not an affliction but a gift."

My mouth gaped but released no sound. A gift or a burden—how did I view my life? "Well, Susanna certainly sees her lot in life as neither burden nor gift but a *right*," I spluttered, trying to divert the attention from myself.

"Be that as it may, I wonder if the two of you have more in common than you realize."

Dalia delivered her observation softly, but I reared back. Unknowingly, she'd placed her finger upon a deeply tender spot. "Please don't compare me with her."

"Oh, I didn't mean it as an insult." Dalia wriggled upright with a dismayed expression. "Simply that you both carry pain. Susanna releases hers onto others, but you—" She stopped, gazing at me with a touch of uncertainty in her face. "I fear you swallow your pain like poison."

"What would you have me do instead? Release it onto others as she does?"

"No, but . . . you could release it onto Adonai. Remember the words you just spoke, Joanna: 'The Lord's right hand will hold you securely as you cling to Him.'"

I recalled Chuza's firm belief that Israel's God was the Lord of individuals as well as nations, that His presence was a promise for every person.

"I don't know what I believe anymore," I admitted, gazing down at my hands. "I want to believe, but faith without proof seems foolish."

"But Adonai *has* given us proof." Dalia spoke earnestly, eyes growing fiercely bright. "You've heard the stories. You've sat beneath Torah. You—"

"I've sat beneath His silence," I interrupted. "We all have, for hundreds of years. When does faith become foolishness?"

Dalia's eyes shimmered with sudden tears.

"I want to believe!" I cried, remorseful over my bitter words. "But faith feels too painful, too risky. Acceptance is so much better."

"Acceptance is good," Dalia admitted, quickly swiping at her eyes. "I've had to embrace acceptance too. But isn't life more bearable when acceptance links arms with hope?"

My heart was thirsty for her belief, but my stubborn mind refused to respond to the nudging in my spirit.

TWELVE

The following morning, I awoke to find Dalia gone. She'd fallen asleep tucked into my bed, and I hadn't been willing to wake her. Rubbing sleep from my eyes, I quietly padded from the room. Voices and laughter pulled me down the hall and to an unoccupied guest room. Gently, I eased the door open to find Dalia and Eden on tiptoe, peering with arched necks through the window.

With a quick hand, I stifled a laugh. Eden was at least two heads shorter than my sister and had positioned a low stool beneath the window so she could reach Dalia's height.

"If you look . . . just there." Eden strained higher on her toes, wobbled, and nearly crashed into Dalia, who braced her with a laugh.

"How did you even discover this view?" Dalia asked in a delighted voice.

Eden huffed with the effort of remaining balanced in such a precarious position. "I was dusting on top . . . of the wardrobe and needed to stand . . . on the bed to reach . . . oh, stop laughing!"

It was the happiest and freest I'd ever seen Eden. Even though our own relationship had mellowed into a comfortable companionship, I knew she was still nervous around me. With Dalia, however, she spoke as if to a long-lost friend.

"What are you looking at?" I grinned, wanting in on the fun, but then Eden fell. With a yelp, she tumbled from the stool and landed squarely on her backside.

She gazed at me from her prostrate position with such mortification that I burst into laughter—it stretched comfortably through my chest, up and out, filling the small room and joining with Dalia's. Eden shifted her gaze between us with a befuddled expression that released into a giggle. Hauling herself to her feet, she smoothed her rumpled tunic.

"I was showing Mistress Dalia the theater."

I quieted. "You can see it from here?"

"It's the only place in the house where you can catch a view." Eden gestured to the window, and I took up station by Dalia, making use of the stool as I craned my own neck.

Sure enough, a portion of the circular theater was just visible in the distance. My palms grew sweaty, knowing it was within my power to give Dalia more than a straining glance at the magnificent structure. "You truly want to see it?"

Dalia's face flooded with embarrassment. "I shouldn't be so curious," she stated dismissively. "Ima certainly wouldn't approve, but I don't know if I'll ever be this close to it again." Her voice trailed off, and in her tight face I recognized my own tendency.

Through long and painful years, she had learned to dismiss her own desire . . . as I had learned to dismiss mine.

"Come." Before I could second-guess myself, I snagged Dalia's hand and led her and Eden back down the hallway and to my room. Settling Dalia into a chair, I tilted her face to the bronze mirror. "Eden, can you do Dalia's hair? We're going to the theater. Well . . . *outside* the theater. I can at least give you a closer view."

"You're sure about this?" Dalia squirmed in the seat.

"We'll be there and back before anyone even notices we're gone," I assured her as Eden opened a drawer for hairpins.

Dalia's subdued mood from the night before evaporated before my eyes as she sighed and wriggled, excitement emanating from her. "A trip to see the theater and then your wedding . . . I'm grateful I'm still able to experience such things!" She left unspoken the fear that it might not always be so.

"What's this?" As Eden began combing her hair, Dalia slipped a hand into a drawer and gently touched the crumpled crown. "Is this . . . ?"

"Yes." My voice cracked. "What remains of it. I think of that moment often."

Silently, Dalia stared at the few faded blooms, before plucking them gingerly from the drawer with long fingers. Grasping my arm, she slowly dotted my wrist with the remnants, as if forming a bracelet.

"Beautiful," she murmured. "You worry others only see your outward beauty, but I see your internal beauty, and I'm proud of you." She brushed the pieces into her palm, then spilled them into mine. Briefly, our hands cupped the remnants—a promise caught between us.

———— ✦ ————

Along with Eden, we snuck from the back of the home. I kept a protective hand on Dalia's arm, nervous and vigilant, yet hopeful that she could enjoy the brief outing without another incident.

As we neared the theater, Dalia openly gawked. "Oh," she breathed. "It's so much bigger than I expected."

The impressive limestone building was built into the north face of the acropolis, arching out and away from the wall in a towering half circle, crowned with a colonnade boasting Corinthian capitals.

"I know you said we would remain outside, but now that

we're here, can't we go in?" Dalia's eyes traveled to the columns. "I've never been so high up in my life." She turned to me with an expectant expression and sharply I recalled her face peering up from the base of a tree, imploring me to please haul her up.

"Mistress, I'm not sure that it's safe." By my side, Eden shifted on restless feet. "It's busier than usual due to the new production."

I tensed, knowing that she was right.

"Joanna?" Dalia's bright, eager face filled my view, anticipation radiating from her like light. How could I snuff it out?

"If . . ." I released a shaky sigh, relenting to her pull. "As long as we're brief."

As we entered, Dalia began to breathe harder, and as we ascended the steps to the colonnade, she grasped my hand tightly the higher we climbed. When we reached the top, she stopped abruptly, eyes casting upward to the overhanging roof and then downward to the stadium seating. She tugged her hand from mine to cover a gasp. "How magnificent!"

For a moment, she swayed like a willow in a storm, and I worried she was about to collapse. But when she turned, there was only wonderment upon her face. "I've never seen anything like it. We're so high up. The scenery looks so real." She grasped at a nearby column and then wildly searched for my hand, trying to tether herself back to reality.

I slipped next to her side, gave her my hand, and together we gazed at the rows and rows of seats that spilled down to the stage in the center, where the production was already underway. A series of tall, three-sided sets adorned the stage, each side painted to represent a different scene. With a swift rotation, the sets transformed from a forest to a palace. Actors strutted across the stage with exaggerated makeup and elaborate clothes, and Dalia soaked it all in.

After a while, Eden softly murmured, "We should get back."

Dalia overheard and spun to face me. "Oh, please! Just a little longer."

"Just a little." I grinned, ignoring Eden's frown.

Men scurried about the stage during a break in the production, adjusting the scenery. Dalia was captivated by all the activity, so I took the opportunity to scan the crowd for familiar faces.

"My mistress invites you and your friend to sit with her." Susanna's handmaid appeared at my elbow, and I followed her pointing finger, grimacing as I saw Susanna close to the stage. She was standing and observing us, although we were too far away to read her expression.

"Your *friend*?" Dalia leaned in close with a low laugh. "I don't think Susanna recognizes me from the other day. I wonder what her reaction would be if she did."

"We're not going to find out!" Alarm leapt into my tone. "When Susanna intends to maim with her tongue, she doesn't miss her mark. I couldn't bear to see you within her sights again."

Dalia's lightheartedness dimmed as she observed me through narrowed eyes. "You're frightened, aren't you?" she murmured. "It's deeper than distaste. She frightens you, but I don't see why. Are you frightened of what she can do to you?"

"I'm not frightened of her," I asserted, but even as the protest left my lips, we both sensed its untruth.

I'm frightened of becoming her.

"You need to face her," Dalia stated matter-of-factly as if crowning me with daisies once again. "Rather than hiding from her, face her. Show her the compassion she so obviously needs."

I shook my head. "Not today . . . not right now."

"If not now, then when?" Dalia cocked her head and lifted a hand to touch the hollow in my cheek where my dimple formed. "I'll go with you. Your wedding is so close and then I'll be gone, and I don't know when I'll see you again."

She put into words the truth I could hardly bear. I twisted from her, but she grasped my shoulder. "I'll go with you so you don't have to go alone when I'm gone."

Long steps were etched between the white limestone seats. Many were taking advantage of the break in the production to move and socialize. Dalia released my shoulder and took one step, then two.

"What are you doing?" I hissed, feet rooted to the spot.

"She can't harm me, not truly. She's not worth fearing, Joanna."

Susanna's cutting accusation at the wedding banquet and the slyness in her eye when she'd slandered my character rose to mind. "Words can be horrible weapons," I managed through gritted teeth.

Dalia stilled, looked over her shoulder. "I understand how hurtful words can be."

"We should leave now, mistress," Eden's voice sounded from behind me, and I cast her a look that communicated my agreement. When I turned back around, however, Dalia had descended even farther.

"Where are you going?" My voice squeaked in alarm.

Dalia twisted to send me a determined look, face open with invitation, eyes serious as they probed mine. "We were never meant to live under the tyranny of fear and grief, Jojo."

With a smile, she descended, quickly becoming obscured from sight in the crowd.

"Wait!" I shouted, finally surrendering to her downward pull and scrambling after her. The chatter from the crowd drowned out my voice as I called to her. Panic nipped at my heels, lending urgency to my feet as I lost sight of my sister. Unconcerned if it was rude, I shoved past a woman and breathed a sigh of relief as I caught sight of Dalia once again.

Foolish, foolish, foolish.

The word echoed in my head, keeping time with the pounding of my heart. I'd been foolish to bring her, foolish to let her get so far away from me. And Dalia was foolish for willingly throwing herself at Susanna. What did she hope to do when she reached her? Did she expect me to say something? How, exactly, was I to show Susanna compassion?

Dalia kept bobbing in and out of sight. She turned once to find me, and I waved wildly, trying to draw her back or, at the very least, stop her forward movement until I reached her. But she seemed to take my gesture as an indication that I was following and so gave me a confident grin and kept going.

A shrill whistle pierced through my anxious pursuit. It echoed against the stone seating, arresting everyone's attention. For a moment, I thought it was part of the production, and looked with confusion at the stage. But the performers appeared as surprised as the audience.

A strangled scream sounded close to the stage and then another until the theater resounded with terror. Fear settled in the center of my chest. My wide eyes took in the scene, but my mind could barely comprehend it. A young man scrambled up the seats, trampling those in his way, screaming of an attack. Behind me, a man fell, crushing me against another woman, who threw me off with a disgruntled cry.

Dalia.

I shoved aside the fear and confusion and focused on getting to my sister. People swarmed upward, and I shoved against their current, alone and desperate. My breaths came in frightened snatches as hands clawed at me, shoving me about like a storm-tossed boat. Fabric pulled from my body, and I realized my head was uncovered, my hair ripped free from its braids. But still I strained and pushed downward.

No, no, no.

More screams of attacks sounded as another shrill whistle rent the air. I stumbled over something and crashed to the ground, where one foot kicked me and then another.

Scrambling on hands and knees, I clutched at a bench with a growing certainty that if I didn't stand soon, I would be trampled to death. Before I could rise, someone kicked me against a seat and my head hit the stone with a sickening thud.

Stand, Joanna.

I blinked rapidly, trying to decipher who'd spoken.

Stand now.

My legs shuddered violently as my head swam, but stubbornly I obeyed the voice, grasping blindly for anything to aid me.

My hand met flesh and I pulled, straining upward, pausing when I realized that I grasped a man's forearm. He looked down at me, and as my vision cleared, I gasped. There was blood on his tunic, but it wasn't his own. Hate simmered in the eyes that locked with mine—deep pits of black, filled with pain and fury.

As he grasped my arms and pulled me up, I released the terror that had been mounting in my breast since the first whistle sounded. I screamed, pulling away, but a shove from behind drove me deeper into his arms. My head crashed against his chest, and my horror knew no bounds as I twisted in his arms, needing to be free of his hands, desperate to fly up and away like the little swift, and to take Dalia with me.

For a wretched moment, we were locked together as I screamed and sobbed with my eyes shut tight. And then I was free and stumbling. He had pushed me, or I'd been torn from his grasp. I caught my balance and found him gone.

Below me, the crowds were thinning, and I began to see the carnage. Multiple bloodied forms lay motionless throughout the theater as people continued to stream upward and away like ants from their nest. I stumbled down the steps, my passageway less obstructed now. Slipping on a smear of blood, I righted myself and screamed Dalia's name.

Please, Adonai. I need to save her.

In answer to my desperate request, a spot of honey caught my eye. Dalia was many rows ahead of me, huddled on the stone steps, her thin arms covering her head as she was buffeted about by the fleeing audience.

"Dalia!" I shrieked her name, but there was no way she could hear me. Strength infused my body and clarity my mind. I needed to leave the center aisle. Taking a swift turn, I jumped onto a row of seats and then leapt to the row below. There were fewer people in the seats, but it was still a treacherous path, requiring the nimble step of a mountain goat.

Breath hitching in my chest, I lifted my tunic and leapt, straining my legs as far as they would go. One row and then another. Was I near her now? On the next leap, I slipped, and the sole of my foot landed on the edge of the seat below, propelling me forward.

My chest landed hard on the seat, knocking the air out of my lungs. I lay panting—a frightened fish on the bottom of a boat—blinking and desperate to right myself. Air sawed painfully in and out of my lungs as I stumbled to my feet, so disoriented that I stepped right into the path of a large man, who crashed into me full force.

And then I was flying.

I landed on a stone bench at an awkward angle, my right leg coming down hard on the edge with a sickening crunch.

Fire leapt through my leg as the edges of my vision blackened. Mulishly I pushed against it, willing myself to stand. I dragged myself into the center aisle, but the fire in my leg was so intense, I couldn't continue.

Adonai, save me!

The blackness encroaching my vision became a blinding light, leaving my head reeling. I closed my eyes to the terror and focused on the voice filling my mind.

Breathe, Joanna.

I took one last breath and gave myself over to the light.

Thirteen

His eyes were pools of tar, sticky and deep. I gazed too long and was trapped, unable to tear myself away. Anchored in their depths, hatred flickered like a torch in the dead of night, but there was nothing to illuminate. The loathing was personal. What had I done to warrant this hate? I needed to look away but couldn't. I wanted to scream, but no noise came.

Adonai, deliver me. I begged God to release me from this vise-like grip.

Awaken, Joanna.

Again, the voice in my mind sounded—quiet and mighty.

Awaken, daughter.

Peace, like a salve, coated my heart. Compelled, I tried to follow the voice into consciousness. As I did so, other voices rose to the surface, tense and fraught with fear.

"Is there nothing else you can do for her?" Abba's voice, tight with attempted control.

"Her senses are dulled from the drink. She's as comfortable as I can make her."

"Will she lose her leg?" Ima's voice, barely discernible as she wept.

"Unlikely, but I must set the bones so they have a chance to heal. She will need to wear a splint and rest for many months."

Large hands moved me, shifting my body, exploring my leg, which throbbed dully. I tried to open my eyes, but lead weights were affixed to my lids and prevented my attempts.

"This will hurt dearly. It's a blessing she's still unconscious."

I'm awake! Please stop! I'm awake!

Desperately, I tried to open my eyes, my lips, anything to communicate my awareness. But large hands gripped my leg, and before I could make a sound, they wrenched my limb apart. Pain seared my body like a branding iron, and I was helpless beneath its heat.

Blackness clawed at me again, and before I succumbed to its depths, I called out to the voice of comfort.

———— ✦ ————

Everything was soft, glowing, and warm. I was a newborn lamb in the folds of a shepherd's cloak—tucked up safe and tight.

Daughter.

The voice was near. Tears of relief and comfort pricked my eyes. Gone was the empty face with the black eyes.

Daughter. Loved one.

My eyelids trembled like a fledgling taking wing.

"Mistress?" A soft hand stroked my forehead. "Are you awake? Oh, mistress! Please say something!"

"Eden?" My voice croaked past cracked lips. Compulsively, I wet them with my tongue and tried again. "Eden?"

A head landed against my side and the sounds of weeping filled the room. I pulled my eyes open to find Eden collapsed over me, shoulders heaving. Increasing degrees of awareness came over me, and I shifted on my bed, the former coziness fleeing as memory, dark and ugly, took its place.

"Where's Dalia?" The searing pain of earlier had faded to a dull throb. I tried moving my leg, but Eden reared upright and placed a restraining hand on me.

"You mustn't move, mistress! The physician said you must remain still to allow the break to heal." Eden's eyes were wide, face streaked with tears. A large bump on her forehead caused panic to rise in me.

"Eden, are you all right? What happened? Where's Dalia?"

"I'm fine." Eden's slender fingers hovered over her forehead. "It's only a bump. You . . . you could have died!" Her young voice cracked as she folded herself over me once again.

A sound in the corner caught my attention. Ima reclined uncomfortably in a chair, head at an awkward angle, mouth agape as she softly snored. As if sensing my attention, she startled awake, blinking rapidly until her eyes alighted upon me. With a soft cry, she stumbled from her chair and to my side. Eden made room for her by my bed, where she collapsed with a sob.

"Daughter, you worried us to no end!"

"Will someone tell me what happened?" My tone was growing into a fevered pitch. "And where's Dalia?"

Ima's face tightened. "There was another attack—this time on a much larger scale. To think that we've come to this—a mass assault, the Zealots waging war upon us! Oh, Joanna, what were you even doing at the theater?" Ima's concerned voice grew raw with disbelief. "You should never have been present, let alone with Dalia."

Regret settled in my breast, a live coal that left me nearly speechless. "Where is she?"

Ima grew deathly pale. When she spoke, her voice shook. "I'm afraid we don't know where she is. There was . . . a lot of confusion. Bodies are still being discovered. Many were trampled."

My breathing quickened. "But she could be okay. You just haven't found her yet?"

A moan escaped Ima's lips. "Perhaps. Get some rest now. I will inform you once we have more to share."

After she left, I slid in and out of dreams, dark and horrible. No matter how I shifted on my bed, there was no comfort to be found. While I was awake, Eden held my head in her lap, gently nudging broth past my cracked lips.

Late into the night, I awoke to strained voices outside my door. Ima was sobbing while Abba talked to her in hushed tones.

"You *must* tell her, Zahava."

"I can't."

"If you won't, then I will."

"It will kill her."

"She is stronger than you think."

The door creaked as Ima entered and I, suddenly frightened, feigned sleep. With a cool hand to my flushed face, Ima hovered above me, humming snatches of a song.

I considered opening my eyes and facing whatever Ima had to say but couldn't. Instead, I lay motionless beneath her touch as she softly began to weep.

"I'm so sorry," she whispered, but I was unsure if she was directing her words to God or to me.

Abba was there in the morning, sitting quiet and alert in the corner, when I opened my eyes. "You're awake. Good."

"What—" Dread, deep and pulsing, worked its way up through my body.

"I must tell you something hard, Joanna."

"Where's Ima?"

"She wouldn't—" Abba's voice broke, hesitation highlighting his face. He looked significantly worn, as if someone had wrung him out like a rag. "She's lying down." He cleared his throat. "She told you we don't know where Dalia is, but . . . your sister, along with so many others, was trampled in the confusion after the attack. Sarah has already left with her . . . body."

My face flushed hot, then grew cold and clammy. Abba's words landed hard between us, demanding to be addressed, but my mind was too numb to respond.

"I'm so sorry." Abba hovered over me for a long moment.

"This can't be true," I said. "Abba?"

"I'm so sorry. For you, for Sarah, for us all. This will be the last we see of Sarah. She says she wants nothing more to do with us."

Dalia—my beautiful, strong sister who had faced a hard life with determination and strength—was gone. Her huddled form on the theater steps rose in my mind, jolting me into understanding.

This is my fault.

Emptiness yawned open inside me, shuddering wide. A wail traveled from the void but refused to leave my body, banging instead like a trapped bird in my chest. I covered my head with my arms and turned to the wall.

Abba was silent. Finally, I felt his hand on my shoulder, but instead of bringing comfort, his touch made me curl into a tight ball.

"You may be tempted to blame yourself." His words were a hoarse whisper. "But you must refuse to shoulder that burden. Dalia would not want you to live with that weight."

What did he know of what Dalia would or would not want? A moan slipped past my lips, and his hand lifted from my shoulder. As he quietly left, I lay staring at the wall, in too much disbelief to feel a thing.

❖

"What do we do when God doesn't give us what we want?" I was twelve and tired—exhausted from waiting for things to change

and on the cusp of abandoning all hope. I'd begun voicing my doubts to my sister, afraid to bring them to my parents.

"Well . . ." Dalia had scrunched up her nose in thought. *"I suppose we trust Him to give us what we need instead."*

"But what if He doesn't answer us at all?"

"Oh, He does, Jojo. You just may not hear it because it's not what you expected."

With a strangled gasp, I reared upright in bed, sweat beading on my face. The sudden movement flared pain throughout my leg, and I eased back into the pillow with a groan.

Never had I met a person with more faith than my sister. She had fed upon it like food, had longed for God like she thirsted for water.

"Eden!" I screeched, desperate to not be alone with the horrible, relentless emptiness. When she came to my side, I clung to her, as a person in a pit might cling to the rope of rescue.

Gently she eased onto the bed and curled against my side while my body broke apart with deep sobs. Eventually I lay limp, hair sticking to my sweaty brow. Silent, hot tears seeped down my cheeks as I stared at the ceiling. There was a hairline crack I hadn't noticed before. I traced it slowly from where it began.

"Do you believe in the immortality of the soul?" I whispered.

"Yes." Eden's answer was immediate, her grip on my hand strong. "Yes, I do."

The crack widened, stopping above the foot of my bed. I began tracing it backward with hungry eyes.

———— ◆ ————

My marriage ceremony would have to be postponed, and Othniel's family was being less than understanding. "They are pushing for a new date. They want it settled now," Abba informed me.

I gazed at him with a hollowed expression. "I can't."

"You're still healing. It would be in everyone's interest to postpone until you're completely well, and of course, we don't know for sure when that will be. I'll see what can be done."

The new production had drawn several notable politicians who, along with a handful of religious leaders, had been the intended victims of what was now the largest attack to date.

With the head of the Sanhedrin as one of the targeted victims, Abba was offered his position—a promotion that he declined. Never one to turn away a chance for advancement, his refusal seemed to shock all but Ima. Whenever Abba left home, multiple bodyguards accompanied him, causing some to speculate that fear was behind his refusal.

The break in my leg, although severe, would heal in time. Ima kept me supplied with a tincture of wine mixed with myrrh for the pain, but nothing could dull the deeper pain in my heart, nor the guilt that now defined me.

I awakened often in the night, sweating and tossing on my bed. Eden began sleeping in my room, and whenever I jerked awake, she would rise as well, holding my hand until I fell back asleep. In some of my deeper dreams, I heard the voice again, as if someone was searching for me, following me into the lowest places, paving a pathway back out.

Fourteen

We sat unhindered and happy in a field of crown daisies as the wind whipped Dalia's hair up into a cloud that softly drifted about her face.

Abba had lied.

Dalia was not dead. She was here with me.

"You're here," I sighed and clasped her hands tightly. "And you're safe."

Dalia smiled and silently threaded a chain of daisies around and around and around my wrist.

"That's enough, sister," I giggled.

But Dalia only wrapped the chain tighter, cinching it like a taut rope with each turn.

"Stop! You're hurting me!"

Tighter, deeper, harder, the chain of daisies dug into my wrist until I lost all feeling in my fingers and my pleas morphed into soft sobs.

"The daisies!"

I awoke with a start and clutched at my wrist where I could still feel the throbbing pressure of the flower chain digging into my skin.

No field and no sister . . . just the fading light of day filtering through my window along with a sinking realization.

I called for Eden and begged her to check the drawer, even though I already knew the answer. It was empty and so was my purse, where I'd slipped the faded blooms before we went to the theater, desiring to keep them on my person once again.

Gone, just like my sister.

———— ✦ ————

"Othniel is requesting to see you." Ima stood in the doorway as Eden served me food. I shoved the dish aside, appetite gone.

Ima worried her hands, refusing to look at me. "From the beginning, Othniel has been asking to see you. At first you were too ill. Now, however, your strength has returned enough for us to move you downstairs."

"I don't wish to see him."

"He is your betrothed, Joanna." Ima's voice wobbled. "He has a right to see you. He's concerned, as he should be."

Othniel's presence was hardly what my heart needed in the moment. He expected a beautiful wife, one who could hold her own in court. How would he respond to a broken bride? I did not want his pity or his rebuke.

"Joanna!" Ima's voice was shrill as she awaited my response.

"I-I can't, Ima." I forced the words out.

She threw up her hands and left, returning later that evening with Abba.

"You will meet with Othniel tomorrow, Joanna." Abba's voice was quiet but firm. "I know his family's insistence on setting a new date seems rushed, but perhaps this is what you need—a husband to help you after such an event. Now, more than ever, you must think of your future."

How could I explain to my parents that Othniel's presence had never brought me comfort and was unlikely to do so now? How could I think of the future when my sister was gone?

The next morning, I was startled awake by Ima shaking my

shoulder. "He's here, Joanna! He comes early and demands to see you."

For a moment, I thought I was dreaming as Ima flew to the wardrobe, where she pulled out several items. "You must do her face quickly, Eden. I've already sent someone to tell Othniel she was sleeping and he must be patient. Even so, we cannot keep him waiting forever!"

Eden quickly withdrew the ornate box of cosmetics and gently pressed on my shoulder, bidding me turn so she could see my face.

Disoriented, I shrank back from her hands and curled into a ball on my side. "I haven't gotten out of bed since—"

"You must meet him. I'll have Akim carry you, if need be," Ima said.

The thought of Akim hauling me downstairs made me shrink back even more. "I can't, Ima. I don't wish to see him."

Ima continued to fly about the room, pulling a fine tunic from the wardrobe and searching my drawer for hairpins.

"I won't go!" I stated, louder and firmer.

Ima stopped, hands fluttering helplessly before her. "But . . . but you *must*," she stuttered in confusion.

Face resolute, I turned toward the wall and waited until she left.

How could I plaster on a smile for Othniel when I was gutted inside? How could I expect him to understand?

Enough time passed that I began to drift into an exhausted sleep, but Abba's sharp cry outside my door jerked me into alertness. He flung my bedroom door wide, and I curled deeper into myself, face toward the wall.

"He left, Joanna. Othniel left in a rage. I've sent a servant after him to try to undo the damage you've caused." His voice shook. "He is your betrothed and yet you refuse to see him. You refuse to allow yourself the comfort he could bring. We will send gifts and plead with him to return, and when he does, you *must* meet with him."

He left on swift and urgent feet, while I pulled a sheet over my head and wished for the oblivion of sleep.

———— ✦ ————

The message arrived early the next morning. Ima's distressed cry pierced the entire household and set everyone on edge. Abba thundered from his study and I, still bleary from sleep, struggled upright. Footfalls sounded on the stairs, and a moment later my parents stood in the doorway with a parchment in hand. Abba's face was ashen.

The lethargy that had gripped me for many days was pushed back by a bite of terror. "W-what is it? What's happened?"

Wordlessly, Abba crossed the room and dropped the parchment on my bed.

Fingers clumsy with dread, I snatched at the parchment, eyes leaping across the words.

It was a certificate of divorce.

Our legal union was now broken. There would be no marriage ceremony. A complex swirl of emotions flooded my breast, the most surprising one being a shot of relief that seared my heart like an arrow finding its target. I was free from his impatient hands and lustful gaze, free from the spirit of ambition that consumed his thoughts. On the heels of relief, however, came the burning sensation of shame—shame so deep it threatened to mark me and my family for life. I was a discarded and unwanted woman.

"As stipulated in the contract, he's returned the dowry." Ima's voice was dazed. "His disdain must run deep if he would forfeit such a large sum."

"He gave his reasons." Abba's voice was hollow. "He writes that he has no use for a wife who cannot get out of bed."

"The ring, Joanna." Ima's voice caught. "You will have to return his token." She looked at my hand and, finding it bare, lifted her brow in surprise.

Numbly, I opened a small box near my bedside and plucked the band from its hiding place, extending it to Ima. When she reached for it, I grasped at her hand, so filled with shame that my voice came out low and husky. "Ima . . . I don't know what to say."

She averted her face, disentangling her hand from mine as she pocketed the ring.

"There is nothing to say, Joanna." Abba's voice cracked, and in a shocking sign of weakness, he sank onto the foot of my bed, covering his face with a hand.

"Abba?"

"He must have interpreted your refusal to see him as a sign that the commitment was over. I know you did not intend it, but shame is now upon our family." He lifted his head, averting his face, but not before I noted the wetness in his eyes.

"Abba!" The cry tore from my heart and leapt from my lips.

He rose slowly, defeated. "Your future . . . I need to ensure that you have a future. If I've pushed you, it's because I'm desirous of this one thing, and now—"

He didn't need to finish the thought.

Now that the future he'd hoped for was terminated, what would remain for me?

❖

I wrote to Livia. Not knowing what I could or should say, I wrote to her anyway, hoping to maintain the friendship between us, but the message was returned unopened. Did she despise me? Perhaps her parents were keeping her from me.

Not long after the divorce was finalized and news of it had leaked through court, I received a visitor. For a moment, I thought it was Mireya—she who knew grief firsthand had come to offer comfort. But no . . . it was Susanna.

"She comes in good will," Eden assured me. "She's heard of how you were poorly treated by Othniel and has come to extend comfort."

"And you believe her?" My eyes widened. "She has come to gloat. She is comfortable in a prestigious marriage, and I sit lame and divorced, a shame to my family, and of no use to anyone."

"You mustn't talk so!" Eden's voice hitched with emotion. "You are not lame. You will regain your strength over time. And the shame . . . surely it is on Othniel's side, for he cast you away in your time of need."

"Perhaps this is Adonai's chastisement. I wish—" I broke off, hesitant to say the words.

"You wish what?"

"I wish it had been me instead of Dalia!" There—I said the words that had burned in my breast ever since I'd learned the awful news. I spewed them as one might emit a rancid stew. "I wish she was alive and I was dead. I cannot stand the thought that I was spared while she was not. How am I to live with this horrible reality?"

Eden grew quiet. I risked a glance to find her gazing at me with a conflicted face.

"You have nothing to say?" I questioned, voice softening as emotion drained away and left me weary.

"I have . . . something to tell you." Eden glanced at the door, confirming it was closed.

"I tried to find you and Dalia in all the chaos. I never did see Dalia, but your location became . . . obvious. People were streaming upward, away from the stage, but in the middle of the swell was this strange opening. Almost like an eddy in a river—a disruption of movement. It was *you*, mistress."

Eden swallowed hard. "You were splayed in the aisle but not a single foot trod upon you. Every single person was moving around you, compelled to give you space. I-I've never seen anything like it. You *should* be dead, mistress." She gazed at me earnestly. "You should have been trampled to death, but you weren't. I cannot pretend to know why, but one thing is clear: God spared your life."

Week pressed into week. Even though the physician encouraged me to exercise my leg, I was afraid to move. The few times I attempted to place weight on my leg, I was met with pain that drove me back to bed. Always accompanying the pain was the memory of the man who had grasped my arms. I avoided movement because the physical pain prompted such emotional pain that I couldn't bear it.

I began watching the comings and goings of people from my window. Twice more Susanna came. Both times, I watched her from behind my latticed window, but her face was too hidden for me to assess.

"Do you still believe she comes to mock?" Eden asked. "When she is so persistent?"

"Some of Dalia's final words were about Susanna, how she was in need of compassion." My tone was listless. "Before her own death, Dalia was thinking of others, of Susanna who is not worthy of her compassion! If it hadn't been for Susanna's mocking invitation—"

I bit my lip and turned away. "I will not see her, Eden. Tell her not to return."

Soon after, we received startling news of Othniel's new betrothal. "He's to marry the daughter of Herod's cousin," Ima disclosed, face pinched. "There are rumors that Herod himself made the match and that the bride is older than the groom and with two small children from a previous marriage. Even so, Ravid's family must see the match as preferable, especially if it came from Herod. Perhaps *this* is the reason he was so quick to put you aside."

On the heels of this news came distressing rumors. It wasn't enough for Othniel to discard me. Now he'd begun spreading word that I was unstable in both body and mind.

"He must be justifying his own actions by depicting you in such a negative light," Ima mused.

Perhaps *this* was why Mireya stayed away and my second note to Livia was returned unopened. Did it matter anymore what others thought of me? What did anything matter now that Dalia was dead? I wanted to ask Ima how she could bear it. How could she bear to take one more breath when Dalia's was gone? But her face was flint. Her true thoughts and emotions sectioned away so securely that there was no use in hunting for them.

I continued to wrestle with the haunting picture of God's mercy in the middle of the attack. I dreamed dreams of deliverance in which God plucked me from danger over and over again.

My frightened prayers as a girl resurfaced, except now they had matured into something deep with jagged edges that tore into me with each breath.

"God of Abraham, Isaac, and Jacob. You who call Yourself the Almighty One. Why?"

I sat in bed and rocked in anguish, lifting my face to the ceiling, clenching my fingers into fists, jaw aching as it released the words, hot and tangled on my breath.

"Why, for once, couldn't it have been me? Why did you take *her* when You should have taken *me*?"

No thundering reply came. Alone in the silence, I wept myself into calmness. I pressed the heels of my hands into my eyes and took long, shuddering breaths.

Daughter.

The endearment came softly, as subtle as the lifting of a breeze.

I exhaled slowly, letting my hands slide down my face as my body relaxed.

Stand.

The voice had urged me to action before, and I'd obeyed, but now I resisted, scared and reluctant.

Stand.

If I continued to sit here alone, then grief, anger, and loneliness would continue to pool about me until I drowned. It was clear that God had spared my life, and if I had any hope of living it, I would need to look to Him.

"The Lord's right hand will hold you securely as you cling to Him." The words of David in my sister's mouth. *"Cling to Him."*

Hesitantly, I stretched out a trembling hand and grasped the edge of my bedside table. Slowly, I swung my legs over the side of the bed and placed the soles of my feet on the floor. Gently, I eased myself forward, hunched and hovering over the table like a woman bent by age. I swayed until the anxious thump of my heart eased into a steadier pace. When I attempted a step, I stumbled hard against the table, knocking the earthen pitcher on its surface to the ground, where it splintered into pieces.

The physician had said it would take time to regain my strength and that the continued pain was only in my head, but as I grasped the table in shaking hands, I knew the pain to be real. Everything in me wanted to sink back into bed, but the gentle command to stand was a firm rod in my back, compelling me. With clenched jaw, I shuffled two steps forward. When I came to the wardrobe, I grasped it with a quick exhale as if I'd run for miles.

"Mistress, are you all right?" Eden appeared in the doorway. "I heard a crash—you're standing!" She yelped in surprise as she flew to my side.

"Something . . . isn't right," I panted. "It shouldn't be this difficult."

"Try again, mistress. Try again with me here."

Together we crossed the room, me leaning heavy against her, but still my steps faltered with a clear limp. "Call Ima." I collapsed onto a chair.

Under Ima's careful eyes I tried again, and it was soon clear to all of us that I now walked with a limp. Abba sent for the physician, and after a thorough examination, during which he measured my legs, he leaned back with a frown. "It's as I feared. The right leg is shorter than the left. This is what causes the limp. The bone healed, but the healing has shortened it in length."

"How can this be? Is there nothing you can do?" Ima moaned.

"I'm afraid there is nothing anyone can do."

After he left, I stared at the leg that had betrayed me. God had spared my life but had left me marked. Instead of dismay, acceptance fell about my shoulders.

I would now bear a reminder of the day I lost my sister.

FIFTEEN

Sunlight kissed the daisies' unfurled faces as they swayed in the field. I stood on the edge, eyes hunting for Dalia. I could feel her. She was here.

A sound like water moving quickly over a pebbled creek bed entered my waiting ear, and I turned. Dalia was laughing. There she was, running with abandon. She was meeting someone she dearly loved and had longed for all her life. I opened my arms, but she rushed past me, nearly leaping with her eagerness—flying just like the little swift.

He caught her around the middle with happiness that rolled like deep thunder. The ground beneath my feet shook, for the world couldn't contain the weight of this joy. My body arched toward them with longing, heart soaring, but my feet were tied to the shuddering earth.

He was holding her, speaking to her, and she was gazing up into His face while I strained toward them, pulling on my earthbound legs, crying out for them, "Wait! I am coming!"

Air sawed into my searching lungs as my eyes flung open. Through tears of delight, I could see that the crack in the ceiling had widened.

With my weight unequally distributed, pain often settled in my hip and lower back. I began using a cane when I walked to help alleviate the extra pressure on my right side. As time passed, the cloak of acceptance tightened around my shoulders. It seemed doubtful that any man would want me—injured and slandered that I was—and yet I knew from whispers among the servants that Abba still had hopes of finding me a spouse, despite how improbable that might be.

Now that I was mobile, I noted how Ima spent hours in her room. Once I heard deep sobs from behind her closed door and stood perched in the hall like a bird in a snare.

"I can't do this anymore, Itamar. I can't." Her words were broken apart and desperate.

Abba, with a husky voice, replied, "You must, Zahava. You will."

Grief and guilt were evident in both their voices—starkly reminding me of my childhood and the moment they'd decided to send Dalia away. They had learned to live with her loss when it had meant a new life in Gennesaret, but now we were confronted with a loss that was deeper.

I was loath to leave our home, even though I knew isolating myself would only add to the spreading rumors of my instability, but I didn't care. Instead, I spent my days in the empty guest room where Dalia had peeked through the window at the theater. Here in this room, where the decision to go had been made, I sat on the bed and talked to God. With closed eyes and open hands, I talked and talked.

WINTER 23 AD

Cold winds descended upon Sepphoris, whipping through the city and lashing at the corners of our home where I continued to hide. When Abba informed me that we were hosting a guest for dinner and that I was expected to be present, I shrank into myself.

"It will be good for you, mistress," Eden assured as she readied my clothes.

I hadn't donned fine apparel or applied cosmetics in so long that the thought of it turned my stomach. I couldn't, however, avoid social gatherings forever, so reluctantly I allowed Eden to do my face.

I made my way to the dining room, hoping that the evening would go by quickly and that little would be required of me in conversation.

Our guest rose as I entered, nearly spilling his cup as he did so. We stood still, staring wide-eyed at each other. My mouth opened but couldn't communicate its surprise, so I shut it quickly and averted my gaze.

"Joanna, you remember Chuza, Herod's financial minister."

I nodded swiftly.

Abba stroked his beard. "Chuza, thank you for joining our humble table."

Our table was anything but humble. My nervous eyes roved over the spread before me. Small pots of garum, a valued condiment, sat next to each seat and in the center of the table rested plates of fish and roasted lamb, fragrant with tarragon. We hadn't feasted this finely since my betrothal ceremony—since the man who now stood solemn and observant had followed my panicked steps out of this very room. The memory warmed my cheeks.

In truth, I'd thought of this kind man often over the last few months, for he had the strong faith of my sister, the unflinching belief in the closeness of God. I wanted to latch onto him and demand answers, grab ahold of his certainty and claim it for my own. *How do you believe? Show me how.*

"Come and sit." Ima gestured to her side.

With all my strength, I tried not to limp. It could not, however, be helped. Chuza's eyes never left me as my cane tapped a weary pattern across the floor and I sank onto a low cushion. My face burned with embarrassment.

As the meal commenced, Chuza leaned toward me. "I was sorry to hear of what happened with your betrothed." He tried to meet my eyes, but I steadfastly stared at the table. "You should know that his words are not taken at face value."

"His treatment of our Joanna was certainly less than honorable," Abba inserted.

Chuza ignored Abba and continued to search for my gaze. "I was sorrier still for the tragic events you endured, both the injury and the loss of your cousin."

I looked at him sharply.

News that we had lost a relation had spread, but hearing Dalia referred to as my cousin only worsened the pain.

"Men like Othniel are often uncomfortable with sorrow," Chuza continued. "It reminds us of life's unpredictability, its brevity. But sorrow also has lessons that are hers alone to teach, and happy is the person who learns them."

I narrowed my eyes, assessing his words. His gentle expression finally loosened my tongue. "That's the second time you've spoken of the lessons sorrow teaches. What sorrows do you carry, Minister? What lessons have you learned?"

Like a shutter closing on a window, Chuza became veiled before me, his open sincerity dimming. The sudden effect of my question ignited my curiosity.

"You would comfort me with lessons learned. Tell me, sir, what lessons are they—for many find sorrow to be a cruel instructor."

"Joanna, do not offend our guest at our own table." Abba's voice was low, face apologetic.

Chuza shook his head with a raised hand, tone firm. "I am not offended." Turning to me, his voice dipped into softness. "I am *not* offended. Yes, sorrow often appears to be cruel." His eyes searched my face. "One lesson I've learned is compassion. I am quicker to recognize pain in others."

"You mean weakness." My chin quivered. "You are quick to discern the weakness of others."

"Pain is not weakness." Chuza's brow furrowed.

"Then you are the most unusual of men. Many would say that pain and its accompanying sorrow amounts to weakness that must be conquered."

Chuza clenched his jaw. "I don't aspire to be like most men."

A spark of attraction flared—not unlike the moment in the garden where I'd longed to bring him comfort—but this time it was accompanied by an unsettling heat that jolted through my body.

As if sensing my internal disruption, Ima darted a questioning look at me.

Embarrassed, I began methodically shredding a piece of bread to give my hands something to do. I shoved a few pieces into my mouth, gagging in my hurry. Face aflame, I tried to hide behind my cup and tamp down the new emotion surging to the surface.

Even with Othniel's good looks, I had never felt this sudden pull, like the room had tilted in Chuza's direction, and I was sliding, falling, slipping closer and closer. He was attractive, but not overwhelmingly handsome the way Othniel was. And yet the room continued to shift as his integrity shone brightly. I blinked under its brilliance, gulped at my cup, and scrambled desperately toward higher ground.

"You will be interested to hear that we've apprehended and tried two men," Abba stated.

"Indeed, that is good news." Chuza's voice was deep and smooth. If he detected my flustered state, he made no mention of it.

"Yes." Abba nodded appreciatively. "They received a proper hearing and were found guilty."

"I pray that the swiftness of justice is enough to deter further attacks," Chuza stated and then turned to me with a lowered voice. "I was supposed to be present at the theater that day but was detained."

I squirmed beneath his continued attention and concern.

"You were caught in the very thick of it." Chuza's voice softened. "I can only imagine the horror of such an experience. Such events can leave a lasting mark upon a person. I don't mean to reopen a wound. I simply hope you are well. In fact, I—"

For the first time his composure shifted. Maybe he'd rethought his words as they left his lips but couldn't stop them in time. "I-I wanted to come sooner but was detained . . . in Tiberias."

He had wanted to come sooner? "You are kind to be concerned." Unusually kind. I forced a small smile.

"You are well, then? You are healing?"

"I think . . . I *want* to heal, but I feel—" I stopped, unsure how to respond to the gentle inquiry from such a prominent and confusing man.

"What do you feel?" he probed.

"I-I feel . . ." At the moment, I felt an overwhelming desire for this man to understand. Taking a deep breath, I closed my eyes and gripped my hands tightly. "I suppose I feel . . . helpless." I took a steadying breath. "In the middle of the attack, I came face-to-face with my own helplessness, and the feeling has lingered." Helpless to save Dalia. Helpless to claim her publicly as my sister.

I glanced at my parents, whose tight expressions begged me to tread carefully with my words.

Chuza leaned back quietly, staring at his half-eaten garum. "No one likes to feel helpless. A man would do just about anything to avoid that feeling."

My parents were silently urging me to stop speaking. I could sense it in the rigid way Ima held her body and in how Abba pressed his lips into a thin line. Their reaction, however, had the opposite effect of loosening my tongue even more.

"I'm beginning to realize that all of this"—I swept my hand above the lavish table—"cannot save us in the moments that matter most. We are more helpless than we realize, and we mask it. In so many ways, we mask our lack of control, and in that moment in the theater, I felt utterly exposed."

Chuza's jaw was firmly set. He'd been unoffended before. Surely now . . . But no, he seemed to want me to continue, for as I clamped my lips shut, he leaned forward. "Go on."

Was that admiration I saw in his dark brown eyes? Dalia was the only one who had seen me clearly, but here was this man asking me to continue. Caution told me to be silent, but I was too weary to listen.

"You claim sorrow has lessons worth learning. Well, I have learned at least one."

A servant stood nearby with a small bowl of water and cloth, ready to wash our hands after the meal. I turned and gestured toward her, took the bowl from her hands, and wet the cloth. Turning back to Chuza with the rag, I wiped firmly at my face, punctuating each motion with my words.

"We live our lives bound up in layers of pretense, and for what? We perform like actors on a stage, but for whose benefit?"

The cosmetics Eden had so generously applied dripped down my cheeks. My words were controlled and methodical as the rising fire in my belly spread through my body. I finished wiping at my eyes and cheeks and stood with a bare face, trembling.

"I felt the hatred of man, and I realized that our layers cannot protect us." I dropped the soiled rag onto the table. "We expect to find life and meaning in them, but all they do is obscure what is true."

Chuza gazed up at me with parted lips, his expression inscrutable.

By my side, Ima released a strangled, "Joanna!" Abba sat next to her, face mottled.

I didn't want to stay for the effects of my demonstration, so I left the table, leaning heavily onto my cane, no longer trying to control the extent of my injury.

Chuza stood quickly and, for a moment, looked like he might follow.

He had wanted honesty and for once I had given it. I limped from the room, fueled by boldness—or perhaps a touch of lunacy.

Sixteen

A handful of days after the dinner with Chuza, my parents sought me out. *Here it is, finally.* I'd expected it sooner—chastisement over my behavior at the table. All they'd done, however, was to remain distant. Had my display shocked them into silence? Now, however, they seemed ready to speak.

"Why do you come here?" Ima questioned, eyes searching the guest room.

"I come to remember Dalia." *To remember her happy and hopeful.*

Ima's eyes skittered from mine and down to her hands, where she nervously twisted the sleeve of her tunic.

"You . . . have a visitor." Abba sank onto the foot of the bed heavily. "He's waiting in the reception hall. He insists on speaking with you—alone."

Coldness seeped into my bones. "I won't face Othniel. What could he possibly have to say to me?"

"It's Chuza," Ima murmured.

"What?" The surprise compelled me awkwardly to my feet, a sudden twist of nervousness snaking through my belly.

Abba patted the bed, urging me to sit and brace myself for his words. My body, however, was a jumble of too many nerves.

"He's asked for your hand in marriage." Abba seared me with a pointed look. "But wants to speak with you before moving forward."

I laughed—a loud, disbelieving sound that crashed into the room, echoed off the floors, and died into strangled silence. "You . . . you jest. That can't possibly be true."

The seriousness was written on their faces. This was not a jest. I collapsed onto the bed.

"I'm just as astonished." Abba took my hand and I jerked away. "Especially after such a rash demonstration . . ." His words held reproof. "Even so, he seeks you as a bride. Such a match is preferrable to Othniel in every way. Chuza is established and reputable, a relative of Herod's own wife. This will, however, place you directly under the king's eye."

Abba's conflicted emotions were discernable by the way he kneaded my hand like dough for the oven. "I can understand if this union gives you pause, but it guarantees your future and I . . . I need to know that your future is secure."

My dumbfounded mind registered that he was talking, but I could only stare at my hand in his while my thoughts whirled.

"Chuza is better equipped to help you navigate court life. His reputation and temperament are proven. He will be a much better husband for you," Abba continued.

Numbly, I pulled my hand from Abba's and clutched at my throat, where my pulse hammered hard, recalling the words I'd overheard in the palace garden. *"I didn't come here for a bride."*

Had he changed his mind? Why? And why *me*?

"He's a Gentile, yes, but he's a proselyte to the faith," Ima interjected, misreading my hesitation.

"He is so . . . prominent," I murmured. "He needs a wife who can walk with ease in his circle of influence. Instead, he seeks a wife who would hobble about the court? I am unsuitable!"

The court flourished upon the very layers of pretense I had

so artlessly railed against. Was the man blind? Hadn't he noted my unease in Herod's company? What was this man thinking?

"All the same, he chooses you." Abba grew even more somber. "Joanna, such a match after what you have been through is unheard of. I've resisted the idea of God's involvement in human affairs, but this confounds me. Perhaps this is God's divine intervention."

Abba's words rushed to my head, filling it with dizziness. "And the minister wants to speak with me . . . now?"

"Before you talk with him, I have something else to share." Abba gathered both of my hands into his firm grasp, rubbing his thumbs across my knuckles, face softening as he spoke. "I have no sons . . . no earthly heirs. I do not have much time left on this earth to ensure your future is set."

"Abba, what are you saying?"

He sighed, head bowed.

"Your father is sick, Joanna." Ima placed a soft hand on Abba's back.

I looked between my parents in confusion. "I know the doctor has been here, but you said it was stress."

"That certainly didn't help," Ima stated. "But it has been going on longer than that—stomach pains that grow worse by the day and prevent him from food."

"And is there nothing—?"

"The doctors have tried their remedies to no avail," Ima murmured.

Abba squeezed my hand. "It's why I turned down the appointment in the Sanhedrin and why I am determined to see you married."

With a sharp breath, I pressed my forehead to our clasped hands. "I didn't realize . . . I did not know you were ill. Oh, Abba—"

All the tangled history of hard decisions and swallowed hurts stretched between us. Years of blaming him one moment and loving him the next.

"I've begun to consider how I want to handle my affairs." Abba swallowed hard. "Between my illness and . . . what has recently transpired—" He broke off with a regretful shake of his head. "You have been through so much and I would see you established before I die. Rather than all my earthly possessions being left to my brother, I will transfer them to you, Joanna, by deeds of gift, beginning with your betrothal to Chuza. I would then gift you another portion of my estates upon your marriage, and at my death, the final portion would be yours."

I tried to take in the full gravity of Abba's announcement—the illness and the gift.

I always knew I would receive a sizable dowry. Such monies, however, would be under my husband's control. Even though I could not acquire Abba's estates and wealth by inheritance, I could receive them as deeds of gift. Unlike a dowry, such gifts would be under my control alone.

"You would give so generously to me?" I questioned softly. "Even after recent events?"

"Especially after recent events," Abba whispered. "If this is indeed God's hand, then I would be a part of it. You were bound to the past, but now you can move forward."

"This is what you want? Me . . . handling your wealth after you are—" I couldn't say it. Tears moistened my eyes, and I released his hand to swipe at them.

"You deserve a future of freedom. No more looking to the past." He hooked a knuckle beneath my chin. "Move forward into the future prepared for you."

Ima drew close and placed a hand on Abba's shoulder. "You are the remaining daughter, Joanna. Through you, our legacy will continue."

"And now you will be strategically placed as Chuza's wife."

Abba's eyes shone with tears, and for the first time in years I felt his pride rest upon me like a benediction. "Who knows what influence you can wield in this new position."

Looking away from Abba's face full of hope, I cast my eyes upon my trembling hands, mind spinning with the mystery of God's incomprehensible plans.

◆

I didn't breathe as I entered the reception hall. I couldn't. Instead, I prayed for strength to make it through the conversation without collapsing at Chuza's feet. He stood near the same potted plant I'd hidden behind during our first encounter. His eyes softened and, upon seeing that I remained frozen by the doorway, he came to me.

"You are confused," he stated, the corners of his lips deepening in a half smile. "There it is, the furrow." He tapped his brow, eyes resting on my own. "I don't blame you for your bewilderment."

I'd spoken to him boldly when I thought I'd never see him again, but now, standing before him as a potential wife, I could not make my sluggish tongue move.

"Honesty is important to you." Chuza's eyes searched mine. A blush crawled up my neck as I held his gaze. "And so I will be honest with you as best I can. I did not enter this court imagining that I would marry, but wiser, older counsel has told me what I've already begun to suspect. Flourishing in this court in my new position means assimilating as much as possible into your culture. It means taking a Jewish wife."

My breast flooded with a strange mixture of admiration and disappointment. This was certainly not a passionate speech. This was not what a maiden would hope for from a man. But it was also refreshingly honest.

"I'm in a difficult position. Because of circumstances in my past—" His words broke off, as did his gaze. A deep breath seemed to catch in his chest. He wrestled with it for a long moment, finally releasing it as his eyes closed. "Because of circumstances in my past," he repeated slowly, "I have chosen to remain celibate. A hard decision, to be sure, but one that I stand by. And yet . . . I find myself in need of a wife."

The blush that had been hinting at my neck now blossomed all over my mortified face. He was willingly celibate? This was unheard of. Procreation was a duty—and childlessness the greatest of ills. Some Essenes practiced celibacy, but a man in Chuza's position? Why would he have made such a rash and impractical decision?

A strangled croak exited my parted lips, and at the sound, Chuza's face tightened, eyes finding mine once more.

"What I'm offering to you is a union in . . . name only." His eyes parted briefly from mine, but he pulled them back, took a deep breath. "A partnership. I respect you and would give you all that is mine to give."

All but himself. I couldn't help it . . . I let my eyes glance at his impressive frame. The pull I'd felt during the dinner was still present. Could I marry this man and yet not enjoy him the way a wife should? A husband . . . but in name only—not a *true* marriage. How could I begin to wrap my head around it?

"You are surprised and skeptical, as I expected you would be."

He would have me as a wife in name only in order to protect his position in court. Unease clutched my chest. "I don't want to live unauthentically," I managed to say.

"And that is why I'm coming to you like this—in order to be forthright on what I am and am not offering to you. We would live authentically with each other, and there are other bedrocks upon which to build a satisfying relationship."

"What could those bedrocks be?"

"Respect, confidence, trust." He drew close, voice quieting, eyes searching mine.

He was being vulnerable with me in a way no one else had ever done, apart from Dalia. He could have kept this to himself and let me make the discovery after the fact, and yet he hadn't.

Chuza was gazing at me with a mixture of apology and hope. "I, too, know what it is to live weary of pretense, tired of answering to the whims of others. You will be safe with me."

My chest clutched unbearably tight. His hope went both ways—he was trusting that he would be safe with me in return.

"We will live outside Tiberias. I understand your hesitation and will not have you compromise your morals by living within its walls. Marry me, and I will respect you, provide for you, and aid you in your new life."

He was speaking compassionate words a brother might utter to a sister or a guardian to someone in his charge. I bit my lip, averted my eyes.

"I would not, however," he continued, "have you contradict your own desires. I realize that this arrangement asks much of you, and I understand if this is not what you want."

"Why?" The bold question left my dry lips, rough as stone scraping stone. "You indeed ask much of me, and therefore I need to know why. Why this commitment to chastity? Why not a *true* marriage?" Heat settled in the base of my stomach as I forced the words out.

He studied me for a long moment before carefully stepping forward with his words.

"I was married before." The admission was delivered quietly. "I was married before but lost my wife, and after that I . . . made the decision."

Throughout his soft admission, he held my gaze, and I did the same. There it was . . . the hidden sorrow that had marked his life. I could see the years of pain behind his eyes and in the way he clenched his shoulders. Compassion warmed my chest but was instantly consumed by an aching, horrible loneliness that pulled me inward, folding me back upon myself into something small, private, and unwanted.

"I . . . I don't want to be a replacement. I don't want to be used," I stated.

"And that is not how I view you. You are not a replacement. You are not something to use and discard as other men might, as Othniel did. Rather, I see this as mutually beneficial. This relationship—it could be an asset to both of us."

A glimmer of understanding flickered in the dark of my mind. He was in an impossible situation—committed to chastity and yet in need of a wife. I was in an impossible situation—lame, slandered, and past marriable age. Shame and embarrassment clawed at my breast. Of course he'd approached me, because who else would agree to a chaste marriage?

I wanted to weep, but he was gazing at me with such clear regard it dried up the bitter tears and checked the humiliation clinging to my heart. He could not fabricate such a look even if he tried, and he would not have risked this conversation with a woman he did not trust.

"You do not need to answer me now. Simply consider it." He held out one large hand, calloused palm up. I stared at the open invitation but did not slide my hand into its grasp.

Seventeen

I took the evening meal alone in my room, barely touching the food for the whirl of emotions swirling in my stomach. Pressing the heels of my hands against heavy eyes, I slumped in a chair.

Could I bear the reality of having no children? Wouldn't tongues wag when I remained childless? But . . . tongues were already loosened thanks to Othniel, and remaining unmarried in Abba's house also meant a childless future.

Perhaps another suitor would arise. And perhaps he would be worse than Othniel. But Chuza . . . he admired me. Not every woman could say the same of her husband. Not every woman's thoughts were welcomed as Chuza clearly welcomed mine. He did not hold the vicious slander against me, and with our union, others' approval of my family's name would follow.

He must have loved his first wife dearly to have made such a decision upon her death. Would I be living in that shadow? This, in the end, gave me the biggest pause. But the memory of Chuza's unflagging gaze as he gave me the truth eased the sting. He was being honest about his past—open in a way no other man had ever been with me, and perhaps that honesty and mutual respect could indeed be a foundation upon which to build.

But I would be close to the throne—unbearably close—in the same circles as Susanna. Bile clawed at my throat at the very thought, but on the heels of the image came Chuza's firm voice. *"I don't aspire to be like most men."* Surely, Abba was right in that Chuza would be a well-suited guide for such waters.

And then there was the matter of Abba's generous gifts and the devastating news of his illness. How long had he known? No wonder he had been so eager to see me settled with Othniel. A woman—even a woman of means—needed the protection of a man, and here was Chuza offering it to me. I would have a husband who respected me, as well as financial freedom. A woman could leverage both in mighty ways.

"One day you will marry a good man. He will love you deeply; I know it. It will be God's good gift to you, and I will be there to see it."

With a sharp exhale, I cast my eyes upward, piercing the ceiling with a fierce gaze, wishing Dalia was here.

"Sister," I said the word aloud, staring harder at the ceiling.

Knowing entered my bones, sliding through my body like silk over bare skin, and I shivered, welcoming the aching sureness. My sister was alive and whole before the very face of God.

"Chuza may not love me," I murmured, "but he respects me. Perhaps *this* is the good man you always knew God would provide."

⁘

For weeks I wrestled with the decision while my parents anxiously waited, probing at first and then giving me space. Chuza hadn't placed pressure for an answer, but even so, I needed to arrive upon one soon.

Finally, I confided in Eden, keeping the strange stipulations private but divulging as much as I could. "How can I step into a future that feels too big for me and too uncertain?" I uttered in a rough whisper. "How can I move forward without Dalia?"

"She wouldn't want you to punish yourself, to remain stuck." Eden's voice was surprisingly firm as she snaked an arm about my shoulders.

"I don't know why God saw fit to spare me. I don't know why He would choose to plant me in high places." I covered my face with my hands. "I'm overwhelmed!"

Eden dropped her arm from my shoulders to worry her hands in her lap. "You asked me once for my own history. I wasn't ready then to share it, but . . ." She turned to me, eyes glinting in the lamplight.

The accident had cracked something open between us. I could see her need written on her face, the desire I'd felt myself all these years, the need to be known. I extended a hand, and she took it, eyes shifting to our joined fingers.

"My name is not Eden," she whispered. "My given name is Achsah—anklet—named after an ornamentation. My *chosen* name is Eden."

I stared at her, openmouthed. "What caused you to call yourself by a different name?"

Eden's face crumpled. "I was a young maid with my heart set on marriage." She gazed up at me with eyes wide and swimming. "I've always longed to be a mother. I know most maids do, but my longing was close to a hunger, a physical need—as if Adonai placed a special thirst within me for little ones."

She slipped her hand from mine to hug herself tightly. "My mother died when I was young, and later, when my father, a stonemason, died in a quarry accident, I became the responsibility of an uncle I barely knew. He sold me, mistress." She was trembling hard. "To settle his own substantial debts, he took my dowry, took what little was left of our estate, and sold me into a life I would never have chosen for myself." She gulped and forced herself to meet my eyes. "That is when I made a decision. I was no longer Achsah. I would be Eden."

"Why *Eden?*" I watched her face, filled with anguish for her, amazed at the tenderness and strength she exhibited.

"Because Eden means a place of pleasure—a delight." Even though she was still trembling and clasping herself furiously, she'd never looked stronger. "I couldn't choose what happened to me, but I could choose this—my name. I could choose how to live moving forward, and so I decided that instead of seeing my life as ending, I would see it as a new beginning."

"Like God in the Garden," I murmured.

"A place where He does new and unexpected things, a place of delight," Eden finished.

I embraced her even as the last words left her lips, clinging to her until she wriggled. But instead of pulling away, she twined her thin arms around me and held fast.

"You must learn to live your life, Jojo. It's the one God gave you. You have to find a way to live in it."

Dalia's voice, as clear and sweet as birdsong, threaded with Eden's own history, leaving me breathless.

"I have to believe you are here for a purpose."

———— ◆ ————

Early in the morning I sought Abba in his study. He sat with elbows on the table, forehead resting in his palms. He'd aged, and his weariness hung from him like a loose cloak. I stood in the doorway, silent and unobserved, finally clearing my throat. His eyes, when they met mine, harbored an emotion I didn't recognize in him.

"I've been thinking of Dalia," I spoke softly. "She is not dead, Abba. Not truly."

"What?" His face instantly grayed.

"She was certain of God's personal care. In truth, I envied her faith, even though I didn't understand it. And she was certain of life beyond death. That certainty gave her the courage to live. She is alive with Adonai now. I know it, and soon you—oh, Abba, I pray you come to know it too and believe it for yourself."

Abba's shoulders dropped, his expression unclenching like a loosened fist, his words an exhale. "Oh . . . I see. The resurrection of the dead, hope of eternal life." He smiled softly, wistful and sad. "There is . . . beauty to the idea."

"Yes!" I pushed from the door to cross the room. "Beauty and *truth*. If Dalia could have such courage, then so can I. If she could face the future without flinching, then so can I. . . . I will marry him, Abba."

Instead of replying, he held his hand out, palm up, waiting.

My hand, when I slid it into his, was cold. He closed his large, warm fingers around mine and squeezed.

"I can be a stubborn mule, Joanna." He studied my hand, traced my knuckles. "You are . . . brave to consider new things. I've held onto certain beliefs, unwilling to question them or let them go. You've been shaken." He cleared his throat, made himself continue. "And so have I."

My gaze landing on our joined hands, I noted how mine was slender and smooth next to his rough calluses and gnarled veins. When he spoke next, that hand shook.

"I am learning that sometimes God gives us things we cannot understand in order to shake us apart. To undo things we believe that we shouldn't. To make room for the things we *must* believe. To finally arrest our attention. If you have found hope, cling to it. If you have found a deeper faith, rejoice."

He stood then, drawing me close, and pressed a lingering kiss to my forehead, tickling my brow with his beard. In his kiss there was a blessing, confession, and apology. I stood still and alert beneath the weight of it all, wondering which things were coming apart and harboring hope for all the room they left behind.

We sent my agreement back to Chuza, after which I lay on my bed in silence and stared at the crack in the ceiling.

I am small, scared, and lame. Who am I that You would place me in such a position?

There was no answer, and suddenly I was restless, eyes jumping from ceiling to floor as I stood quickly and lost my balance, dropping to my knees, yelping at the pain in my leg.

Yahweh!

I called upon the name He gave to Moses, His sacred, covenant name.

Yahweh!

I stared hard at the wall with gritted teeth.

If this is to be a new beginning, then I cannot walk into it without Your strength.

It was the one thing I knew, and so I clung to it.

I cannot do this without You!

My heart cried and cried again as it learned to talk to Him in a new way—as someone who was claiming Him for herself.

In the midst of the cries came a quietness, a hush—the memory of comfort carried by the voice that named me Daughter.

For he has not despised or scorned the suffering of the afflicted one; he has not hidden his face from him but has listened to his cry for help.

Psalm 22:24 NIV

PART
TWO

Eighteen

Spring 28 AD
Tiberias, Israel
Five Years Later

My mother's eyes were misty, clouded, unseeing. I held her hand and hoped that this time she would hear me, speak to me. Her lips parted and so did mine, both of us mimicking speech. "Yes, Ima? Yes?" But no sound came from either of us and soon I couldn't breathe, my lips perpetually parting, waiting, straining. "Yes, Ima? What is it?"

I gasped awake, forcibly dragging myself from the dream, rearing upright, breath sticking in my throat for a long, disoriented moment. Slowly, the captured breath left my body, and I sagged back onto the bed. These dreams, they came more often now—ever since I buried Ima four months ago.

With a groan, I eased my legs over the side of the bed. Pushing back the dream and its accompanying grief, I kneaded my right leg with habitual strokes, readying myself to stand.

"Does it pain you this morning, mistress?" Eden stood in the doorway, wide eyes pooling with gentleness in the morning light.

"No pain at the moment." I gave a half smile to the woman who had become less handmaid and more of a sister.

I allowed Eden to help me to my feet and then limped to my

155

dressing table. By midmorning, pain would crawl up to my hip and grip my lower back as my body accommodated the shorter leg. The sturdy cane I continued to carry helped—some—but my joints still groaned in protest with a near-constant achiness.

I eased into a seat. "My meeting with Matthias was moved up. After you're finished here, can you inform the kitchen that I'll be entertaining a guest for the noonday meal?"

"Certainly." Eden took up station behind me and began sectioning my thick hair for braids.

Reconstruction on the synagogue in Sepphoris was going well, and Matthias, the chief architect on the project, was arriving today to update me on the progress. I found great joy in funding such projects. This latest one focused on reconstructing the synagogue located in the poorer district of Sepphoris. It had fallen into disrepair, and with the congregation unable to fund its renewal, they had been forced to worship elsewhere. Over the last five years, I'd funded many such projects, channeling the earnings from Abba's estates into various worthy causes and attaining a reputation within the court as a generous patroness.

"Who knows what influence you can wield in this new position." Would Abba have been pleased with the way I managed his wealth? I hoped so. He had passed only a few months after my betrothal—pale, weak, and wracked with stomach pains. There had been nothing the physicians could do.

"Are you all right, mistress?" Eden gently lifted my head. "You keep drooping as if something weighs you down. Another dream?"

"Yes—and they always leave memories behind." I raised my chin, took a deep breath. "Busyness drives them away, though, so it's a good thing I have a full schedule today."

Eden pursed her lips. I knew the look well and all it represented. "I know you think I'm *too* preoccupied, Eden, but I've had to be since Ima—" I cleared my throat. "Now that she's gone, the sale of her home has kept me busy."

For years I'd invited Ima to live with Chuza and me at our villa sprawled on a hillside outside Tiberias. At the invitation, however, Ima had grown pale and strangely distant, steadfastly refusing all mention of relocation.

"*Our home in Sepphoris, then,*" I'd offered. "*Chuza has a fine home, and you can move there.*"

"*Thank you, but no. This place makes me think of your father and of—*"

"*Dalia?*" I'd finished. Ima never said her name, but I kept it alive in my heart and mind and sometimes forced it out between us.

Her eyes had glistened, words barely audible. "*Yes,*" she'd gasped. "*Yes.*"

In the past year, she'd acted as though someone from the past might walk through the door at any moment—Abba, Dalia, or Aunt Sarah, who remained, as far as I knew, in Gennesaret. For a woman who refused to talk about the past, Ima had been stuck in it, lived in it, and eventually died in it, so delirious at the end that she'd repeatedly called me by my sister's name.

I closed my eyes, willing that particular memory away. My hand in Ima's while she wept Dalia's name and stroked my face. Her mind had been so scattered after Abba's death.

"You seem especially somber this morning, so let me distract you with some news." Eden paused to squeeze my shoulder. "Susanna has experienced a full recovery."

"Manaen must be so grateful."

"Some are calling it a miracle." Eden's words were careful, for she knew what a tender subject Susanna was.

The memory of Susanna calling Dalia down the theater steps continued to haunt me, so I maintained distance from her as I could—a distance she had come to respect.

Recently she, along with many others, had fallen ill from a contaminated water source within the city. The malaise had sucked its victims of life, with high fevers and insufferable cramps driving many to their beds, where they wasted away.

"I'm glad she is well."

Eden began slowly twisting my curls. "Perhaps . . . perhaps now the two of you can—"

"I doubt it," I interrupted with a soft yet firm voice.

Eden huffed an irritated breath. "You're about as stubborn as these knots in your hair." She pulled gently on one for emphasis.

"You're one to talk about stubbornness," I retorted with a laugh.

Eden was a freedwoman now, and I'd encouraged her to return to her hometown, seek a husband, and have the children she'd always longed for. But she'd adamantly refused to leave me. Like Ruth binding herself to Naomi, she'd decided to remain in her new life with me rather than return to the old.

"You know," Eden quipped, comb snagging on another knot in my tresses, "ill will, if nurtured, breeds hatred and births regret." She picked at the knot in short, aggressive strokes.

Biting the inside of my cheek, I shook my head. "Another of your wise sayings? How about we talk about something else instead? Oh, I don't know . . ." I tapped my chin thoughtfully. "Perhaps we could discuss Asher."

Eden froze, my knotted curl slipping from her fingers. "The boy who works in the stables?" she squeaked.

"Oh, come now." I smirked, pleased with myself because in Eden's reaction I saw I'd deduced correctly—she was infatuated with the young man. "He is hardly a *boy*."

Quiet and stocky, Asher was not much taller than Eden herself and tended to draw little attention in word or manner. The only time I'd seen him animated was when he caught sight of Eden, and then his broad face blossomed in such a self-forgetful manner that he became close to beautiful.

"He's handsome, isn't he?" I prodded with a grin.

"I've not thought about it." As quickly as they'd frozen, her fingers leapt to life, attacking the knot with new vengeance. "I suppose he is. I don't know. I don't talk to him. I mean, he doesn't say anything to me. Why would he? Why would you even ask such a thing?"

"I've seen the way he looks at you when you're not watching." I yelped as she tugged a little harder than was strictly necessary.

A bubble of nervous laughter left Eden's lips. "What an imagination you have!"

"I thought you should know," I said as my scalp began to scream under her frantic fingers. "I'm happy for you."

She stilled again, and I took the opportunity to twist out of her hands and stare into her conflicted face. "You're deserving of all good things, Eden. Your happiness means a great deal to me."

Her large eyes searched mine before she turned me back around with a gentle nudge. Threading her fingers softly into my hair, she rested her chin briefly on the crown of my head. "I could say the same about you."

❦

Midmorning brought the usual pains. I leaned heavy on the cane and ignored the discomfort, shoulders easing downward as the lovely scent of lily lifted in the breeze. It was spring in Tiberias, and the flowers were bursting with color, opening thrilled faces to their Maker.

How I loved my garden. It flowed in a chaotic sprawl outside my window, along the whole eastern side of our home. Now that spring had arrived, it was time to fill my basket with blooms. Every year, I brought the outdoors inside, leaving bouquets all over the villa. I had time before Matthias' arrival to harvest fresh blooms for the triclinium.

With a soft ache in my heart, I entered the largest portion of the garden—a splash of crown daisies, and in the middle of the flashes of yellow, a stone bench where I came to pray to the God who held my sister. It had become the dearest part of my garden, the heart from which everything else sprung.

Cutting some of the blooms, I nestled them in my basket, gently fingering their petaled faces before turning to another portion of the garden. Chuza, however, intercepted me, rounding a wild tangle of Commicarpus and catching me off guard.

"O-oh." I nearly dropped my basket. "Pardon, I didn't see you there." Flustered, I moved aside to allow him passage, but he stood silently in the middle of the path.

Dreams of Ima weren't the only ones that plagued my nights. Sometimes I dreamed of Chuza and awoke restless and confused. We'd settled into a companionable relationship, so when the errant dreams came, disrupting that calm, I ruthlessly shoved them aside.

"I came to find you," Chuza stated, eyes bright. "I have a favor to ask."

Surprise lifted my eyes to his, for he didn't typically ask for favors.

"We've been invited to a dinner party, but I'm unable to attend since I'll be traveling. It would be rude not to show, so I'm wondering if you would attend in my stead." His words were hesitant, warm eyes easing into uncertainty.

I frowned. "This seems a small favor to ask. If the invitation was for us both and you cannot attend, then it makes good sense for me to go."

"Even though the invitation was for us both, I hadn't intended to ask you to go." Chuza bit his lip and sighed. "It's from Manaen and is at his home."

My body clenched. Chuza was aware that I avoided Susanna when I could. Honesty, respect, and trust—these were the bedrocks upon which we'd built a satisfying relationship and yet . . . there was not complete openness between us. He did not speak about his first wife, nor the circumstances leading to her death, and I did not disclose the root of my hurt with Susanna nor the secret of beautiful Dalia.

"Susanna has never extended such an invitation before. . . ."

"This comes from Manaen. I'm unsure if Susanna knows." Chuza's voice was hesitant. "I realize it's asking a lot of you, but Manaen is a close colleague. He's holding this dinner party in honor of his wife's recovery. It would mean quite a bit to me if you went and extended my personal greeting to Manaen."

Thoughtfully, I studied his worried eyes, heart softening the longer I examined their depths. The connection between us was solid and strong, each respecting the boundaries of the other. He'd been supportive of my many philanthropic pursuits, not questioning how or when I used my father's funds. He'd even joined me in some of my endeavors, contributing from his own finances.

Any lingering slander from Othniel had died upon my marriage to Chuza. Our relationship had indeed become mutually beneficial, each of us contributing to the good name of the other. It was a relationship that few, if they understood its stipulations, would understand, but we were content with each other. Abba had been right—Chuza had proven to be a good guide in deep waters, so couldn't I do this small favor for him?

"I'll go," I finally murmured.

"Thank you." He dipped his head, and for a moment, I thought he'd reach for me. "I leave early tomorrow for the port of Acre. Herod is returning from Rome, and I must be there to meet him." He broke off, looking conflicted.

He was often like this when he left me—nervous and tightly bound.

"So far away?" I regretted my words as something close to fear leapt into Chuza's face.

"It won't be for long," he quickly assured me, and then he did reach for me, and I let him take my upper arms in his large hands. He squeezed gently, and I nearly drifted into his arms before catching myself. Physical contact between us was sparse, although I welcomed it when it came.

"I'll be sure to extend your personal regard to Manaen." I eased back, breaking his hold and turning away, mistrusting the expression on my own face.

NINETEEN

Susanna glowed with health as she cuddled her youngest on her lap. Having been confined to her bed for so long, she seemed determined to keep those dearest to her close, welcoming her children's embraces and feeding them from her own plate. I sat nearby and watched her with a growing lump in my throat.

I'd entered my union with Chuza knowing that we would not have children and yet . . . seeing Susanna expectant and happy, welcoming one babe and then another, had placed a desperate pit into my stomach. If I was honest, part of my avoidance of her was because I didn't want to feel the sting of my own lack.

Despite my childlessness, I was held with great regard due to my patronage. The honor my beneficiaries bestowed, however, didn't quite satisfy the deep ache that now grew sharper the longer I observed Susanna's joyful demeanor.

"Thank you all for joining us on such short notice." Manaen sat upright at the head of the table. He'd grayed considerably in the last few years, his silver beard lending him a distinguished look.

"As most of you have heard, Susanna has experienced healing. When many still lie on their beds desperately sick, when some of our own friends and family have died from this illness, my

Susanna . . ." He broke off, voice catching. "My Susanna not only lives but is completely healed, strong in mind, body, and spirit." He pushed the last words out on the ends of a sob, catching his face with a palm.

Susanna reached a slender hand to him, enmeshing her fingers in his beard as she lovingly cupped his cheek. He turned into her hand, planting a kiss on her wrist. The love between them was beautiful and apparent, and the room quieted in the face of their affection.

I'd observed the couple often from afar but never in such an intimate setting. A new pang entered my breast. What must it be like to stroke your husband's cheek unhindered and happy because you knew he would welcome your touch? What must it be like to hear his tone flood with love as he said your name?

"What brought about this healing?" a man asked, face earnest. "I have a cousin close to death from this sickness. Please tell me how you found healing."

"It's a miracle," Susanna whispered.

Manaen nodded and spoke loudly for all to hear. "It is indeed a miracle. I have a friend in Capernaum whose son was at the point of death. He went to a teacher who had performed a miracle in Cana and begged him to heal his son. This teacher told my friend his son would live and that very hour the boy was healed. That very hour! When I heard of this, I knew I had to seek him for Susanna."

"I could not even rise to greet him, but lay helpless on a litter." Susanna wept. "The teacher placed his hands on my face and healed me with his words."

Amazement rippled throughout the room.

"What is his name, and where is he now?" The man from earlier rose to his feet. "Tell me, and I'll take my cousin to him."

"Jesus of Nazareth," Manaen replied.

"Nothing good comes from Nazareth!" a woman hissed.

The small village sat four miles south of my hometown of Sepphoris, small and unimportant.

"He's preaching all throughout Galilee," Manaen continued. "The last we heard he was near Chorazin."

"I've heard of this man," someone exclaimed. "He teaches as one with authority and even casts out demons."

"Has his teaching spread to Judea? Do our religious leaders know of him? They are beside themselves as it is with Pilate's appointment, so how will they respond to a new teacher and miracle worker?"

My chest tightened at the mention of the new Roman prefect in Judea—a man appointed by Sejanus himself.

"Surely he's not garnered the attention of the Sanhedrin or Rome—yet," a man asserted.

One interested voice after another joined in the speculation. I watched silent and wide-eyed, unsure how to respond or what to think until my gaze snagged on Susanna. She was watching me, eyes soft with invitation. I let myself return her look, squirming uncomfortably beneath her calm focus.

"Do you believe what they say?" Mireya drawled, voice hot against my ear.

"Whether or not this new rabbi has divine power, I cannot say, but we cannot deny the change before us," I replied, nodding to Susanna who was physically whole, internally at rest.

Mireya laughed. "At the very least, this teacher is a curiosity I would dearly love to see."

To Mireya, everything was a curiosity and ripe for enjoyment. Having married a wealthy nobleman, she spent her days for pleasure and looked upon me with open confusion, for I did not indulge in the baths and never frequented the theater.

The talk died down as the evening drew to a close. I gave Chuza's personal message to Manaen and made preparations to leave, hoping I could do so without Susanna noticing. My cane tapped a refrain on the tiled floor as I neared the open front door.

"Wait!" Susanna's voice rang out behind me as she hurried to my side. "Joanna, please wait."

Why was she bridging the comfortable gap that had grown between us? I couldn't even recall the last time we'd spoken.

"I'm happy for you, Susanna." I attempted to leave, but she stayed me with a firm hand.

"I'm sorry for the way I used to be. I've wanted to talk to you, but when it was clear you didn't want the same, I allowed my own shame to keep me away. I dare not hope for your forgiveness."

Surprise consumed all rational thought. I gazed out into the night, staring at a jewel-studded sky as Dalia's voice filled my mind. *"You need to face her. . . . Show her the compassion she so obviously needs."*

Adonai, I can't.

"I-I could offer excuses for my behavior, but I won't. I've changed, Joanna, and I'm sorry."

"You have indeed changed," I stated slowly. "This rabbi . . . he has changed you."

"Yes, and you could experience it too."

Her words and hopeful tone gave me pause. "What do you mean?"

"Come with me." Her voice was breathless, urgent. "Come with me to see him and experience his power." Her eyes dropped to my leg. "Come with me, and we can ask for healing."

Pain lapped through my body like a flame as I recalled the day that had marked me. "What makes you think I want or need such healing?"

Susanna blinked rapidly. "It's just . . . your leg . . . I've always . . ."

"You've always what?" I whispered roughly, grief lying low beneath my skin.

"It was *me* who so rashly invited you that day!" Susanna cried, averting her face. "I only extended the invitation to humiliate your cousin, and then you came and I called to you and . . ."

"Please don't speak of that day or of my . . . cousin."

Was she truly sorry for how spiteful she had been? Or was she simply riddled with guilt? Was this whole conversation an attempt to assuage her own culpability?

"You've experienced healing," I managed to say. "I'm happy for you. But please don't extend to me your pity." I bit down on the last word. As quickly as my leg would allow, I descended the steps, and as I entered a cushioned litter, her voice, soft and pained, reached me.

"It's not pity, Joanna. It's not. If you would come and see . . ."

But I did not stay to listen. With a sharp rap of my cane, I indicated I was ready, and on the backs of two servants, I was carried from Susanna's sight, out of earshot, and away—at last—from her pity.

✦

Standing in the doorway of the new synagogue, I ran a pleased eye over the interior while Matthias finished going over the particulars.

"We will be ready to begin services within a fortnight. The congregation will be pleased with the renovations. We were able to reuse more materials than we originally thought. The funds we saved were then able to go toward the additional *mikvah* and the double colonnade."

I cast my eye down the length of the room to the *bema*, the raised platform for the reading of Scripture, and recalled the respite Dalia had found as she'd learned at the synagogue in Gennesaret. *May this building be a safe place for any who need it.*

Progress on the synagogue was further along than I'd anticipated, so I'd extended my visit by several days in order to review all the improvements. Satisfied with the results, I took my leave of Matthias and reentered the litter, where Eden awaited me.

With the last few days so full, I'd pushed aside the memory of Susanna's pleading eyes. But now, in the quiet of my litter, they rose up to plague me.

Over the years, Susanna had become inseparably linked to the loss of my sister, and I still mistrusted her motives. Had the earnestness in her voice been authentic? It sounded like this Jesus was healing people's souls as well as their bodies, so was it possible that Susanna might, in fact, be a transformed woman?

Word had reached court that Jesus had forgiven a paralytic man's sins, even referring to himself as the Son of Man—the Messianic title from Daniel, the coming deliverer to whom dominion and glory and a kingdom were given.

Surely not . . . but then the paralytic man had stood up and walked.

It was one of many reports that made its way to court. Many journeyed to see him, some coming back restored from all kinds of ailments. A prophet from Nazareth? The mind balked at the very idea, and yet . . . his works were speaking for themselves.

"Come and see." Susanna's invitation resounded. Dare I go and assess for myself this man who healed with a touch, a word?

Lately, he'd spent most of his time around the northern borders of the Sea of Galilee. Last I heard, he was in the Korazim Plateau, north of Capernaum.

I sucked in a sharp breath, letting my imagination journey to a time when I was young and achingly hopeful that God would come and help me. And now a healer had arisen, performing miracles near the same locations where Dalia used to walk. Oh, that this Jesus had come sooner.

The lump in my throat grew painful.

"Come and see."

———— ✦ ————

The road from Sepphoris to Tiberias was broad and well-traveled. Our litter ambled along comfortably, but the closer we drew to home, the more agitated I became.

Eden rested across from me, eyes half-closed. I stared through the curtain with a restless gaze that flitted from tree to rock to sky. For an hour, I wrestled with my thoughts, shifting in my cushioned seat like it was a bed of pikes. Finally, we neared the Sea of Galilee, where the road cut south to Tiberias.

I shoved my head from the litter, words pouring from my lips like floodwater. "Turn north up ahead."

"What are you doing?" Eden's voice was thick with drowsiness. "Home is south."

"Even so, we're going north."

"But why?"

"Because *he's* there." My voice shook, then grew more certain. "And I want to go and see."

TWENTY

The wind whipped off the Sea of Galilee and sent shivers down my spine. Gently, I pulled the curtain aside to peer at the scene before me. We'd encountered dozens of people along the road, all traveling in the same direction. With the swell of the crowd, my curiosity mounted. Surely if Herod got word of such crowds, he'd be displeased. I shivered again, this time from uneasiness.

"Do you see him?" Eden joined me in thrusting her head from the litter.

We were on a road winding around a sloping mountain that ended in the Sea of Galilee. At the base of the mountain, a throng of people formed, and from the center of the throng came excited shouts.

"Do you know what's happening?" I questioned someone who had come from the thick of the crowd.

"He's healing all who come to him!" the woman cried, face shining.

Her joy matched so many others. As servants bore our litter closer to the heart of the crowd, we encountered many more who claimed healing. When we could draw no closer, Eden and I exited to stand by the side of the road, our gazes straining forward.

It was impossible to tell who Jesus was, and for hours we

waited as more people came broken and left restored. Eventually a group of men broke from the crowd and began ascending the mountain.

"Those are some of his followers." A woman pointed to the men picking their way up the craggy mountainside. When they parted, I saw him. From a distance, he looked like any other man as he sat on a large rock and raised his hands for silence.

"Blessed are the poor in spirit, for theirs is the Kingdom of heaven."

He spoke loudly and with great authority. His position on the mountain served to amplify his voice, which came leaping downward, bursting off the rock and into our waiting ears.

"Blessed are those who mourn, for they shall be comforted. Blessed are the meek, for they shall inherit the earth."

The meek? The words of his message began penetrating my mind, distracting me from the crowd.

"Blessed are those who hunger and thirst for righteousness, for they shall be satisfied."

Both his words and his delivery were authoritative, eliciting everyone's attention. Eden and I stood riveted to the road. We were close enough to hear his words as they carried across the plain, but the crowd had spread far and wide behind us, and soon some of his disciples descended the slope to repeat his words throughout the crowd so that those in the back could hear.

My jaw loosened as I listened, a slow warmth spreading from my chest outward. Rather than elevating the pious, he highlighted the necessity of spiritual bankruptcy. Those who achieved happiness were those who acknowledged their own need before God—those who accepted mercy and then gave it to others. He spoke of authenticity of heart, of motives, and of desires. Piety, under his definition, was nearly impossible, for who could act with pure motives at all times? And yet he led us away from despair and toward confidence in God.

The Kingdom—he mentioned it repeatedly, but in terms I'd never heard before. This kingdom wasn't about nations and autonomy but about humbling oneself beneath God's rule. He spoke of mercy and forgiveness as if these things were in his hand, ready and immediate. Not once did he reference another rabbi. Not once did he claim the authority of another teacher. He spoke his words like they came directly from heaven . . . like he *knew* these things and was simply revealing them to us.

The longer he spoke, the harder I began to tremble. A crack began forming in my mind, spreading, widening, making room for belief. In his words I saw life as I'd always hoped it could be—stripped of pretense. Was this way of life even possible?

"When you pray, do not be like stage actors, who position themselves outside the synagogue in the most prominent places in order to be seen and praised. I tell you the truth, this is the only reward they will receive! Instead, when you pray, shut yourself up in your room and address God as your Father. And then your Father, who sees you, will reward you."

I gasped aloud and stretched a hand to Eden, who clasped it in both of her own. Addressing God as one's abba? I scoured my mind, searching our Scriptures. Israel had known God as Father, and certainly He had chastised the nation as a father would a son. But for each person to claim Him as their own abba? This spoke directly to what Dalia always knew—God was listening. But to listen as an abba to a child? This denoted a level of intimacy that was scandalous, outrageous . . . beautiful.

As Jesus began speaking of earthly treasure, many prominent people in the audience grew restless, and some even began to leave. Jesus, who clearly held no wealth of his own, nonetheless seemed to understand its pull and spoke strongly but without condemnation. Rather, he urged our hearts toward eternal riches that were impervious to rust and decay. Wealth was a master, and those who sought it would be ruled by it, but those with a good eye lived generously no matter how much they owned. The body with its desires would then follow after that good eye.

His words were pulling back layers like flesh from bone, exposing the tender truth beneath, until I could no longer stand upright. I sat down hard, right there in the dirt on the side of the road. The warmth in my chest spread, pooling in my joints, loosening the constant ache in my back, turning my body into an open vessel for his words to come, come, and fill me to the brim.

I sat on the side of the road—there in the dirt in all my fine clothes—until he finished speaking. The crowd slowly began to disperse, but I remained unmoving, even as many jostled past me. I didn't care how I looked, how I appeared, only how his words had left me.

Eden crouched by my side. "Will you go to him?"

The soft question jolted me. "Go to him? Why?"

"For healing." She pressed a loving hand to my knee.

No.

I shook my head, unable to even utter the word for the new worry that gripped me.

No.

How could I present myself to this man? Surely all he would notice was my glittering affluence. If he saw me, would he despise me? I could not bear to sit beneath such reproach. I wobbled to my feet, grasping Eden's hand for support as I shook my head with enough finality that she acquiesced with a sigh.

"I won't go to him, but . . ." My purse was heavy upon my person, and Jesus' words heavy on my mind. If ever there had been a worthy cause, this was it.

"Could you go and find someone from his company?" I asked with pleading eyes. "I will wait here."

Eden's face filled with questions, but she left quietly to do as

I'd asked. Anxiously, I waited by the litter, heart in my throat until she reappeared. I frowned in confusion, for a young woman followed her.

"I was hoping to speak with one of Jesus' disciples." My voice faltered awkwardly.

The young woman glanced past me to the litter, quickly taking in the ornate curtains, before blinking with surprise and refocusing on me with a small smile. "I *am* one of his disciples." Her voice was thin and airy, so quiet I had to lean forward. "I am one of many who follow him."

A rabbi who welcomed women as disciples? I had never heard of such a thing.

"I am Mary of Magdala."

I was too surprised and flustered to reciprocate with my own name so instead withdrew my purse. "I'd like to make a contribution to your rabbi's ministry." I slid coins into my palm and extended them toward Mary, whose own hand fluttered hesitantly by her side.

"You are skeptical, and I do not blame you." I gave her a smile that I hoped would dispel her worry. "I'm not seeking to establish a patron-client relationship." I stepped closer and reached for her hand, turning it up between us, nestling the coins in her palm. "I expect nothing in return. This treasure, it is fleeting." I closed her hand over the coins. "Please accept it. Let me use it for a greater purpose."

Mary met my eyes, and I could see her uneasiness slowly fade as she examined me. "This is good of you," she murmured as she tucked the coins into her own purse. "But won't you come and meet him yourself?"

Susanna, Eden, and now Mary—everyone was urging me to place myself before this rabbi. I shook my head, smile slipping. "Thank you, but no. It is enough to contribute from afar."

I expected Mary to leave, to hurry gratefully from my presence, but instead she continued to observe me with shrewd eyes.

"I recognize your sadness."

A rush of air left me—half laugh, half cry. My lips opened to correct her, but nothing came out.

"Whatever you are facing, bring it to him. He will welcome you. I know how capable he is." Mary's face softened. "I am filled with his love and healing now, but it wasn't always so. There was a time when I was filled with spirits so evil and dark that I despaired of life itself."

Astonishment filled me. This beautiful, meek woman had once been controlled by demons? "Jesus . . . healed you?"

"Seven—the number of completion. I was completely consumed by seven evil spirits, driven from my family, from those who had formerly loved me."

My breath caught as I saw Dalia's broken face that first time we'd left her—when she'd understood what abandonment was.

"No one would touch me. No one dared come near me."

"Stop," I pleaded, trembling before this woman, Dalia's face stark in my mind.

Mary looked at me with furrowed brow. "Oh, but it doesn't end there. He came to me." Her face lifted with delight. "I did nothing to deserve it. I didn't even know of his existence, and even if I did, I would not have been able to seek him. He came to me. He sought me when no one else would. He placed his hands on me, called me by name, and demanded the spirits leave. Who am I to expect such mercy? I am no one, and yet he chose me when I could not choose him. He gave me wholeness, and now I get to live with new purpose."

The settled certainty in this woman was stunning, and my mind whirled with the story she'd laid at my feet. Who was this man, this rabbi, who ran toward the oppressed? He sought out those who could give him nothing in return? I shook my head in bewilderment, for I had never seen power modeled this way.

If only Dalia was alive. I would expend all the effort and money in the world to bring her to Jesus. If only—

"You are weeping." Mary was looking at me with eyes full of compassion, and for a moment I considered letting her take me to Jesus so I could be near the man who used his power in such remarkable ways. But I couldn't speak. I could only gaze at Mary as I pictured Dalia's face. I could only feel the pounding of my own yearning heart.

"Thank you again for the gift." Mary was leaving, and my heart was calling after her to come and take me with her. But my grief and guilt rooted me to the road, my own history binding up my limbs as I watched her slender form disappear into the distance.

◆

We stayed overnight at an inn and began journeying home early the next morning. I was eager to be home, surrounded by the quiet of my flowers. We traveled south along the dusty road that wrapped around the western shore of the Sea of Galilee.

"You're punishing yourself, as you always do." Eden had softly chastised me last night. *"Why deny yourself meeting this man? When will you stop punishing yourself for that day?"*

I'd pushed away her words, denying them, retreating into myself. Now, an hour into our journey, Eden was silent, allowing space for my thoughts, which were dark and brooding.

Easing back on my cushion, I pulled back the curtain to peek at the sky and trace the wandering shapes of the clouds with tired eyes.

I hadn't slept. For hours, I'd lain awake, dry-eyed and hopelessly alert, heart pounding like I was running from something. When sleep came, it was in spurts. I'd tossed, half-dreaming upon my bed, fully waking before the dawn, hair sticking to my sweaty brow as I'd shaken Eden alert.

Now the lolling motion of the litter threatened to carry me back to sleep. My eyes fought a losing battle until Eden's sudden exclamation jerked me upright.

"Aren't these some of Jesus' company?" She was glancing outside the litter, and I joined her by the curtain.

Foot travelers clogged the road. At our litter's approach, they parted, most willingly but some with dark expressions that filled my stomach with unease. As we passed, I caught sight of Mary and quickly fell back inside, panting against my cushion.

"Close the curtains!" I hissed.

The disciples' conversations swirled about our litter as we were borne through their midst. I listened to their voices, holding as still as possible, barely daring to breathe.

"Do you fear them?" Eden whispered.

I shushed her with a wild hand in the air.

The voices dimmed and grew fainter until it was clear we'd passed them. With a deep sigh, I released my clenched shoulders until a shout drew me tightly into myself once again.

A man's voice cried out from behind us.

"Is he calling to us?" Eden asked.

"Keep moving," I instructed the litter bearers, but the shout came again, closer this time, and then he was upon us, beseeching the litter to stop. Mulishly we pressed onward, but the man's insistence was as biting as a bee sting until I was compelled to respond.

"Stop!" I pushed the curtain aside as the litter came to a sudden halt.

A man fidgeted in the middle of the road, shifting his weight from one muscled leg to the other. His strong build spoke of intentional physical training as he flexed his shoulders with a nervous gesture. Having succeeded in his errand to stop me, he now appeared speechless.

"Yes? How can I help you?"

He looked me in the eye, and I startled. It wasn't nervousness that filled his body with jitteriness. It was *distaste*. This—this was the look I had hoped to avoid. He took in my litter, the silk curtains and plush cushions, with a sneer that he quickly tried to hide. Clearing his throat again, he seemed to be struggling to get his words out.

"My rabbi . . . he sent me to come and get you."

Shock slithered through my body and left me trembling. I glanced back down the road to where the disciples had come to a stop. They stood in clusters, observing our interchange.

"Why me?" I turned a bewildered expression to the man.

He rubbed a large hand against the back of his neck. "Believe me, I'm just as confused."

I was too overwhelmed to be offended. "I-I can't."

"He was very adamant that I come and fetch you." The man sighed. "Please. It will only be a moment." He glanced back over his shoulder, and I followed his gaze to where Jesus stood next to the road, Mary close to his side.

Mary must have recognized the litter, must have told Jesus of my financial contribution. Did he wish to thank me? Or perhaps solicit even more funds?

"Go," Eden hissed. "Please, mistress. Go."

I searched her eyes for a single, wild moment before scrambling from the litter and onto the ground, where I swayed for a moment with indecision. But I went. I allowed the man to lead me toward Jesus.

My companion kept his eyes averted. He did, however, note my use of the cane and my pronounced limp, for he adjusted his pace as he realized I couldn't keep up with him. Together we approached Jesus, him taking painfully small steps and me limping by his side.

As the disciples near Jesus saw me approach, they parted until, at last, there was no one remaining between Jesus and me. He watched me approach, and I forced myself to meet his eyes. There was no distaste to be found in their brown depths.

"Thank you, Simon." He clapped a hand on my guide's thick shoulder and then faced me with a smile playing about his lips. "Ah, Joanna. How glad I am to see you."

How did he know my name? I hadn't given it to Mary. Someone must have seen and recognized me yesterday. I tried and failed to speak.

He watched me quietly for a moment before continuing. "You're likely wondering why I asked for you."

From the look of it, everyone was wondering the same.

"I thought perhaps you were concerned . . . about the funds." My gaze shifted to the woman by his side. "But as I explained to Mary yesterday, I do not expect anything in return."

Jesus' face softened. "Thank you for that. You gave freely, not reluctantly or under compulsion. But that is not why I sought you out." He held my gaze with such intensity that my throat dried up.

"I have a question for you."

My mind whirled. Did he know my connection to Herod's court? Did he want inside information? He'd spoken of a kingdom under God's reign, but perhaps his talk was a front for more political aspirations. What question could this man possibly have for me? What kind of answer dare I give him?

I wet cracked lips. "What question would that be, Rabbi?"

He moved close and placed both hands on my shoulders, waiting patiently for me to look him in the eye. "Joanna, do you want to be healed?"

The blood drained from my body. I shook beneath his hands, beneath his question, and dropped my face to stare at the ground.

"You don't need to feel beholden to me. I told Mary . . . I don't expect anything. You don't have to—"

"This is not repayment." His voice cut through my anxious chatter.

Healing . . . it was being held out to me, but my heart pushed it away. How could I accept healing when my sister was dead? How could I walk away unscathed from a moment that had ended her life? It was unthinkable that I might live completely restored when she had suffered all her short life.

He was waiting for my answer; they all were. I forced myself to lift my eyes to his. "Rabbi, the injury that caused this limp . . . it comes from the worst moment of my life." I swallowed hard and uttered the words that unmasked my deepest belief about myself. "What I bear is what I deserve."

Adonai, Dalia needed this man's healing! Not me!

"Rabbi, no—" I sobbed. "I cannot accept your healing. If you only knew—"

He increased the pressure on my shoulders, and through my tears, I saw his own.

"Whatever you are facing, bring it to him." Mary's calm assurance as she'd joyfully testified to this man's power echoed in my mind. He had gone to her when she could not go to him and now, it appeared, he was doing the same with me.

Jesus closed his eyes briefly before releasing me. When he opened his eyes, they shone with compassion. "Remember my words. The poor in spirit are blessed, Joanna. The poor in spirit are given the Kingdom of God." He took a step back and spread his hands wide. "As it is written, 'I will have mercy on whom I have mercy, and I will have compassion on whom I have compassion.'"

My mouth gaped as the words of God to Moses left this man's lips. Words God had given before displaying His glory. Words God had given after promising Moses His presence. Here was this man with the words of God in his mouth extending to me exactly what I needed but didn't deserve.

Mercy.

In his pointed question, I recognized a new responsibility. Healing would require a new way of thinking—of myself and of my past.

"I-I think I need to be changed on the inside before I'm healed on the outside." The confession came wobbling from my lips. I did not expect his response—a deepening in his eyes, my words pleasing to him.

"The Son of Man comes not only to give sight to the blind and good news to the poor, but also to bind up the brokenhearted and comfort those who mourn." He moved his hands in time with his words as if shaping something from nothing, molding and working the air with the breath from his mouth and his two strong hands.

"I come to bestow a garment of praise instead of a spirit of despair." One of his dancing hands dropped to my arm where he circled my wrist with his fingers, the pressure strong and firm. "A crown of beauty instead of ashes."

"I'll make you a crown, Jojo."

A spasm clutched at my throat, and I grabbed at Jesus' hand where it rested on my wrist. I pressed that hand closer, my heart crying out as his fingers covered the spot where Dalia had once dotted a line of broken daises.

"I need that beauty," I confessed, voice breaking. "The comfort, the binding up . . . I need it."

Gently, Jesus placed his other hand over mine. "Then I ask you again, Joanna. Do you want to be healed?"

"Yes," I rasped, not recognizing the hollow voice as my own. "Yes, I want your healing." I bent my head over our hands and wet his knuckles with my tears. "Please—inside and out—I need it."

His lips rested briefly on the top of my head, his voice dipping low as he said, "Then receive it. Be healed, Joanna."

Strength entered my body as peace pierced my heart. I stood

upright and gazed at him, blinking away tears so I could see clearly. I dropped his hand to take a step and then another. Out of habit, I leaned heavy on the cane, loath to let it go, but my legs were steady, my conflicted heart steadfast.

I stretched out my right leg. The pain was gone, and so was my limp. I took a handful of eager steps to be sure. Those around me shouted for joy, but all I could do was stand in the road with my face in my hands and weep. For the first time, I distinctly sensed God smiling upon me, and the brightness of His joy was more than I could bear.

Yahweh! All I could do was cry out His holy name. All I could do was abandon the cane, cast it aside on the edge of the road as I turned to Jesus and ran on my two strong legs into his arms.

TWENTY-ONE

My heart and mind remained full with the happiness of God, His smile impressed indelibly upon me. I'd allowed myself to become defined by the wound. Could I learn to be defined by His joy?

"We were never meant to live under the tyranny of fear and grief." Dalia's last words had been a testament of her very life. She'd stubbornly clung to God, refusing to be ruled by anything else. Could I do the same? Could this Jesus' vision of the Kingdom truly come?

With excitement close to giddiness, I thought of Chuza. He wouldn't return from Acre for several more days, but I imagined the surprise on his face when he did, the jaw-dropping disbelief when he beheld my healing. I closed my eyes and played his face full of delight over and over in my mind.

As we entered the villa courtyard, our steward quickly approached. "Mistress Joanna! We've been expecting you. Master Chuza came home early. You're to go to him immediately upon arrival. He's in his study." His worried expression and tone sent foreboding throughout my body.

With a breathless thank-you, I hurried off, leaving a wake of astounded servants who watched me depart on unfaltering, steady legs.

———— ✦ ————

Chuza stood by a table, hands threaded behind his head. Upon my entrance he whirled, and before I could speak, he had crossed the distance between us, pulling me roughly into his arms, capturing me against his chest.

"What are you doing? Chuza, what—" Every muscle in my body tensed with shock as my face pressed against his pounding heart.

"I'm sorry, I shouldn't have—" As quickly as he'd grabbed me, he let go, jerking back, face conflicted and distraught.

I stared at him, wide-eyed. Never had he drawn me directly into a firm embrace. Every part of my body that he'd just touched was now ablaze with awareness.

"What has happened?" I asked, avoiding his eyes as I clasped myself with shaking arms.

"I-I returned home early to find you gone." His voice was equally unsteady.

"I had business to oversee in Sepphoris and stayed longer than I'd anticipated. Surely the servants told you . . ."

"Yes, yes they did." Chuza was stepping away from me, eyes refusing to meet mine.

This was unlike him. He was unsettled in a way I'd never seen before. And so was I, but most certainly for a different reason. His chest had been solid and warm. I hugged myself harder.

"They expected you home a few days ago," Chuza stated in a tight voice.

My brow lifted in confusion. "Is *that* why you're upset?" Certainly, Chuza was always nervous to be away from me, but this seemed like an overreaction. "I'm sorry if my delay worried you, but I didn't expect you home yet. Why *are* you home early?"

Wearily, he moved to a table and poured himself a drink of water, which he promptly ignored in favor of pacing. Heart in my throat, I eased onto a low couch and watched him stride about the room.

"Herod returned from Rome as scheduled, and I met him at Acre. I traveled with him to Caesarea, where he plans to stay for at least another week as he meets with Pilate, but he brought back news from Rome that was so troublesome I made an excuse to leave early."

"I know he has plans to mint his own coins." I frowned. "But I thought you were in favor of that. Did he not receive permission from Emperor Tiberius?"

"He did." Chuza stopped pacing to run a hand through his thick hair. It stuck up in all directions. "He received permission to strike his own coins, but he also received permission of a different sort." Chuza groaned and sank onto the couch beside me where he rested his forearms on his thighs, head hanging low.

I stared at his bowed head, my hand fluttering over his shoulders briefly before I snatched it back to my lap.

"He received permission to marry Herodias . . . and divorce Phasaelis."

"No!" I clutched at my chest. "Herodias—the wife of his half brother Herod Philip?"

Chuza nodded. "The very same."

"Such a union makes no sense."

"It makes some sense." He clenched his jaw. "Herod wants to marry close to Roman power, and Herodias is related to Antonia, the emperor's sister-in-law."

"But to risk upsetting the Jews . . . not to mention the political scandal—"

"Exactly." Chuza scrubbed a large hand over his face. "Not only does he violate Jewish law by marrying his brother's wife, but he also personally insults Phasaelis and her father."

Once again, Herod was ignoring the clear teaching of the law, but this time he would be angering a king. Nabatea, the powerful nation nestled just southeast of Herod's own Perea, was no small power to toy with.

"Why would he upset Aretas?" I questioned. "He risks decades of peace with this divorce," I continued, eyes widening.

"I well know it, but Herod has the backing of Sejanus, which is the only reason he would attempt such a move. He celebrated the prefect's birthday while in Rome and received his support for the divorce."

The prefect of the emperor's guard had grown in power, and there were rumors he had his eye on the throne. If Herod indeed had Sejanus' backing, then perhaps he was safe from Aretas— for now.

My mind continued to make horrifying connections, leaping from one distressing thought to another. "You're Nabatean," I spluttered. "You're a relation to the Nabatean royal family. Oh, what does this mean for you?" Without thinking, I buried my face into his shoulder.

Chuza placed a strong hand on my back. "It means I walk a precarious line. It means I must give Herod no reason to distrust me . . . at least on the surface."

I pulled back to look searchingly into his face. "On the surface?"

"When I heard the news, I knew one thing immediately." Chuza grasped my hand. "I must tell Phasaelis, warn her what Herod is about to do. It was she, after all, who asked Herod to appoint me to this position. I owe her, but beyond that, she is my kinswoman, and I could not live with myself if I stood by silently while these events unfold."

My heart softened. "Of course, you must tell her."

"You understand, then?" He questioned, eyes searching mine. "If she leaves now, then Herod loses face. He will not take kindly to a wife deserting him so publicly. I will have to keep my involvement strictly hidden."

"She is family." My voice cracked. "Do what you must for your family."

"*You* are my family," he murmured. "I never want my actions to place you in harm's way . . . ever."

At his fervent words, the press of my body against his was more than I could bear. As calmly as I could, I removed my hand from his own and sat back, increasing the distance between us.

"I'll go to Phasaelis first thing in the morning." He was calmer now; his tone and temperament evened out after sharing the heaviness of his news.

"Yes, yes you must." I rose and paced to the table where he'd left his full cup. Greedily, I gulped the water, trying to temper my emotions as I processed his news.

"Joanna?" His voice was strange. I turned to find him standing, face pale as he stared at my legs.

"What?"

Oh.

I'd been so eager to share my healing with him but had become completely befuddled by his touch and his news.

"Come here."

Trembling entered my body at his husky tone. Silently, I obeyed, crossing the room on slow, steady legs. With a shuddering breath, Chuza sank to his knees in front of me, hands sliding to my tunic, grasping at its folds, wonder written on every line of his face.

"What? How?"

He was so close. I could feel the heat of his hand through the linen. I'd imagined this moment as a sharp burst of happiness but not this—this slowly building tension, ripe with wonder and joy too deep for words.

I took a step back, still facing him. Slowly, I lifted my tunic, exposing my leg as I stretched it forward. He let out a sharp breath, snagged my tunic, and yanked me close again.

"No, it can't be. There isn't even a hint of your limp. Your leg was shortened after the break, wasn't it? So how . . . how?"

A blush, deep and instant, crawled up my face as he buried his hands beneath my tunic and ran curious fingers down the entire length of my leg.

"What are you doing? Wait, Chuza, I—" I couldn't breathe, couldn't think, could barely stand. With a flailing hand, I sought support, but the only stability to be found was Chuza's own broad shoulders. As soon as my hands landed on him, he let out an exultant shout.

"Oh, this is a miracle! I've never seen such a thing!" He surged to his feet, taking me with him, lifting me up, up into his arms with another shout.

This joy was too much. His closeness was too much. I wept, unsure if the tears were happy or desperately, hopelessly sad.

"Joanna!" He seemed oblivious, too caught up in the miracle to notice how he pressed me to his heart or how I shivered in his arms. Landing me solidly back on my feet, he captured my face in his hands and then, only then, did awareness seem to settle upon him. He stilled, eyes widening, but instead of pulling away, he drew me closer until I was flush against him, my tear-streaked face still cupped in his hands.

"Oh, Joanna," he breathed, gaze dropping for the briefest of moments to my lips and then back to my eyes, where I thought I saw desire flicker in their depths.

I twisted from his hands in a whirl of confusion, angrily swiping at my cheeks. The door to desire between us was closed—intentionally and carefully closed. He had no business knocking on that door. Agitatedly, I returned to the table, placing it between us.

Chuza's eyes were shimmering with apparent embarrassment. If not for the miracle staring both of us in the face, he certainly would have left the room. Instead, he remained frozen in place, gaze traveling once again to my legs.

"Tell me how this healing happened." His request was soft, emotions tightly back under control even as he continued to avoid my eyes.

Adonai, what do I say?

What would Herod think if he knew his Nabatean financial minister's wife was connected to a man who spoke of a new kingdom? Panic flared in my chest. And what would Chuza himself think? Would he react the way my parents had with Dalia? Would he see Jesus as someone with whom association must be prohibited at all costs for the good of the family?

I could deny Jesus' work in my life. I could attempt to explain it away.

No.

Chuza was astute and would see through a falsehood. But an even deeper reason tugged at my heart. How could I accept the miraculous work of God and then lie about it? I had experienced the very power of God. Would I then keep that from him?

I bit my lip so hard, I tasted blood.

"You are nervous. Please don't be," Chuza stated, finally holding my gaze. His expression had settled into the earnest look I knew, and the familiar, calm tone of his voice and openness of his gaze loosened my tongue.

Please let this not be a mistake.

"After leaving Sepphoris, I traveled north to hear the new teacher—Jesus of Nazareth."

With a sharp release of air, Chuza sat down hard on the couch. "I'd heard he's the one who healed Susanna. *He* did this? Is he a physician?"

I shook my head. "He has the power of God, Chuza." My hands clenched the table until my knuckles shone white. "He singled me out; he knew my name. He healed me with the words from his mouth, as if the power of God resided within him, as if all of heaven was at his command."

Chuza looked so overwhelmed that it swept away my earlier flustered reaction to him.

"He healed you . . . with a word from his mouth?"

"Yes!" I moved from behind the table, hands splayed before me. The warmth I'd experienced on the side of the road as Jesus spoke now filled my body again. How I wanted Chuza to understand.

"When he spoke, his words came from God."

"That reeks of blasphemy." His brow furrowed.

"But if he is the Messiah?" The word caught on my lips. I held it, tasted it, said it again—slower this time. "The Messiah will come from God, won't He? The Messiah will speak God's words."

"You've been shaken. And so have I." Abba's voice as I'd never heard it before, uncertain, pained, and hopeful.

"I am a daughter of the Sadducees." I began to pace agitatedly, releasing the confusion in my breast. "My whole life has been under the influence of their teaching, and they do not believe in a Messiah. How could one man arise who was so powerful, so influential that he could bring down the strength of Rome?"

I came to a restless stop before him. In my earnestness, I took his hand but then dropped it just as quickly with a rising lump in my throat. "I was taught that any writings mentioning a deliverer depict time-bound events in our people's past as God brought deliverance from Assyria and Babylon. Such writings were not prophecies waiting to be fulfilled, and yet—"

My breath came fast as the crack in my heart widened, stretching to accommodate this new belief.

"And yet what if we *are* to expect a Messiah? I do not want to miss Him because I've been told not to expect Him."

"This Jesus, is he claiming to be the Messiah?" Chuza's voice was tight, expression impossible to read.

"I don't believe so, but—" My voice grew faint. "He speaks of a kingdom."

At that, Chuza's eyes flooded with alarm. "That's dangerous talk."

"No, he speaks not as an insurrectionist, but as a prophet. Oh, I wish you could have heard him." Again, I snagged his hand without thinking.

"He seems more concerned about people's hearts than anything else. Almost—" I broke off when Chuza enmeshed his fingers with mine.

"Almost what?" Chuza's voice went hoarse.

Tears pooled in my eyes as longing swelled within me. How I wanted this new vision of a Kingdom to be true! "As if our *hearts* could be under God's reign even if our bodies are still under Roman control. He was inviting us to God's rule *right now*. Can such a thing be possible, no matter our political situation?"

Silence. The room was full of a heavy silence. The pressure of Chuza's fingers entwined between mine grew more and more noticeable but neither of us made a move to untangle them.

Then he sighed—one long breath he'd been holding the entire time. He stood, retaining my hand as he explored my face. "I was first drawn to your religion by the idea of a God whose eyes are always on His people. A God who is not limited the way we are, utterly independent of human hands."

A shadow of sorrow crossed Chuza's face. "Mankind . . . we're so bound by place. Bound by the insufficiency of our own resources. It makes sense to worship a God who experiences no such limitations, whose actions aren't dependent on our own ability to appease Him."

There it was—the sorrow that still lurked beneath the surface— the gaping wound that was caused by his first wife's death.

I pulled my hand from his, but he reclaimed it, captured it again with pleading and deepening eyes. "I've studied the prophets and believe in the coming of a Messiah who will gather God's people under God's reign. It is good for your heart to be open to such teachings."

His free hand unexpectedly moved toward my face, fingers nestling in the curls at the nape of my neck, thumb anchored at my jawline as he tilted my face toward him. "Could it be that the God who moves as a spirit is now building a kingdom in the hearts of His people?"

Chuza's soft question pulled between us like a cord, tethering and tethering. He increased the pressure at my neck, and I placed a hand to his chest to steady myself, head at a sharp angle as I looked up, up to where his face hovered above mine.

No.

I twisted from his grasp once more, heart thudding.

No. I could not want him in that way.

"I plan to provide financial support to Jesus' ministry." With all the strength I could muster, I pulled myself farther away from Chuza.

"I don't know his financial situation. Most of his closest followers seem to own very little. I . . . I would like to offer what aid I can."

Chuza watched me quietly. "Of course you do. The man miraculously healed you. How could you not?"

His eyes were pooling with understanding but also with a deep caution, which his next words confirmed. "But Joanna, whether this kingdom exists only in the hearts of the people—for now—it is still dangerous speech. Herod will not appreciate talk of a kingdom and where that could lead."

"I realize that, and with what you've shared, I also understand that this places you in a dangerous position."

"Herod is now aware of Jesus," Chuza drew out the words slowly. "With so many in the court experiencing healing, Jesus' reputation is that of a miracle worker. The few times Herod has mentioned him, he's done so in a light manner, and maybe he is simply curious. At least for the moment, he doesn't perceive Jesus as a threat."

"If I am discreet . . ."

Chuza crossed the room to grasp my shoulders in his large hands. "If you are discreet, then yes . . . I don't see why you couldn't provide funds to this Jesus."

"Thank you." I attempted to lay a hand over his, but he was pulling away, crossing the room to a table overflowing with parchments.

"I must reach out to some contacts before speaking with Phasaelis." He shuffled rolls of parchment, indicating that the conversation was over.

"Y-yes, I'll leave you to it." Bearing down under a wave of confusion, I left the room, daring to glance back just before closing the door to see Chuza averting his face, as if he'd been watching me.

TWENTY-TWO

For days on end, I was tormented with thoughts of my interchange with Chuza and with worry over the situation he now faced. In agonizing detail, I recalled every touch and look, finally convincing myself that I must have misread him. He'd been caught up in the aftermath of a miracle—that's all. For his part, Chuza remained distant, avoiding intimate settings, as he was consumed with plans for helping Phasaelis.

He spoke with his cousin, informing her of Herod's intent. With great calm and secrecy, Phasaelis quickly gathered her personal items and attendants together and sent word to Herod, asking if she could go to Machaerus, Herod's southernmost fortress on the east coast of the Dead Sea. Request granted, she traveled south. Chuza then made arrangements for Phasaelis' safe passage from Machaerus to Petra, the Nabatean capital, where she informed her father of Herod's intent.

I spent many sleepless nights out on my balcony, alone beneath the stars, chewing my nails until they bled, imagining what Herod would do if he found out that his financial minister had aided Phasaelis in deserting him. But Chuza was careful and knew which connections to call upon without drawing attention to himself.

To show his appreciation, Aretas offered Chuza a staggering reward, which he refused. "I will not take a single coin from that man. I did this for the sake of my cousin—not him, not even Nabatea!"

Chuza paced his study with shaking hands, shoving furiously at his desk while I watched, startled and quiet.

"He dares to congratulate himself on appointing me for Phasaelis' entourage all those years ago, as if he had great foresight in choosing me." Chuza spat. "I cannot stomach his gratitude!" He flung a roll of parchments against the wall and laced his hands behind his neck.

"What did he do to you?" I asked past trembling lips. "Why this great rage? Why does his gratitude anger you so?"

Chuza merely growled deeply in his throat, the sound lodging in my belly. "It's nothing. Nothing."

But it wasn't nothing, and the bedrock of our relationship shifted and shuddered.

As anticipated, Herod was livid that he'd been so publicly outmaneuvered. Phasaelis' flight made him out to be an incompetent ruler who lacked control even over his own household. But there was nothing left for him to do other than officially divorce her and marry Herodias. Much of the country despised Herod already, but with this newest development, he alienated even some of his staunchest supporters. As his brother's wife entered his court and his bed, Herod swiftly silenced any who dared speak against the union. One voice, however, refused to be silenced.

Deep in the south in the lower Jordan Valley came a teacher with such fiery words that their heat spread north, lapping at Tiberias' city gates and setting Herod's ego aflame. It was said he wore camel's hair and ate locusts in the wilderness, a wild-eyed wanderer with a sharp tongue and keen sense of justice. With great acuity he preached throughout Perea, one of Herod's own provinces, and his message was one of repentance. Like an ax at the root or a winnowing fork in the hand, God was near and ready to move. People came to him in droves to be baptized, earning him the name John the Baptizer.

Preaching from afar wasn't enough. The man with fire on his tongue pushed his way directly into Herod's presence. I, along with many others, packed ourselves into the throne room to see the man who was causing such a commotion.

"It is against God's law for you to marry this woman!" John stood upright in the middle of the room, pointing a long finger to where Herodias sat on her throne. He spoke what many were thinking, and yet the gasp throughout the room was audible.

"It is against God's law for you to take your brother's wife!" John thumped a fist into his palm as he emphasized each word.

The effect on Herodias was palpable. Her jaw clenched atop her long and regal neck, her fingers dug into Herod's arm, and her face contorted with rage as she whispered into his ear.

Rather than react rashly, as many feared he might, Herod remained calm, benevolent even. His eyes flashed with interest as he shushed Herodias with a firm hand and, to everyone's surprise, extended an invitation for John to appear before him the following day.

Every day for a week, John appeared in court, and Herod listened to him with great relish. "It is clear that you are a holy and good man," he stated. "And the people clearly revere you as a prophet."

"I am but a voice crying out in the wilderness. My role is to clear the road for the one to come. And behold, he is here."

In the light of Herod's interest, Herodias grew desperate until finally—and to no one's surprise—Herod sent soldiers to arrest and imprison John.

"He does it as a favor to Herodias," Chuza confided. "But also, ironically, to protect John. Such is Herodias' hate for the man, Herod is afraid she will act covertly and have him killed and thereby incite a public uprising. He'd rather John languish in prison, safe from Herodias, and away from the public eye."

And so John was locked up in the depths of Machaerus, this baptizer who'd ignited the fury of a queen and the interest of a king, this bold man who claimed to clear the way for his cousin—Jesus of Nazareth, the man who'd healed and changed me.

Covertly, I sent funds to Jesus along with news about John the Baptist. While my thoughts traveled to Jesus, Chuza's remained close to home as he kept an eye on Herod's temperament. "His interest is becoming more than casual curiosity," he disclosed one night. "By now, Herod has heard that Jesus is related to John and is expressing a desire to meet him."

"That can't be good, can it?"

"Herod certainly respected John and enjoyed listening to him, but in the end, that wasn't enough to save the man from prison. John was outspoken, and it seems this Jesus is the same." Chuza's face was grim. "I don't want to see the man who healed you thrown into a dungeon. It would be in his best interest to leave the region, at least until Herod's interest dies down. Perhaps you could send word . . . ?"

I would do something better. I would go to him myself before Herod could act on his curiosity.

TWENTY-THREE

Mary's eyes glowed softly, warming me more than the fire before us. "I'm glad to see you again."

Her kindness dispelled some of my uneasiness. Still, I cast a swift look about the courtyard in Capernaum. It was filled with Jesus' disciples, most of whom were giving us a wide berth. Eden was happily acquainting herself with other women in the company, and at the sight of her joyful face, more of my tension eased.

"Jesus will be happy to see you too."

"You don't know where he's gone?" I questioned Mary, trying to conceal my worry. "Shouldn't some of the men be with him?"

"You sound like Andrew." Mary laughed. "Jesus often does this. In the evenings or early mornings, he'll go away by himself to pray. He needs the time alone, I think, for he's so often around others."

"Will he be back in the morning?"

"Oh yes, he always comes back." Mary's face creased in a reassuring smile. "I'm happy you came so we can thank you in person for all the funds you've sent. Your gifts have eased a burden from many."

"I'm glad. I wasn't sure of the financial situation."

"Many have families to support and are unable to contribute as much as they'd like."

"I'm happy to supply whatever you need." Discreetly, I pulled out my purse. "While I'm here, I can offer even more. Surely, as your company grows, so do the financial demands." I was about to extend the purse to Mary when a harsh snort sounded from behind me. I turned to see Simon observing me with hooded eyes.

"Are you seeking to repay the teacher?" he questioned. "Keep your money."

"Enough, Simon!" A man I had yet to meet quickly joined us. "Let her give as she is able. It's what all of us have done, isn't it?"

"Simon is right to be worried," another man stated. "She is standing with one foot on each side."

"Nathaniel," Mary murmured, tone full of gentle warning.

"I do not trust those in Herod's court." Nathaniel shrugged, eyes hardening as he gestured to Simon and some of the others. "Many of us don't."

"If you are honest with yourself, Mary, you don't either," Simon muttered. "We do not know her true motives."

My cheeks flamed at such pointed words, eyes casting about to the others. Was it true? Did they all question me? Did Mary? I wanted to both melt into the ground and surge to my feet in defense.

"Are you forgetting *my* own history?" the first man continued, voice calm and firm. "Jesus called me by name, just as he called you. He calls whom he wishes, so why not someone from Herod's court? Isn't this why he's here? To unite Israel under her Messiah?"

A huff of air left Simon's lips, and he bowed his head. When his gaze rose again, his face had softened, although more with resignation than acceptance. With a nod to Nathaniel, they both left without saying another word as the man who'd defended me sat by my side.

"I apologize on their behalf. If you knew Simon's history, you'd understand why this is so hard for him."

"He was a Zealot," Mary breathed quietly. "And from what I hear, he was high-ranking and—"

"We don't need to expound upon his past, Mary," the man gently reproved. "It's his to share if or when he chooses to do so."

Zealot. A sliver of fear snaked its way through me, leaving me shivering despite the fire. I was a girl again, alone in the theater in the arms of a man who would not let me go. I'd dreamed of his eyes over the years, haunted by the way they'd unmasked me and how they'd despised what they'd uncovered.

"Joanna?" Mary's soft voice pierced the fog that had descended upon me.

Blinking away the image of those eyes, I refocused on Mary and the man who was observing me so kindly.

"I'm Matthew." The man smiled. He was older than most in the company, his hair streaked with silver. "Before this, I was a tax collector."

"A tax collector?" I gaped at him, quickly shutting my mouth but not before he laughed out loud.

"I do not blame you for being dumbfounded. I was a customs collector along the trade route from Damascus to the Mediterranean, based in this very town." His laughter faded as he talked, eyes growing distant, the lines around his mouth smoothing out, looking like he was more comfortable with somberness than mirth. "For many years, I collected taxes for Herod Antipas."

"My husband is Herod's financial minister," I said. "Part of his job is to oversee the appointment of and revenues from tax collectors." I spoke the words in one long rush before I could think better of them, Matthew's honesty inciting my own.

We stared at one another—each on our own end of such a

despised system. And then I laughed, a short sound that I quickly stifled with a hand to my lips.

Mary smirked at my outburst and then Matthew was chuckling as well, his shoulders relaxing, face easing once more into a smile.

"Your husband, he is high-ranking." Matthew's eyes turned serious. "Does he know that you are here?"

"Yes, he is aware."

"I know many in court, such as yourself, have experienced healing, and it has led even some high officials to belief."

His words prompted memories of Manaen and Susanna. I had yet to connect with Susanna since my healing. Perhaps by now she had heard of the news, but silence stretched between us.

"Does your husband join you in your support of Jesus?" Matthew questioned, eyes alight.

"He's certainly interested." I paused. "My husband is a kind man, a good man. He's honorable, and his faith far exceeds my own. We have always been . . . partners."

"Your love for him is evident," Mary stated softly.

I was stunned into momentary silence. Love him? No. I had entered this union knowing that true and deep love was something we would not share, not when he still loved his first wife.

"I respect him," I quietly corrected.

"And you trust him?" Matthew gestured to the purse in my lap. "He must know how you are using such funds."

"He does, and I do. Our marriage is built upon honesty and trust." Unexpectedly, tears stung behind my eyes as I recalled his rage against the Nabatean king before I left. There was something, though, something he wasn't sharing, which had to do with Aretas.

"He's never aspired to be like most men," I stated. "When others are compelled by greed, he looks to the interests of others."

Mary placed a warm hand on my knee. "It sounds like God uniquely placed the two of you together. What a blessing."

Ducking my head, I stared hard at the scarlet cords of my purse. "Perhaps," I whispered. "Here . . ." I turned Mary's hand over where it rested on my knee and slipped the entire purse into her palm. "Please accept this. I never meant for it to be an offense."

Mary accepted the purse. "Thank you for your generosity, and please know that Simon doesn't speak for all of us."

Her eyes were sincere, but a part of me wondered. Would she accept my wealth one moment and then despise it the next, the way Aunt Sarah had with my parents?

"I hope that those who doubt my motives will be reassured," I stated carefully. "I want to put Jesus' words into practice, and this is one way I can do that. Use it to build the kingdom Jesus talks about."

Matthew's eyes glowed softly in the firelight. "God bless you, Joanna, and be with you wherever you go. May His face shine upon you and give you peace."

The benediction fell upon me like a warm cloak. My eyes slid closed as I took the words in and held them close.

Eden and I spent the night in a nearby home with Mary Magdala, Mary of Clopas, and Salome, the mother of two of the disciples. In the morning, we returned to Andrew's courtyard to discover that the entire village had beat us to the door. From inside the home, we could hear Jesus' voice. He'd returned and was speaking loudly for the benefit of those gathered.

"If any of you wants to come after me, you must deny yourself, take up your cross daily, and follow me."

Take up a cross? I grimaced at the gruesome words. Who would voluntarily pick up the rough wooden crossbeam that would eventually hold their own tortured form?

"Whoever tries to save his life will lose it, but whoever loses his life for my sake will save it. For what do you benefit if you gain the whole world yet lose your very self?"

A man nearby grumbled under his breath and turned away, face twisted with disgust. "This man's words are lunacy," he muttered before leaving. Several others followed him, leaving enough of a gap for us to slither into the courtyard.

Jesus stood in the center, arms raised as, once again, he used his hands to illustrate his words. Palms lifted upward, he stretched his arms wide. The image of a cross flashed quickly before me, and I winced. Why had he spoken of the need to carry a cross? If it was a *daily* death, then surely it was a figurative death. What, then, was he asking us to die to?

"If anyone is ashamed of me and of my words, the Son of Man will be ashamed of that person when he comes in his glory and the glory of the Father and of the holy angels. I tell you the truth, some standing here right now will not die before they see the Kingdom of God."

There it was again, the Kingdom that Jesus kept preaching. A Kingdom under God's reign—and the path to this Kingdom was death?

Jesus quieted, his arms dropping to his side, chest heaving. Many began to leave as I watched Andrew approach him with water, urging him to drink.

Conflicted, I let myself be buffeted about by those leaving. The message I had to deliver now seemed hollow after hearing Jesus speak.

Jesus drank deeply from the cup Andrew offered, some of the water spilling and wetting his thick beard. With a sigh of satisfaction and gratitude, he returned the cup and then looked directly at me where I stood against the wall with the other women. His face split into a smile as he extended a hand of welcome.

How did he always do this? He seemed to know exactly where I was and refused to let me stay there. Part of me wanted to scurry after the muttering man, confused and put off. I had no desire to die for this man in order to follow him. Under the steadiness of his gaze, however, I sensed an invitation. Perhaps the death he spoke of was a necessary step toward the new life in his Kingdom.

"Joanna! They told me you had come."

I went to him, the muttering man a distant memory as I accepted the hand Jesus offered. "Rabbi, I've been following your movements, and my husband has been keeping a close eye on Herod's temperament."

Jesus studied my face. "They said you had a message for me?"

"As you know, your cousin is now being held at Machaerus."

"Yes." Jesus' eyes saddened. He dropped my hand to run his own across his face in a tired gesture that made my chest hitch with compassion. "He sent two of his disciples to find me."

"I used to be one of John's disciples," Andrew interjected. "I know John. He is a man of action. He grows weary while waiting in prison and longs for the Kingdom more than most. He sent his disciples for affirmation."

"God blesses those who do not fall away because of me." Jesus gazed south with eyes full of longing. His love for John was evident and spurred my next words.

"Ever since his arrest, word of you swells. Herod enjoyed listening to John speak, even though his words were blunt and honest. With John imprisoned, Herod's curiosity over you is piqued, especially since he's learned of your connection to John."

I hesitated before delivering the next words as gently as I could. "My husband is an astute man, and he believes Herod will begin exerting more . . . direct efforts to find you. I know what it's like to stand before the face of the king. From girlhood, I have understood his power. One moment he is simply curious, and the next he acts—swiftly and boldly. Rabbi, you are deep in his territory. Please, for your own safety, consider leaving Galilee."

Those around Jesus grew quiet. Out of the corner of my eye, I saw Simon and Nathaniel studying me.

"Thank you, Joanna." Jesus' eyes were full of warmth and understanding as he placed a hand on my shoulder. "But my hour has not yet come."

The steadiness of purpose was evident behind his words. "You are not afraid, then?" I asked incredulously.

"I have come not to do my own will but the will of the One who sent me, whose purposes cannot be thwarted. Don't be afraid of those who want to kill your body, for they cannot touch your soul. Fear only God."

Sharply, I recalled Dalia's final moments, her tenacious insistence on abolishing my fear. Like the man standing before me, she had looked to God's strength.

The morning sun blazed into the courtyard, throwing heat and shadows across the earthen floor while I stood in the light of this man's bravery. He was resolute and seemed to be inviting me into that strength. I'd come with urgency to warn *him*, and yet Jesus seemed to be warning *me* away from misplaced fear and toward confidence in God.

Who was this rabbi who seemed wholly unaffected by Herod? And how could I share in his certainty and strength?

Twenty-Four

Spring 29 AD

Jesus remained in Galilee, teaching and preaching with a growing fervor and following. I traced his movements, sent funds, and followed those monies myself when I could. Each time I entered their company, Jesus welcomed me openly, pressing a kiss of blessing to my forehead. In the light of Jesus' approval, others began warming to me, or at least kept their doubts quiet. Although I still harbored worry that Mary and Matthew's gracious attitude toward me might shift, I began tentatively thinking of them as friends. With each visit, I allowed the seed of friendship to take deeper root within me.

As Herod's birthday drew close, he made preparations to throw an elaborate party. It was the first birthday since his new marriage and he was desirous to show off his wealth and power. This year, he would spend his birthday in Machaerus, on the border between Israel and Nabatea, for with his divorce, he was eager to keep Aretas well within his sights.

Chuza, along with numerous other noblemen, was a part of a northern deputation that would travel south to honor Herod. I would be traveling with him, for Herodias had received permission to host her own banquet for the women of the court.

"You will be close to John." Mary's eyes had flown wide as I'd told her of my travel plans. "Perhaps you can learn from his disciples how he fares. I'm sure Jesus would appreciate any news you could bring."

I promised to keep my eyes and ears open. It was the least I could do for the group of disciples. Perhaps in doing so, I could quiet any lingering doubt some of them carried.

✦

Not since Susanna's own wedding had I been to a banquet as lavish as this one. I reclined with other women of the court as servants brought out trays of luxurious foods. Herodias was partial to roasted pheasant, a costly meat, and so the tables groaned beneath platters of entire birds stuffed with choice herbs, along with dishes of soft curds nestled in pools of honey, boiled quail eggs with a garum relish, and platters of fish baked in a pepper-rosemary sauce.

Machaerus was an imposing stone fortress crowning the peak of a mountain. Undulating hills rippled outward, and over a few of their rises one could glimpse the dark waters of the Dead Sea. Our rooms were simple and well-furnished, with northeastern windows that overlooked the lower city.

I'd seen little of Chuza along the way since I'd traveled in a two-wheeled carriage while he'd ridden horseback. With separate rooms and entourages, our interactions had been sparse, but he'd managed to catch me before leaving for the evening. "You will be careful?" His hand on my arm had been warm, matching the look in his eyes. "Word of your healing has spread, and many will now see it for themselves."

Did he expect me to conceal the source of my healing? I couldn't do that. He knew I couldn't. I wasn't the only one, after all, who had experienced Jesus' miraculous power. Many sat among us, benefiting from Jesus' touch. My eyes flitted to the table opposite me where Susanna reclined. I kept my gaze trained on her, waiting for a look, but none came.

Upon our arrival, I'd discovered that the dungeon was directly beneath Herodias' banquet hall and that she'd requested the hall specifically, seeking to keep the Baptizer beneath her heel. The feast would last days—enough time for me to discover the location of John's disciples. To expediate matters, I slipped a handful of coins to a guard. His findings, however, were somber. John's disciples were in the lower city and hadn't been allowed entrance for quite some time, not with the influx of guests and festivities. Many had already left the city altogether. The news sat within me like a smoldering coal in my gut.

The banquet hall buzzed with easy enjoyment, but I could not join in the festivities. Mireya tried to engage me in gossip and finally distanced herself in disgust, muttering that I was "far too serious" and always had been. But how could I relax when I knew who sat directly below me?

With each sumptuous dish, the sensation remained as my thoughts continued to travel downward to where a man sat in solitary confinement—a man cut off from his friends, all but deserted, and why? Because he'd dared to expect that the man who called himself king would follow God's law. Because he'd spoken up when others remained silent. Because he refused to bow to the fear of man.

I sat on a cushioned seat with succulent pheasant in my mouth and wrestled with myself in a new and uncomfortable way. It'd been easy to give my money. It'd been easy to give my words. Did I dare to risk more? Could I go back to Mary and the others with no news? Could I tell them that I'd feasted right above John without another thought of his welfare?

I could make an excuse that would sound reasonable. I could shrug my shoulders and say, *"What could I have done? His disciples were barred from entering, scattered and fleeing. What more could I have done?"*

"Don't be afraid of those who want to kill your body, for they cannot touch your soul." Jesus' words of confidence sounded heavily in my ear.

And yet it took me days—days of wrestling on my cushioned couch among the finest of the court—before I surrendered to the prompting in my spirit. I would not sit by, separated and safe, when it was within my power to talk to this man, to discover for myself how he fared, and to bring back word to Jesus.

The guard who'd brought me the news of John's disciples was more than willing to accept more coin in exchange for an escort. I told him when and where to expect me, and on the final day of the feast, I excused myself early. The sounds of revelry were heavy in the air as I hurried through the colonnaded courtyard to the prearranged meeting place. As I passed through the southern wing of the guest rooms, a door opened, and instinctively, I pressed myself into the shadows.

A man and a woman who was clearly not his wife exited and returned in the direction of the banqueting halls. I waited until they'd passed from sight before continuing, but another door opened, this one almost directly in my face. Heart leaping into my throat, I froze in place as a man half stumbled from the room, accompanied by a flurry of feminine giggles. Even though the man was obviously disoriented from drink, he still seemed to sense my presence, body lurching as he turned, eyes lifting to lock with mine.

My heart tumbled straight from my throat to my toes.

"Where are *you* headed in such a hurry?" he purred, words slightly slurred as he cocked a hip against the door.

"Back to my room, as you certainly should be, Othniel." I

glanced at the closed door. "I suggest you sleep off your drink and rid yourself of that perfume before confronting your wife."

"We have an understanding." Othniel waved an unconcerned hand and pushed himself off the door and toward me. "What I do and who I do it with is none of your concern."

"I could say the same to you." Swiftly, I tried to step past him, but his next words reached out like a silken cord, ensnaring me.

"That husband of yours is a hard man to figure out."

A chill spread across my arms. Since my marriage, I'd gone out of my way to avoid Othniel, which hadn't been hard to do since Herod had stationed him in Jericho. Hearing him speak of Chuza both terrified and infuriated me. "He is a man of integrity, which might explain why it's hard for you to understand him."

The barb was out before I could think. Instead of offense, delight crossed Othniel's bronze features. He circled me now like a vulture until he faced me directly.

"I remember you as a kitten—all soft, beautiful, and big-eyed." His right cheek twitched with the beginnings of a grin. "When did you grow claws?" His lower jaw jutted forward as he slid his eyes down the length of me.

"And I used to think of you as a wolf—perpetually hungry." I raised my chin. "But now I see you as the fox you are."

This barb reached its home. Othniel's amused expression hardened into anger. "Be careful, kitten." He spoke the words softly around a clenched jaw. "I was influential in separating you from Livia, and I can act again."

Livia—a name I used to associate with innocence and friendship. She'd been married off to a prosperous merchant years ago and lived many miles away in the southern port city of Joppa. I'd never seen or heard from her again.

"Enough. You will not take one more thing from me, Othniel."

"You act erudite and assured, but it's your husband's position that allows you to speak so. I see you hiding behind him. You think his position is your safety, but you forget how quickly a man's title can be stripped from him."

With a disgruntled shake of the head, I attempted to push past Othniel, but he snagged my arm with a firm hand. My head hovered at his shoulder, the heat of him encompassing me.

"Ah, lovely Joanna. I know much more than you realize."

Slowly, I peered up at him.

"Do you forget my position? I oversee the trade of goods from Nabatea. I have many connections with merchants from Jericho to Petra." His grip on my arm tightened.

Despite my best efforts, I began to tremble.

Othniel must have felt the tremors, for he glanced down at me. "I have many connections, and they talk, especially when gold is on the table."

"Release me," I hissed.

With a sharp laugh, Othniel complied, shoving me away from himself. "Tell that husband you hide behind that I'm on to him. I know he had something to do with Phasaelis' flight, and he's a fool if he thinks he can hide his involvement." He took a large stride toward me, and I stepped backward, bumping against the stone wall as he loomed before me. With a grin, he placed a hand next to my head, ducking his own to peer into my eyes.

"Providing the means and funds for the former queen's flight? Such actions, especially given Chuza's connection to Aretas' court, *could* be seen as treasonous. Where do his loyalties really lie? Does the Nabatean find himself homesick?" Othniel bent lower, lips brushing my ear. "I simply need to prove it, and then when he's gone and out of the way, where will you be, kitten? When you have no husband to hide behind, I'll be waiting."

"How dare you!" I spat the words, shrouding my terror with fury. "How dare you speak to me in this way! You talk of hiding behind position, but take care of your own. Your tangential marriage into the royal family is no credit to you, Othniel. Herod placed you close to keep an eye on you because you're too volatile to trust!"

His hand on the wall moved down to grasp my arm painfully, and for a moment it seemed he'd shake me, but with a deep breath, he regained control. "You simple woman. You know nothing."

"No, Othniel, it is *you* who knows nothing. You've made up an imagined plot in hopes of advancement. As always, you want more. You want what you can't have, so you make up stories to rob those who are honorable. But you can prove nothing, and you know nothing!"

My words released in a long rush, leaving me shuddering beneath his hands. I'd hoped to demolish his suspicions with the weight of my anger. Instead, Othniel was assessing me with narrowed eyes that seemed to settle into certainty the more I talked. I pressed my lips together, stopping further speech as my nose flared with ragged breath.

He said nothing more. Slowly, he removed his hand, easing back as he caught his lower lip with his teeth and raised a brow at me. His gaze was decided as it roamed my face. His full lips yawned into a smile, then abruptly, he left.

———— ◆ ————

Cool air caressed my heated cheeks as we entered the lowest portion of the dungeon. It was moist and dank, the air cold and thick with poor ventilation. Torches lined the walls, illuminating the uneven stones beneath my slippered feet. Rats skittered in the shadows. I stayed close to my guide with my heart in my throat and tried not to gag as the smell worsened.

"This is it." The guard stopped in front of a small cell with iron bars. "I'll wait up the stairs." He left quickly, eager to reach higher elevation and sweeter air.

A series of wet coughs echoed from the cell as I drew closer.

Nervously, I plucked a torch from the wall and held it high to illuminate the dank interior. A man crouched in the corner on a pallet, his thin form heaving as another series of coughs gripped him. His lungs sounded full of water, his coughs doing little by way of relief. I winced as he painfully drew in air, my own breath catching in my chest as I listened to him struggle.

"John?" I questioned softly. In the warm glow of torchlight, his wide eyes met and held mine.

His hair was thick and tangled, sticking out in a burst of matted curls around his head. The last time I'd seen him had been in court, where he'd stood erect, his impressive frame commanding full attention as his voice filled the room like thunder. Now he was doubled, almost in two. The transformation was so startling, I had to push back tears.

Slowly, he rose to his feet and stumbled a few paces. One hand reached toward me, grabbed a bar, and held it tight. He pulled the rest of his body close, face coming fully into the light. "Yes, I'm John."

His eyes were clear and somber, voice hoarse from the coughs but lifting with a hopeful tone. "I'm John," he repeated, his words breaking off with another cough. "Who are you?"

"I've seen you before, when you confronted Herod, but we haven't met. I'm Joanna, and I'm . . . a follower of Jesus of Nazareth."

As soon as I said the words, doubt seized me. Was I a true follower like Mary? Or, like Nathaniel had insisted, did I live with one foot in both worlds?

"Or at least . . . I would like to think of myself as one of his followers," I amended.

At the name of Jesus, John's eyes grew bright, and the same longing I'd noted in Jesus' face entered his own. "Oh, how happy I am to meet you, then." He gripped the bars in both hands. "Tell me, how is he?"

"He is well," I assured him, grateful that I could bring him some good news. "For now, at least. I did warn him recently to leave Herod's territory until the king's curiosity dies down." I cast my eyes upward where—even now—Herodias celebrated above us.

John laughed, his rough chuckles turning into spasms of coughs. "I'm sure he didn't listen to you," he croaked, eyes gleaming.

"That's correct." I smiled and then grew somber. "He speaks highly of you, John. He loves you deeply, thinks of you fondly, and upholds your faith as exemplary."

A soft sadness entered John's face. He bowed his head, welcoming my words like a warm mantle on a brisk day. "Sometimes that faith flickers." He raised his eyes to my torch. "Like a small spark in the wind."

"'A bruised reed he will not break, and a smoldering wick he will not snuff out.'" My heart swelled with compassion as I gripped a bar with my free hand, the torch throwing shadows into John's face.

He peered with fresh interest at me. "The words of Isaiah. Jesus also quoted that prophet to encourage me. I asked him directly: Are you the Messiah?" John broke off, bowed his head before continuing. "And in response, he pointed to his works: the blind see, the lame walk, the deaf hear, the dead are raised, and the Good News is being preached to the poor."

John lifted his head, eyes pooling with tears. "But what else does Isaiah say? Within that very passage, the prophet records how the Messiah will proclaim freedom for the captives and release for the prisoners!" His voice echoed throughout his cell.

"Because of my own experience, I allowed doubt to flourish. Because that particular promise was not fulfilled in my life in the way I expected, I was willing to overlook the miraculous; I was willing to question the miracle worker." He clutched my hand, pressed it tightly against the cold, iron bar, anchoring me into place.

"Instead of rebuke, Jesus met me with mercy. Instead of condemnation, he redirected me to the truth. In one reply, he unmasked the root of my problem and gave me the solution. The works of God are now among us, and blessed is the one who does not stumble. Blessed is the one who endures, holding onto truth, suffering persecution for the sake of righteousness. The Kingdom of heaven belongs to such as these!"

He was shouting now, perhaps in an attempt to push the truth up and out through the layers of stone separating us from Herodias. I bent over his hand where it captured mine and pressed my forehead to his raw knuckles, staring at the dank ground slick with human waste.

"Faith in what? Faith that Adonai would heal me at a certain age? That's not really faith, Joanna. Faith is founded on Adonai Himself and not on the condition that He act in a certain way at a certain time."

"With all my heart, I want the vision of his Kingdom to come true," I whispered, so quietly I thought John hadn't heard.

He placed his other hand on the back of my head. "It is, Joanna. The Kingdom of God is in our midst. We may experience insults, persecution, and slander from others, but in the end, we are blessed. In the end, we inherit the Kingdom."

I was close enough to see the sores on John's arms, the bruises on his angular jawline. "Even so, I hate to see you suffering."

John shook his head. "My suffering is temporary, and it is forming patience within me. I'm not known to be a patient man." His lips quirked. "I'm learning that the Christ follows his own timing. I'm still learning what it means to surrender to his way."

"You are brave to suffer well for his sake." The words caught in my throat, tears pressing hot against the back of my eyes. "I don't believe I have the same bravery."

John studied me gently. "Then ask for it. Our Father in heaven gives good gifts to those who ask. But I wonder if perhaps you don't see yourself clearly yet." He nodded to where I stood. "You are here. And not up there." He cast his eyes upward. "Some would call that bravery."

"Some would call it duplicity." I laughed shakily.

"And what does Jesus call it? Does he scorn your station?"

"No. He seems to welcome people from all walks of life."

John nodded. "Then think on that. Dwell upon yourself less and upon him more."

"I can see that is what you have done, even encouraging your own disciples to follow Jesus."

"I'm fulfilling what God put me on this earth to do." Fire leapt into John's eyes. "My life is to pave the way for his, my voice to precede his own. As the friend of the bridegroom, I have no cause for sorrow when he comes to collect his bride."

I studied his face, knowing that some would interpret his words as madness, but he was sane, calm, and sure. Even in the worst of circumstances, he was absolutely resolute.

"You know your purpose," I murmured. "And that steadies you."

"I must decrease, and if that means I languish here so that his Kingdom might increase, I am learning to be content."

Quick footfalls sounded behind me, causing me to startle and nearly drop my torch. The guard returned, eyes wide. "You need to go."

"I'm not finished speaking with the prisoner." Quickly, I withdrew my purse. "If it's a matter of money—"

"Keep your money!" the guard spat. "I never should have taken it in the first place, but I thought it an easy assignment. In and out and no one would know. But they come!"

"Who?"

"The captain of the guard. I hear him even now. We must leave before he sees us."

More voices and the sound of clanking armor filtered down the steps and off the walls, thrusting panic deep into my chest. I turned to John, who stood still and calm. I couldn't abandon him.

"If you won't go, I'll be forced to leave you behind." The guard backed away, toward a different hall and an alternative exit.

If I let him leave, I wouldn't be able to find my own way back out, and I would be stuck confronting the captain of the guard. Everything within me screamed to run. I looked back at John, who was nodding at me.

No, I couldn't leave him alone.

"Go," I whispered hoarsely to the guard, who needed no further encouragement. As he fled down the hall, light from multiple torches illuminated John's small cell as a gathering of men rounded the corner.

A burly man stopped short at the sight of me. "What are you doing here?"

With all the strength I could manage, I drew myself up, lifted my chin, and forced myself to meet his eyes. "I was curious about Herod's prisoner. I've heard many things about him and wanted to see him for myself."

"You can't be here." The man frowned. "You need to leave." He nodded to a man behind him. "Escort her back upstairs."

As the man moved to obey, I gained a clearer view of the others. Six men in all . . . and one holding a sword.

"What do you intend to do?" I backed up against the bars. "I refuse to leave until you tell me why you are here."

"We have direct orders from Herod," the burly man stated. The guard with the sword shifted it impatiently from hand to hand.

"Do not harm this man." I poured all the authority I could muster into my voice.

The burly man laughed, the sound bouncing back from the ceiling and filling the cell. "You have no authority here. In fact, by standing in our way, you are directly defying Herod himself. Move aside."

"Joanna." John's calm voice came from behind me, and I whirled around. "Do as they say."

"No," I said, tears clogging my throat.

A guard snagged the torch from my hand and grasped my arm. I wrested it from his hand, but he grabbed hold again, fingers firmer and unflinching as he dragged me from the cell.

With strength born from desperation, I pushed myself close to the guard, throwing him slightly off-balance before yanking my arm from his hand once again and throwing myself back at the iron bars.

"This isn't right." I grasped at John's hand, and he caught it, pressing it tightly to his cracked and bleeding lips.

"God is fanning the smoldering wick of my faith into a bright flame," he murmured. His eyes, when they lifted to mine, were steady. "I am unafraid, Joanna. In fact, I am blessed. Let me go."

Two men came this time, one on each side. "She has resisted long enough. Detain her in her room, and let Herod decide what to do with her."

My heart barely registered the dire words as the guards pulled me back down the hall. The cell door groaned open, and I twisted at the sound just in time to see the guard with the sword entering before the door clanged shut behind him.

TWENTY-FIVE

A shaken Eden watched as I frantically paced my room. From the bed on one end to the table at the other and back again, I took quick strides, stopping intermittently to shake my hands, trying to rid my body of all the rage, fear, and sorrow by flinging it from my fingertips.

"Mistress, please . . . what happened?" Eden's voice was small. She'd been preparing my things for bed when the guards had dumped me unceremoniously in my room, locking her in here with me. Since then, I hadn't ceased to move, too distraught to answer her questions.

I stopped now by the small window etched into the wall, placed my trembling hands against the sill, and peered out. Rows of buildings cascaded down the slope. I imagined John's remaining disciples in one of them—alone and with no knowledge that John had been executed.

Spinning from the window, I shoved a fist to my lips as a scream clawed up my throat. With great effort, I pressed it down. Someone needed to tell John's disciples. Someone needed to ensure that they came and retrieved his body, for I couldn't bear to think of him receiving no burial.

Eden placed a hand on my arm. "Mistress?"

I clutched at her hand, pressing it tightly between both my own. The guard outside the door ensured that, at least for the time being, I was trapped within the four walls of my room. Who could help me? Who cared as much as I did for Jesus and those connected to him? I could send for Chuza, but would he be able to act discreetly, without Herod's knowledge?

Susanna.

With a groan, I released Eden's hand and sank onto a cushioned seat, head drooping as the name resounded like a gong in my head. Dare I trust her with this?

"Eden, I need you to listen closely." I barely recognized the harsh scrape of my voice, the terror of the last hour having carved my throat raw. "I need you to get a message to Susanna. Can you relay it from memory? For your own safety, I don't want to put anything into writing."

"Y-yes, I'm sure I can remember it. What is so urgent and dangerous that you cannot commit it to writing?"

"Herod had John the Baptist executed in prison." Speaking the words out loud solidified the horrific events. "Some of his disciples are still in the lower city but haven't been able to gain entrance. I need you to find Susanna and tell her what has happened. Tell her . . ." I choked on the words, forcing them out. "Tell her to do whatever she can to ensure John's disciples can retrieve the body. And then after you've found Susanna, see if you can get word to Chuza. Tell him—" The longing for Chuza's presence was so intense I could barely finish. "Let him know I'm here."

"What if they won't let me leave?" The fear was evident in Eden's voice.

Quickly, I strode to the door and rapped with my knuckles. When no reply came, I used my fist.

"Quiet in there!" the guard snapped through the door.

"Would you keep my maid under house arrest too? She's done nothing. At least let her leave."

After some hesitation, the guard unlocked the door and eased it open just enough to show his disgruntled expression, which shifted to Eden, assessing her small and quaking frame. "She won't be allowed back in," he muttered, shoving the door wider with a grunt.

With a quick glance at me, Eden silently slipped out the door.

Alone for the first time, I swayed slightly in the middle of the room, mind trying and failing to make sense of everything that was happening. With a small cry, I slumped to the floor and gave vent to the tears I'd been trying so valiantly to suppress.

◆

Hours passed, during which time I grew faint with dread. Had Eden found Susanna? And would Susanna help? Had Eden sent word to Chuza? Where was he now? I had nothing other than frantic questions to keep my mind occupied. I tried to pray, but my body was so tied up with worry, no words would come.

The view from my window told me it was the dead of night by the time four guards came to fetch me. They led me down several corridors in the direction of the banquet halls, the sound of revelry still obvious. A rushing began in my ears as we swiftly traversed the corridor. Were they taking me to Herod?

Adonai. The fright in my body was so sharp, I could only pray two words. *Adonai, help.*

With each step, the rushing in my ears intensified. For a wretched moment, I feared they'd lead me directly into Herod's banquet hall to parade me before the entire assembly, but we pivoted and entered a separate room.

Torches lined the walls, and I stood squinting in the light, my eyes more accustomed to the darkness of my room. When my gaze focused, I could see we were in a small audience chamber. Ornate tapestries lined the walls, plush rugs spread across the floor, and a small triclinium graced the back wall. Herod stretched like a cat on a low cushioned bench, but my eyes and heart went straight to the man by his side.

Chuza sat upright, as did his hair. At the sight of him, something inside me crumbled. I stretched out a hand as he surged to his feet. With a few quick strides, he was by my side.

"Chuza." Herod's tone was tired, clipped, and full of warning. Chuza's face tightened. He swallowed hard, grasped my hand, and turned.

Herod raised a hand. "Come."

As we approached, Herod pushed himself upright with a sigh. My eyes were adjusted enough to note the other occupants in the room. Othniel, along with a handful of others, relaxed by Herod's side. Othniel smiled at the look on my face and raised a goblet in my direction, toasting me.

"Is this any way to treat a lady of the court?" Herod's voice was slurred from drink, eyes bleary. "Leave." He nodded to the guards, who quickly drew back and left the room. "My apologies, Lady Joanna." Herod faced me as I pulled my hand from Chuza's and dipped into a low bow, remaining there, hovering above the floor like a bird mid-flight.

"I'd planned to deal with this in the light of day, but when your husband learned of what happened, he caused enough commotion to nearly bring down the entire fortress." He barked a laugh. The warm congeniality of his tone was disorienting in light of the circumstances.

"What is this about you worming your way into places you shouldn't?" Herod leaned back to gaze at me with hooded eyes. "My captain of the guard says he found you talking to John the Baptist. But that cannot be true. Why would a noblewoman such as yourself want anything to do with such a man?"

With great effort, I wet my lips, hoping my voice didn't waver. "I-I was curious, my king."

At my soft reply, Herod smiled, as if he was speaking with a child who was no threat to anyone. When he remained silent, I continued, "I apologize, my king. I wasn't thinking rationally."

Herod flicked a hand, and a servant appeared to refill his goblet. As the sounds of trickling wine filled the small room, Herod kept his eyes trained on his cup. When it was full, he lifted it and, instead of drinking, twisted the goblet slightly between his fingers, observing as the dark liquid swirled and glimmered in the torchlight.

"You were curious," he stated, his voice sounding less slurred. Swiftly, he set down the cup. Some of the wine sloshed onto the table, soaking into the linen cloth. As Herod observed the slowly spreading stain, his lips twitched. "You were merely curious." His eyes flicked to mine. "Which is why you interfered with my direct orders. You were simply being *curious*."

In a moment, I saw that he'd been leaning into his slurred speech and disinterest as a ploy to disarm me. Weakness entered my legs, and my head became light.

"I'm sure what my wife means to say—" Chuza's voice was level and calm, and I knew how much strength he was exerting to keep it that way.

Herod raised a hand. "Let your wife answer for her own actions. If there's anything I've learned this night, it's that wives are capable of more than we realize." He snorted a laugh and others joined in, which seemed to displease him, for his gaze darkened.

Was Chuza in danger because of me? Fresh worry pierced my heart as I pushed my bow lower, flowing robes kissing the floor as my mind raced. What could I possibly say or do to defuse this situation, to divert the attention back to myself and away from my husband?

"Forgive me, my king. As you yourself attested, John was a holy and good man, overwhelmingly revered by the people. When I'd heard how he'd captivated your attention, I wasn't surprised, for you have always willingly entertained notable men."

I risked a glance up to find something flickering in Herod's eyes . . . something that looked remarkably like regret. "The man had a keen sense of God's justice," he muttered.

"It's widely known among the court how you enjoyed listening to him speak, even after his imprisonment. Can you forgive a woman her desire to see the man who had so captured your attention?" With effort, I infused my tone with flattery.

The couch creaked as Herod rose. I kept my gaze trained on the ground until his sandaled feet came into view, and then I studied those feet, not daring to look or breathe or think.

Abba, help.

His jeweled fingers found and grasped my chin. In a swift movement, he twisted my face upward, and I blinked into his eyes as into the sun.

"Lady Joanna, your reputation as a generous patroness precedes you, and, in turn, incites my own generosity of heart." He angled my face, studying me, one of his jewels impressing deeply into my throat. "I shouldn't wonder that the Baptizer caught your attention."

He turned my face back and locked my gaze with his own, which was full of masculine appreciation. Bile rose in my throat. I wanted his fingers off me. I wanted out of his presence, never to return. I wanted freedom from this game of pretense.

I wanted the reign of the Christ in the Kingdom of God.

A sob tangled with the bile in my throat, and my eyes watered with the effort of holding them both at bay.

The look in Herod's eyes deepened as he released my face. "I do not condemn your curiosity, but never let it interfere with your king's will again, Lady Joanna." He took a step back, sank onto his couch, and flicked a hand. "It's late. Chuza, take your wife to bed and let's be done with this."

In a moment, Chuza was by my side, hand grasping mine as I rose on unsteady legs. Herod nodded for us to leave, and the door creaked open behind us. Freedom—at least for the moment—was on the other side.

Dazed, I allowed Chuza to lead me back toward the door. We'd reached the threshold when a loud voice stopped us short.

"Wait!"

At the command to stop, Chuza tensed and then slowly urged us both around.

Othniel stood towering over the table. "Wait a moment. My king, her limp is gone. She entered this court with a pronounced limp, do you recall?"

Herod shook his head, irritated with this triviality, expression clouding in thought before clearing. "Ah yes, she did. A shame for a beautiful woman to be crippled in such a way. The limp is gone?"

"Yes, my king. I've heard rumors of some in your court experiencing miraculous healing from that new teacher, Jesus of Nazareth."

Herod stroked his chin. "Yes, I've heard the same."

Othniel extended a long arm in our direction, pointing at me with excitement mounting in his voice. "There can be no other explanation for her healing."

"Was it this miracle man everyone's talking about?" Herod questioned me. "Or perhaps a physician?"

Up until this moment, Chuza had been quietly enduring the events as they unfolded, but now he moved quickly, turning to block me slightly from those at the table. His face held tenderness threaded with such a desperate look that my lips parted. He didn't speak, only pressed his lips together tightly with the smallest shake of his head.

Did he want me to lie? I gazed into Chuza's eyes laced with fear, noted how his broad chest expanded with deepening breaths, his hand trembling slightly as it grasped mine.

In my current situation, he must consider my connection to

Jesus too dangerous to disclose. But how could I accept Jesus' miraculous mercy and then publicly deny what he'd done? I couldn't. Not even to protect this man who had become so dear to me.

Herod raised slightly from his couch, expression lifting with interest and impatience. "Come now. Speak up!"

"I'm still learning what it means to surrender to his way." John's steady words, moments before his faith burst into full flame, moments before he'd gone to be with God.

Could I have faith that clung to God despite my circumstances? Faith that didn't demand God move in a predictable and comfortable way? Could I have the faith of Dalia . . . and of John?

Abba, help. I am weak and afraid.

I slid my fingers to my wrist, remembering Jesus' hand there. *Give me the strength to pick up this cross.*

"It was Jesus." I pushed past my husband to face the men at the end of the room. "It was Jesus who healed me."

Behind me I heard Chuza's sharp inhalation. Before me, Herod rose to standing, eyes alight with fascination.

"I'd be interested in hearing the details. Is he a doctor? Magician?"

I'd been prepared for Herod's anger, so I was taken aback by his intense curiosity. "No, he is neither of those things, my king."

With a swift, impatient gesture, he indicated for me to return to him and, as I did so, he observed my steps carefully. "Remarkable. No lingering trace of your limp. What did he use to heal you?"

"Only his words, my king. His words and his touch." I closed my eyes and longed for that dusty stretch of road by the Sea of Galilee when I'd first heard him speak.

"He gives sight to the blind and legs to the lame." I opened my eyes and looked steadfastly into Herod's own. "The words from his mouth were enough to flood my body with healing."

"Joanna." Chuza's voice was quiet and raw. He'd come to stand by my side, face ashen.

"Only his words." Herod stalked closer until I could smell the wine on his breath. "And what did it feel like?"

The words poured smoothly over his lips—a slight pause between each one—and I understood that this was entertaining to him. The knowledge stunned me into silence, and I blinked up into his face, trying to form a response as sickness roiled in my stomach.

"Both my body and mind were instantly strengthened." Tears threatened at the hungry way Herod looked at me.

"As you've said, my king, the hour is late, and my wife is tired . . ." Chuza's strong voice cracked.

Herod raised a firm hand in Chuza's direction, his gaze darkening at my husband's impudence. "And do you still see this Jesus of Nazareth?"

"Sometimes, my king."

Herod pursed his lips. Finally, he paced to the table, tipping his goblet and draining his cup.

"You aren't the first, Lady Joanna, and I sense you won't be the last. This Jesus is healing both the lowly and the highborn. Did he request money for his services?"

"N-no." My hands were beginning to shake the longer I sat beneath his questions. Best to keep my willing contributions secret.

"Interesting. Most charlatans perform for monetary compensation, but this man hands out miracles for free!" He barked a laugh. "I wonder if he would come and speak with me the way his cousin did. I wonder if his tongue is as sharp." He quieted, then grew thoughtful. "If nothing else, I would dearly love a miracle."

His eyes grew distant before he roused himself with a shake. "Well, if you *do* see him again, tell him that his king would like an audience. A miracle man." He smirked. "From Nazareth."

"Y-yes, my king, of course."

"Good." Herod nodded and swept a hand toward the door. Chuza snagged my arm with firm pressure and led me away.

As we reached the exit, I dared to glance back. Othniel was by Herod's side, lips to his ear, eyes expectant and hungry.

———— ✦ ————

Chuza drew me down the hall and into his room with powerful steps and thundering breath. As soon as the door closed, I clung to him, not thinking about the careful years of habit that stood between us. I dug my fingers into his back, burrowed my face into his chest, and released the tears I'd been holding back.

"Joanna!" Roughly, he removed himself from my arms, pinning my face between his hands and capturing my eyes with his own, which were wide and disbelieving. "Joanna . . . why did you . . . of all the dangerous things you could have done!"

His eyes raced across my features as if seeing me for the first time. "Oh, you brave, infuriating woman." He shook his head, breath catching in his chest. "Holding yourself before Herod like a queen—calm and authoritative. You were radiant and foolish and brave."

He pulled me back into his arms, dipping his head to press his face into the crook of my neck. "How you found the strength to conduct yourself in such a manner . . . more poised than a seasoned official!"

My head was swimming and light as Chuza's lips moved against my throat and then up to my jaw. I should push him away, demand that he honor the terms of our relationship that he'd so carefully stipulated and we'd so intentionally upheld, but neither of us seemed to care as his mouth moved to my face and he kissed away my tears with soft and roaming lips.

"I can't do this again," he murmured against my brow, my ear, the corner of my mouth. "Now I'm the foolish one. I'm the foolish one."

My lips remained raised and hopeful, but he bypassed them with a groan, pushing me back and turning away.

His hands sought the table, where he planted two fists, arching his back and bowing his head. I stood trembling behind him, missing his warmth. What had just happened? With Herod—and with us? Everything that was ordered and understood in my life was now flung in the air, scattered and disorienting.

Deep, rasping sounds came from Chuza, and I watched in disbelief as his broad shoulders began to shake. He was weeping. Weeping!

A new desire shuddered open inside me as I crossed the room and slid my arms around his waist, clasping him tightly from behind.

He quieted at my touch, voice barely audible. "I cannot bear to lose you. It would kill me."

When he'd composed himself enough to face me, he twisted in my arms, gathering me to himself once again.

Love—I could see it in his eyes, feel it in his touch, hear it in his voice. Exultation and confusion warred within as I hid my face against his breast.

All these years, I'd understood our relationship to be entirely chaste, and never once had he breached that wall between us. I'd thought, at times, that he viewed me as a sister, but this? This was not a brother's touch. I shivered and pressed closer. Something had changed between us and now continued to shift.

With a strong hand, he cupped my head. "What were you thinking, Joanna?"

"I wasn't thinking beyond the desire to see John, to bring a report of him back to Jesus." My voice faltered as I imagined Jesus' face upon hearing this grisly news. Easing back, I peered up at Chuza. "How could I have known that Herod would do such a thing? He's always catered to the people when it's in his power to do so. Why would he have John executed?"

Chuza's grip on me tightened. "Herod was enraptured by Herodias' daughter, Salome. She performed a dance, and he promised her up to half his kingdom."

"And she requested John's death?"

"His head . . . delivered on a platter."

With a low moan, I pressed my forehead to Chuza's chest.

"I was there when the request was made and when the head was . . . delivered."

I couldn't suppress the gag that spasmed my throat. "I shouldn't be surprised that Herod was willing to put an innocent man to death to save face."

"He did so with reluctance, but now . . . now he knows that you are connected with John's cousin. I'm afraid his eye will remain upon you."

"And upon you," I muttered. "Not just Herod's eye . . . but Othniel's." I grimaced.

"Othniel? Did he say something to you?" Chuza's voice hardened.

I nodded against his chest, unwilling to meet his eyes and face the confusing love I might see there. "He accosted me in the hallway earlier."

Chuza growled deep in his throat, the sound rumbling throughout his chest. "That man is a snake. Did he put his hands on you? Harm you?"

"No, I-I am fine. But he claims to know that you helped Phasaelis and is working to prove it. He said such actions, given your background, will be seen as treasonous. He seems intent on taking you down."

Pulling back, I found Chuza's face close. "Do you think he bluffs?" I questioned, daring to place a hand briefly to his cheek.

"Oh, I'm worried—so worried for you."

Chuza's eyes flooded with a soft, unguarded look that swirled my stomach into a flustered mess. "Perhaps he bluffs, but I will

230

need to exercise wisdom." He sank onto a couch, retaining one of my hands in his own.

"Herod is well aware of the political implications of his divorce, and as a result he's not eager to draw any further ire from Aretas. Up until now, he has been circumspect with the remaining Nabatean connections within his court, but if Othniel presents this information to him—" Chuza released my hand to scrub his face. "I do not see it going over well. I would be remiss to ignore such threats, even coming from such a snake as Othniel."

This man was caught between two courts, and I'd just made things even more complicated for him. "What will you do?" I whispered, voice tight.

Chuza quieted, studying his hands before lifting his gaze to mine. "There is one move that no one would expect and that would utterly undermine anything Othniel could attempt. It is, however, risky . . . perhaps too risky." He took a long, steadying breath. "I could tell Herod Antipas the truth."

TWENTY-SIX

Our wooden-paneled carriage jostled along the rutted road, dipping into a hole and throwing me against Eden, who squeaked her surprise. It was a five-day journey from Machaerus to Tiberias. Our carriage was one of many in the large company traveling back north. Five days of uncomfortable travel. Five days to fret over Chuza's idea and to replay his lips on my face again and again. I sighed and cast my gaze out the window.

In the end, could it be the truth that saved us? Could Chuza get ahead of Othniel by disclosing his own involvement in Phasaelis' flight? Could he describe his own actions in a way that did not come across as treasonous? Could he, in fact, use this to secure a firmer place in Herod's court? Fear clenched at my stomach with a firm grip, twisting the knife of uncertainty deeper.

The pair of mules pulling our carriage balked at something in the road, throwing me, once again, against Eden.

"I delivered your message." Eden had been waiting for me in my room after I'd left Chuza. *"But I don't know what happened afterward. Susanna seemed resolute and thankful you sent me to her."*

"Are you okay, mistress?" Asher's concerned face appeared at the carriage door. Although he directed his question to me, his eyes were upon Eden, who blushed and squirmed.

"I'm fine. We both are." As Asher returned to the mules, Eden craned her neck to follow his movement. She'd been distracted the entire journey to Machaerus, and I was sure it would be the same on the return trip. Her and Asher's stolen glances and obvious mutual admiration had delighted me earlier, but now it put a hitch in my chest.

I snuck another glance out the opposite window. Chuza was ahead of us on his horse but had stopped when our carriage did. His steed did an impatient dance in the middle of the road.

We'd talked for hours as I relayed in greater detail everything that had transpired between Othniel and me. Longing to be back in Chuza's arms had left me flustered while we talked, but he'd been distracted and serious and had made no more moves to hold me.

I shivered despite the warm weather. His touch had stirred hidden embers and cast doubt on the narrative I'd held in my mind. Perhaps it wasn't a continued love for his first wife that kept him from me. But if not that . . . then what? If he loved me, desired me, then why refrain from a true marriage?

When I'd left with the first hints of morning on the horizon, it was without his kiss. He'd settled again into a calm exterior, a familiar, impenetrable comradery that had been our relationship's foundation. I shivered again, pulling my mantle tightly about my frame.

Later that evening, we stopped at an inn, weary and ragged from the day's journey. As Eden followed my trunk into a room, I lingered in the central courtyard, hoping to speak to Chuza when he returned with Asher from tending to the animals.

"Joanna."

I jolted at the urgent yet quiet voice, eyes roving to the covered gallery surrounding the courtyard. Susanna emerged from the shadows and gestured for me to follow her, leading me to her room and then fastening the door.

"Did you—?" My voice cracked into silence.

Susanna nodded. "Yes, I took care of it."

I released a long, shaky sigh, eyes lifting upward in gratitude.

"I made sure his disciples were able to recover his body." Now it was Susanna's voice that broke. "I'm thankful you notified me, that the prophet received an honorable burial."

"Thank you," I breathed.

"You chose to trust me." Susanna's voice shook. "Even after all we've been through, all the sharp words I've used . . . you chose to trust me." Her voice caught as she hunched over with a sharp sob.

Compassion broke through—the compassion Dalia always knew Susanna needed, the compassion I'd so resolutely withheld. It was here, compelling my arms to reach for her, to hold her as she wept.

"I can't begin to tell you what it means to me . . . that you would trust me. I've stayed away from you . . . too ashamed to do otherwise, too convinced that you would never forgive me. Even after your healing! Even then, I couldn't face you."

In the wake of Susanna's deep relief, I realized I'd been treating her with the same suspicion that Simon and Nathaniel had treated me. But if we were united under Jesus' vision of the Kingdom, then didn't that supersede anything that had come before?

"I spent so many years envying you." Susanna's tears quieted as her voice grew somber. "Envy and ambition were twin masters of my heart and led me to resent you. You had everything I thought I wanted. But I could tell you didn't seem to *need* it the way I did, and I confess that this infuriated me. Please forgive me, Joanna."

Grasping her hand, I managed to speak past the lump in my throat. "It shouldn't have taken a desperate situation for me to trust you. I should have let go of past hurts long before now. I forgive you, Susanna, and I hope you can forgive me."

"Of course, and I don't blame you." Susanna pulled away to swipe at her face. "Now, more than ever, we need to know who our allies are. I was present when Salome came to Herodias, asking what she should request from Herod. When she demanded his head, many responded with enthusiasm, but not all. John was highly regarded."

"Herod himself appeared regretful," I mused.

"Manaen seems to think Herod will turn his efforts inward, focus on his secret police in an attempt to get a handle on public opinion."

"Chuza didn't mention that." My heart constricted as I recalled our long hours of conversation. "You and Manaen are close." I didn't realize I'd stated my observation aloud until Susanna replied.

"We are indeed." Her cheeks grew rosy. "It wasn't always so. After all, he's more mature than I . . . in age and disposition." She laughed. "But his steadiness has grounded me in a way I didn't even know I needed. When Jesus healed me—" She broke off, overcome by emotion. "Manaen didn't hesitate in his unequivocal joy and belief."

The memory of my husband's exuberance upon my own healing swelled like an underground spring. "Chuza also responded with joy, but I'm not sure about the belief . . . not yet."

‹ ◆ ›

When the sprawling walls of our villa came into view, the knotted worry in my chest loosened. Finally—*home*. There had been no chance on the road for Chuza and me to speak privately. Indeed, he'd spent most of his time ahead of the carriage, and as soon as we neared home, he nudged his steed toward the stables.

Wearily, I allowed our steward to help me from the carriage and Eden to assist in removing my dusty and rumpled travel clothes. She served distractedly with bright eyes and fumbling hands, her mind somewhere else entirely. Normally, I would gently tease her, goad her into speaking of Asher, but my mind, body, and spirit were sore and desirous of one thing—to crawl into my bed and seek the relief of sleep.

As Eden finished combing my hair, a swift knock sounded at the door. I twisted in surprise as she opened it to reveal a disheveled Chuza. He was still dirty from the road and carried his pack. Rising quickly to my feet, I motioned for Eden to leave us.

He entered my room, eyes widening as he took in my bed with its abundance of cushions, the feminine array of perfumes on the table, and me clothed in only a loose tunic. His eyes snagged on my black curls, which were unbound and flowing. I pushed past the rising lump in my throat and heat in my cheeks as I gestured for him to sit and offered him water.

Settling his pack at his feet, Chuza took the cup from my hand, fingers lingering over my own as his eyes continued to drink me in. We'd never been in each other's private quarters, and his expression showed how it rattled him. I could bear it as long as he did not touch me, as long as he stopped looking at me with that new softness. I took refuge behind a table and waited for him to speak.

"I detest the idea that Othniel thinks of you, is watching you."

Regret nipped at my mind. I'd unnecessarily burdened him by relaying all of Othniel's threats, including the ones directed at me. "He's a braggart and was intoxicated. I doubt he actively thinks of me."

Chuza's eyes held clear skepticism. "He sounds determined to take me down and get to you. A man like that is willing to act with or without the truth. If he can find nothing concrete, then he will use slander. We both know this."

"Herod first valued you for your connections," I said, trying to control my worry. "Your contacts within the spice trade from Rome to Petra are part of what make you so invaluable. You've been good for his administration, so do you think Herod will listen to Othniel over you?"

Chuza's face softened the longer I talked. "You're frightened." He rose and crossed the room to the table but kept it between us. "I've been thinking of little else the entire trip home, and I don't see a way forward unless I outmaneuver Othniel, try to get ahead of this with a portion of the truth."

I turned away, unwilling for him to see my face.

Both of us were caught between two worlds. This union was supposed to be mutually beneficial, but here we were, each of us endangering the other in our own way.

Weakness threatened my limbs as I stumbled out from behind the table and to a low couch, keeping my body turned from him, face hidden in my hands.

He moved to me, reached for me, but I shrank away from the promise of comfort. What comfort could we derive from each other? We who were not a *true* husband and wife? My heart was hollowed out of my chest, and I spoke from that void. "I'm afraid I . . . I've outstayed my usefulness to you."

Deep silence penetrated the room before he drew in a breath. "What do you mean?"

"You needed a Jewish wife. You've always been clear on what this marriage was . . . and was not." Emptiness spread from my chest outward. "With these latest developments, I have become useless to you, an additional liability on top of everything you face—a wife who openly defied Herod's guards, a wife who is following a teacher who preaches about a kingdom." I bowed my head, not daring to look at him. "I would understand if you wanted to put me away."

With strong hands, he pulled me to standing and twisted me toward him. His eyes were fire, his voice low. "Is that what you want?"

My face was full of his scent—oud, vanilla, and leather, mixed with smells from the stables. No, it wasn't what I wanted. I couldn't have what I wanted, which I now realized was him—all of him.

"It's . . . it's not about what I want. It's about protecting you, and if I'm making things worse, then surely . . . because I can't, Chuza. I won't stop supporting Jesus." I was tripping over my own words in an effort to keep emotion at bay.

He studied me with narrowed eyes. "Did I ask you to stop?"

"N-no." I blinked up at him in surprise. "But I assumed you would."

"Didn't I tell you that I've never aspired to be like most men? I will *not* put you aside. You expect to be used and discarded, but I will not do that to you, Joanna." Anger rippled through his body like a rolling wave at the mere thought of our parting ways.

"I was frightened you might ask it of me," I confessed, "that you might make me choose between you and Jesus. I've had to deny so much of myself for the sake of appearances, and I will do so no longer."

He tugged me into his arms, my temple colliding with his collarbone as he crushed me to his chest. "I know what it's like to have a choice foisted upon you." He spoke the words into my hair, hand pressing into the small of my back. "And I will not do that to you." His voice was gently rolling thunder. I pressed closer to the echoes of its rumble and allowed myself this moment—this moment where it felt like we were one.

Twenty-Seven

The road was cluttered with people. I stood next to Susanna beneath a wild sycamore tree and strained my ears to hear Jesus. He sat on a large boulder on a slope, talking, with hands that danced with each word.

We were halfway between Capernaum and Chorazin. Jesus had finished teaching in the Capernaum synagogue, but the crowds had followed him, streaming down the road, unwilling for him to leave.

"He draws people like flies to honey," Susanna observed quietly.

Mary Magdalene was nearby and glanced at us with a sad smile. "Not all people. Some hate his words, fueled by the pride in their hearts."

"Or do you think it's fear?" I wondered. "Fear over what his message requires from them?"

"Fear, pride . . . I wonder if sometimes they're two sides of the same coin," Mary said.

Now that I was about to see Jesus again, I couldn't shake Herod's eyes or the memory of his fingers on my chin. *"If you do see him again, tell him that his king would like an audience."* I would do no such thing, but the question rattled in my head: Had I endangered Jesus by testifying to his work in my life?

"Jesus needs to keep moving if we're to make Chorazin before evening." Simon approached us like a gust of wind tearing into the sea, glancing briefly at Susanna and me before drawing close to Mary.

"He moves according to his own purposes. You know this," Mary remarked.

"Even so, I'll remind him." Simon began pushing his way through the crowd when a loud commotion by the road drew everyone's attention. A group of women holding children stood in the road, pointing to where Jesus sat. Peter, John, and several other disciples were blocking their way.

"Why are they stopping those women?" Mary questioned.

Simon shook his head. "Of course they're stopping them. Jesus doesn't have time for children. He needs to get on the road."

"Enough!" Jesus' voice washed over the gathered crowd, halting the disciples, who looked to him in confusion. "Let them through. Do not hinder them!" He rose to his feet, face thunderous.

I had yet to witness such ferocity from him and watched amazed as the disciples quickly obeyed, parting so that the women could pass through.

A young woman with an infant reached him first, and Jesus stretched his arms forward in invitation. Gladness broke open on the woman's face as she gratefully transferred the small bundle into his waiting arms. Jesus' eyes brightened as he peered into the small face, placed a hand over the child's forehead, and pronounced a blessing. Before transferring the child back, he nuzzled the infant's neck with his nose, eliciting a wet gurgle from the small bundle.

Child after child was deposited into Jesus' arms. He clasped each one close, offering hugs and tickles and grins. He allowed one little boy to yank on his beard, releasing a groan as if in agony, much to the boy's delight.

Jesus paused with a young girl, no more than four, in his arms. "Do you see this child?" he called and shifted her so that she sat on his shoulder, towering over those gathered. Her eyes widened in enjoyment, two chubby hands coming up to hide her dimpled grin. "To such belongs the Kingdom of God."

Murmurs rippled throughout the crowd. The Kingdom of God belonged to those with the least power?

"I tell you the truth . . . if you would receive the Kingdom of God, you must do so like a little child."

Not earned but received—with the readiness and openness of a child accepting a good gift from her father.

Tears clouded my vision as I stared at Jesus' hands—the powerful hands that had healed me. Hands that even now were lifting up a little girl and calling us to be like her. I'd been trained to believe it was the role of the powerful to separate from the weak. But here was this man who used his power to stoop beneath others and lift them up.

✦

The disciples were abashed after Jesus' open rebuke of them and so the gathering that night was tense. Jesus had left late in the evening to pray alone, and those of us who remained sat around the fire in our host's open courtyard.

"We've all heard of John's beheading." Mary softly broke the silence. "But none of us have heard an account from someone who was there." She looked expectantly at Susanna and me.

Slowly, painfully, we retold the events of that night. When I reached the part where I'd spoken with Herod, Simon jumped agitatedly to his feet.

"He knows you're connected to Jesus, doesn't he?"

With a lump in my throat, I watched Simon pace, his face appearing severe in the firelight.

Susanna placed a steadying hand on my knee. "Yes, he knows," she answered for me.

"And yet you're here." Simon extended his hands outward in disbelief.

"I shouldn't have told you," I murmured. Facing the fire, I watched the flames writhe and lick at the wood. A charred branch collapsed, shooting embers into the night. One landed on my tunic, burned the flesh beneath, but I let it be, enduring the momentary sting.

"What did you say?" Simon asked sharply.

"I said I shouldn't have told you about my encounter with Herod." I swiped the lingering spark off my lap, eyes jumping upward, weariness and defensiveness warring within my breast. "I debated disclosing my interaction with Herod because I feared this reaction. But I am committed to telling you the truth, Simon. Even if you don't believe me."

"You stood before Herod with Jesus' name on your lips. It is natural to be concerned, Joanna," Judas chimed in. The treasurer, the one who always accepted my coin with eagerness, now observed me with a tight and conflicted expression.

"I would never do anything to endanger Jesus. You know that." I looked with alarm from one face to another.

"Perhaps not intentionally," Judas stated.

Simon grunted. "Your husband—*both* of your husbands—walk too close to the throne for my comfort."

"When has this ever been about your comfort?" Matthew spoke up from the other side of the fire.

"Ah, I forget that you are a man of precise words, Matthew." Simon stopped pacing to shove a hand through his hair. "It's not my comfort I'm concerned with. It's *his* safety." He gestured out into the night in the vague direction of Jesus.

"You saw him today," Peter spoke up. Typically, a loud, boisterous man, he was subdued tonight. "Jesus doesn't approve when people are hindered from coming to him."

Simon shrugged. "And your point is?"

"Let them come!" Fire leapt back into Peter's eyes as he raised his head and stood. "Let these women come, Simon." He gestured to Susanna and me. "Who are you or Judas or anyone to hinder his Kingdom from spreading where it will?"

For a moment, the two men stood toe to toe, both large, broad, and imposing. Finally, Simon jerked away, seeming to bite back whatever reply was in his mouth before leaving swiftly.

"You didn't have to sound so superior." Judas shoved aside his pack with a sharp look at Peter and stood, following Simon into the night.

"I apologize for my brothers' behavior," Peter muttered before sitting back down.

"Your brothers?" I questioned, looking at Andrew. "But I thought . . ."

"Yes, Andrew is my brother by blood, but lately I've begun thinking differently of the word."

"Jesus pointed to us and said, 'Here are my mother and brothers,'" Andrew clarified. "He said that not to devalue blood relations but to expand our understanding of those terms. He said that anyone who does the will of God in heaven is his brother, sister, and mother."

Peter's large hands dangled between his knees as he gazed at me across the fire. "Since then, those words have held new meaning for me. Simon and Judas, as infuriating as they can be at times, are brothers to Jesus." He raised a hand to pound his chest. "As am I. So that makes all of us brothers, one to another."

As many heads nodded around the fire, a deep longing filled me. Despite their differences, these disciples laid claim to one another as siblings. Instead of seeking their own interests, they laid down those interests for the sake of their brothers, their sisters. Could I enter into this relationship with them? Peter, Mary, and Matthew seemed to think so, but then there were times like tonight when I doubted.

Some, like Nathaniel and Simon, still avoided my presence. Even though Judas accepted my gifts, was he accepting of me? Perhaps not if he viewed me as a potential hazard to Jesus.

Was I? Could I inadvertently hurt the one who'd healed me?

TWENTY-EIGHT

WINTER 29 AD

As Jesus' ministry spread in and around Galilee, Susanna and I continued to offer our support. I had contributed financially to other endeavors and now used those established relationships as a guise in traveling to meet Jesus. As much as I appreciated Peter's defense, Simon's worry mirrored my own. Whereas he was uncertain of my loyalty, I was uncertain of how closely I was watched.

The easy companionship between Chuza and me had been shattered, for now we'd experienced a hint of true intimacy. At Machaerus, the warmth that had always existed between us had ignited in a single, crashing moment. I'd been so certain that things between us would now change, but as weeks bled into months, Chuza pulled inward, and I saw less and less of him, until I was sure it was intentional avoidance. I longed to confront him but didn't know how—not when he spent long periods of time away from home, not when his mind was so preoccupied. He was waiting for the most opportune time to approach Herod, all while maintaining a close eye on Othniel. The longer he tarried, the more anxious I became.

Honesty and trust—he'd named these traits as supremely important, but increasingly I harbored doubt. He was withholding something from me. Could I blame him when I held my own secrets?

In the brief times we were together, I brought Chuza news of Jesus, which he always welcomed with eagerness. The common people revered Jesus as a prophet, and many traveled long distances for a chance to listen to him and be healed. The religious leaders, however, were far more skeptical and openly rebuked Jesus for healing on the Sabbath, even claiming his power came from Satan.

"He called them hypocrites!" I relayed to Chuza one evening.

"Hypocrites." Chuza repeated the word slowly. "He likens the religious leaders to stage actors?"

I nodded. "He differentiates between man-made traditions and God's law, even equating the Pharisees with Isaiah's own prophecy about lips that honor while the heart remains far removed."

"Such worship is a farce," Chuza quoted, eyes alight. I noted the interest in his face at the mention of Isaiah.

"He opens the eyes of the blind."

Chuza observed me quietly before reciting the prophecy. "'You will be a light to guide the nations. You will open the eyes of the blind.'"

That night belief shone in Chuza's eyes, brief but present. I saw its flame before he turned his face from me.

With the rise of Jesus' ministry, I was becoming increasingly convinced that all earthly power must ultimately bow before the power of heaven. Even Solomon knew that the heart of a king was but a stream of water turning in the hand of the Lord. Daily I prayed over the heart of Herod, pleading with God to turn it within His mighty hand.

My prayers were frequent and took on a new tone. Jesus had told us to seek God as Abba, and innately I'd called out to Him as such in Herod's presence. Now, I continued the practice with a fumbling tongue. "Abba . . . Daddy."

It was shockingly intimate, but if I was to accept the Kingdom, Jesus said it was to be from the position of a child. And so I prayed my outrageous prayers, trusting Jesus' word, for there was no doubt that he had the power of God in his hands and the words of life on his tongue. What he had, he used for others as he preached of a kingdom in the hearts of God's people. I witnessed firsthand the expansion of his vision as Jesus continued to collect hearts wherever he went.

"The Kingdom of God is like a farmer who scatters seed on the ground," he said. "And while the farmer goes about his life, that seed sprouts and grows. First a leaf here and then a head of wheat there until finally the grain is ready."

And so it was with us, faith unfurling a leaf here, producing a head of grain there—the work of God invisible and active in our midst.

———— ✦ ————

When Chuza finally approached Herod, it was humbly and in the presence of only a handful of others. Calmly he stated his case, how some in the administration distrusted him due to his connection to the Nabatean court. Rather than let such suspicions lie and rather than risk Herod's own distrust, Chuza was coming to him with the truth.

Yes, he had informed Phasaelis, but no, he was not loyal to the Nabatean court. Downplaying his personal relationship to Phasaelis, Chuza instead highlighted the fact that he owed his very position in Herod's administration to her. The loyalty she had elicited from him was now firmly in Herod's own hand. So much so, in fact, that he'd turned down a large sum of money from Aretas. He could have taken the money and fled, but he'd refused and now he placed himself at the king's mercy.

Herod had begun to suspect as much and had watched Chuza closely. Now, in light of his honesty, Herod was inclined to be merciful to the man who'd turned down a king's reward.

Chuza's hands shook as he relayed the events to me. My relief knew no bounds, but he was shaken to the core. Far from easing his mental distress, the audience with Herod had heightened his anxiety. "His eyes will be upon me even more. I will have to prove my loyalty in tangible ways. I don't know what he will require of me, but there will be something."

We were standing beneath the growing night, a blanket of stars above our heads, preparing to retire.

"You've done the wisest thing." I attempted to soothe. "You think Herod will require a sign of your loyalty, but you've already given it with your honesty. You turned down a fortune, after all."

"Maybe I should have accepted the reward and left while I could!" Chuza groaned.

I'd never seen him so distraught—not since the night he'd kissed away my tears. The urge to comfort him was unbearable. Silently, I slid my hand to his arm, ran my fingers along the firm curve of his muscles and up to his shoulder. But instead of entering my embrace as I'd hoped he would, he pulled away, and my hand was left achingly suspended between us.

"It's unfair," I whispered the words before I could think better of them.

He shot me a glance. "What's unfair?"

"You. This." I backed away, tired and desperately confused. "You claim to be a man of honesty. I've always admired that about you, from the very beginning." The words rushed from me like blood, and I was powerless to stop. "In fact, you're so honest that you told a king your most well-guarded secret." I shook my head, arms furiously clasping myself as I backed away from him. "You're open and honest with everyone but me!"

"No, I—" He moved toward me, regret clearly etched across his face, hands seeking me, but I pulled away.

"Do not touch me! You have no right to touch me."

He stopped short, aghast at the vehemence in my tone.

"You once spoke of bedrocks upon which to build a relationship . . . a foundation of respect, confidence, and trust. But those bedrocks are shaken, Chuza, and I don't know what to believe about us anymore."

"Joanna—"

"Did you forget? It was *you* who created this chaste marriage. It was *you* who outlined the stipulations. And it was *you* who then broke that agreement and held me, kissed me in such a way that—" I broke off, blinded by angry tears. "You had no right and yet you did and now I . . . I . . ."

And now I was sick with love and longing.

"I'm so sorry," he rasped, tears shining in his own eyes.

"I don't know what's going on inside your head or heart because you won't tell me." My chin trembled, but my voice remained firm and steady. "I'd accepted that it was love for your first wife that kept you removed, but when you look at me like that—*stop* looking at me like that!"

Yanking my veil before my face, I turned away from him.

"I'm sorry," he repeated in a helpless voice.

His words brought no comfort, for they came with no explanation. Shivering, I hugged myself hard. "We will not touch again, Chuza, not unless you're willing to be open with me about what this relationship is."

Twenty-Nine

SUMMER 30 AD

The cool of the stone nipped through my tunic as I leaned against a column and listened to Jesus retell the parable of the soils. We were in the synagogue at Magadan, a fishing village on the west coast of the Sea of Galilee, halfway between Tiberias and Capernaum.

My eyes took in those gathered. All of us were sacrificing something by being here, whether it was the good opinion of the religious leaders or of our own family members. Following Jesus came with a cost.

Everything came with a cost.

Chuza had been right. Not long after his audience with Herod, he'd been called into meetings to discuss Gabalis, a district on the Perean frontier. There were rumors that Aretas had his eye on the region, for it was a strategic location along the trade routes. Chuza was being called upon to make use of his former trade connections, to gather what information he could about Aretas' intent. The ever-present strain was evident on his face, almost making me regret the direct words I'd used with him months ago.

My eyes and heart rested upon Jesus. *Your Kingdom come.* It was a short prayer, one I'd begun praying when I didn't know what else to pray. *Your Kingdom come.* Oh, let it come soon—soon! Like the promise of growth from a mustard seed or a lump of leaven, the Kingdom was ready to expand. It must. It had to. *Soon.*

Mary shifted by my side, her face wreathed with a frown. This particular trip was costing her more than the others.

"Do you find it hard to be back in Magadan?" I leaned close, whispering my question in her ear.

Mary paused before replying. "At first, no. I was too changed by Jesus to care what others might think. Too altered for this place and its memories to touch me." Her smile grew rueful. "But it's strange how time can work against you." She nodded to where Jesus stood in the center of the room. "Not unlike those thorns he's talking about. Time gives rise to worries and dims our memory. Even the miraculous can be pushed aside by immediate concerns."

She turned to me with sad eyes. "So yes, at times I find it hard to be back. As if my past was waiting for the miracle in my life to grow old enough so that shame's voice can be heard again."

I slipped an arm around her back. "You and I, we must think less of ourselves and more of him and his message—his Kingdom."

Beyond Mary, movement by the door arrested my attention. A group of religious leaders stood outside, their heads clustered together as they observed Jesus. But these were not simply local elders and scribes. I recognized several of them from Herod's own court. My heart did a skittish dance.

"Joanna, what is it?"

"I just—nothing," I stammered. "I thought I saw someone I know." I risked another glance to find the group moving away. "I'll be right back." Swiftly I skirted the room, pausing by the door to squint in the sudden light.

As my eyes focused, I saw the men standing behind a nearby

column. I had not been mistaken in my recognition. Two of the men were in Herod's own administration. Some of the others were Pharisees, and yet others Sadducees, all distinguishable by their dress. What were these three groups of men doing together? My stomach churned with uneasiness as one of the Herodians glanced my way. His eyes lingered on my face, traveling briefly over the rest of me before he turned back to his companions. His look had been cursory, and yet something in the way he held himself afterward indicated his continued awareness of my presence.

"Is everything all right?"

I jumped at Simon's voice.

"I saw you leave quickly," he stated.

Nervously, I ducked around the corner of the synagogue, indicating for Simon to follow. "I recognize some of those men," I whispered urgently.

Simon reared back to glance around the building, and impatiently I yanked on his mantle to stop him. "What are you doing?" I hissed. "Don't let them see you."

"Bah, let them see me," Simon muttered and then stopped as he saw my face. "You're frightened."

"Two of them are Herodians, staunch supporters of the throne. I recognize them from Herod's administration. I think one of them might have recognized me." I twisted my hands nervously, nearly biting my tongue as I regretted my words, for they caused Simon's eyes to narrow and his nose to flare. "Pharisees, Sadducees, *and* Herodians all joining together?" My tone lifted, emphasizing each word. "You know as well as I how unusual that is."

"Indeed, it is. Well . . . at least the Pharisees and Sadducees." Simon continued to look at me, but it was impossible to read his expression. "I would imagine the Sadducees and Herodians often consult with one another."

I blew an irritated huff of air from my lips, causing the curl on my forehead to dance. "They all have different concerns—some political, some religious—and they all dislike one another, so what has brought them together like this?"

"Do you think the men you recognized are sent by Herod himself?"

"I doubt it. He has larger concerns at the moment." *Like Gabalis and proving the loyalty of my husband.*

Before I could say more, a swell of people emerged from inside. Jesus' teaching must be over, for we were surrounded by the departing crowd. When the synagogue had cleared, we risked another look around the corner to find the group of men entering. Swiftly, Simon pushed past me and followed them. Heart in my throat, I silently slipped inside after him, keeping to the wall so as not to draw attention.

"Jesus of Nazareth, you would assume a position of authority among us, coming into our synagogue and sitting in the seat of Moses, speaking as if you alone hold the correct interpretation of the Law." A Pharisee stood rigid in front of Jesus, nearly spitting in his face, so vehement were his words.

"We demand that you show us a miraculous sign from heaven to prove your authority," a Sadducee added, hand lifted, pointing to the sky beyond the synagogue roof.

A miraculous sign? I held such a sign in my own body, as did Mary and countless others. There were signs I hadn't even observed. The way he'd fed thousands with a young boy's meal. How he'd walked on water and even raised a young man from the dead. What else could Jesus do that would satisfy these men?

Quietly, I observed their expressions, disbelief already evident on their faces. They had come here with decided rather than open minds. The soil of their hearts was a footpath, hardened through years of plodding in the same direction. What could the seed do but be snatched from such a path? There was no entry point for it to take root.

"You know the saying." Jesus spoke evenly with squared shoulders, appearing utterly untroubled by the men before him. "Red sky at night means fair weather tomorrow; red sky in the morning means foul weather all day."

Jesus held his hands uncharacteristically still, resting by his sides. "You know how to discern the face of the sky, but you refuse to discern the signs of the times. Hypocrites!" His right hand rose, pointing at each man in turn. "You hypocrites!"

In another man's mouth, these words would be weapons, angry and furled with an intent to maim. But in the mouth of Jesus, they were calm and exact. Rather than accusatory, his words were a lifted curtain, showing people the truth, even if the truth was uncomfortable.

"You would accuse us?" one of the Pharisees said, the rage evident in his voice.

"Only an evil, adulterous generation would demand a miraculous sign," Jesus stated. "But the only sign I will give them is the sign of the prophet Jonah."

He had mentioned this sign once before, and the explanation had filled everyone with dread. As Jonah was in the belly of a fish for three days and nights, so would he be in the heart of the earth for three days and nights.

He emerged now from the synagogue. Quickly and decisively leaving the group of men behind, he exited with long, purposeful strides, drawing the rest of us with him out and into the light, as if leaving a tomb.

❖

Later that night, after crossing the Sea of Galilee for the region just north of Hippos, the men in our group made camp in a hasty, agitated manner. Seeing so many religious leaders united against Jesus had set everyone on edge. The repetition of his teaching on Jonah also did little to lift everyone's mood.

As he so often did, Jesus had withdrawn to pray. I was helping Mary gather brush for the fire when she clucked her tongue. "Ah, we left Magadan in such haste that we forgot to bring bread!"

Nathaniel approached us with a bundle of sticks and cast them down in a frustrated gesture. "It grows late, and Hippos is the nearest town."

"Are you volunteering to walk into Gentile territory for bread, Nathaniel?" James poked, intending it for fun, but Nathaniel snorted, clearly not receiving the words as such.

"Don't you think you're better suited for that task, Son of Thunder?"

With a grimace, I watched as Andrew joined in and the men lobbed their words at one another, some playful but some simmering with irritation and blame. As abruptly as the gentle quarreling had commenced, it stopped, as Jesus entered camp, face tight.

With a sigh, he took a bundle of wood from Andrew and brought it to where the women stood. Gently, he eased the load to the ground and began collecting Nathaniel's scattered sticks until all the wood was in a neat pile. Then, taking a piece of flint from the script at his waist, he began building a fire.

Mary stooped to offer him dried leaves, which he took with a murmured thanks. For a moment, we simply watched him, hands working the flint against stone, coaxing a flame to take hold of the brush. A spark flared, and Jesus squatted back on his heels in satisfaction.

"You must watch out. Every one of you be alert." His eyes were gentle yet firm as they lifted to us.

Jesus took a burning twig and held it upright, letting the flame lap downward, close to his fingers before dropping it onto a nest of dry leaves. The flame ate at the leaves, consuming, crumbling, encroaching. "You must beware of the leaven of the Pharisees and Sadducees."

Guilt crossed Nathaniel's features as he muttered to James, "He knows we forgot the bread. Now the master will go hungry tonight due to our carelessness."

"Well, whose fault is that?" James muttered back.

"Enough." Jesus twisted to look at the pair behind him, turned back to the fire for a long moment, then rose slowly to his feet. "Your faith in this moment is small." He clapped a hand on both men's shoulders. "Why are you arguing about bread? Especially after all you have seen and heard? Do you not understand, even now? Remember that I said my food is to do the will of Him who sent me. Remember that I said I am the Bread of Life. Remember that I fed a multitude with one meal and you yourselves filled baskets with the leftovers."

Jesus' hands now cupped each man's head, increasing in pressure until all three heads nearly touched. "Why do you not see? I'm not talking about bread. So again, I tell you to be on guard. Beware of the leaven of the Pharisees and Sadducees." He pulled back with weary eyes and retired to his tent.

James bowed his head. "Sometimes I forget. I get so caught up in the moment, and I forget."

"It's not only the seed of the Kingdom that spreads." I surprised myself by speaking. Heads swiveled in my direction, and I cast my eyes to the fire Jesus had begun. It was sputtering but strong. Bending, I added enough brush to fuel it without snuffing it out.

"False teaching . . . deceptive ideas . . . they must be recognized so they can be abandoned. I confess I'm still learning what needs to be uprooted in my own mind." I grew quiet, contemplative as I poked at the flames. When I glanced up, they were all watching me without a single look of judgment. In fact, they seemed to be waiting for me to say more.

"I am a daughter of the Sadducees." With some difficulty, I swallowed hard and made myself continue. "I was trained to take pride in my lineage—even to look down upon others whose station in life differed from mine. I've seen firsthand how deceptive ideas can become family legacy, false views so engrained in our way of life that we need someone outside us to unveil the truth. I think . . . I think my father was beginning to understand this. That sometimes false ideas must be shaken from us. Sometimes this is what's needed in order to make room for the truth."

Tears escaped as I cradled the precious memory of Dalia in aching hands—her startling faith in the midst of adversity, her tenacious belief in the presence of God, and her unrelenting hope that I would come to love Him with an open heart. My sister had kept my heart open when otherwise it might have ended up as hard and trodden as a footpath.

Mary sank to her knees by my side, resting an arm about my shoulders.

I swiped at my face, sniffed, and lifted swollen eyes to the others. "I . . . I had a sister."

This confession was one I'd been forbidden to state. The open and honest truth I'd been forced to conceal—unable to lay claim to Dalia and hating myself for it.

"Her life . . . and death . . . forever altered me. It was she who taught me courage and faith, and I think—I *know*—she is the reason my heart was ready for his message." I glanced to where Jesus lay sleeping. "In the end, sorrow indeed has lessons that are hers alone to teach."

"That's a deep thought." Mary sighed. "And a true one. Sorrow can crack us open like a nut from its shell. I am so sorry for your loss."

Gratefully, I leaned into Mary's embrace as the disciples began talking in hushed tones for the sake of the sleeping Jesus, whose gentle snores could be heard from his tent. Behind Mary, movement caught my eye. It was Simon, turning brusquely away, walking into the growing night and away from the tender flame.

THIRTY

FALL 30 AD

"I heard your name in court."

The wind whipped Chuza's dire words away as alarm stirred in my belly. He stood with shoulders hunched against the gusts, jaw set as he watched Asher train a young stallion in the field behind our stables.

Ever since that night beneath the stars when I'd spoken so directly, we'd avoided each other. I could hardly bear to be in his presence for the confusing swirl of frustration and longing it produced, and he seemed just as eager to stay apart, shame coloring his cheeks every time our eyes met. When he did need to speak to me, it was always in the presence of others. Perhaps he no longer trusted himself to be alone with me.

"What did you hear?"

Chuza's gaze remained fixed on the field. "Someone noted your presence with Jesus' disciples, wondering if you were one of them. I'm sure it's been noted before, but this time the . . . intimacy of your connection seemed to be apparent. There is now talk that you consider yourself to be one of them—not just a patroness but an actual disciple."

A disciple, a follower of Jesus' new way of living and being. Yes, I wanted this role and did not want to hide it. But I also did not want to be foolish and endanger Jesus or the infuriating man by my side.

"What would you have me do?" I whispered, and when he remained silent, I wondered if he'd even heard me. Finally, I forced myself to look at him, study his strong profile. He'd heard me.

His deep-set eyes darted across the field, landing on Asher, the steed, the tree line in the distance—everything but me. He'd recently trimmed his beard. I could see the sharp line of his jaw and . . . were those strands of white hair? He was only thirty-two. My gaze softened as it traveled up his head where yes, there were a few additional hints of white at his temple. He worked his jaw slowly, tasting his words, testing each one before releasing it, eyes closing as his head bowed with acceptance.

When he turned to me, there were deep, furrowed lines on his brow. *Oh, husband.* He was aging before my eyes—he who was still so young and strong and vibrant. He must have seen the concern in my face, and it seemed to anguish him even more, for he drew in a quick breath and turned away from me again.

"I once told you that I would not make you abandon Jesus and his teachings for my sake. My own safety—" He broke off, glanced down at his feet. "My own safety does not concern me, but you—" He extended a hand but caught himself before it reached me, pulling it back just in time. He'd honored my words that night beneath the stars. He had not touched me once since then.

"I'm worried over your safety," he said. "I've considered asking you to withhold your involvement and active support, at least for a time."

My lips parted, preparing their protest, but he was speaking again.

"But I won't make that request of you. Partly because I understand your desire to support Jesus, but also because Herod has larger concerns at the moment. There may be talk about you in court, but he isn't listening. This business with Gabalis, yes, but Pilate's brutality is quickly consuming Herod's attention and efforts."

The Roman prefect of Judea was proving to be as ruthless as the man who'd appointed him. He'd massacred some Galilean pilgrims during Passover, mixing their blood with their sacrifices and throwing the nation into an uproar. I'd been present when people came to Jesus with the news. In their eyes was the question I'd held in my heart since childhood: *Why?*

Why the suffering of the innocent? Why did such a horrific thing happen to these people?

They came to Jesus with the question but had already formed an answer. Surely it was those pilgrims' sin. It had to be. It was the only explanation that made sense of a senseless situation. As was his way, Jesus received their news with tenderness and strength.

"Do you think those Galileans were worse sinners than anyone else? Is that why they suffered?" He'd exposed their reasoning, laying it upon the table for examination. And then he'd torn it apart. *"No! Not at all! Unless you repent of your sins and turn to God, you too will perish."*

He'd redirected the focus from *why* to the immediate concern of the state of their hearts. All of us sinners—all of us in need of mercy—none worse than another.

The wind was growing stronger. Chuza turned his back to it, eyes watering, body shielding me from the wind's relentless bite. "Herod is furious that pilgrims from his region were treated in such a manner. He's thought of little else. And now, with Pilate's latest overstep, Herod's anger is compounded."

"You mean because of the votives?"

Chuza nodded. "We are preparing to travel to Jerusalem with Herod and many others to confront Pilate about them."

I'd heard the recent reports of how Pilate had placed gilded votive shields in Herod's Jerusalem palace. These shields, although not bearing the image of the emperor, contained inscriptions claiming his divinity.

"Do you believe his anger with Pilate is enough to distract him from Jesus?" Without thinking, I moved closer to avoid the wind that tore through the field, battering Chuza's back and throwing his hair into chaos. "I respect your concern, but perhaps I am safer than you think despite the court gossip. Besides, as you said, Herod will be out of the region for quite a while."

Out in the field, the stallion lunged, but Asher held his ground, waiting for him to calm. The muscular animal snorted and stomped, steam rising from his flanks.

"Yes, I'm hopeful that with Herod so distracted and out of the region, you will be safe to continue your involvement, but, Joanna . . ."

At the sound of my name, I turned back to Chuza and froze. I was nearly in his arms, standing sheltered and warm beneath his hunched form. Steadfastly he kept his hands at his sides, but his eyes were soft.

"Joanna." My name on his lips was sweet.

My gaze moved rapidly from his tempting lips to his serious brown eyes, throat running dry with embarrassment.

"Please be careful." Not since Machaerus had he sounded so plaintive, not since he'd wept the words, *"I cannot bear to lose you."*

He loves me. The knowledge was a splinter deep within the hand, throbbing and painful, obviously and undeniably present.

Beyond us, Asher was exerting pressure on the stallion, who tugged and whinnied. With each movement in the desired direction, Asher released some of the tension, voice raised to be heard above the driving wind.

My eyes flicked away and then back to Chuza's intense gaze as he awaited my response. "I-I will," I assured him. "As you should be careful . . . husband." My voice caught on the last word, for we did not often address each other in those terms.

Slowly, his shoulders eased, gaze drifting to my mouth, lingering there. "That's all I ask."

Out in the field, the stallion was beginning to grow impatient, pulling at his reins with loud whinnies. Chuza tore his eyes from me, cleared his throat, and moved away, calling out to Asher, "That's enough for today."

Asher nodded and began to lead the horse back to the stable.

With a deepening sadness, I watched Chuza stride briskly away. He would be gone for so long. Not only was he aiding with the delicate negotiations in Jerusalem, but he was meeting with former associates at the behest of Herod, gathering as much information as he could about Gabalis. What was he clinging to so desperately that he would deny himself my love?

Turning to leave, I caught sight of Eden. She stood silently against the stone wall surrounding the field, eyes trained on Asher as he neared the stables. He was so focused on the stallion that he didn't see Eden where she stood in the shadow of the wall. I recognized the fire in her face—that awful, aching hopefulness for something so close at hand it hurt.

THIRTY-ONE

A steady influx of bizarre dreams began plaguing my nights. Dalia, hiding in Gabalis, waiting for Chuza to find her. Chuza, detained in Jerusalem, forced before Pilate to answer impossible questions. Jesus, trapped in Machaerus, searching for John. In every dream I was alone, observing the unfolding events with no power to help, no power to rise up and come to anyone's aid.

The worst dream, however, was the one in which Herod's police followed me straight to Jesus, where they captured him and threw him in the prison beneath the Sepphoris palace.

"Abba!" I would awaken calling out to my Father in heaven, sweat coating my body, sheets twisted and damp.

News arrived from Jerusalem. Pilate had refused the Jewish delegation's demands that he remove the votive shields from Herod's palace, most likely relying upon his connection to Sejanus.

"We've written to Emperor Tiberius," Chuza solemnly relayed. Hidden in his words was a calm assurance of success. "I, along with others, have urged Herod to involve Antonia. He is, after all, now related to her through marriage." Tiberius' sister-in-law was beloved and above reproach, a woman both the emperor and Sejanus would listen to.

As Chuza was delayed in Jerusalem, I wrestled with worry, unable to shake the effects of the dreams nor the memory of my husband from the last time I'd seen him—hair whipping in the wind, body hunched, eyes desperately sad and full of love. *"Please be careful."*

◆

Eden rested a hand on my knee as our litter jostled along the road. Gratefully, I took her hand in my own. She'd been unusually quiet lately. Whenever I tried to talk openly with her, a wall went up. She listened, but with none of our former intimacy, and offered very little of herself in return. If I hadn't been so worried over Chuza and Jesus, I would have pushed harder. Guilt that I hadn't now laced my heart as I squeezed her hand.

"Eden, what is happening with you?" I murmured and watched as she hastily constructed her walled defense.

She pulled her hand from mine, averting her face. "What do you mean?"

"You seem subdued. Is it Asher? Has he broken your heart?"

Eden shifted farther away from me. "Let's not speak of it."

"But—"

"Please."

Her voice was low and authoritative, a new tone she'd never taken with me before.

Color rose in her cheeks as irritation flared in my chest, but as quickly as the new emotion rose, I let it go. This woman had long been more of a sister than handmaid, and with our joint belief in Jesus, that made her a true sister. I would not hold this against her.

"Very well. We won't speak of it." I turned away, sensing her regret as she threw furtive glances my way.

The sun was low in the sky as the air swelled with evening sounds—carts wending along dirt streets; women chattering on their way home from the well; children shrieking in play during the last light of day; and over, under, and permeating it all was the clear scent of fish.

We'd entered Capernaum.

It'd been weeks since I'd seen Jesus or anyone from his company. Susanna had sent word that she was stopping at Capernaum on her way home from Caesarea Philippi and urged me to meet her there.

I instructed the servants in the direction of the inn where I knew Susanna would be staying. When we arrived, however, her servants informed us that she was with the disciples at the home of Peter and Andrew.

"We should retire for the night," Eden urged me. "You can join them in the morning."

Despite my exhaustion, I had no desire for bed, where I would simply toss and turn under the weight of terrifying dreams. "I can't wait. I'll go now," I told Eden, ignoring her protests, leaving her to unpack our things while I departed.

Ever since Chuza had left and the dreams had begun, I'd been tightly bound. The thought of being in Jesus' company tonight promised sorely needed refreshment.

Exiting the inn, I hastened my steps into the growing night, bumping into a man who lingered just outside. Mumbling an apology, I picked up my pace as the sun dipped below the horizon and darkness yawned through the emptied streets.

My thoughts were focused on my destination, and I did not hear the footfalls behind me until they grew close enough to become obvious. I stopped, heart pounding. The steps stopped as well.

I glanced over my shoulder in time to see a dark form blending into the shadows.

I continued on, this time more slowly and with ears at the alert.

After several long moments, I twisted again. I didn't see anyone but detected soft scraping as of feet moving quickly over a rocky surface.

Fear from my dreams now spilled into the dark streets of Capernaum as I surged forward with faltering breath.

Rounding a corner, I saw light flowing into the street from Peter's courtyard. I was so close.

"I would never do anything to endanger Jesus."

My own words rang in my head as did Judas' response.

"Perhaps not intentionally."

Beyond that pool of light, I could imagine the group of men and women gathered around a fire, a conglomeration of followers whose lives Jesus had upended and transformed. They were the closest thing to family I'd experienced in a long time, and my heart yearned to be with them, even while my steps slowed to a halt.

Foolish—I'd been recklessly foolish. What had I been thinking leaving alone this late at night? I'd allowed urgency to be in Jesus' presence to outweigh common sense.

I would return to the inn. If someone was following me, their reason could hardly be benign, and I would not risk leading them straight to Jesus where he was relaxing, safe and unguarded.

Loath to return the way I'd come and possibly run straight into my pursuer, I darted down a side road, seeking an alternative route back. There was no more shuffling behind me and slowly my breath evened as I made another turn and then another.

But now I was lost.

The hour was late, and the streets were empty. Even though I was now convinced no one was following me, I was still alone at night, in a vulnerable position that I never should have placed myself in. *Oh, Joanna. Foolish, foolish.*

Making a swift decision, I darted down another street. The moon made for poor lighting, its silver curve insufficient to guide my steps. The darkness and my own increasing alarm disoriented me until I found myself thoroughly lost in what appeared to be the fish market. I paused, heart thudding painfully in my breast.

Someone else was breathing.

No, it can't be. I whirled, glancing wildly about but seeing no one.

Blindly, I ran down the first road I saw and came face-to-face with a stone wall that stretched impossibly high. The only way out was to go back.

Lips pinched tightly, I drew a long breath in through my nose, held it, released it. Swiftly, I backtracked. When I reached the fish stalls, I saw him.

He was standing utterly still and silent in the shadows of one of the stalls. If I hadn't already detected his presence a moment before, I never would have seen him, but my awareness was heightened, drawing my eyes immediately to his bulk.

The man I'd bumped into at the inn.

Seeing that I'd spotted him, he peeled himself from the wall. I stood trembling in the road, surrounded by rank-smelling baskets, and watched as the man stopped short, face cloaked in shadows.

"Who are you and what do you want?" My voice was strong even though I felt as gutted as a fish.

"You are a slippery one, I grant you that." His voice was deep and unfamiliar.

"Who are you and what do you want?" I repeated the words, slow and firm.

He shifted, and the scant moonlight slanted across his face. "Such an authoritative tone for someone who is caught."

"Who sent you to follow me?" My voice wavered, and quickly I spoke again, strengthening my tone. "Your clothes denote you as a hired man. What job are you to complete? And for what purpose?"

Fury flashed across his angular features. "You would do well to consider your own position rather than question my own."

I attempted to push past him, but he snagged my elbow in a large hand. "We're not finished here."

Gritting my teeth, I yanked myself free, taking two steps back.

He was shaking his head, muttering under his breath. "He's not paying me enough for this."

A name separated in my mind like oil on water, rising to the surface. "Othniel?"

The man's gaze flickered in surprise. I'd been right.

Othniel, who was stationed many miles away in Jericho. Othniel, whose attack on my husband had been undermined. What did he hope to gain by this new tactic?

"Inform your master that I am not afraid of him."

"You dare to cross Herod twice—once at Machaerus and now in your blatant support of a blasphemous man. You say you are not afraid. You should be."

"*This* is what your master hopes to bring to Herod's attention?" I laughed to keep from crying. "Our king has larger interests to concern himself with. It's your master who is small enough to worry about who I see or where I go." My words were strong, but I was shaking and trying hard to hide it.

The man snorted in disgust, grabbing my arm once again. I sucked in a sharp breath and gazed into the face that loomed above mine.

But it wasn't his face. It was another's, with eyes so black they were endless. I was trapped in a moment that had shattered and re-made me. Memories from the theater resurfaced with a vengeance.

"Let me go," I begged as I clawed my way upward, out of that memory, back toward the light.

"You talk big for such a small woman. Your bravado is sorely misplaced, adrift as you are between two worlds. Take care of yourself and that loose tongue."

"You have no right to touch me. Let me go."

"You heard the woman. Let her go." Out of the shadows

stepped a large figure. My breath caught in surprise as Simon approached us. His face was a storm on the Sea of Galilee—clouded and roiling. Swiftly, he reached my side and clapped a strong hand on the man's shoulder, fingers digging into flesh, pushing him away from me.

The man dropped my arm, swinging his own up in a calculated move, coming into contact with Simon's wrist and breaking his hold.

Simon reacted immediately, roughly shoving the man backward and inserting himself between us. "Oh, you don't want this fight. Trust me." He released an airy laugh full of ease, rolling his shoulders once, twice, completely unperturbed as he bunched his fingers into fists.

The man pivoted to approach me from a different direction. Simon merely moved with him, bouncing lightly on the balls of his feet, fists still clenching and unclenching. "Back away, turn around, and leave. Immediately."

Simon's stance, however, suggested he'd rather the man stay and fight.

The man growled deep in his throat. "This doesn't concern you."

"This absolutely concerns me. This woman is my family."

Confusion flickered in the man's eyes as he looked from Simon to me and back again. "You know who this is, don't you?"

"I know exactly who she is. She is my sister, and if you have a problem, you will direct it to me."

The man wavered, clearly unsettled by Simon's response.

"Leave!" Simon barked, taking a step forward and then another.

The man stepped back.

"Report to your master that Joanna is far from adrift and that he will have a fight if he goes after her again."

The man glared at Simon, gave him one last, long look, before spitting in the dust at his feet and striding off.

"Ha!" Simon crowed. "What a coward." He smashed his fist

into his palm, needing to release the fight in him. When the man was out of sight, he turned to me. "Are you okay?"

Whatever look was on my face caused his own to soften. All the fight in his eyes drained away, leaving behind a new openness.

Simon spread his arms wide, but I was already halfway in them, clutching him tightly. He smelled of sweat and smoke and felt like safety. I exhaled shakily, long and deep, in the arms of my brother.

THIRTY-TWO

The firelight flickered off concerned faces as I sat beneath a warm blanket and tried to still the trembling in my limbs. I was safe. Hours later, and my body still refused to believe it, tensing at every sound.

Simon had been keeping watch, had caught me turning from Peter's door and followed my frantic flight, losing me multiple times as I'd dodged and weaved my way through Capernaum. When he'd found me and intervened, he'd been so confident. But now, as he sat by the fire, his face seemed to release its strength, his expression finally indicating distress.

By my side, Susanna sat rigid, her hand in my lap, fingers threaded through mine. From the moment I'd arrived, she'd not let me go.

"I had no idea you were being followed," Mary softly stated from where she sat on my other side.

"I didn't know either. Please believe me!" With a low cry, I dropped my face into my palm. "Oh, I would never do anything to endanger you! To endanger *him*. Never."

"We know." Simon's voice was low and hoarse.

The gathered crowd was solemn. I longed for Jesus' presence, longed to directly assure him of my love and loyalty, but he was away with Peter, James, and John, and no one knew when they would be back.

"My husband has been carefully tracking Herod's attention." I sniffed, heart desperately eager for Chuza. "But I'm afraid both of us underestimated Othniel's vindictive nature."

"I don't think it's vindictiveness." Susanna whispered so quietly that I was the only one who heard.

"What do you mean?" I whispered back.

Susanna's face whipped up, surprised she'd spoken aloud. "He's very much like I used to be—utterly consumed with himself." She gazed back down at her lap. "God protected me from my own nature by humbling me and joining me to a man who would urge me toward righteousness, but Othniel . . ." She shook her head sadly. "Othniel's nature has done nothing but feed upon itself. He wants the best of everything at any given moment, and he'll do what he needs to get it. I'm sure he cannot stand seeing you thrive without him, Joanna."

"Hired or not, I'm shocked that man dared to confront you, an influential woman of the court," Mary muttered. "Does he have no honor or sense of self-preservation? Isn't he worried what you might do?"

"If he was hired by Othniel, it doesn't surprise me," Susanna answered in my stead. "He attracts people who are like him."

"And Othniel certainly doesn't see me as any sort of threat," I finished.

"He needs to watch himself," Susanna continued. "Herod is well aware of Othniel's nature. He keeps him in court out of deference to his father."

Simon lurched to his feet. "Herod is shrewd and ruthless. I'm sure he sees himself in the young man." He strode out of the light, hand on his hip.

"Be that as it may, he has enough on his mind with Pilate's offenses against the nation." I shook my head. "No, his mind is fully occupied with Rome at the moment. Let us hope that Othniel's attention span is as short as his temper."

From where he paced outside the circle, Simon groaned. "Even though Herod is furious with Pilate at the moment, he is too willing to cooperate with Rome."

"You speak as someone with personal experience," I stated softly. Simon stopped pacing opposite me, the fire dancing between us. My breath caught at his expression, for I recognized it, knew that place of deep and relentless pain.

"My uncle—" His voice broke. "I don't speak about this much." He glanced at others around the fire. "Not many people know this part of my history."

Everyone sat alert, waiting.

"Some boys know from an early age that active resistance against Rome is their destiny, but that wasn't so for me. I come from a family too poor and desperate to think or act beyond attaining the next meal. My uncle began thieving as a way to survive. During one of his robberies, the landowner caught him and gave chase. The man fell from a roof, and my uncle stopped to assist him, but the man was already dead. My uncle's moment of compassion was his undoing, for he was apprehended. It didn't matter that he hadn't spilled the man's blood. He was tried and condemned, held responsible for killing the man. Herod handed him to Rome. He was crucified with others along the road west of Sepphoris."

Simon stopped speaking, breathless and with a heaving chest. The silence that followed was flooded with sympathy.

"And that compelled you," I murmured. "It compelled you into the life of a Zealot?"

Simon met my gaze across the flames, his eyes full of sorrow and regret. "I've committed worse crimes than my uncle." His confession, surprising and humble, left his lips quickly. "And yet, here I remain—not only alive but forgiven!" He shook his head, eyes still holding mine but seeing through me to something beyond. "Chosen, of all things!" His voice rose with incredulity. "But some days the gift of it is lost on me as I remember what my uncle endured and what I myself deserve but didn't receive."

Compassion warmed me like a long swallow of hot tea—burning, searing my chest. "You and I . . . we're not so different, Simon."

His eyes refocused on me.

"I know what it's like trying to live after someone you love has died, trying to find hope among the injustice." I held his gaze, honoring his honesty by offering my own. "Learning to live with the weight of the gift."

I shifted my eyes to Mary. "I spoke once of a sister." I expected pain to sear my heart as the words left my lips but instead, I was lifted up—sustained.

"She was afflicted by a disease from an early age, cast aside by our family for fear of what others would say. Her disease shook her, immobilized her. She would crash to the ground and could never remember anything afterward. She suffered for something utterly out of her control while I—I lived unscathed."

I stopped for breath, then made myself continue. "Her life taught me what true courage looks like. It's smaller and more pervasive than one would think. It looks like hope in the heart of a girl." I closed my eyes, seeing Dalia's face once again. "She believed each of us had a purpose, planted where God intended us to be."

Opening my eyes, I looked at Simon, who was blurred behind my tears. "Like your uncle, whose life was taken abruptly, her life came to an end while mine . . . mine continues on. And here I am, still learning what it means to be brave, to live out the gift of life."

"I know what it's like to be cast aside." Mary's voice was tender. "Did she have someone to love her?"

"She lived in Gennesaret with my aunt and uncle. They took her in when my parents were unwilling to bring her to Sepphoris."

"I'm sorry to hear of your great loss." Matthew's eyes shone in the firelight. "Was it the disease that took her?"

"No." I dipped my head to study my fingers, which were still enmeshed with Susanna's. "There was an attack at the theater in Sepphoris. Only a handful of targets but many deaths in the aftermath."

Susanna sucked in a sharp breath. The hand in mine shook, but I held on tight.

"I recall the incident," Simon murmured.

"I'm sure we all do," Philip added. "News of it spread throughout Galilee."

"And down to Judea," Judas affirmed.

Andrew shook his head. "To think you were present . . ."

"I think of that day often and the pain it caused my Aunt Sarah. She left before I was even conscious, before I could say anything, before—"

I broke off then, pressing my face to Susanna's shoulder. She wrapped an arm about me, holding me tight as if to keep me together.

———— ✦ ————

There were no dreams that night, just a deep, deadened sleep. I was jarred from that sleep by a pounding on the door.

"Mistress! A visitor. He says it's urgent." More pounding.

Stumbling from bed, bleary-eyed and disoriented, I cracked the door open to find one of the innkeeper's servants outside.

"I'm sorry to awaken you at such a late hour, but he was adamant, said it couldn't wait until morning. He seemed so distressed that I let him into the kitchen."

"Who? Did he give a name?"

"No . . . I'm sorry, mistress. He was so distraught and urgent that I failed to ask."

"I'll be there as quickly as I can."

Closing the door, I found Eden upright in her bed, eyes as wide and confused as my own. We both dressed quickly, and as we lit lamps and followed the servant to the kitchen, I began to tremble.

"Eden, what if it's news about Chuza?" I whispered. "What if something has happened to him?"

"There is no use in imagining the worst," she responded with a firm tone and hand. "We will find out soon enough."

The kitchen was dimly lit, but even so, I recognized him immediately.

"Nathaniel?"

He spun at the sound of his name, one hand coming up to clutch at his hair, the other propped on a hip.

My earlier fear over Chuza shifted. "Nathaniel, is Jesus safe?"

Swiftly, I crossed the room, breath rushing from my body. "Tell me he is okay! Did the man who followed me find him?"

Nathaniel was shaking his head. "No, no, I'm sorry, I didn't mean to alarm you so."

He looked like he hadn't slept one bit since I'd seen him earlier in the evening.

"Then what could possibly be so urgent?"

"It's just . . . when you shared so openly with us tonight, I—" He broke off, eyes misting as they met mine. He'd listened attentively while I'd spoken, leaning forward, hands on thighs, body poised as if to stand, expression clenched and earnest.

This man had largely avoided my presence but now sought me out in such dramatic fashion, and my heart thudded hard.

"Joanna, I am from Cana, just five miles north of Sepphoris."

"Yes. Yes, of course I know where Cana is. I lived there myself until I was seven."

"When the attack happened, it affected us too. People from my town were present. Someone I knew was trampled, nearly killed."

"I don't see why you needed to wake me for—"

"Cana experienced an influx of travelers after the attack as some left Sepphoris and still others journeyed to it to be with loved ones."

"Nathaniel, I'm sorry if my past made you relive painful moments from your own, but—"

"Joanna, I think I saw your sister!"

I stared openmouthed at him. "Don't be cruel," I rasped. "That can't possibly be true."

"I didn't want to say anything in case I was wrong, but there is a deep unrest in my spirit, an urging, a fire." Nathaniel began to pace. "I saw some of the wounded. Some were just passing through on their way home. Others stayed. A woman and her daughter stayed many months while the daughter recovered, a daughter who experienced seizures that some said were a result from the attack."

I sat down hard on the ground in the middle of the dark kitchen. Eden sank onto her knees by my side.

"We . . . we still have some connections in Cana."

"Is it so impossible that your aunt stayed with them while your sister recovered?"

Impossible. Yes, impossible. And yet . . .

Nathaniel crouched on the ground, eyes alive and warm.

"You . . . you saw Dalia?" My voice was small, nearly frightened. The hope was too powerful, too big. It would undo me.

Nathaniel rested a hand on my shoulder. "Tall and slender with unusual hair, ruddy in color, like—"

"Hair like honey."

A slow smile spread across Nathaniel's face. "Like honey," he murmured.

My heart dipped at his next words, dipped and then soared like the swift, up, up with a wild, mounting hope on its wings.

"Joanna, your sister is very much alive."

Thirty-Three

"My help comes from Yahweh, who made heaven and earth. He will not let you stumble; the one who watches over you will not slumber."

I was a sleepy seven-year-old watching my mother stroke my sister's hair on the night before she left her.

"Yahweh keeps you from all harm and watches over your life. Yahweh keeps watch over you as you come and go, both now and forever."

"What if He doesn't?" I'd sat up in bed, staring at Dalia's slumbering form, panic clutching my young heart. *"What if He doesn't watch over her?"*

Ima had weaved her hand in and out of Dalia's curls, refusing to meet my gaze, refusing to speak. Perhaps not knowing the answer.

The first night back home, I sequestered myself in my room. Chuza was still away and wouldn't be back for many more days. My heart and mind flew to him, then to Dalia, back to him, and then to Susanna, churning my mind into an uproar that expressed itself through furious pacing.

For weeks I'd investigated Nathaniel's story, traveling first to Gennesaret, where I discovered that Dalia had returned and remained with Aunt Sarah until three years ago upon Aunt Sarah's death. Afterward, she'd left, accompanied by a young scribe named Judah and his sister, Tirza.

No one could tell me with certainty where they had gone. Some said to relations in Caesarea Philippi, while others claimed they had gone in search of a physician in Antioch—a large, bustling city many miles north of us in Syria. Either way, they had never returned.

"To think of her alone, without family," I'd worried to Susanna.

"It sounds as if these friends are as good as family to her," she'd soothed.

Since Caesarea Philippi was closer, about thirty miles north of the Sea of Galilee, I journeyed there first, accompanied by Susanna. After a few fretful and frustrating days, our errand proved more difficult than hunting for a gnat in a lion's thick mane.

"Manaen has connections in Antioch," Susanna had assured me. "Go home; rest. I will see what he can do."

Rest? There could be no rest, for Dalia was alive in the world but still lost to me.

"Do you think they knew?" I'd asked Eden as we'd journeyed home, weary and ragged.

She hadn't needed to ask what I meant. "Someone must have known the truth and concealed it from both you and Dalia, otherwise you would have sought each other."

Had my parents lied, or were they, themselves, deceived?

Abba! My heart continued to cry to my Father in heaven as I wrestled with how to view my earthly parents.

Feverishly I paced my room. It was just as well that Chuza was still away. If he was here, I would not have been able to keep my distance. I needed comfort and longed for it from him.

A knock sounded at the door, stalling my frantic movement. Eden entered on quiet feet, head bowed. She carried a tray of food that she slid onto the table. "Any news?" Her voice was soft and pained.

"Nothing yet, but it's too soon for Manaen to have found anything." I gnawed at my nail, sat at the table, then stood again. "I'm wondering if Judah, a scribe by trade, is connected to one of the synagogues there. Perhaps that could be a place to start."

"Take some refreshment, mistress. You need it. You'll make yourself sick."

She was right. I'd already lost weight in the past few weeks. I plucked a round of bread from the tray and took a bite, but it turned to dust in my mouth. I dropped it and sat down hard, hands flying to my face.

Eden remained silent by the door. As a soft sob escaped her lips, I raised my head in alarm. She stood small and shaking, grasping her elbows in a tight embrace, shoulders hunched.

"Are you missing Dalia tonight too, or is it something else?" I slipped from the chair and to her side, pulled her hands free, held them in my own. "I can't remember the last time we talked in depth, and I'm sorry for that. I've been so self-absorbed. For a long time now."

"No, mistress. You do not need to apologize."

"But I do, Eden. I'm sorry."

At my apology, her face seemed to crack open. She tugged her hands free, arching away from me.

"What's wrong? Won't you tell me? Please, Eden. You're like a sister to me." I pushed the words out as my throat tightened. "I haven't told you that before, but I should have. You're like a sister to me, Eden. Please talk to me."

My words, rather than bringing comfort, seemed to heighten Eden's distress, as she dropped her face into her hands with a wail. "Oh, that's the problem, that's the problem! You're like a sister to me too."

"How is that a problem?"

"Because I cannot abandon you! I won't!" Her eyes were deep and languid as she lifted her face to me. "You are my family."

"I feel the same—"

"And you've already lost so much. Your parents, your sister—" She broke off and bit her lip. "And so I told him no. I told him no!"

"Who? No to what?"

"He wanted a family, and he wanted it with me. A whole slew of children. As many arrows as our quiver could hold, he said! But I told him no, and now he refuses to look at me. I-I've hurt him so deeply, and he will never ask again. Never."

She dropped her face back into her hands with a low sob.

"Asher?" My voice squeaked with confusion and alarm. "But why would you turn him down? Marrying him wouldn't separate us."

"He purchased his freedom." Eden gnawed at her lip with flushed cheeks, eyes jumping to and from mine. "Master Chuza has agreed to lease land to him west of Sepphoris."

"Oh, I see." I grew solemn, contemplative as I gazed at her.

She still wasn't meeting my eyes. "I would be the wife of a tenant farmer, unable to serve as your maid anymore."

"You would give up your future with Asher for me?" I shook my head, amazed, before pulling her into a snug embrace, bowing my head next to hers, and breathing in slow and deep. "I've not felt so loved in quite a long time."

She let out a low cry and clung to me. "I won't abandon you!"

"You wouldn't be abandoning me."

"I made a pledge to you."

"You are a freedwoman. You can do as you like, and I won't hold it against you. Eden, this is not an ending."

She pulled back, and I grasped her arms tightly, peered into her face. "This is another new beginning. Take it with joy. Marry him."

"But I've hurt him. He won't ask—"

"The man will take you, Eden. Go to him. Go to him even now with my blessing."

Eden shook her head in disbelief. "You truly think he will? And you wouldn't feel hurt or . . . alone? You're sure of this?"

Her plaintive question gave me pause. *Would* I be okay left alone in a marriage that wasn't a true marriage? The answer came softly and strong.

"I've never been surer. In fact, if you don't go to him, I will go myself and drag you with me." One eyebrow lifted. "You know I will."

A surprised laugh released from Eden's hopeful lips as her face grew radiant. My permission seemed to uncork a whole reservoir of admiration inside her that had been simmering, waiting, yearning to be released.

"He is the best of men," she said, breathlessly eager. "The life of a tenant farmer's wife will be different from anything this stonemason's daughter has known." Her big eyes widened, as did her lips in a large smile. "Master Chuza has been so kind to him . . ."

She continued on in a rambling, hopeful voice. I listened through tears and a growing numbness. How I loved this strong woman who'd been willing to give up her future for me. There was no doubt in my mind that Asher would receive her back and then she would start a new life away from me.

And I would be left with a husband whom I desperately loved but couldn't have.

Thirty-Four

Winter 30 AD

An owl swooped low, nabbing a mouse from the tall grass before departing in a flurry of feathers as I reached the distant pond on our land.

Since my conversation with Eden, I'd snuck out here night after night, finding solace in my smallness. This portion of our estate was far from the villa, its land still untended and teeming with life outside our control.

Asher had received Eden with deep enthusiasm. She would remain with me during the betrothal period, and then I would let her go.

My feet were bare and cold, my toes sinking into the softness of the ground as I neared the pond's edge and stared, once again, into the vast sky.

Somewhere, perhaps many miles away from here, my sister might also be looking up, up, and wondering.

Nearby, a cluster of almond trees was blooming, throwing their late pink and white blossoms out into the frigid world. So outrageous, their display, so provocatively hopeful and yet so brief. Blink, and the blooms were gone until next season.

A new year was coming in a few months and then Passover, and the weather would shift toward drier, warmer winds. But for now, the world was wet, the air was cold, and life was surging just beneath the ground. I dug my toes deep into the mud, and it moved to accommodate my feet.

The moon was low in the sky. I stared at it and fiercely fought to empty my mind, to think of nothing, to feel nothing—not one single thing. I pressed my hands to my heart and stood utterly still.

Time passed, and living things moved about me. An animal lapped at the water nearby. From the sound of its footfall, it was large. I remained quiet, not even turning to see what it was, releasing my breath when it left.

Rain came suddenly and with no warning, or perhaps there had been signs, but I hadn't listened to them. It started, remained strong, and I let it pierce my tunic and soak the skin beneath.

I remained this way until the night deepened into a lovely black beneath the thickening and thunderous clouds, only moving once to tip my face upward so the rain had fuller access.

His voice was deeper than the distant thunder and more driving than the rain. It called for me with such ferocity my heart shifted in my chest, my eyes blinking open. I knew the voice and loved the man.

Chuza was coming for me.

His presence was an intrusion in all the right ways. His voice was warmth seeping into cold bones, and my body responded by turning, my eyes beginning their hunt.

The grass shifted noisily at his approach, slapping at his legs, flattening beneath his feet as he came barreling forward through the thick night. My searching eyes found him, lingered, softened.

He stopped at the sight of me. His steps, so urgent before, became slow, hesitant. His voice, when it came again, was soft and broken.

My name on his lips was music. As he came closer, his face became clearer. I watched his lips and longed to kiss my name right off them.

His eyes were wild with worry as the rain sluiced over his hair, his face, his body. Closer and closer he came until he'd snuck within arm's reach. He lunged at me like a dying man for water, snatching me back from the pond's edge, pressing me hard against his chest.

I pulled away and watched his lips move, full of words and fear. His arms were trembling. I snaked a hand up and rested it along the dip of his neck where it joined his shoulder, felt his sharp collarbone jut against my palm.

Had my life as I knew it been nothing but a lie?

Perhaps I could hold onto this man, this real man in my arms. Perhaps I could find truth with him.

He buried his face in the side of my neck, his lips to my throat. A shudder passed through his body. He needed me to return to him. Like the roaming swift finally coming to rest in her cliffside nest, he needed me to return.

I held him, kissed his shoulder, inhaled his scent, and exhaled the words I'd been holding onto for a lifetime.

"I have a sister."

THIRTY-FIVE

With wide and hungry eyes, Chuza gazed at me. He'd returned home from his travels late to find my door yawning open, room empty, servants ignorant of my whereabouts. His search had taken hours, and now that he'd found me, his expression remained aching and broken.

He'd carried me home, attempting to leave me in my room so Eden could tend to my needs, but I'd clung to him, refused to be parted, refused for anyone else to help me, and so he'd taken me to his own room. Vaguely I'd registered his shaking hands as he'd gently peeled off my wet garments, keeping his eyes averted as he slipped one of his own tunics over my shivering frame.

Now I sat by his side on a low couch, burrowed deeply in a blanket with a cup of hot tea in hand. Eventually, my chattering teeth began to settle, as did the numbness in my mind and body. I glanced down, noted the new tunic, then eased my eyes upward, heat simmering in my stomach as I stared directly into Chuza's face.

"What happened?" he whispered hoarsely. "Talk to me."

And so I did.

Pushing through embarrassment and the hollowness in my chest, I told him the pieces of my past that no one else knew.

The horrible, beautiful secret of Dalia. The unfairness, the faith, the fear, the loneliness. I told him the darkest pieces—the ones where I still wrestled with shame and guilt and had to surrender those feelings over and over to God. The theater, her death, the lies, the truth.

The truth—how necessary it was. From this moment on, I would be wholly committed to it. I would not bear lies in my life anymore. On my lips, in my life, from this moment on—the truth.

When I finally stumbled to a stop, Chuza took the cup from my hands and wordlessly gathered me into his arms. My mind was clearer now, body tensing out of habit, but I yearned for his comfort and so allowed myself to melt into his embrace. He noted the moment my body relaxed and responded by drawing me even closer.

"I've searched for her." I spoke into his chest, voice muffled. "But all I can find is that she left with some friends over three years ago. Perhaps Caesarea Philippi or Antioch. No one is sure. I can hardly stand the idea that she is out there somewhere . . . without me."

I'd held myself together for endless weeks, but now that he was here, I allowed myself to fall apart. A sob clutched at my throat. Fisting Chuza's tunic in my hands, I pulled myself closer, speaking my words through a clenched jaw, pressing my face deeper into his breast. "This joy . . . knowing Dalia is alive . . . it's consumed by the thought that my parents intentionally lied."

Chuza ran his hand up and down my back in long, firm strokes as he spoke into my hair. "You feel betrayed by those closest to you."

"My parents made so many choices—some I know of and many that I do not. Some I understand—and many, many, I do not. They buried the truth, thinking that was love, but isn't love uncovering the truth and *fighting* for it?" I reared back with a ragged breath, searing his eyes with my own. "Shouldn't we lay

287

claim to the truth, grasp it boldly, tightly with both hands, refuse to let it go?"

Chuza's eyes roamed my features. "Lessons that sorrow has taught you," he whispered. Gently he ran long fingers over my brow, around my ear, trailing down my neck. "It pains my heart that you've had to learn so many."

"Jesus often speaks of his message of the Kingdom as seed." I was quieting now beneath Chuza's touch, leaning into his hand. "My father spoke of being shaken apart—like the hard soil from Jesus' lesson, the soil that needs tilling before it can receive truth." My breath caught. "Oh, Chuza . . . I'm afraid my parents . . . perhaps their hearts were conflicted and the truth was choked . . ."

"You fear the truth fell among thorns for them." Chuza's eyes deepened with understanding.

"Yes," I breathed, easing into his arms and slipping my own about him, palms pressing into his back as I relished the feel of him solid and warm beneath my hands.

"From what you've described and I've observed, they seemed to wrestle with regret." Chuza's voice rumbled gently beneath my cheek. "People make choices for all kinds of reasons. I know from experience that sometimes people do the inexcusable because they think they have no other choice."

"But if they lied to me . . . How can I possibly forgive them?" All the desperate years thinking Dalia was dead stretched behind me like a wasteland. "It's impossible—all the years of unnecessary pain."

"Forgiveness often does seem impossible," Chuza admitted, leaning back to look at my face. "You have every right to be hurt and confused, but now you must decide what to do with it." Warmth pooled in his eyes as he placed a hand to my neck, threading his fingers into my hair as he cupped my jaw, traced its line with a thumb.

"Forgiveness is hard, but I know that being the one who *needs* the forgiveness is also a place of pain." His brow furrowed as his next words seemed to stick in his throat. "And if that forgiveness never comes . . . well, that's its own torment. You will learn to forgive them—in time. You must release them from whatever untruths they knowingly or unknowingly harbored. You must do this for yourself."

My mind was soft and unguarded, warmed through by the blanket and my husband's comforting words and embrace. I hardly cared about anything else. He was pulling away, hand dropping from my face, and the small distance between us was too great.

I loved him deeply and dearly. This was the truth. And I would fight for the truth.

Grabbing his tunic, I pulled him back. His eyes flew wide at the look on my face. "Joanna—"

I stilled his startled mouth with a kiss. His lips were smooth and warm, just as I'd imagined.

Chuza tensed like an animal caught in a snare. My lips moved against his, slow and firm as I kissed him deeper, coaxing a response.

"Joanna," he murmured against my mouth, resistance slipping as his hands found my waist. "Joanna."

I silenced his fading protests.

With a groan, he scooped me into his lap and took over— kissing me back until I was breathless and gasping, with not a single coherent thought left in my head.

"N-no!" He pulled back as if coming up through deep water for air.

I tumbled from his lap as he jerked to his feet to stride agitatedly across the room. Scrambling upright, I tripped on the billowy folds of his tunic, which was laughably huge on me.

He had his hands laced behind his head, back turned to me.

"Chuza—" My voice cracked. There could be no going back, no avoidance or pretending we didn't love each other. Not this time.

I waited with suspended breath as he unlaced his fingers, dropped his hands to his side, and faced me. His eyes held an expression I'd never seen on him before.

"You said we would not touch again unless I'm willing to be open with you about this relationship." His voice was low and even. "You were right to demand this of me. Your desire for honesty has always . . . endeared you to me." He forced himself to hold my gaze. "I have not lied to you, Joanna. It's important that you know this. I've been open with you, but only up to a certain point. I've withheld the whole truth from you because I cannot bear . . ." He broke off, looking away from me.

I took a few halting steps until I stood before him.

"Our future must involve complete honesty. I see that now." He slid a hand to my waist, hidden beneath volumes of fabric. "You've lived under deception for far too long, and so even though I fear you will despise me, never view me the same way again, I will give that honesty. If . . . if you are willing to hear it."

"I am willing. I will listen," I whispered.

His eyes closed for a moment, hand slipping from my waist to scrub his face. "I need to begin by telling you more about my first wife."

An uneasy hole opened in my chest, but I bit my lip, waiting.

Sinking onto his bed, Chuza rested his forearms on his thighs, hands dangling between his knees. "We married young. It was arranged by our parents. Huldu was eager, but I was . . . reluctant." A sad smile played about his lips. "We struggled to conceive. Some couples pull apart during such a time, but it drew us together, and I came to love her."

Pain seared my heart afresh.

He was looking off into the distance now, his mind was carrying him far away from me. "Finally, we conceived, after years of barrenness. As her time drew close, the midwife speculated it was twins. Huldu was so large, so uncomfortable. I was helpless." He gazed down at his hands again, where they had begun twisting the fabric of his tunic. "Her time came early—not uncommon for twins."

He stood abruptly, striding halfway to the door, one hand on his hip, the other raking through his hair over and over. When he turned, the wild look in his eyes frightened me.

"This is the part I never wanted you—or anyone—to know."

"You can say it," I managed to whisper. "Whatever it is, you can say it to me."

His conflicted eyes plumbed the depths of mine. He nodded, settling into his decision.

"Huldu had just gone into labor when I received a summons from King Aretas himself. He wanted me to help oversee a delicate trade negotiation with Rome. I asked him to send someone else in my stead, given my personal circumstances." Chuza sank once more onto the edge of his bed, half-turned from me. "He said the personal circumstances were why he chose me."

"What?" Confusion furrowed my brow. "He asked you to leave *because* your wife was in labor?"

Chuza bit his lip. "It's the way of Aretas. He often vetted men by placing an impossible choice before them."

"He was testing your loyalty? But you're related!"

"Sometimes family needs the most testing," Chuza stated wryly. He sighed before continuing. "Huldu begged me to defy the king's orders. Her labor had just begun, and it was going well. There was no cause for alarm, but she was frightened. She was alone and frightened and wanted me near."

Chuza's voice wavered. "I pushed Aretas as much as I could, drawing upon our personal connection, but he was firm. Still . . . I could have defied him." He shook his head angrily. "I could have defied him and let the consequences fall as they may, but I didn't want to risk it. At best, he could have stripped me of my position, leaving me with nothing. At worst, he could have executed me, but I knew he wouldn't go that far." Chuza's words were tense and rushed. "I wasn't willing to risk losing everything—my position, my honor."

Crossing the room, I sat at his feet and peered up into his conflicted face. "You're punishing yourself." I rested a hand on his knee.

"You don't know the worst of it," Chuza stated, words hollow.

"Then tell me."

"I chose obedience to my king over my wife. It's a decision most men would have made and commended. I ignored her pleas for me to stay, and I left."

Understanding began to open in my breast, love filling in the cracks. "You talk as though you were cruel and heartless, but I know you are not so. You did not leave her happily or willingly." I opened my hand in invitation where it rested on his knee, but he kept his hands twisted in his lap.

"Perhaps not, but still . . . I mark this as the weakest moment of my life."

"Weak? You are the strongest man I know." My words tripped over themselves, hasty and earnest, embarrassment crawling up my neck and heating my cheeks. No matter that I'd recently been in his lap, lips tangled with his, somehow voicing my deep admiration left me with a new, uncomfortable vulnerability.

Chuza's eyes found mine, expression shifting rapidly like clouds crossing a stormy sky, love fighting like the sun to push through.

"Any strength or maturity you see in me comes after this moment." He was silent for a long while. "Word reached me while I was away that her labor lasted days. Everything crumbled after I left. The babes refused to come, and her labor became difficult."

He still would not take my hand, and so I took his, grasping it firmly between my own.

"She delivered one stillborn baby after days of excruciating pain. Hours later, she delivered the second. Also stillborn."

The air was snuffed from the room, everything close and tight. I gulped, clung to his hand.

"She died without me there to comfort her. She endured the unimaginable . . . alone." He shed no tears, as if the many years of grief had dried them up.

"My decision proved my loyalty to Aretas, who was strategically choosing men from his own court to send to Phasaelis. My greatest moment of weakness landed me here, and I promised myself—" He swallowed hard, hand limp in my own. "I promised myself that I would never make such a wrong decision again. I would never again choose a king over my wife."

The tang of salt was sharp on my tongue as tears wet my cheeks. I pressed my lips to the back of his hand. No wonder he'd taken such grave offense at the offer of Aretas' reward.

"I understand how one decision can lead to years of regret. I've asked for Huldu's forgiveness over and over again, but of course she has no way to extend it, and I am left to imagine her final moments. The midwife said she called for me unceasingly—no other words, only my name. When the first babe came and she held him by herself, did she hate me? Surely when the second babe came, she despised me. When she drew her final breath, was she cursing my name?" Chuza's voice was thin with aching.

"No!" I thought hearing of Chuza's first wife would be too hard to bear, but his uncertainty over Huldu's love was somehow worse. "No, you cannot think that!"

I lifted my face from his hand and raised myself to kneeling. "I cannot imagine that she called your name in hate." The words came swiftly and strong like an archer's arrow finding its mark.

"A woman does not call for her husband in her darkest moment from a place of hate—only longing. Deep and abiding longing."

Chuza's eyes, when they met mine, were filled with such tenderness that it transformed his handsome features into something beautiful. "You do not think she despised me?"

The lump in my throat was painful, and I was having a hard time speaking around it. A hard time, too, meeting his captivating eyes.

"Of course I cannot know for sure, but, Chuza . . . dark and desperate times have a way of clarifying the things we love. If she loved you the way you described, then how could she not remain so to the end?"

Slowly, Chuza lifted a hand to capture my face, eyes lingering on my hair, my cheeks, my brow—drinking in all of me. "I do not deserve your kindness."

I released a shaky breath, recalling my own reticence when confronted by the startling mercy of Jesus. "I don't think any of us deserves the kindness God Himself gives."

Chuza smiled, his face breaking open in a mixture of joy and sadness. "El-Olam," he said softly. "The everlasting God, free of time's constraints, preexisting and all-powerful. This deep sorrow led me to find solace in your Scriptures—in the God who responds to repentance with mercy." He shook his head in bewilderment. "A God who doesn't need appeasement or require proof of loyalty but simply desires a heart turned toward Him."

"A lesson that only sorrow could teach," I whispered. "I entered this union accepting that you loved your first wife. Is that why you made the commitment to chastity?" I forced the hard words out, laid them directly between us.

He withdrew his hand from my face, eyes dimming. "I did love her dearly, but I confess that my decision was driven by fear." He groaned and averted his face. "How could I risk binding another woman to myself? How could I risk bringing life into this world again? Another wife would mean children, and I can't . . . I can't . . ."

With a gentle hand, I turned his face to me, settling my palm below his cheekbone.

Chuza's eyes misted. "I would not use a woman to sate my thirst without giving her the reward of children, and so I committed myself to remaining unattached. When it became clear that maintaining such a status was unwise in my new position, I did the only thing I could think to do."

I moved my hand to his neck, felt his pulse pounding beneath my palm.

"I thought in being direct with you, I could spare you any hurt," Chuza murmured. "Oh, I was foolish, Joanna. I thought I could marry you without wanting you."

Shivers of pleasure drove straight to my heart, and I increased the pressure on his neck, pulled him closer.

He was refusing to look me in the eye and instead gazed upon my hair cascading over my shoulders. "When it became abundantly clear in my own mind that I loved you, I remained committed to the terms of our union. I never wanted to hurt you or draw you into a desire for something I could not fulfill. But then everything changed—Phasaelis, your healing. Everything was shifting so rapidly, and you're right—desperate times have a way of clarifying the things we love."

I rose to my feet, stumbling as my legs ached from being crouched for so long. I stood before him on tingling legs, heart pounding with a deeper love. "I am going to tell you the last words my sister told me," I whispered, sliding my hands into his hair the way I'd wanted to do from the very beginning. "'We were never meant to live under the tyranny of fear and grief.'"

Chuza's eyes slid closed. I sank my fingers deeper into his hair and pulled back gently so his face was laid bare to me.

"You are frightened to accept God's abundance, as was I once. You say His mercy is what drew you to Him, and yet you push that mercy back in His face."

He opened his eyes, surprise flickering in their depths.

"Chuza, He is also Yahweh-Rapha—the Lord who heals in both body and soul, pardoning our iniquities. You've affirmed this truth without claiming it for yourself. Or did you forget?" I dipped my face to murmur into his ear. "Did you forget that it was you who first urged me to place myself in the care of a God who keeps His word, who engraves us on His very hands?"

He tugged me into his lap and buried his face in my curls. "How can you love a man who abandoned his wife?"

My hands clutched his shoulders as I tried to steady my breath and voice. "I do not judge you, husband. How can I take the role of judge when it is God's alone? I cannot speak to the man you were then, only the man I know now, and he is a person of integrity."

Chuza lifted his face, and heat flooded my cheeks at the look in his eyes. Suddenly, the room was incredibly warm, even though it was cold and blustery outside. The rain had been pounding the walls the entire time, the wind tearing at the window, and now the outer turmoil settled within me at the continued look in his eyes.

"I don't know how to do this again," he whispered.

"We could learn—together."

"I don't want to fail you."

"You won't. You aren't."

"If you were to conceive . . ."

"Then we would be in God's hands—the babe and me." I reached for his face, forced his eyes to meet mine. "An infinite God who promises His presence is worth trusting."

Hope eased across his features, rousing itself from a long slumber, and then he was flushed, looking at me like a bashful youth who couldn't believe his own good fortune.

A small laugh escaped me, surprising and light.

He grasped my chin, thumb catching on my bottom lip, quieting my laughter as quickly as it'd come with a serious look that was now anything but youthful or cowed.

"Oh, I love you. I love you." His voice dipped impossibly low.

"I-I love you too."

Earlier I'd leapt at him, but now all I could do was hide my blushing face in his shoulder and weep tears of gratitude for words I never thought to hear and had convinced myself I didn't need.

He kissed my tears away as he'd done at Machaerus, and when I turned hopeful lips to him, he took them, firm and decisive.

What grace was this? A gift coming when least expected, a careful tipping into happiness.

Outside everything was wind and fury, but here, right here with him, was truth and mercy as we found what it meant to be fully seen and thoroughly loved.

THIRTY-SIX

SPRING 31 AD

Instructions came from the emperor for Pilate to remove the votive shields—immediately. The directive was harsh, for Tiberius downplayed emperor worship, especially in client states, and did not appreciate Pilate unnecessarily stirring up unrest.

The appeal to Antonia had neatly circumvented Sejanus, who was caught in his own nest of trouble. After years of manipulation, Sejanus had fallen under suspicion of sedition and was growing increasingly out of favor with the emperor. With the ire of the emperor and the waning of Sejanus' power, Pilate was doubly humbled.

More word came, this time from Chuza's connections. Far from overlooking the deep insult done to the royal family, King Aretas was simply biding his time, and yes, his eye was upon Gabalis. The question wasn't a matter of if but when, and Herod would do well to fortify the eastern Perean border.

Even as the political climate continued to shift, so did my own raw and wondering emotions. As Manaen called upon his contacts in Antioch, Chuza joined his efforts, expanding the search into Caesarea Philippi. "It's only a matter of time," he assured me.

I had entrusted my sister into Adonai's hands before, and now I would have to do so again.

After hearing of my encounter in Capernaum, Chuza insisted that I never leave home without an escort. It wasn't my own safety, however, that consumed me. Jesus continued to cause unrest wherever he went. As the devotion of his followers increased, the hatred from his enemies surged hot, rending my heart with worry.

Beneath the waiting and uncertainty, however, there was a new steadiness born from a growing trust and intimacy with Chuza. This man of hidden sorrows who had chosen to risk love with me was a source of delight in days that felt dark. His eyes, when they rested upon me, sang with joy. His mouth, when it opened, was full of endearments. His hands, when they touched me, trembled as if receiving a gift.

As his heart opened, I helped him toward deeper truth. He'd wrestled with his wounding, refusing to forgive himself for a choice he couldn't undo. It had taken the direct intervention of Jesus to release my tight grip on my own wound. With tears, I recounted to Chuza in greater detail that moment on the road, Jesus' hand on my wrist as he'd surrounded me with the gift of his knowledge, blessing, and forgiveness, as he'd released me to new life. How I wanted this for Chuza too!

The more we unraveled Chuza's pain and laid it bare for healing, the more I realized I needed Jesus' healing, again, for myself. My parents' choices, both the known and the unknown, were a weight I would have to release. I'd allowed Jesus access to the one wound, but now here was another, and what would I do with this newest hurt?

"You must release them from whatever untruths they knowingly or unknowingly harbored. You must do this for yourself."

As I gently held Chuza's pain, so he did with mine—each of us helping one another toward hope.

———— ✦ ————

We lay in bed, and he traced the tender skin along the inside of my arm. I shivered and pressed closer, head pillowed on his shoulder.

Passover was mere weeks away, and soon we would depart for Jerusalem. Each year, Herod spent the festival in the lavish Hasmonean palace just west of the Temple Mount. Knowing now how closely Othniel watched my movements, I feared I would need to stay near the palace rather than with Jesus. It was still unclear whether Othniel intended harm for me or for Jesus, but with the current political and religious climate, I would do nothing to draw more unwanted attention to the Messiah.

Jesus—his message and ministry, his strength and strong resolve—flooded my mind as I turned in my husband's arms.

"Will you come with me to meet him?" I whispered. "Perhaps after Passover, once we're all safely away from Jerusalem. Will you come meet Jesus?"

Lightly, he danced his fingers on my shoulder before replying. "Yes, I will come. The more you've spoken of him and the more reports I hear, the more I come to understand that a man like Jesus demands wholehearted commitment."

He paused and stretched, jostling my cheek from his shoulder as he rested an arm behind his head and turned to me. "I'm used to living circumspectly, and this Jesus . . . when I meet him, I will have to definitively give him my loyalty—or not. Lukewarm loyalty is worse than no loyalty at all."

I propped myself up on an elbow. "He will like you," I stated with conviction. "And once you meet him, you will see for yourself." My hand slid to his hip as I burrowed into his arms once more. "If only we can get through Passover," I muttered, words cracking open with fear. "He is adamant on going to Jerusalem, even though many have urged him to stay in Galilee. But Jesus is driven by a higher purpose. Like John, that purpose seems to prevail over everything else."

"He is surrounded by faithful followers," Chuza consoled. "They will urge him to exercise discretion." He paused, placing a gentle hand to my back, bracing me for his next words. "I've been saving some good news."

I stilled in Chuza's arms, breath catching, hope swelling in my chest—a caged animal, trapped and feral, ready for release.

"Dalia indeed spent time in Caesarea Philippi, but it appears to have been a stop on her way to Antioch. She was searching for a physician who is renowned in that region, and Manaen was able to learn his identity—a Greek God-fearer named Luke, who sometimes passes through Galilee on his way to the Holy City. I'm sure that's how your sister and her friends heard of him in the first place."

Chuza trailed his fingers from my shoulder down to my wrist and back again.

"It seems probable that he'll be in Jerusalem for Passover. I'll station myself in the Court of the Gentiles, make inquiries. I'll stay there however long it takes to find him. I'll—"

Twisting, I captured his earnest face in my hands and stilled his beautiful mouth with kisses. "I love you," I murmured against his lips and then made sure he had no chance or breath to respond.

THIRTY-SEVEN

"I took my troubles to Yahweh; I cried out to Him, and He answered my prayer." I spoke the psalm of ascent, carrying hope toward Jerusalem. The journey to the Holy City from Tiberias was laborious and long, but I held the songs of David in my heart and sang them back to the Lord along the road.

"I was glad when they said to me, 'Let us go to the house of Yahweh.'" Yes, glad—for there was much to anticipate on the other side of Passover. With the news from Gabalis and Rome, Chuza no longer felt the heat of Herod's testing, and the ease of that burden was evident. He walked taller, with a smooth brow and unfettered expression.

"I lift my eyes to you, O God, enthroned in heaven. We keep looking to Yahweh our God for His mercy." Eden joined me in song, fingers threaded with mine.

We would find her. We would find Dalia, bring her to Jesus, and she would experience in her body what I had—healing inside and out. For years Dalia had planted in tears, but now she would harvest with joy.

"Yahweh is good; He has cut me free from the ropes of the ungodly," Eden continued.

I closed my eyes and envisioned the Lord's deliverance and

protection surrounding His Messiah, His Promised One. Surely the Lord would not allow Jesus to come to harm—not while he was in the Holy City worshiping his Father.

"And now here we are, standing inside your gates, O Jerusalem," I whispered. Her beautiful walls and towers stretched to the sky, welcoming pilgrims in. And hourly they came—thousands upon thousands until the seams of the city were bursting.

We entered the Hasmonean palace late in the day, passing several contingents of Roman soldiers. The hope I'd experienced on the road flickered as cohort upon cohort of soldiers entered the Antonia Fortress north of the Temple Mount.

"So many," I murmured. "I wonder if Jesus knows that Rome has increased their presence this year."

The entire city was talking about Jesus' entrance—riding a donkey and accompanied by cries of "Hosanna!" Far from being discreet, he seemed to be gathering momentum. *Adonai, protect Your Messiah.*

"He's never before entered the city in such a way," I mused to Chuza. "Many have followed him from Galilee. All the disciples seem to believe his ministry is reaching its culmination."

But culminating to what? Jesus had never indicated he would attempt to wrest power from Rome. Instead, he'd preached about hearts that belonged to God. How would that vision come to completion in the presence of soldiers intent on silencing anything they deemed suspicious?

One relief was that Jesus was spending his nights in Bethany, a village two miles east of Jerusalem. But his days were spent in the city, and the worry settled in my stomach like a stone.

The first morning after our arrival, that uneasy feeling in my stomach had multiplied into a bout of sickness so intense, I was lightheaded. Chuza's face crumpled with concern as Eden plied me with water.

"You're warm," he muttered, pressing a hand to my cheek. "Is it something you ate? Or perhaps you've overtaxed yourself." He sat on the edge of our bed and caressed my back while I curled into a ball and moaned.

"I'll stay with you today," he said.

"No." I groaned as another wave of nausea hit. "Please go to the Temple as you'd planned. I'll be fine. This will pass."

Chuza's gaze flickered with concern, but he left for the Temple Mount. As soon as the door closed behind him, Eden took his place upon the bed, eyes widening with alarm as I gave in to the sickness. Instead of the expected relief, however, I felt worse. The nausea lingered, but even when it lifted, I stayed in my quarters, too exhausted to leave.

I awoke from a nap late in the afternoon as Chuza returned. His dark complexion now appeared ashen, and for a moment I wondered if perhaps we'd both been struck with the same ailment.

"It's Jesus," he exclaimed. "I saw him do things that no other man has done!"

Fear and joy mingled in my breast as I snatched Chuza's hand. He sank onto the bed next to me. "I was in the Court of the Gentiles, asking after our physician. The court is loud and raucous, cluttered with vendors. It's hard to think straight, let alone worship. But still I managed to be vigilant, when . . . when *he* came."

"Jesus?"

Chuza nodded, a dazed look in his eyes. "When he saw the vendors, he began violently overturning their tables."

"What?"

"He scattered the coins of the moneychangers and threw the benches of those selling doves. Money and animals were everywhere, people shouting, running to get out of his way, and above it all—his voice." Chuza drew a long breath. "He quoted Isaiah. He delivered the words with the authority of a king. He spoke them as if . . . as if they were *his own words*." Tears gathered in Chuza's eyes. "He said, 'My house will be called a house of prayer for all nations!'"

He turned to me then, dark eyes shimmering. "A Jewish rabbi standing in the middle of a courtyard full of Gentiles saying such things? He was defending our right to worship in God's house, and he quoted Isaiah with such . . . *intimacy*. I saw it, Joanna," Chuza rasped. "I know you've described it to me many times and I've witnessed the aftereffects in your own body, but now I've seen it with my own eyes. He began healing—the lame, the blind—he healed them all."

The wonder in his voice was unmistakable. I could see his heart scrambling to higher ground right before my eyes.

"Children in the courts sang out a refrain, and it's been sounding in my head ever since." Chuza placed a large hand over his face. "Hosanna to the Son of David."

I opened my arms, gathered him into my embrace, and held him close as his heart beat hard with belief.

✦

Chuza was detained with Herod the next morning while I, feeling better from the previous day, sought Susanna's presence. Together we made our way to the Temple.

Jesus had been teaching on the Temple steps daily. News of him traveled throughout Jerusalem like fire lapping at a dry field. Far from concealing his presence, Jesus appeared to be intentionally drawing people's attention.

"My presence can hardly endanger him at this point," I mused to Susanna. "Since he so publicly addresses the crowds."

"Are you afraid of what Othniel might do?"

I shook my head. "Othniel is the least of Jesus' concerns now."

"And for yourself?" Susanna pressed. "If he sees you with Jesus . . ."

"Let him see me," I stated firmly. "Let him take his observations to Herod. I won't be afraid of him any longer, nor let him keep me away from Jesus."

We neared the wide Temple steps, the crowd thinning enough that we could see Jesus standing in a tight cluster of people outside the western Huldah Gate. My heart swelled with eagerness as we ascended the stone steps but then stuttered to a stop as we saw whom Jesus was speaking to.

Othniel stood with a handful of courtiers and Pharisees, forming a ring around Jesus. Susanna's horrified expression mirrored my own as we scurried within earshot.

"Herod has long sought you, Rabbi." Othniel's smooth voice was unmistakable. "And I confess, I've been filled with curiosity and wonder myself."

I scoffed, certain that Othniel spoke disingenuously, but as I caught sight of his face, I was taken aback by its apparent openness.

Othniel gestured to the courtiers with him. "We know that you are an honest man, one full of integrity, and that you teach the way of God truthfully."

My heart began to sink as I detected the false humility in Othniel's tone. What game was he playing?

"You are impartial and do not care about others' opinions. You're not swayed by appearances." Othniel stretched his arms wide.

The nausea that had blessedly eluded me threatened to return.

"So, tell us, Teacher," Othniel continued, and the fox in him could finally be detected. "Tell us what you think of the matter. Is it permissible under the Law of God to pay taxes to Caesar?"

Jesus looked at Othniel as if regarding an obstinate mule. With eyes full of disappointment, he placed a hand on Othniel's shoulder. "Why are you trying to trap me?" He shook his head and sighed deeply. "Ah, you stage actor." He dropped his hand from

Othniel's shoulder and lifted his arms to encompass the others, his voice rising with indignation. "Hypocrites! Show me the coin used for the tax."

Someone placed a denarius in his palm, and Jesus held it up for everyone to see. "Whose image is stamped on this coin?"

A dull silence greeted him. Finally, a Pharisee spoke up, stating the obvious. "Caesar's."

"Well, then, give to Caesar what belongs to Caesar." Jesus extended the coin to the Pharisee. When he took it, Jesus grasped his hand, anchoring him in place. The man looked up, startled. Jesus placed a hand to the man's chest. "And give to God what belongs to God."

Amazement rippled through the crowd. Othniel stiffened, body tense like a wolf being denied its prey. When he turned from Jesus and pushed through the crowd, his expression was tight like a crumpled parchment.

As the people began to disperse and Jesus entered the Temple, Nathaniel caught sight of us and pushed his way through the crowd. "Joanna! Susanna! We've missed you." It'd only been a few months since I'd seen him, but his face seemed aged and tired.

"And we've missed all of you," I said. "I've been afraid to draw attention to Jesus, but now I see—"

"That he's doing very well on that account himself?" Nathaniel laughed, but there was no genuine mirth behind it. His eyes were strained and full of sadness.

"Is there anything you need?" Susanna gently asked.

"No. We are with him," Nathaniel replied. "We have all we need."

"Are you well, Joanna?" Simon approached with Andrew, concerned eyes studying me. "You look altered from when we saw you last."

Waving a hand, I offered a small laugh. "I was unwell yesterday, but it has since passed."

"Do you have more news of your sister?" Andrew wondered.

"Yes, we're looking for a Greek physician, a God-fearer from Antioch named Luke. Dalia was searching for him. If she was successful, then perhaps he will remember her. It's a thin thread to follow, I'm afraid."

Simon elbowed Andrew eagerly. "Didn't Philip come to you about some Greeks?"

"He did," Andrew affirmed. "Yesterday some Greeks approached Philip asking to see Jesus, but I don't believe any of them matched your description." His voice trailed off, eyes apologetic.

"Even so, perhaps Philip could find where they're staying," Simon said.

"Yes, of course. I'll speak to Philip and see what he knows." Andrew smiled, although I could tell he expected to find nothing.

There was a small flame of hope in my breast. I would nurture that spark and pray for a flame.

THIRTY-EIGHT

The next day was Passover. I awoke dry-mouthed and with a turned stomach. "Not again," I moaned to Eden. "I thought this had passed."

"Let me fetch Master Chuza," Eden consoled as she urged a steaming bowl of broth upon me.

The smell of the broth was a kick to my gut, and I pushed it away. "He'll just worry himself when there's nothing he can do."

As it'd done before, the sickness passed by midday, but left a sour taste in my mouth. Later in the day, I partook in the Passover meal as sparingly as I could without drawing Chuza's attention.

"Manaen says Jesus is celebrating Passover in the Essene Quarter," Chuza shared with me as we prepared for bed.

"I pray he isn't within sight of Caiaphas' home." I frowned, imagining Jesus near the high priest's stately residence. "Why does he keep himself so close to those who wish him harm? I will breathe easier once he's away from Jerusalem."

"Soon enough he will be, and then I will go with you to meet him for myself," Chuza murmured, drawing me into his arms and nuzzling my neck.

Nervously, I pushed him away, stomach still too riotous for my liking. "I-I'm afraid I'm worn out tonight."

"Are you still experiencing sickness?" Chuza placed a hand to my cheek, brows lifting with alarm. "I thought that had passed."

"It seems to come and go," I assured him, trying to keep my tone light. "I'm sure a good night's sleep is all I need."

And yet rest remained elusive. While Chuza slumbered peacefully, I flopped on the bed, the meal sitting precariously on my stomach, until eventually I drifted into a fitful sleep.

The next thing I knew, I was startled awake. I sat upright, dizzy and disoriented, forgetting for a moment where I was. As my heartbeat slowed, I took several deep breaths and pushed back the irrational panic. I was safe in my room with my husband. My hand slid to his side of the bed . . . and found it empty. The sheets were tossed, thrown off in a hurry, but the bed where he'd lain was still warm.

Scrambling from the bed, I called out for him. "Chuza?"

He was dressing quickly in the dark but paused at my voice. "I was trying not to disturb you. I'm sorry, love."

"What's happening? Is it morning?"

"Not quite." Chuza cinched his sash about his waist. "Herod has requested the presence of his military officials and administration in the reception hall."

"At this hour? Why?"

Chuza stopped his frantic movement to face me. "Come here." He opened his arms, and quickly I entered them. "I don't know much. Only that something is happening . . . with Jesus."

"What?" I reared back.

"He was arrested sometime in the night and ended up in the praetorium before Pilate."

A shudder passed through me. Chuza felt it, drew me close, and delivered the next words into my hair. "Pilate just sent him to Herod."

With a groan, I sank into Chuza's chest, too horrified for tears.

"Why did they arrest him? On what grounds? Where is Mary, Simon . . . ?"

Chuza placed firm hands on my shoulders, eased me back, and stared into my face with a grim expression. "We'll have more answers soon, but I must go. I'll send word to you as soon as I can."

He turned to leave, but I clung to him. "I'll go too."

"No, it's not safe." But there was hesitation in his face, and I leapt upon that look with a vengeance.

"I'll stay in the gallery. No one will see me."

Chuza sighed deeply and ran his hands down my arms. "I have to go . . . now. I don't have time to argue."

"There's no need for argument." Quickly, I released him, snagging my mantle from a nearby chair. "Go, and I will follow discreetly."

Chuza let out a frustrated grunt and opened the door. Beyond him I could see the palace courtyard, the dark sky, the barest hint of morning's light. "The gallery," he stated, tone somber.

"The gallery," I agreed, rushing him out the door.

When he'd left, I finished dressing in a hurry, focusing my thoughts on the tangible items before me—the strap of my sandal, the sash at my waist, a heavy veil to hide my face. I tethered myself to each small task, pushing back the terror that threatened to consume me, ignoring the irritating sickness in my stomach.

With shaking hands, I lit an oil lamp and left our room. The entire palace complex was in an uproar. I stood on the second floor in a covered gallery that wrapped around the central courtyard. Numerous people were leaving their rooms. A contingent of Roman soldiers stood below, and frantically I searched for Jesus in their midst. But he was nowhere to be found.

Our room was adjacent to the reception hall, whose doors now groaned open to release a stream of men into the courtyard. I took a large step back, holding my flame in trembling hands as their angry voices rose in the early morning air.

"We are wasting our time here. Pilate is unwilling to act and shifts the problem to Herod, who does not have the authority to condemn Jesus."

They moved away, taking their conversation with them.

"Joanna." Her face came into the light, eerily gaunt and beautiful as shadow leapt across her features.

"Susanna." I pressed her hand to mine. "They've arrested . . ." I couldn't finish.

She nodded jerkily, tugging at my hand. Together we scurried down the gallery, panic nipping at our heels.

There were so many people milling about that it was easy for us to enter the reception hall unnoticed. I led Susanna to the gallery overlooking the hall, both of us quickly ascending the steps to find it swarming with people. Pushing my way to the rail, I breathed heavily into the veil covering my face, Susanna close behind me.

Focus on getting to the rail, Joanna. One breath in and out. The scratch of the fabric against my cheek. The dampness of the linen from my breath. The smoothness of stone as my hand found the rail and grasped it tightly. My eyes landing on *him.*

Jesus stood bound in the middle of the room with his torn garments hanging loose upon his frame. His face was bruised, one eye badly swollen. At the sight of him, all air left my body in a single rush.

"Jesus of Nazareth!" Herod stood opposite Jesus with open arms, as if greeting a long-lost friend. "At last I meet you!" He approached with a wide smile and clapped both his hands on Jesus' shoulders. "You, sir, are an enigma. On and off I've searched for you, but you remained elusive. Here we are . . . all the way in Jerusalem before we meet." He chortled, shaking Jesus' shoulders, rocking him back on his heels.

"At first, I thought to myself . . . can this be John the Baptizer back from the dead?" Herod turned and stretched an arm to the officials behind him. "We saw what happened to that loud-mouth."

Some chuckled in response. My eyes immediately found Chuza. He stood close to Manaen, the two of them silent and somber. Not two paces away, Othniel lurked in the shadows, satisfaction splayed across his face.

Herod turned back to Jesus and clucked his tongue in disapproval of his bonds. "Take these things off, will you?"

Immediately a guard released Jesus, who rubbed his wrists where they had been scraped raw.

"There now." Herod beamed. "That's better." He took several large steps back, propping his chin on his hand, inspecting Jesus. "Now then, I hear you are a miracle worker. Is this true?"

Jesus stood quietly, observing Herod. At his question, he remained silent.

Herod frowned. "Well, man, speak up! Now is your moment. Give me a sign of your power, and I will see what I can do with our friend Pilate."

Still no response from Jesus.

"You've healed some in my own court, fed crowds, performed wonders—and yet you can't be bothered to show even one sign to your sovereign?"

"That is part of the problem." A chief priest stepped from the side. "This man recognizes no sovereign, for he, himself, claims to be a king."

"Is that so?" Herod laughed, the loud sound flooding the room, bouncing off the walls. As the echoes of his laughter died, he drew up close to Jesus, mood abruptly shifting.

"You must share how you came by that title when the emperor has yet to bestow it upon this lowly tetrarch." He bowed, hands splayed in mock admiration, each word a blade wielded with spite. "A king?" Herod rose, voice lifting with incredulity.

"And yet here you stand—at my mercy. Some *king* you are." He spat on the ground at Jesus' feet and lifted his chin to the guard.

Swiftly, Jesus was bound once again. With another nod, Herod indicated for the chief priests and scribes to bring forward their charges.

"This man said that he will destroy the Temple and, in three days' time, build another made without human hands."

"It took us forty-six years to construct that majestic building!" Herod snorted. "I'm disappointed, Jesus of Nazareth. I'd heard you were a man of wonders, but now I see you are a lunatic."

"He is misleading the nation by claiming kingship!" another chief priest cried.

"He promotes insurrection by forbidding us to pay our taxes!" A scribe pointed an accusatory finger.

"Would he bring down the wrath of Rome upon us?" a man shouted.

"He calls himself the Son of Man, the fulfillment of Daniel's prophecy!"

"He speaks blasphemy and consorts with demons!"

On and on the accusations came; the room was heavy with hate, the air thick and nearly unbreathable. I grasped the rail until my knuckles shone white as I listened to the lies flow from one mouth to another—lies and hate as suffocating and oppressive as the plague of darkness. Susanna's fingers fluttered over mine and then clutched my hand where it held onto the rail, both of us desperately searching for stability as the world continued to tilt.

Why wasn't Jesus saying anything? I held his healing in my body, proof of his miraculous power. And even though I'd never seen him wield that power for himself, surely now . . . *now* when darkness was so close and thick, *now* was the time to use that power to silence these men. But he stood calm and still. The bruises on his face were beginning to deepen, one eye nearly swollen shut.

"What kind of king stirs up such dissension?" Herod's voice rose above the others. "You think yourself a king? Well then . . ." He took a long sweeping bow before Jesus, and the room erupted into laughter. "Let me bring you my tribute, *King* Jesus." He rose and struck him across the face.

I yelped and pressed the veil tighter against me, eyes hungrily searching for Chuza.

He stood, slightly obscured now, in the back of the room, fists clenched by his side. Not everyone was enjoying the show. Some faces were twisted in mockery, but others were ashen with dismay.

"Hail, King of the Jews!" The head of Herod's bodyguard saluted Jesus, then thrust his hand to Jesus' face, grasped his beard, and yanked out a fistful of hair.

I bit down hard on my veil to keep from screaming as I stumbled back from the rail. The air was sucked from the room, which was strangely silent but for the roaring in my ears. I couldn't breathe. The nausea that had plagued me for days demanded release. My heart lodged in my throat, banging like a trapped bird.

I pressed my eyes closed, transported to the roadside near Chorazin. The air there was heavy with the laughter of children. One child in particular had his hands deep in Jesus' beard while he—full of life and power—gave them the Kingdom.

"Hail, King of the Jews!"

My eyes sprang open.

The chief priests and scribes had stepped back, making room for Herod and his soldiers to encircle Jesus. They took turns bowing and, one after another, struck him.

Susanna's hand trembled in mine. I clung to her and pressed my veil closer. Those in the gallery were shouting, urging on the brutality as if we were spectators and the mockery below was unfolding upon a stage. Opposite me, across the courtyard, Mireya laughed, long and loud as she leaned over the rail and pointed.

To see the enjoyment on faces I'd known most of my life broke my heart in a new way. *Abba, they are blind! They don't see him. They don't understand.*

"Hail, King of the Jews!"

I clung to the rail and focused my eyes upon Jesus, refusing to look away as I bore witness to his pain. The bile on my tongue was sharp. I swallowed it back.

The mockery continued until finally Herod brought out a brilliant white robe. "I've had my fun. Pilate has sufficiently made amends for his recent misconduct by sending me such a fine gift, and now I will send that gift back. A little worse for the wear, maybe." He shrugged as his military commanders shouted their enjoyment.

"Let's remedy that, shall we?" Herod draped the white robe over Jesus' shoulders. "Much better." He nodded with approval. "Befitting a true king."

Herod turned to the chief priests. "Return him to Pilate with my deepest regard. This man is none of my concern."

They were taking him away. They were going to deposit him back into the brutal lap of Rome.

No. The nausea clawed up my throat, leaving me faint.

The chief priests and scribes began to escort Jesus from the room to where I'd seen a gathering of Roman soldiers outside. Once Jesus left, what would become of him? The desire to keep him in my sight overwhelmed me.

As the men began escorting him from the room, I pushed back the sickness and fear, yanked the veil from my face, and leaned over the rail, barefaced and weeping.

I am here.

Jesus was parallel to me now, almost obscured by the number of chief priests and scribes surrounding him.

Releasing Susanna's hand in my hurry, I shoved through those gathered in the gallery. Hand over hand on the rail, I pulled myself forward, keeping in step with Jesus and his captors. Below me, Jesus faced resolutely forward, eyes looking neither to the left nor to the right.

I am here. Do not listen to them. You are my king. Rise up and show them! Show them who you are.

They neared the door as I stumbled down the steps leading from the gallery. Splaying my hands against the stairwell, I pressed hard, shaking as I tried not to faint.

He passed by me briefly as they left the hall, and for a moment he turned. His face was bloodied from the torn beard, one eye now completely shut. I gazed into the other, and then he was gone.

No. No. No. I waited for them to leave, then slipped out as well. The courtyard was filled with noise. I hurried to my room, where I would have a better view.

They were leaving the palace compound. I couldn't see him. There were too many, and now they were gone. The clang of their armor still rang in my ears. Their voices still haunted my mind. His one open eye still stared deeply into mine . . .

Even though the sun was on the horizon, darkness spread across my vision. I couldn't breathe. What would happen to him? Chuza would find out. I would go back to him.

Someone called my name. I attempted to respond but the ground spun upward, meeting me with a silencing embrace.

Thirty-Nine

"Joanna!" Her face floated in and out of sight, a distant cloud on a warm summer's day. My eyes refused to stay open, my mind refused to stay present, and so I could not hold onto her. Instead, I drifted back to the dark.

"Joanna!" Her voice was louder, and this time I could feel her hands on my arms, shaking me from the darkness. I moaned and she shook me harder, grasping my face. I longed for the oblivion of darkness, but she was too insistent. My mind crawled upward until my eyes pulled open.

"Susanna?"

"Thank God!" She sagged by my bedside.

My lips were cracked, my throat as dry and raw as the Judean wilderness. I shifted on the bed and frowned as I realized my head was in someone's lap. Twisting, I peered up into Eden's face. Her wide eyes were rimmed in red, as if she'd been crying.

"What happened? Where are we?" I croaked.

"You collapsed," Eden whispered. "Susanna helped me carry you back to your room."

"Where is he?" I asked Susanna, voice growing stronger.

"Chuza? Both he and Manaen are still with Herod."

I shook my head vehemently, the terror returning as memories resurfaced. "No . . . Jesus. Where is he?" Lurching upright, I pushed at Susanna. "It's light out. How much time has passed? Has Pilate released Jesus? Or is he still detained?"

"We've heard nothing yet. He's appearing a second time before Pilate. That's all we know at the moment." Susanna placed a palm on my cheek. "You're warm, Joanna, and weak. You frightened us. When was the last time you took food or water?"

I brushed at her hand. "I haven't been able to keep anything down lately. I'm sure it's nothing."

"You are understating your condition, mistress," Eden said as I swung my legs over the side of the bed. "She's been insisting all is fine," she muttered to Susanna. "But she isn't herself. She has no energy and can hardly keep anything down, including water."

As if to prove her point, I rose to my feet and swayed, made for the door but stopped as my head grew dangerously light. The room tilted, and I doubled over, gagging.

"How long has this been going on?" Susanna rushed to my side, placed a firm arm about my shoulders, and drew me back to the bed.

"Just after we arrived in Jerusalem," Eden answered.

"Fatigue and nausea . . . what other symptoms do you have?"

I sank onto the bed with a moan. "Why are we talking about *me* when even now Jesus is suffering?"

"What other symptoms?" Susanna gently pressed.

With a sigh, I eased onto my pillow. "Mainly the nausea. It's gripped me most mornings, but often passes by midday. The smell of food aggravates it. I'm achy all over, but that's from traveling."

"Oh, Joanna." Susanna's settled expression confused me. "Your time of the month . . . have you missed it?"

Understanding landed heavily on my mind. "I-I'm late, but that happens sometimes, and so I didn't think . . . with everything going on . . . searching for Dalia and now Jesus—" I broke off and curled onto my side, hands resting on my belly in disbelief.

Susanna placed a tender hand on my back. "I know the signs well. You are most certainly with child, my friend."

Eden released a soft gasp. "A babe! Oh, mistress, a babe!"

I pressed my hands against my stomach and imagined a child there, nestled deeply inside me, small and full of life. "A babe." I breathed the words, hardly able to comprehend them. "A babe so soon. Oh, Chuza—Can you find him for me?" I asked Susanna, breath catching as I recalled the last time I'd seen my husband—grim-faced and distraught as Jesus was beaten right in front of him. He had just begun to heal, to believe, and now this—how would his heart respond?

"Certainly." Susanna nodded and made for the door. "I will try to get word to him. And I will go to the praetorium myself to see what I can learn."

"I should go with you."

"Absolutely not." A familiar authority infused Susanna's voice. It was the tone she used to take when trying to make me feel small, but this time it was clear that she wielded it out of love.

"If you won't consider your own health, then think of the babe." Susanna pointed a finger at me but with soft eyes. "Your priority right now is to rest and drink." She turned her finger upon Eden, who leapt to her feet and scurried to a pitcher of water. "I'm sure Chuza will want a physician to look at you."

"But don't tell him—"

"I won't." Susanna opened the door. "That's for you to share." Her voice gentled. "Now rest."

After she left, Eden pressed a cup into my hand and stroked my hair. "I can understand your fear in light of all that is happening, but this is good news, mistress—a gift in the middle of darkness, a new beginning."

"How can I feel anything but fear when Jesus—" I broke

off, breath catching. "Surely, at any moment, he will show his power?"

Eden scrunched her eyes closed, teeth catching her lower lip. "May it be so."

I managed to empty the cup at Eden's insistence and promised to rest, but how could I sleep after such events? The weight of grief, the joy of new life, and fear over the future mingled in my mind until the whirl of emotion finally conquered my resistance, pulling me into a dead sleep.

———— ✦ ————

I awoke to his hands on my shoulders, his deep voice in my ear. Mind immediately alert, my eyes pulled open to find Chuza on the bed, face hovering above mine, gaze full of love and worry.

With a cry of relief, I pulled him close. He descended willingly, wrapping me in his arms where I lay on the bed, nestling his face into my neck.

"What time is it?" I twisted in his arms to look at the window.

"Late morning."

"Chuza!" I shoved at him and sat upright. "Why did no one wake me?"

"I couldn't get away sooner."

"Is Susanna back?"

"I haven't seen her. She said you felt ill . . ."

"Oh, forget about that. Forget about that!" Throwing the sheet aside, I stumbled to my feet, crossed the room, and flung open the door as if Jesus himself was waiting right on the other side. "Pilate must have released him by now. He has no grounds to detain him. How badly is he hurt?"

A distinct sound from the bed stopped my frantic rambling. I'd heard that sound only once before, when Chuza had wept over the thought of losing me. He was slumped on the bed, face in his hands.

"Chuza?" I returned to him on trembling legs, rested a hand on his shoulder.

"There is no easy way to tell you this." Chuza lifted his face and placed a hand over mine, eyes bright with tears.

"Pilate wanted to release Jesus, but the chief priests were adamant. He gave them what they demanded. Jesus received a death sentence . . . crucifixion."

"Crucifixion." I stated the word as if I'd misheard. "Crucifixion."

Chuza tugged on my hand, urging me into his arms, but my whole being was snagged on the one word and the detailed images that followed.

Iron nails driven into flesh. Twisted limbs and wrenching screams. Tearing flesh, slow asphyxiation, nakedness, humiliation. Men screaming for death, praying for death, begging for death to relieve them. Torture only befitting a demon.

This was to be the death of Jesus?

I collapsed, but Chuza caught me, easing us both to the floor where I released a long, low wail, shuddering in his arms. "When? When?"

"It is done," Chuza rasped, holding me tight.

"But it cannot be. It cannot be!" Wildly, I looked about the room as if to anchor myself in my surroundings. "Where was it done?" I pulled myself to standing. "Was anyone with him when—" A sob stopped my words.

Chuza rose and drew me into his arms, saying nothing, simply letting me weep until my grief turned quiet. I swallowed it into my being, held it next to Jesus' miraculous healing. Now this would mark me too.

"It was on the road leading west to Emmaus—Golgotha." Chuza answered my earlier question, voice cracking.

Golgotha, so named for its infamous skull shape, was one of many execution sites around Jerusalem. This particular site was extremely public, for it was on a hill by the side of a major road.

"Herod is pleased with Pilate's acquiescence to the chief priests and even more so by his 'gift' of Jesus this morning." Chuza's voice was terse. From the weariness etching his handsome features, I could tell he'd spent long hours holding his tongue.

"The two of them—Pilate and Herod—have forged a new bond over these events. Many are urging Herod not to be zealous in jumping into such a precarious friendship, but Herod is too flattered to listen. Pilate has used Jesus to ingratiate himself with Herod and the religious leaders, to undo some of the damage he's caused of late . . . and it's working." Tears resurfaced in Chuza's eyes. Gruffly, he wiped them clear. "To see Jesus used as a political pawn—it's unbearable."

Bowing my head, my eyes landed on my stomach. How could I bring a child into a world that had brutally killed the Messiah?

I was beginning to feel lightheaded again and clung to Chuza. He placed a strong arm about my waist, grasped my chin, and studied my tear-streaked face. "It's more than grief that affects you. I didn't realize how strong your illness was. I will ask for Herod's personal physician."

A protest was on my lips when the room suddenly darkened. Both of us startled and turned toward the one window in the room, which only a moment ago had let in the midday light. Chuza slowly released me, and I followed him to the door, which was still cracked open. He swung it wide, and we both gazed out into darkness as deep as the dead of night.

Wordlessly, I threaded my fingers through his as we left our room and gazed up into the sky.

Shouts rang throughout the palace compound as doors banged open and others joined us on the gallery and streamed into the open courtyard below. Chuza released my hand and quickly entered our room, returning a moment later with an oil lamp, its flames throwing light onto his face. We gazed at each other, neither one of us speaking as I slipped my hand back into his.

It began to rain, a slow drizzle as the heavens wept. Those in the open courtyard sought shelter, while those of us in the gallery remained dry. The ground quaked, and Chuza pressed me to his side.

Just as I'd wrapped my arms about him, a servant came. Herod was gathering his administration. Chuza gently disentangled himself from my arms and transferred the lamp to my hands.

"Go inside and wait for me." He pressed his lips to my brow and then moved to my cheek, my jaw, and finally my lips—brief and firm.

He turned and was quickly swallowed up by the unnatural darkness. The moment his broad shoulders vanished, I experienced such panic I nearly cried aloud. Quickly, I entered our room, closed the door, and pressed my back against the carved wood.

Alone—I was utterly alone as the world around me shifted and shuddered. Shakily, I took a deep breath and then another and called upon God with all the strength I could muster.

Do You see what is happening? Do You care?

A roll of thunder crossed the sky, causing me to slide to the ground in terror.

The world is mad. We are held captive by men drunk with power and flattery. We need the Kingdom of the Christ! But now all hope of that Kingdom is gone. How can You allow Your Messiah to be killed? Do You see? Do You care?

A swift knock at the door startled me.

"Mistress?" Eden's voice, thin and small.

Surging to my feet, I swung the door wide, pulling her inside and into my arms.

Eden—her chosen name, a place of delight and new beginnings. I held her and wept for everything we had just lost.

Lord, we need You! Come to us. Help us. They have murdered him.

"I've been praying unceasingly since—" Eden's voice wobbled into the silence as she clung to me. "Is this God answering our prayers? Is it judgment? Is the world ending?"

It felt like it—the end of everything good.

Placing my flame on the table, I knelt on the ground, pulling Eden along with me. We were silent for a long moment, entombed in darkness.

How could I bring forth new life when the vision of Christ's Kingdom was over?

He told us to call You Abba. Do You truly care for us as Your children? How could You let this happen?

Next to me, Eden cried God's name aloud, pulled her hand from mine to cover her face, and hunched over her knees. I joined my voice to hers, and together we prayed until our breath ran out, and still the day was as dark as night, deepening, pressing down upon us.

Eden remained curled into a ball, and I lay prostrate, simply breathing Adonai's name for what felt like hours, until the darkness began to feel more like a womb—a temporary holding place, a breath that was held in anticipation of release.

Even when the darkness lifted, we remained as we were until Chuza found us—Eden crouched, and me lying on my face in the light with my sputtering flame, hands raised, waiting to receive.

———— ✦ ————

Often the corpse was left hanging from the cross, a welcome feast for beasts and birds of the air. But the chief priests wanted the crosses cleared before the Sabbath, and so the guards had expedited death by breaking the legs. Jesus, however, had already died.

Instead of being thrown into a mass grave, Jesus was removed from the cross by Joseph of Arimathea, a prominent merchant and member of the Sanhedrin who had requested the body from Pilate. Jesus would enter his final resting place in Joseph's new tomb.

Horrified news extended from the Temple that the thick curtain partitioning the Holy of Holies had been torn from top to bottom, as if God had reached down and wrenched it apart Himself. How fitting for the veil to be torn, for I also sensed a wrenching apart of our dreams, hopes, and expectations.

I lay somber and alert in Chuza's arms that night. He was sleeping with one arm draped over my hip, large hand resting lightly on my stomach. I swallowed hard and pressed my hand over his, anchoring life beneath our palms.

⁕

News spread to Herod's court the next day that Pilate, at the insistence of the religious leaders, had placed a seal on Jesus' tomb and posted a guard.

"They don't understand Jesus or his disciples," I stated to Chuza. "They do not understand the way of Jesus at all. The foundation of his teaching was truth." My voice cracked. "They imagine we would try to continue his teaching through blatant lies? Through deception? In doing so, we would utterly desecrate his memory."

Mary Magdalene and some of the other women had already prepared spices and invited me to join them the next morning to anoint Jesus' body. Joseph of Arimathea had done what he could to prepare the body, but time had been limited, and so the women would finish what he'd begun.

Chuza expressed concern over my involvement since I was still pale and weak, but I made a point of sipping water throughout the day, even managing to force down food as proof that I was sound of body, or at least sound enough to perform this last kindness to the one who had so graciously shown me mercy.

News of Jesus' trial and execution continued to swirl about court. It stung anew at the way he was passed from mouth to mouth, a curiosity to be examined from every angle.

He'd been humiliated . . . utterly ridiculed for his talk of the Kingdom. The charge placed above his cross had stated *Jesus of Nazareth, the King of the Jews* in three languages so that no one would miss it, emphasizing his origin in humble Nazareth to further mock him. But the news that brought me to my knees was the way they'd draped him in scarlet and shoved thorns upon his head. I sat in my room and held my wrist, recalling his eyes full of compassion as he gently led me toward healing. The man who had promised me a crown of beauty had been forced to wear a crown of thorns.

During that long and hopeless Sabbath, I sat with the knowledge of life in my body while mourning the death around me. All my life, faith had been a flickering flame threatening to snuff out, but then Jesus had breathed upon that flame. And I had seen him do the same in so many others. In the sad and sure eyes of John the Baptist, I had recognized the flame. In the pained and strong eyes of Simon, I had recognized the flame. In the wondering and hopeful eyes of my husband, I had recognized the flame.

What would we do now that Jesus was dead? Surely the flame would also die, in each and every one of us. The flame would eventually die.

FORTY

I shuddered awake and lay in bed, clinging to the sheets. The ground had moved, I was sure of it. Easing myself upward, I cast my eyes about the room. A shattered pitcher confirmed that the ground indeed had moved. Gingerly, I swung my bare feet to the floor and padded softly to the window. A hint of daylight was on the horizon. It was time.

Returning to the bed, I lingered for a moment, gazing at Chuza's slumbering form. How was he still asleep? He lay on his back, lips slightly parted, one arm extending upward to cushion his head. I leaned over him, curls spilling about my shoulders and curtaining his face as I slid my hand to the now-familiar hollow beneath his breast. Gently I pressed my lips to his.

I would tell him. This very morning, I would tell him that he was a father, and we would weather what followed together. But first I would go to my Lord to lavish this last gift of love upon him.

Quickly I dressed and, even though Chuza knew where I was headed, left him a note. I pulled my cloak about me and slipped from the room, tightly clutching my contribution of a vial of pure nard.

The Hasmonean palace was near the north wall and close to the Gennath Gate, to which I now hurried. My stomach roiled within me, but I distracted myself from the discomfort by focusing on the task at hand.

Outside the gate stood the Towers Pool, a water reservoir fed by the upper aqueduct—our prearranged meeting place. As I approached, a solitary form rose to greet me, opening her arms in invitation. I entered them, held her tight, and breathed her name. "Mary."

The last time I'd seen her had been before the terror and injustice of the last few days. This, I realized, was how we would now mark time—before and after. "Where are the others? I thought there would be more."

"They're coming. They'll be here soon, but I wanted to speak with you first—privately." Mary's eyes shone in the dim, predawn light.

"Oh, Mary, did you see . . . ? Were you there when . . . ?" I broke off, nearly too afraid to ask.

"Yes."

I didn't need to ask if it was horrible. I knew full well that it was. "How are the others?" I questioned.

"Most of them are together except for Peter. When directly asked, he . . . he denied knowing Jesus. Three times he denied him. He's been alienated from the rest ever since. Only John keeps him company." Mary's voice was pained.

Peter earnestly loved Jesus, was utterly devoted to him, so news of his denial was unthinkable. Any thoughts of judgment, however, were obliterated as I recalled my own moments of weakness and fear. I knew what it was to stand directly before the face of power as it scrutinized you.

"I wanted to speak to you privately, Joanna, for I have news." The air was biting and cold. I shivered, and Mary threaded an arm through mine. "We found your physician," she murmured. "The day before Passover, Philip was able to locate the Greeks who'd approached him. Luke was among them. I wanted to tell you right away but then—" She broke off, voice thick. "He remembers Dalia. She remained in Antioch, unable to travel. But as news of Jesus spread, her friends managed to bring her here. Oh, Joanna, they brought her to the Holy City to find him. To think, Jesus' fame was beginning to spread so far and wide and now . . . and now . . ."

My arm slipped from Mary's as I collapsed. I pressed my hands to the ground, dug my fingers into the earth, gathered dirt within my hands, and wailed.

She was here in Jerusalem. My sister was here. My sister was too late.

Abba! God of heaven, why?

Dalia needed the healing touch of the Christ, had traveled so far to now come up short. The injustice raged in my body.

"Do you want to be healed?" Jesus' gentle question tore into me. How could I live out his healing when he, himself, was dead? When my sister was left to suffer?

Mary met me on the ground, gathered me into her arms, and there we remained, huddled and weeping until the others joined us.

Mary of Clopas and Salome came with arms full of spices. As Mary and I rose on shaking feet, I managed to ask, "How will we find the tomb?"

"We followed Joseph that night," Mary assured me. "We saw exactly where he was laid."

I clutched at my vial of nard and allowed Mary to lead us to the road headed north. As we neared the western road to Emmaus, my eyes searched compulsively for Golgotha. It was still dark, but I found the looming outline of the craggy hill. The upright beams would still be standing—permanent, jagged knives shoving upward to heaven, waiting for their next victim to stumble to their feet with his crossbeam on his back. There, just there, he had suffered and died . . . and I had been too physically weak to be present. Tears streamed down my face as regret coursed through my body.

We reached the crossroad and continued north. To our left stretched a quiet garden, full of tombs. Many members of the Sanhedrin had graves here in sight of the Temple. Mary led us off the road, and together we threaded our way through olive trees and flower beds.

"How will we remove the stone?" Salome wondered. "It took five soldiers to get it into place."

"Then they can help us open it," Mary stated, voice flat.

Salome sighed deeply. "But *will* they help us? That's the question."

"They will," Mary snapped, uncharacteristically sharp.

Her steps had been brisk, purposeful, but now she slowed. "I-I'm sorry, Salome." Her voice shook. "They must help us. They must, for I need to see him. I need to—"

Salome placed a hand on Mary's shoulder. "It's all right," she whispered. "Yes, surely they will help a handful of women. We are hardly a threat. Don't worry. You will see him one last time."

The garden was still dark, the sun only a hint on the horizon as Mary led us to a far corner of the garden. I braced myself to come face-to-face with the Roman guards, some of whom might have been present at Jesus' death, some of whom might have mocked him, spat on him, humiliated him.

"It's over here," Mary breathed as we entered a small clearing.

Before us lay a gaping tomb, its stone rolled open. "I don't see it, Mary," I whispered and then startled as she dropped to her knees. "What's wrong?"

Alarm flooded me as she began rocking on her knees, a low keen forming deep in her throat.

I looked wildly at Mary of Clopas, who stood swaying on her feet, looking ill. "Where is the tomb? What's wrong?"

"This is the tomb," Mary of Clopas stated, voice hollow.

I tore my gaze from her to the open tomb. "You must be mistaken. It's dark out. This can't be the right tomb."

"No, this is it," Mary of Clopas insisted. "We saw exactly where he was laid. This site is separate from the others."

I looked around and saw she was right. There was no other tomb in sight.

"Has someone taken him?" Salome whispered, hands covering her mouth.

"Isn't that why they posted the guard? To ensure that very thing wouldn't happen?" I stammered.

Salome dropped her hands. "Where *is* the guard? They would never abandon a post—never!"

"Someone has taken him." Mary spoke from her knees, staring in disbelief at the tomb. "Someone has robbed his grave."

I supported her as she rose shakily to her feet. "Peter . . . I must go and get him. He will know what to do." Mary's voice strengthened with resolve. She deposited her load of spices into Salome's hands, eyes painfully wide as she looked at me. "I'll run as quickly as I can. I know where he's staying. I'll bring him back." She was breathless and backing away from us, nearly tripping as she whirled around and then disappeared back through the trees.

Mary of Clopas, Salome, and I stood with arms full of spices and perfumes, feet rooted to the earth.

Mary broke the silence. "It must have happened sometime this morning. No Hebrew would rob a grave and become unclean on the Sabbath."

"Perhaps it wasn't a Hebrew," Salome speculated.

I shook my head. "What reason would Rome have to do such a thing?"

We stood awkwardly with one another for several long and pained moments.

"We should wait for Peter," Mary finally spoke.

"But what if—" Salome broke off, swallowed hard. "What if the robbers were interrupted and he's still in there?"

We shuddered.

"I hate to think of his body mishandled . . . dishonored even in death," I whispered.

"Let's enter and see." Salome's voice was hard with resolve.

Together we approached the gaping tomb. The air from inside was cold, and we entered that chill, breathless. As my eyes adjusted to the dim light, I could see the long benches on each side of the chamber—both empty.

"Look." Mary pointed to the left.

Strips of linen lay loosely on the bench. The smell of myrrh and aloe hung in the air. The *sudarium*, the linen cloth that covered the body's face, lay neatly to the side, looking intentionally folded.

Slowly, I approached the bench, staring at it in disbelief. "If someone took him, they wouldn't have *unbound* him."

The other women joined me, but before anyone could speak, a deep tremor rippled through the ground as a bright light flashed around us.

I turned but couldn't see. The suddenness of the light had blinded me, and I blinked rapidly, rosy spots in my vision.

"Why do you search for the living among the dead?"

The voice was smooth—silk sliding over skin. The voice was warm—bread fresh from the oven, bidding to come and taste.

As my vision cleared, I saw two men with robes so white and faces so beautiful I was blinded by their brilliance, confronted by the sun itself. With a cry, I fell to my knees, gaze dropping, heart pounding.

"Do not be afraid," one of the men spoke, voice swelling with delight. "You are looking for Jesus, who was crucified. But he is not here. He has risen from the dead!"

The air was sucked from the tomb, replaced by light and a

strange heaviness. My limbs were unable to move, nor my body to breathe, but there was no burning sensation in my lungs. Instead, my body was in need of nothing—everything was stilled and hushed within and without.

"Now go, tell his disciples. Tell Peter. Jesus is going ahead of you to Galilee, and there you will see him."

As quickly as they came, they left, and the air returned, blasting into my lungs with searing heat.

◆

We stumbled from the tomb and lay in the light, trembling and panting. The sun had presented itself. The day was now here.

I crouched on the ground with grass crushed beneath my hands. The early morning air slid briskly beneath my tunic, gooseflesh crawling up my spine and out through the crown of my head. I shook all over.

Someone was weeping. Salome's lips were moving, but I couldn't hear her. I peered up at the sky, down at the garden. Everything was painfully present and immediate. Linen brushing against my thighs, whiffs of nard from the vial I'd dropped, Mary's hands on me, shaking, shaking. Her words came in snatches. *Go and tell.*

Yes, go and tell.

We ran. Our offering of spices and perfume scattered behind us, utterly unnecessary.

A loud roaring entered my ears, and in its center pounded the words in time with my heart. *He is not here. He is not here.*

We weaved in and out of the trees, finding and losing one another again and again. I took a wrong turn and doubled back, found Salome, lost her again.

He has risen. He has risen.

Had Mary returned with Peter? Did she know?

I stumbled to a stop and bent over, hands on my knees, pulling air into my lungs in deep gulps, restless and hungry for something I couldn't name. With one hand I covered my face, and with the other I blindly reached for a tree. My hand connected with its gnarled trunk, body sagging.

A footfall and then another. I opened my eyes, expecting Mary or Salome, but instead came face-to-face with him.

All strength left me in a rush as I sank to my knees. I would have fallen onto my face at his feet, but he snagged my hand, held it tight. I blinked the lingering tears from my lashes and stared at his hand on mine, fingers encircling my wrist. At the base of his palm where it met his own wrist, there was a hole, jagged and deep.

He exhaled, and his breath hung white between us.

Behind him the sun was playing with the silver leaves of the olive trees, lifting them, dancing them, calling them to movement and life.

A deep trembling entered my body where I knelt in the dew-soaked grass. He was gazing upon me with a radiant, vibrant face. I clung to him as he pulled me up with a strong right hand until I was standing on shaking feet, fully before his face. The lines deepened around his eyes, his lips parted, and he spoke one word in a voice I knew, the voice that had been with me from the beginning.

"Daughter."

———— ✦ ————

Dust flung into the air from my sandaled feet as I ran and ran.

In the early morning air, the birds were singing urgently as they announced the new day. Branches reached for my head, and I shoved them away, ducking under and out—out from the garden and onto the road, stumbling, laughing, sobbing.

Before me the grand ashlars of Jerusalem rose upward, and

behind them men and women were blinking awake. They didn't know. They didn't know yet.

To my left Mary ran and to my right was Salome, each of us streaming back to the city with life and truth on our tongues.

Everything I'd known was being rearranged.

With a shout, I leapt into the air as if I truly had wings and could soar like the swift, higher and faster.

As I ran, all the faces I'd worn peeled away, one by one, streaming behind me until I was barefaced and beaming. Now—here—after this moment, I would don no other face than this one.

The one that had beheld God in the garden.

Mary and Salome were headed to the disciples, but I would go to my husband. I would tell him first. And I would not stop telling.

I placed a firm hand over my belly. Life teemed within and without. Chuza and I—we would bring this babe into a world made new by God's unstoppable Kingdom that crossed all boundaries and united hearts beneath God's rule.

The sun had risen, lighting the road. To my right was Golgotha and there, in the distance, those upright beams. Ahead lay the Gennath Gate, and beyond it, nestled in the womb of the city, was my sister, waiting to be found.

I ran beneath the lengthening rays of the sun with a hot flame in my heart—down the dusty road, toward the city walls, near the gently sloping western fields that rippled with a brilliant golden hue. I ran past those laughing fields that winked hopefully beneath the sun, alive and afire with swaths of crown daisies.

author's note

Joanna is named only twice in Scripture—first in Luke 8:2–3 as someone whom Jesus healed and who supported him from her own means, and second in Luke 24:10 as eyewitness to the empty tomb. Given how briefly she's mentioned in Scripture, can we know anything at all about her life? Astoundingly, the answer is yes, and the key lies with her husband.

Luke tells us that Joanna was the wife of Chuza, Herod Antipas' steward. This statement contains two significant pieces of information. First, Chuza is not a Jewish name; rather, it's Nabatean. Nestled in northwest Arabia, just southeast of Herod's own territory of Perea, Nabatea was one of the major world powers at the time. Herod's own grandmother was Nabatean, as was his first wife, therefore Nabateans within his court and administration would not have been unusual.

Chuza's position of steward is better translated as "procurator." The idea is one who manages the estate of another and, in the case of a king, would include his financial business. Rather than merely one of many procurators for the king, some scholars suggest that Chuza was the financial minister more generally, stationed in Galilee and overseeing Herod's revenues.

From these two pieces of information, we see that Joanna was most likely married to a Gentile high up in Herod's administration, and this leads to some interesting questions. Most Jewish families would not see such a union as desirable, for there was a strong taboo against both Herod's court and intermarriage with Gentiles. Because marriages were typically arranged within the same socioeconomic circles, it's highly probable that Joanna came from an elite Jewish family that would have seen an alliance with the Herodian court as advantageous.

The lay nobility of Jesus' day consisted mainly of Sadducees, those connected to the temple and its services. In general, the Sadducees were compliant with Rome and its representatives, for this allowed them to retain their economic and religious power. A Sadducean family would be more liberal in their politics; therefore, I decided to place Joanna within such a family.

I located Joanna's family in Sepphoris because it served as Herod's capital until construction on Tiberias concluded sometime between the years 18 and 23 AD. Described by Josephus as "the ornament of all Galilee," Sepphoris was a bustling, cultured city, complete with a four-thousand-seat theater. Whether or not Joanna originated from Sepphoris specifically, there's little doubt her world was far removed from many of the other disciples. An educated and cultured daughter of an elite, possibly Sadducean, family; married to a Gentile; walking in circles close to the throne—how astounding that Joanna, wife of Chuza, followed Jesus Christ!

Many scholars agree that Joanna's support was ongoing and financial in nature and that scriptural accounts depicting Herod's attitude and events at court were possibly derived from her. The beheading of John the Baptist, Herod's deep interest in Jesus, and Jesus' own trial before Herod—details of these accounts could have flowed from Joanna's lips to the Gospel writers' ears.

Another member of Herod's inner circle who could have reported court details was Manaen. Mentioned only once in Scripture in Acts 13:1 as a founding member of the church in Antioch, Manaen is listed as an intimate friend of Herod Antipas and could also have been an informant. His pairing with Susanna (who is mentioned in Luke 8:2–3 as another woman healed by Jesus who then supported his ministry) is fictional.

From Mark's account of John's beheading, we learn that Herod, although "perplexed" by John, liked to listen to him speak and desired to protect him from Herodias (6:20). Rather than contradicting Matthew's account in 14:1–12, scholars see the differences as indicative of the Gospel writers' varying aims. Matthew's abbreviated account gets directly to the point, whereas Mark's fleshes out deeper motives. In constructing these events, I relied upon Mark's more detailed account and chose to highlight Herod's interest in John and the deep distress he felt at the request for his head (6:26). The problem of John's disciples being barred from the palace is fictional and was my way of sparking Joanna and Susanna's reconciliation.

The relationship between Chuza and Phasaelis, Herod's first wife, is fiction, as is Chuza's aid in helping with Phasaelis' historical flight to Machaerus and King Aretas' offer of a reward. But the political interplay and growing animosity between the Nabatean and Herodian courts is grounded in history. Just as Joanna was "caught between two courts" (that of Herod and Jesus Christ), I depicted Chuza caught between the Nabatean and Herodian courts.

King Aretas wasn't the only foreign dignitary at odds with Herod. Pilate, the Roman prefect of Judea, had a long history of stirring up unrest. Luke 13:1–5 details the slaughter of Galilean pilgrims in which Pilate mixes their blood with their sacrifices. It's likely that this event caused deep discord between Pilate and Herod. The incident with the votive shields is lifted straight from history. This event earned Pilate a direct reprimand from

Emperor Tiberius. Scholars place the timing of these events just before Jesus' crucifixion, which would mean that Pilate entered Passover week at odds with the emperor and would have been especially interested in appeasing both Herod and the Jewish people. Luke 23:12 tells us that Herod and Pilate were "at enmity" with each other prior to Jesus' crucifixion and that Pilate's "gift" of Jesus to Herod solidified their friendship.

Even though Joanna isn't named during the crucifixion, she very well might have been present. Luke 23:49 states that women who had followed Jesus from Galilee observed the crucifixion, and verse 55 details how they followed Joseph of Arimathea and saw exactly where Jesus was buried. It's these same women who then prepared spices and brought them to the tomb that first Easter morning. Luke goes on to place Joanna at that tomb-side discovery (24:10), so it's certainly possible that Joanna observed the full extent of Jesus' sacrifice from cross to grave to resurrected life. In constructing the story, however, I chose to keep Joanna closer to Herod's court, giving the readers a more direct view of Jesus' trial by Herod rather than the moment of his crucifixion. However, the very real possibility remains—Joanna could have been present for the entirety of that emotional weekend.

The Gospel of John records how Jesus appeared to Mary Magdalene in the garden (20:14), but Mary wasn't the only woman to enjoy this privilege. Matthew 28:9 states that Jesus met the other women as they were leaving the tomb to tell his disciples the good news. He meets them with a greeting, and they hold onto his feet in overwhelmed worship.

In depicting these first encounters with the resurrected Jesus, I intentionally left the timeframe a tad ambiguous. There is general consensus that Jesus appeared to Mary Magdalene first, but she was also the one to run back for Peter and John. In the interim between Mary leaving and returning, the other women enter the tomb and encounter the angels. Sometime after they exit the tomb, Peter and John both arrive and leave while Mary Magdalene lingers and encounters Christ. It's after this initial encounter that Jesus appears to the other women as well.

Whereas some of the particulars are up for scholarly debate, certain truths remain clear: The women knew exactly where the body was laid, and when they arrived, that body was not there. Jesus—God in the flesh—met them, greeted them, and they worshiped at his feet.

Dear reader, go to the Word, soak your heart and mind within its pages, and let it transform you from the inside out. In constructing this story, my heart was to remain true to historical and scriptural accounts. Where I inevitably get it wrong, I beg your grace and exhort you to plant yourself within the Word, which is inherently true and trustworthy.

God is still using ordinary people to do extraordinary things. The commission to go and tell remains for us who follow. Like those women on that first Easter morning, may we carry the flame hot in our hearts with lips and life declaring the truth that cannot, will not be suppressed: "He is not here. He is risen!"

For more detailed historical information, including source material and recommended resources, visit HMKStories.com/BeforetheKing.

acknowledgments

Dear reader, I have an honest confession. I was profoundly intimidated approaching this story. Because Joanna is mentioned so infrequently in Scripture, I wondered if I could know anything about her. I spent quite a bit of time crying out to God for help, and at nearly every point in the writing process, when I came up against a hard wall of questions, He faithfully directed me to the right resources. In particular, Richard Bauckham's *Gospel Women* played a foundational role in fleshing out Joanna. What a gift to benefit from theologians who have peered long and hard into Scripture and history, capturing their findings for us who follow. My thanks also extends to Dr. Matthew Easter for listening and offering input as I outlined the early stages of this story. Thank you for directing me to Lynn Cohick, whose work became yet another bedrock for this book.

To those who continue to help me navigate the deep waters of the publishing world—my profound thanks! Cynthia Ruchti, agent extraordinaire, I count you as one of God's good gifts to me. Rochelle Gloege and Jen Veilleux, your confidence in my writing humbles me, and I greatly appreciate your wisdom, guidance, and encouragement. To other team members at Bethany

House—Raela, Anne, and Joyce—partnering with you is a dream! Thank you for answering my many questions and welcoming me so enthusiastically into the Bethany House family.

A special thanks to my sister Laura, who patiently listened while I rambled over particular plot points ad nauseum and who offered input when I stopped for breath. To all my siblings, their spouses, and my dear parents—thank you for being so supportive! To my fellow authors in the St. Louis ACFW chapter, you're amazing! I'm deeply blessed by our group. My church family, and especially those in my Choosing Hope Connection Group, continue to cheer me on so faithfully. What a joy to be surrounded by a strong community who loves Jesus.

As a fellow reader with a lengthy to-be-read stack, it humbles me when someone not only picks up my book but also takes the time to let me know how it impacted them. I've received many kind messages from readers, and God has used each one to uplift my spirit and keep my hand to the plow. So, to you, dear reader, I extend my heartfelt thanks. If ever we meet in person, be prepared for a hearty hug!

And to my husband, Andrew . . . "thank you" isn't quite enough. I couldn't do what I do without your support. Thank you for your steadfast love and the well-timed, "You're being too hard on yourself. Everything will be fine." To the three kids God gave me, how I hope we connect over these stories when you're older! My middle son keeps asking me with glowing eyes, "Are you famous, Mom? Are you famous?" No, sweet boy, but Jesus is.

Abba, this is because of You and for You. Thank You for faithfully meeting me in my weakness with the fullness of Your strength. With a hopeful heart, I place this book within Your hands. Please use it to build Your Kingdom.

discussion questions

1. Joanna calls herself a "daughter of the Sadducees," and throughout the book she learns to abandon false ideas to make room for the truth. Did you find anything surprising about Sadducean beliefs? What ideas must Joanna abandon in order to embrace Jesus' message?

2. Compare and contrast the two sets of sisters: Zahava / Sarah and Joanna / Dalia. Likewise, compare and contrast the mothers with their daughters. How does each view the concept of truth and respond to hardship? How are their beliefs evident in their choices?

3. Joanna's father says, "I am learning that sometimes God gives us things we cannot understand in order to shake us apart. To undo things we believe that we shouldn't. To make room for the things we must believe." Have these words proven true in his own life?

4. Discuss the transformation of Joanna and Susanna's relationship. How do trust, compassion, and forgiveness play out between them?

5. In choosing a new name, Eden decides to view her life "as a new beginning." What events in the story could be viewed as an ending and how are they instead proven to be new beginnings?

6. Read Jesus' parable of the four soils in Matthew 13:3–9, 18–23. Discuss how this parable relates to the hearts of various characters in *Before the King*.

7. In Part 1, Joanna observes, "We lived in a world that drew firm lines between people and did not treat those who crossed them with kindness." In Part 2, Joanna crosses those lines as she supports Jesus and follows him. Discuss the tension that unfolds between Joanna and some of Jesus' disciples. How is that tension resolved?

8. How does the faith of John the Baptist impact Joanna? In what ways is his faith similar to Dalia's? In which moments do we see Joanna embracing that faith for herself?

9. Discuss the times in which Joanna stands before the kings—King Herod and King Jesus. Compare and contrast these kings and their kingdoms.

10. At the heart of the story is a horrible lie from which Joanna must heal. Discuss what you see as her parents' involvement in the lie surrounding Dalia's "death." Do you think Joanna will ever uncover the full truth? Have you ever had to forgive someone who was no longer present?

11. Both Joanna and Chuza are clinging to past wounds. How have they let those wounds define them? As Chuza begins to heal, Joanna tells him, "You are frightened to accept God's abundance, as was I once." Have you ever been afraid to accept God's abundance? His mercy, forgiveness, or grace? Have you affirmed these things for others but denied them for yourself?

12. *Before the King* opens and closes with Joanna running out of a garden, and yet the circumstances are entirely different. How has Joanna learned "that God is as near as our own breath"?

Coming Soon:
Look for Salome's story in
the third book in
the WOMEN OF THE WAY series.

Every stone sings as it finds its purpose—as it's pulled from the earth, shaped and hewn with care, given over to a new calling. This is the lesson Salome learns from her stonemason father. Constantly restless and searching for her own place in the world, Salome is known as the girl with the startling eyes, wild and free with a tongue full of fire, and—if the gossip proves true—she is the girl with no future. As Salome comes of age along the shores of the Sea of Galilee, she begins praying for a place and a purpose, never imagining that she'd find it in the most unexpected person.

This third book in WOMEN OF THE WAY presents the untold story of Salome, mother of the Sons of Thunder, James and John. From the birth of her boys to their appointment as disciples of an esteemed rabbi, the once-untamable Salome must learn that success looks less like control and more like surrender.

Available Spring 2026.

Heather Kaufman is the author of multiple books, and her devotional writing has appeared in such publications as *Portals of Prayer*, *Open Windows*, and *Guideposts*. An editor-turned-writer, Heather worked eight years in the publishing industry while earning her master's degree and spinning tales late into the night. When she fell in love with studying the Bible through a cultural lens, the words of Scripture came springing to life, and Jesus became even more astoundingly beautiful. Now she delights in crafting stories that highlight the goodness of God and compel readers deeper into the Bible. When not reading, writing, or accumulating mounds of books, Heather can be found exploring new parks with her husband and three children near their home in St. Louis, Missouri. Learn more and stay in touch at HMKStories.com.

Sign Up for Heather's Newsletter

Keep up to date with Heather's latest news on book releases and events by signing up for her email list at the link below.

HMKStories.com

FOLLOW HEATHER ON SOCIAL MEDIA

Heather Kaufman, Author   @HMKStories   @HMKStories

More from Heather Kaufman

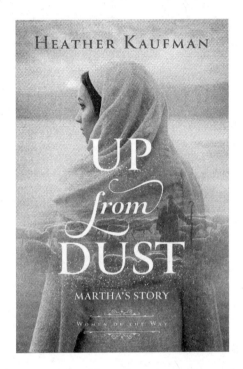

Responsible for raising her siblings, Lazarus and Mary, after her mother's untimely death, Martha finds solace in friendship and the beginnings of first love, until adversity strikes again. Many years later, a life-changing encounter with Jesus of Nazareth reawakens Martha's heart, even as she faces an unknown future.

Up from Dust
WOMEN OF THE WAY